OTHER BOOKS IN *THE OAK CREEK SERIES*

Each book can be read as a stand-alone

Secrets in Oak Creek

Beneath The Surface

BOOK 3 IN THE OAK CREEK SERIES

Scars of the Past

A WOUNDED WARRIOR NOVEL

B. K. STUBBLEFIELD

Scars Of The Past: *Book 3 In The Oak Creek Series*
Copyright © 2019 by B.K. Stubblefield. All rights reserved.
First Print Edition: April 2020

ISBN 9798643611394

Developemtal Editor: Ann Leslie Tuttle
Copy Editor: Jim Corbitt, ScribePower
Proofreader: Amanda Uphill, LaLinc Proofreading

Cover Design: Cover Me Darling

Interior Design: Andie Hansen, Blue Valley Author Services

No part of this book may be reproduced, scanned, or distributed in any printed or electronic form without permission. Please do not participate in or encourage piracy of copyrighted materials in violation of the author's rights. Thank you for respecting the hard work of this author.

This is a work of fiction. Names, characters, places, and incidents either are the product of the author's imagination or are used fictitiously, and any resemblance to locales, events, business establishments, or actual persons—living or dead—is entirely coincidental.

To all veterans – past, present, and future.

Thank you for your service!

TO MY READERS:

Thank you for purchasing 'Scars of The Past.' I hope you will enjoy this romance as much I enjoyed writing it.

I wrote this book in honor of all veterans—past and present—and for those who lost their fight with PTSD upon returning home from the horrors of war.

It is a celebration of every man and woman whose courage prevailed under the most harrowing sacrifices, and a tribute to those who 'soldier on' after their uniforms are hung up, and their boots are stowed away. And to honor those who climbed incredible heights, despite their physical challenges.

This is a story of hope, love, and happy endings. Some readers might be sensitive as it touches on the subject of veteran suicide.

If you could take some time to post a review on your favorite store site, I would be extremely thankful.

Much love,

B.K. Stubblefield

TABLE OF CONTENTS

Prologue	1
Chapter 1	5
Chapter 2	18
Chapter 3	24
Chapter 4	30
Chapter 5	40
Chapter 6	56
Chapter 7	63
Chapter 8	70
Chapter 9	77
Chapter 10	86
Chapter 11	92
Chapter 12	102
Chapter 13	108
Chapter 14	113
Chapter 15	122
Chapter 16	131
Chapter 17	140
Chapter 18	148
Chapter 19	156
Chapter 20	168
Chapter 21	174
Chapter 22	182
Chapter 23	190
Chapter 24	203

Chapter 25	219
Chapter 26	226
Chapter 27	241
Chapter 28	249
Chapter 29	261
Chapter 30	279
Chapter 31	285
Chapter 32	299
Chapter 33	307
Chapter 34	324
Epilogue	346
Acknowledgments	359
Contact The Author	361
About B.K. Stubblefield	362

Scars Of the Past: Book 3 In The Oak Creek Series

"In war, there are no unwounded soldiers."
– JOSE NAROSKY

B.K. Stubblefield

PROLOGUE

THE HOUSE STOOD IN UTTER silence. No outside sounds disturbed the unsettling hush; even the low hum of the A/C had paused for the moment. On this hot August day, no air penetrated the moist and sweltering summer heat that wrapped suburbia in a sticky blanket.

The bantering voices of children had fallen quiet, the neighbor's constant squabbles with each other had seized, and the anxious yaps of the black Lab tied to a pole on the property next to his had stopped. Neither did he make out the roar of the Mustang belonging to the little punk up the street.

All activity seemed suspended in this cauldron of heat. As if the house and the outside world were united in holding a collective breath—listening, quietly expecting, and waiting for the shot to ring out.

It would be over in a moment. Finally, he'd welcome the long-sought peace.

Alone in his basement, he sat in the old red rocker his wife had banished from the upstairs sitting room. Big unsightly spots, caused by his wife's miniature schnauzer, ruined the fabric on the armrests. The neurotic animal had developed a penchant for the chair's suede-like texture. The fondness expressed itself in excessive licking across the material, leaving nasty marks in its place. But the dog wouldn't lick the chair this afternoon; his wife had taken him to the pet spa. For a moment he considered the stains, and it occurred to him they might mingle with his own. As this thought interrupted the raging war in his head, he almost laughed out loud.

Closed window shades kept the basement cool, yet sweat drenched his body. It soaked his T-shirt and dripped from his temples. With eyes shut tight and feeling every muscle stretched taut across his face, his neck vein bulged and throbbed. His strong, masculine features were contorted into a mask of pain. His heart raced, his breath came in short, hard bursts, and he gasped for air as if he'd just completed a marathon race.

His mind sped, too. Although silence surrounded him, the noises in his head thundered. He hadn't slept an entire night in what seemed like ages. Every night, without fail, relentless nightmares visited to show him the ugly pictures of humanity and remind him that sleep was a luxury he couldn't afford. He needed to stay vigilant, look over his shoulders, and remain hyper-aware of his surroundings. When asleep, the touch of someone else's hand flashed danger, putting his brain and body in attack mode.

The first night back at home after his deployment into the brutal world of war was also the first time his wife had experienced his changed behavior. The assault came suddenly—pushing her down, restraining her, while at the whole time screaming at an unseen enemy. With no chance of defending herself, she had feared for her life. Until he snapped out of attack mode. When the war zone faded and gave way to the safety of his bedroom, he felt drained, angry, and disgusted with himself. The image of hurting the one he loved most horrified him. He did not fear his own mortality, but accidentally harming his wife or children became a gnawing, unbearable thought. With his back against the wall, he was tired of fighting. So tired. And with a few hours of sleep here and there, he lived on the edge of sanity.

Earlier this day, the shrill whine of a firecracker and the following explosion had pulled a number on him. The blast, too close for comfort, played tricks with his mind. Instantly on alert, his surroundings turned into the battleground. He heard the high pitch whoosh of missiles and had scrambled for cover. He had to protect himself. Once the noise died, he surveilled the house and neighborhood with his gun drawn. He didn't understand the frenzied gestures of the people around him, waving and pointing. These were his enemies; they had to be neutralized. When, at last, he snapped out of his daze, embarrassment shot through him. The threat had existed in his head only. Exhausted, and angry, he separated himself from the surrounding crowd, seeking solitude. No longer fitting in, he needed to be alone.

His right hand trembled as he held the gun, weighing it, feeling it. With his left he touched the metal affectionately, tracing every ridge. His grip tightened around the rosewood handle. The voice in his head shouted and coached. *Do it!*

You want peace ... . Do it! Keep your family safe ... . Do it! You don't want to go insane ... . Do It!

Now was the time to escape the battlefield. Releasing the pain would be fast, mending all scars. *DO IT!*

Probingly, he lifted the weapon and pressed the short barrel against his sweaty temple where the cold steel rested and remained steady for a moment.

His hand sunk back into his lap as a picture of his family from a happier time—not so long ago—entered his mind. The voice inside his head fell silent as sadness washed over him, squeezing his chest with pain. A sob lodged in his throat and, as he opened his eyes, a wet stream traveled down his cheek and mingled with his sweat. He swiped at the tears, but that didn't take away the darkness that overshadowed his heart. Loneliness pressed on his shoulders with the weight of a ton of bricks. This time, the voice rose more forceful. *NOW*, it shouted.

Your old life is gone … . You can't go back … . You're not a good father to your children, anymore … . And you're too fucked up to lead a useful life … . The BATTLEFIELD is your life!

The voice consumed his mind and soul, making him believe that he'd never be free of the pain. *DO IT NOW.*

The voice was right; he wouldn't escape. It was time to silence it.

He lifted the gun and opened his mouth. As if in a trance, he inserted the barrel, pointing it downwards, knowing the bullet would damage the spinal column where it met the base of the skull. He'd make sure of a successful kill.

BANG!

The front door slammed shut, and sudden loud noises filled the house, reaching into the basement. His wife and three rambunctious boys were home from their afternoon trip to the city pool. In an instant, the atmosphere transformed. Life had returned. Shocked about the act he'd come so close to committing, his eyes snapped wide open. The prospect of his children making the gruesome discovery of his suicide horrified him even more. A hot wave of remorse and shame crashed over him. He lowered his gun, engaged the safety and put the weapon in its safe and rightful place. The damaging voice in his head retreated, slithering into the shadows of his memories. His racing heart slowed. As his mind cleared, a crystal clear thought formed. He needed help.

CHAPTER 1

On this bittersweet April day, Houston Miller strutted off the bus and entered the airport's terminal. The bounce in his step spoke of contained excitement as he made his way to the automated check-in station. The release papers in his briefcase established his honorable discharge from the Army, making him a brand-new civilian. His laptop, on the other hand, held the many bits and pieces to his astonishing dream.

Soon he'd be in Oak Creek, the rural Kentucky town he called home. He checked the time and, with still an hour and a half until boarding, Houston picked a bar and grill inside the terminal, claimed the vacant corner booth, and opened his laptop. A few keystrokes and the document named "Heroes Rise Vision" launched. By the time the waiter brought his beer, Houston barely noticed. He never tired of reading and tweaking the document to bring the dream to life.

Three months earlier he'd laid on his bunk at base camp, flipping through the TV channels when a documentary caught his attention.

A handsome man in climbing gear, rugged like the mountains around him, was the focus of the feature. His breath puffed in harsh gusts with every struggling step towards the mountain top. "Ten more steps … you got this, man!" Someone from behind coached with mounting excitement and increasing volume in his voice. "You did it, man! You did it!"

On screen, the climber reached the summit. Ecstatic at the colossal triumph, he pumped his arms in the air as a celebratory scream from deep inside his chest—a glorious, earth-shaking one—ripped from his throat.

On TV, the commentator applauded the astonishing feat while inside the barracks room, Houston pumped his fist in admiration for the stranger on the mountain. "You did it, brother," he shouted out loud, echoing the voices on-screen. "Heroes Rise!"

The screen switched to a packed pub erupting into applause for the climber. Family and friends, and most of this tiny community had gathered to watch the triumphant climb via life feed at the local watering spot. The name of a non-profit veterans group scrolled across the screen, calling for donations.

Behind the bar, the pub's owner rang a cowbell, the dull, metallic clang silencing the patrons. "Hey, folks. Listen up for a second …" The index finger of his free hand jabbed at the TV. "This amazing group just made the impossible possible for our hometown boy. Let's give 'em a round of applause."

Two climbers, arms loped around each other's shoulders, smiled from large mounted screens. Tribulations and teamwork had turned them into brothers. With similar skullcaps, bearded faces, and wide, toothy grins, there was only one difference between them—one man had accomplished the difficult climb on two leg prostheses.

The clanging cow bell silenced the room for a second time. "In honor of our boy, Nick, I'll be donating today's proceeds." Hollers and whistles of cheer greeted the announcement. "So, don't be shy … but don't be stupid. See me if you need a ride home. This here," with a swift move he lifted a bucket onto the bar, "will help you get rid of that annoying change. "That's right folks, keep it coming." Enthusiasm glowed in his eyes as the first coins hit the bottom. "Oh, and bills are welcome, too."

On screen the national average suicide rate for veterans flashed, and an epiphany had struck Houston. With the force of a lightning bolt it hauled him off his bed. *That's it!* Folks in small-town America raising funds for local veterans. What if … ?

He paced, his restless brain pitching fastballs of possibilities. Start a nonprofit for vets and their families, create an environment of support, provide therapy, and a quiet place to unwind. As in the story of *Jack and the Beanstalk*, the seed planted in the fertile grounds of his mind blew up overnight. Only the sky was the limit. A plan formed. His mountains to climb weren't of the snow-capped kind, but they were just as difficult to conquer. Houston had no time to waste. A name. He needed a name for his organization. A name that carried strength. Houston kept pacing; the energy wouldn't let him sit still. In mid-stride he stopped, slapped his forehead as his reaction of Nick on the mountaintop pushed to the forefront. Of course. *Heroes Rise!* That's it. It couldn't be more perfect.

It's settled, he wrote in an email to his parents. I'll trade my combat boots for hiking boots.

Just a few months ago he had no clear vision of what life after separation from the Army would look like. Now he had a plan. Fourteen years in the Army had prepared him for this challenge. Houston's ambitious vision hurled him towards the future. Serving the physically wounded, the psychologically damaged, and those who only wanted ultimate peace from unimaginable horrors, it was the flaming blaze that burned a new purpose into his life. But first thing's first: he needed money. Lots of money.

A boarding call from the nearby gate interrupted his thinking and shot him back into the present. Draining his beer, Houston called for the check and stowed the laptop. Boarding would begin in ten minutes. His new life as a civilian waited at the end of that flight.

***

On Friday, two days after Houston's return to Oak Creek, Helen Miller threw a massive welcome home party.

"What did you do, Mom? Take out an ad in the paper?" Houston smiled and smacked a kiss on top of her head. His homecoming had been a hero's celebration; Helen Miller had made sure.

His baby sister, Tessa, flew into his arms, moisture sparkling in her eyes. Aunts, uncles, and cousins came out to welcome him back. Plus, it seemed half the town of Oak Creek stopped in to shake his hand and slap his back. To have his family together, meeting old friends, the sizzling aroma coming from the commercial-size grill—those simple pleasures felt just right.

Most folks at the party had heard of the attack on his convoy and, before the night ended, nosy questions of the Afghan *incident* came up. A nerve under his left eye started ticking; his leg bounced in rapid motion. Houston appreciated the empathy and concerns—they were real—but the thinly disguised thirst for gory details sickened him. He needed to block the prattle from the man sitting in a lawn chair next to him. Houston weighed his options and settled on a half-truth. "You know what? Hold that thought, will ya? Gotta water my horse ... if you know what I mean." He winked and pushed to his feet.

With no intention of returning, Houston headed to a flight of stairs that led to a finished space above his dad's workshop, closed the door behind him, and welcomed the solitude of his apartment.

After his return to Oak Creek, he'd settled in the considerable space Helen Miller had turned into a comfortable sanctuary. The entry led straight into the living area. Houston's gaze swept over the walls painted in a soothing shade of gray, a charcoal-colored sofa and chair that contrasted with the blonde wood of the floor. A white shelf room divider hid the queen-sized bed and dresser. The nearby rustic barn door led to the bathroom, while to the right a minimalist kitchen gleamed in white and stainless steel. This airy, modern space was everything he needed. Houston leaned against the entry door, sucking a deep breath. No, he would not return to the party tonight.

***

Reid's eyes flew open, his body shot upright. Perspiration covered his forehead as confusion stretched into eternity. Deep and greedily, he sucked air until the moment passed. When he found his bearings at the end of the nightmarish memory, he raked his hands across his face and swallowed hard. *Jesus Christ!* Not the battlefield, he realized, but a damn nightmare.

A routine patrol.

The convoy rumbled along a rough-and-rocky dirt road, heavy-duty tires crushing and flattening as it snaked through the inhospitable terrain of the Afghan mountains.

Under ordinary circumstances, Sergeant Reid McCabe would have described the harsh mountains and the abrasive, untouched landscape as astonishing. But these circumstances were anything but ordinary.

It was his third tour to Afghanistan. One more week in this godforsaken war pit and he'd be heading home to the lush countryside of his native Kentucky for a much-needed R&R.

The band of armored vehicles came to an unscheduled stop. Ahead, a vehicle had broken down. Damn! His eyes darted, scanned for life in this desolate wilderness, but the scraggly mountainside appeared uninhabited. Sergeant McCabe knew better than to let his guard slip; vigilance had been branded into his brain and flowed through his veins.

Securing the area had highest priority, and it was his responsibility to cover his vehicle's right side. Snatching his weapon, he opened the door and jumped onto the hard-packed dirt, tossing up a plume of dust that encased his legs and settled on his boots. His radio crackled. He reached to push the button ...

BOOM!

The eardrum-shattering sound split the air. Time slowed to a snail's pace as the blast lifted him off the ground.

The explosive sound had come from a backfiring car, and the bed he woke up in stood in the same room of the house he'd left eleven years ago. His parent's home. But the pain ... the crushing pain was back. It burned, and throbbed, and threatened to blow him over.

Reid grunted from behind clenched teeth, hurled aside the bedcover, and sat, gripping the edge of the mattress. Sweat slicked his forehead. He didn't switch on the lamp on top of the nightstand—the neon greenish glow of the digital alarm clock showed the time as three fifty-eight. Not that it mattered. Most mornings he didn't sleep past four o'clock anyway.

He clutched his knee. Fingers digging, kneading and rubbing across the stump, trying to ease the fiery burn. As he knew from experience, the motions were useless. The fierce massage didn't erase the throb. Even though it wasn't a part of him anymore, his missing limb pounded like hell. The doctor's talk of phantom pain echoed in his mind, but that didn't make the experience less real. Since his release from Walter Reed, this happened less frequently.

"A matter of time," he mocked, a cynical edge spiking his tone. In time, they'd said, it might disappear altogether. *Damn if I don't beat this.*

With still an hour before dawn, Reid grabbed the shorts and T-shirt he'd tossed to the floor before crashing into bed last night. When he finished pulling the shirt over his head, Reid reached for the prosthesis leaning against the nightstand. His new reality, they'd told him encouragingly. He despised the term.

Fifteen months! Had it been fifteen months since he'd gotten his first orthopedic device? On some days it felt as if it had been just the other day. He'd handled getting used to the artificial limb all right; yet coping with the emotional trauma from the explosion that had happened two years ago had been another matter. And hadn't he just let his anger rip at the physical therapist? But the guy had been cool, saw right through his B.S. and gave him no slack. Nope, he'd called him out on it. Turned out it was what he needed. He'd prevailed. Grit and determination were as much of Reid's make-up as that rebellious swirl of hair growing in the wrong direction at the front of his hairline. He'd learned to tame that annoying cowlick, too. Donning the artificial leg below the knee was now a part of his routine.

He made his way to the kitchen, switched on the coffeemaker his mother had prepared the night before, and opened his MacBook. They'd stayed in touch, he and his former team, so checking in the quiet hours of the morning had become a routine. As he scanned, his eye caught an email from his buddy, Tex. Reid scratched the stubble of his chin, itching to open it right away. But coffee first. When the machine stopped brewing, he filled his mug and sat to read.

On that disastrous day in Afghanistan, not everyone came out as lucky as he—if losing a limb was something to call lucky. Two of his comrades had lost their lives in that roadside blast. The surviving brothers had rallied around the wounded and now shared a bond most of his hometown buddies wouldn't understand. How could they? It was not their fault.

"Good Morning, Son." Amanda McCabe came into the kitchen as Reid filled his mug a second time.

"Hey, Mom. You're up early. Want some coffee?"

"Sure, hon. But why aren't you asleep?"

Reid's steel-gray eyes hardened as he caught Amanda's gaze shift to the artificial limb. He couldn't stand the glimmer of pity that crept into strangers' faces when they glanced at that. But this was his mother, so he kept his voice neutral when he spoke. "Been getting up this early for years now, Mom. Life in the Army conditions you."

Life in the Army. Reid missed it—the brothers, the camaraderie, the bonds, even the rigid discipline of ceaseless training that prepared them for war. *But it didn't prepare me for this,* he thought. Moving in with his parents at age twenty-nine to lick his wounds knocked his pride. Oh, the petite woman who cooked his favorite meals and offered food as a way of soothing his soul consoled him. Or maybe his mother found much-needed comfort in doing *something*. Because God knows, there wasn't anything else to do but to let him rest and heal. And he was thankful for his dad—the quiet thinker—whose eyes dampened when he spoke of the respect he held for

Reid. Gratitude washed through him, but it was time to retake charge of his life.

The email he'd read earlier had been from Houston Miller, his former Platoon leader. It swirled around his mind and filled his chest with excitement. A one-year walk across the U.S. to raise awareness for the staggering veteran suicide rate. To fund a nonprofit organization that would focus on preventing the outrageous number of veterans committing suicide every single day. And Houston had convinced him, a leg-amputee, to become part of the journey. It would start a new chapter of Reid's life and be his rite of passage.

No doubt, it would take time to condition for this endeavor. A final departure date hadn't been set yet but, by the end of summer, their boots would hit the road. Reid would move to Oak Creek, Kentucky, where he and Houston would train together and support each other once again. Like they had in the past. And once again, it was time to leave the comfort of home and stride towards a new beginning.

Give me two weeks, Reid had responded without a second thought. He had a hunch that this bizarre endeavor just might offer a semblance of normal; whatever that may look like.

First, he needed to break the news to his mother. Reid had kept the lengthy talks and Facetime calls with Houston to himself. The project had given him purpose and hope. His mom wouldn't care for it, and he understood. But Reid counted on Amanda's support. In two weeks, he'd pack a duffel bag and move 140 miles south to Oak Creek. At least he wasn't going to war.

"Did that car backfiring wake you?"

"Yes," Amanda said. "Who in the blue blazes was that at this hour?"

"Maybe, for a change, the paper came early?"

The answer to the question came right after he opened the front door. On the horizon, fingers of gray slid open the curtain of darkness; the early morning's air smelled as fresh as the dew covering the lawn, preceding an unusual warm April day.

There, in the dimming light of the street lantern huddled a form Reid didn't immediately identify. Instantly alert, he cursed himself for not having brought his gun. Amanda followed Reid out onto the porch and promptly felt herself prodded backward. "Get back inside," Reid snapped the order as coffee sloshed over her terrycloth robe.

Damn! A burst of air cleared his lungs.

He need not have worried. The irregular shape was a dog tied to the lamppost. Scampering to his fours, it appeared to be a mutt of medium size with a dark coat, sporting a white blaze, chest, and paws. Reid's anger flared. *You've got to be kidding me. Someone dumped a freaking dog!* He—or she—hadn't barked and still didn't. *Thank God.* The old sourpuss next door surely would have something to say about that. Instead, the dog panted with its tongue lolling.

As Reid approached the animal, the pooches' eyes struck him as knowing. They spoke a language of their own. Even from a distance, Reid recognized the intensity with which they latched onto him, penetrating Reid's soul with focus and expectation. Cautiously, he approached. The dog scampered to his feet, circled the lamppost, and realization smacked Reid broad in the face. Instead on four, the mutt paced on three legs; its right hind leg was missing. What the hell?

In that moment, compassion expanded his chest for the dog who shared a similar fate as his own. "Hey, buddy," he whispered. Reaching to pet the dog's head, he noticed the folded note sticking out from under the collar. "What happened to you, kiddo? Who left you here?" A warm tongue flicked against Reid's wrist.

He slipped the note from the collar and unfolded the piece of paper.

His name is Yard. You know ... as in three feet. He was just a puppy when they took the leg, and he probably doesn't remember what it's like to have four paws. So, it's all right.

Reid's jaw clenched, and the words blurred before his eyes. Gulping a deep breath, he glanced at the space where the dog's leg should be before he continued reading.

He is a two-year-old border collie mix, neutered, with shots up-to-date, and a clean bill of health. I'm not allowed to keep him. The new landlord said he has to go. I begged and cried. But the heartless louse said Yard was too big for the apartment. Yard was my companion, but the scumbag landlord didn't care, and I can't afford to move to a new place. So, perhaps this is meant to be. You don't know me, but I saw you at Progressive Physical Therapy where I was a patient ... same as you. You looked so sad. And that's when I knew Yard and you belonged together. He's been a good dog. I beg you to give him a chance, you won't regret it. Please, don't judge me. I just want what's best for him. He deserves to be with a kind person, and if my intuition is right, you'll be that fellow. He'll be a good dog for you, too. Oh, and in the black nylon bag you'll find his bowls, the treats he likes best, and his absolute favorite red Frisbee. God Bless You.

Heartbroken in Florence

"Fuck! That's rich!" Reid folded the note, shoving it into his pocket. He ran a hand through his short-cropped hair. "So … your name is Yard. And you're damaged goods. Just like me, huh?" The dog tilted his head, listening with attentive eyes. Reid dropped to his knee and ran both hands along the dog's face. Yard gave a small whine, his eyes darting to a spot behind Reid.

"What's going on?" Amanda asked, not lifting her eyes from the animal.

Reid stood, and when he spoke again, his voice packed heat. "Someone dropped him off, saying he and I would make a good pair." Reid clenched his teeth, swallowing the four-letter word from leaving the tip of his tongue. "Tell me, what am I supposed to do with him?" Jerking the note from his pocket, he handed the piece of paper to Amanda.

Amanda wiped at her eyes as she read the message. When she finished, a fat tear rolled over her cheek. "I don't know, honey, but, maybe it's a sign from the universe. Remember your therapist's recommendation of looking into a companion animal?"

Yes, he had played with the idea of adopting a dog, but that was before the walk across America came up. Adopting a dog now would complicate things, unless the animal was able to go on the road with him.

Calm and unafraid, Yard's eyes didn't stray from Reid's face as if reading his thoughts. A small moan pushed from his throat, and lifting a paw, he gently grazed Reid's leg— an unexpected, yet comforting gesture from this abandoned animal. In that moment, Reid's initial reaction of taking him to the pound dissolved with the nudge of a cold canine nose.

Smoothing his hand over the dog's head, he stared at his mom. "Well, then …" he growled, "it looks like I've got myself a dog."

Jeez, he thought. *Did the universe not have the damnedest sense of humor?*

CHAPTER 2

How had this day gone so sideways?

As Keira maneuvered her sunflower yellow VW Beetle into her driveway, she reflected on the comfortable pace of her rural Kentucky town where folks knew their neighbors and friendly hellos were considered good manners. She felt lucky to live in such a tight-knit community and even tighter family. Lucky to have gotten the teacher's job at Oak Creek Middle School. But, jeez, sixth graders were such a tangle of emotions, and with the excitement of the school year ending soon, attention spans rapidly declined.

Was this why she lately felt so out of sorts? Keira closed her eyes, and she remembered the summer after her college graduation when she'd backpacked across Europe with two friends. They'd departed one day after graduation, traveling light and unencumbered. For the tiniest moment, she heard the gondolier's sweet serenade in Venice, wrapped herself in the warmth and cheer of her Irish relatives, breathed the crisp alpine air in Austria, and swooned in the French waiter's poetic language at a Parisian street café. A longing to recapture this sense of excitement flowed through her soul. Was that it? Had her classroom become her cage? No, she quickly dismissed the thought. She loved her kids; she enjoyed teaching. Although, right now, summer break couldn't come quick enough.

Keira pursed her lips and considered Ryan, her best friend's fiancée, who traveled the globe in his profession as a freelance photographer. His independence and freedom sparked a sliver of envy. Ah, but hadn't she experienced the steep price of this freedom through her friend's eyes?

Keira smiled, but couldn't deny the pang of jealousy as she thought of Emily and Ryan. She cheered for their happiness, although at one time she would have been thrilled to squeeze Ryan's neck. Because preceding their engagement, he'd bailed on Emily, just ended the relationship with a hollow reason. Keira, too, had once found herself in that desperate pit of heartbreak and emotional suffering Emily went through. She could relate. No man was worth this agony, and so she'd kept relationships at an arm's length.

In the end, her friends' breakup had been no match for the magnetism of their love. Keira saw it in the flicker of Emily's eyes when Ryan was near, and in Ryan's touches that said he couldn't keep his hands off Emily. *He really loves her.* As she thought of her friend's happiness, a dull ache slid over her heart. With sudden clarity, she realized that she, too, wanted that kind of love. Yes, she could admit to that. But, with her failed dating record, she had no expectations of this happening any time soon.

Irritated, she tucked a lock behind her ear. Could this be the source of her frustration? Or was it that caged feeling combined with no expectation of finding a love like theirs? Keira emptied her lungs in a huff as the day paraded through her mind.

And today she felt as if life had just flipped her the bird.

Unfortunately, her unhappy mood started shortly after arriving at the school. Like most mornings, she headed to the teacher's lounge with a hot brew on her mind. Keira opened the door and stepped straight into Jace's usual flippant greeting. "Hey, gorgeous." Only today, his eyes didn't match the smile on his lips.

The cheerfulness struck Keira as forced, even though she supposed he was unaware. Something occupied his mind; something he'd kept to himself, she suspected. Signal received.

"Hey, Jace." With measured strides she closed the distance to the coffee machine and reached for a paper cup. Pouring the steaming liquid, she said, "I missed you at Pat's yesterday."

The townsfolk seldom referred to the pub by its official name, The Bluegrass Craft Beer Brewery. To them, it was just a sign by the door. Pat, sociable, easy-going, and co-owner of the pub, stood as the face of BCBB. Since Thursday evening was karaoke night, it was the place to meet and share a pitcher. "You missed a great time."

Her stomach pinched as Keira struggled to deliver the statement without accusation. The question stood between them, soundless and uncomfortable. Seconds stretched like a rubber band, feeling like minutes. Could he peer inside Keira, Jace would see the bunching nerves, the speeding pulse. Instead, she leaned against the counter, appearing calm and collected. Only her jade-green eyes met his in question.

"Keira." Jace lifted his hand and raked his fingers through tousled hair, making a mess of the stylish tangle with the beautiful blonde streaks in it. Her stomach flipped at the telltale gesture and the sorrow she'd heard in the single word.

"What's happening, Jace? Care to fill me in?"

The door opened, and before it fully swung out, Jace fixed his eyes on hers. "Not now, Keira. Let's talk later. Lunch?" Spoken in a quiet voice, she understood what her gut already knew. In the wordless language of locked gazes, she'd recognized the guilt, remorse, and even a hint of regret. *Sad* popped into her mind. But she dismissed the thought right away because she'd seen the signs. Had known this day would come and couldn't even be angry.

The relationship was ending. From the start, she'd known this day would come. Frankly, whatever they'd shared, it had lasted beyond expectations. Lately, though, she'd surprised herself by hoping. Who was she kidding? Only her closest friends knew Jace was more than a colleague, but in truth, she'd warmed to the idea of a future with him. A fantasy. A stupid, teenage-like fantasy. A crushing sadness settled over her as she pushed away from the counter. The coffee suddenly tasted like battery fluid.

They met at lunch. Jace was going to leave Oak Creek and, at the end of the school year, he'd move back to California. Home. He'd return home to family and friends. An only child, his parents needed him. That she could understand. Yet ...

***

The afternoon crept at a pace slower than a snail on a lunch break. At last, when the bell signaled the end of classes, Keira just wanted to get out of there. On top of the break-up, her already crappy day only got worse. Her students had behaved like rowdy little monsters—arguing, out of their chairs, disrupting. Had they all caught the stupid bug? Apparently. *Lord, do I really want to put up with this, year after year?* She'd kept her cool, but admittedly, she'd come close to losing her temper.

Keira's neck and shoulders ached; invisible fingers reached into her head and squeezed. All she wanted was to burrow into the soft nest of her bed, pull the duvet over her head, and have an ugly cry.

She'd made it halfway across the parking lot when the phone sounded out her current favorite country tune. Not surprising, the upbeat notes grated on her nerves. Emily Carmichael. Her friend who would be getting married at the end of August. And, who'd scheduled an appointment with the bridal boutique for today. *Today!* Freshly dumped and on the feel-good side of bitchy, she'd help Emily shop for her wedding dress. *Sweet injustice of life, why not rub it in a little more?*

Could this day get any worse?

"Hold on a sec ..." Keira let her bag slide off the shoulder and reached for the key to her little hippie car, a yellow VW Beetle.

Keira puffed air through pursed lips, lifting the stray strand of hair on her cheek. She screwed her face into a grimace and dropped into her seat; the pinching clasp at the nape of her neck had to come off. A flick of her fingers, and curls tumbled to her shoulders. Relief! Not much, but enough to release the nagging pressure. At least a little.

"What's up?" Keira dipped a hand inside the mysterious black hole of the enormous hobo bag and searched for the mini-size bottle of aspirin she knew was in there somewhere.

Emily's voice bubbled from the speaker, "Hey, you. What's up with yourself?"

"Dammit. In what corner of this universe does this stupid container hide?"

"Keira? What the heck are you talking about?"

"Aspirin. I need a blasted aspirin. I've got a ginormous headache right now, courtesy of a shitty day."

"Oh, no, Keira. What happened?"

Sigh. "Later, all right? Meet you at Mona's Bridal Creations right at five?

An exaggerated exhale floated from the speaker, prompting Keira to lift her eyes to the ceiling. Since Ryan's unexpected beach proposal in October, Emily, her strong, independent, kick-ass friend had turned into a walloping mess.

"Um, Mona pushed the appointment back to six o'clock. Please tell me you'll make it?"

Another hour added to this doggone day. The selfish thought quickly deflated by a tiny prick of guilt. Her own party of sorrow probably wasn't a good plan, anyway.

"Stop worrying, Em ... of course I'll be there. I'll go home first, find something that'll slay the pounding in my head, and get out of my fancies."

"Oh, good. I guess by fancies you mean to get out of the comfy slacks and shirt I bet you're wearing right now, just to change into that Mossy Oak gear of yours? Seriously, Keira?"

Keira sniggered. "Only if you don't prefer sweats. Besides, Em, don't you just *love* that bling on my cap?" The lilt in tone hinted at how much she enjoyed ribbing her friend.

"Keira!"

"What? See you at six, marshmallow."

"Heh, heh." Headache or not, the prospect of strolling into the elegant boutique with its delicate dresses, hats, gloves, and other whimsical nonsense, teased a smirk out of Keira. What contemptuous thoughts would Mona, the ethereal lady of poise and etiquette, hide inside that neatly coiffed head when Emily asked Keira's opinion on various dresses? She didn't care. The shirt itched, and the new shoes rubbed against her heels.

But before she headed to an evening of torture, she'd duck into Pet Stop to pick up some kibble.

CHAPTER 3

Two weeks after receiving Houston's email, Reid drove out of Florence with the wipers of the Jeep Wrangler sloshing across the windshield, when he spotted Oak Creek's welcome marker through the downpour.

On the backseat Yard had curled into a tight ball, snoozing the entire trip. Now, as Reid slowed his speed, the dog stretched his limbs with an intense yawn. "What do you know, he's alive! Check out this freaking downpour," Reid said, glancing at the animal in the rear-view mirror. The way Yard's ears lifted and his head tilted, Reid could have sworn he understood.

Yard drew out a whimper in response. "Whoa …" The headlights cut through the curtain of rain but when Reid slammed on the brakes, Yard lost his footing, crashing against the passenger seat. "I need to get you one of those stupid dog seatbelts," he said as he pulled the Jeep to the shoulder. Yard was unhurt. Scampering back into place, the dog yipped at what Reid had spotted a second before. A little brown shadow dragged himself across the street and huddled along the roadside barrier. "Jesus, Yard, I just about hit him."

A firm command to "stay," and Reid threw open the driver door. Damn if his raincoat wasn't thrown atop his bags in the cargo space. Much good it did him there. As if it would make a difference against the driving rain, he hunched over and tucked his chin against his chest. By the time he'd rushed to the rear door and pulled on the slicker, the rainstorm had soaked his clothes.

From the shoulder, tired brown eyes in a matted body watched with caution as Reid approached.

"Hey, little guy. What in the hell are you doing out here in this wash-out?" The dog eyed him wearily but didn't take off. *Déjà vu.* Reid crouched, cautiously extending a hand. He didn't need to touch the soaked mat of the fur to realize the animal's ribs stuck out like sticks. "Ah, shit! You're just a bag of bones. When is the last time you ate?" The dog's teeth chattered. Clearly a miserable creature. Yet, Reid detected what he supposed to be hope in two dull, brown eyes.

With a gentleness that hid well in the planes of a masculine face and strong six-foot frame, Reid carefully lifted the scared dog into the crook of his arm. An anxious growl rumbled, but, too tired to fight, he just watched Reid with terrified eyes. "Shhh, relax." The dog seemed to understand this man meant no harm.

"Holy crap!" Steel turned to ice as his gaze passed over a bloody paw, and dry, cracked pads. Now what? He couldn't just leave him here. Not in this torrential rain, and not in this condition. It would be a death sentence. Nope, not an option.

From inside the truck, Yard stared wide-eyed at Reid's every move. With ears perked and standing tall, he watched as Reid walked to the Jeep and pulled a rag from the back. Wrapped in the old towel, Reid kept the dog close to his chest. Rain dripped from the hood of the raincoat and the tips of his fingers as he scooted onto the backseat. "Hey, boy," he called out to Yard. "Check this out; he's nothing but a bag of bones. So be nice," he warned the mutt. Yard pushed out a yawn that sounded much like a moan.

What were the odds of rescuing two dogs in as many weeks? Hell if he knew. If he'd thought the universe must have a damn weird sense of humor when it plopped Yard on his doorsteps, it must be cracking up now. "Let's call him Bones," he said. "And let's hope he's microchipped."

Yard finished checking out the bundle and determined the furry rag didn't pose a threat. Reid wiped the bleeding paw clean and wrapped it up with gauze from the first-aid kit. "Watch him," he instructed, moving Bones to the floorboard before he climbed out of the backseat and slid behind the wheel.

Turning into the parking space of a gas station he'd spotted as he drove into town, he Googled local animal shelters on his phone. They would patch him up and maybe even find his owners. Reid had adopted Yard—the mutt had turned out to be a real comfort—but he'd be nuts thinking about caring for a second dog while crisscrossing the country. He'd drop Bones off at the shelter and head to Houston's place.

The inquiry brought up two nearby rescue facilities; both calls went to voicemail. He left messages. His next search for a veterinarian showed the address of a single business listed in Oak Creek. Another voicemail, another message.

"All right," Reid ran a hand through short cropped hair. "I guess, we'll have no choice." Yard's eyes skipped between Bones and Reid. "He'll have to come with us, bud, until we hear from one of the shelters." The dog had to have food—canned meat, and something for dehydration, and his paws would need attention. If Reid guessed right, he'd get everything he needed at the Pet Stop. Plus, while he was there, he'd buy that seatbelt for Yard.

***

As fast as the heavy shower had started, it stopped. Patches of blue sky slipped through parting clouds, shafts of sunrays cranking up the heat. April in Kentucky was where the four seasons met—often in one day. It didn't change the fact that Reid's clothes were still soaked or that his prosthesis had gotten wet. Puddle jumping would do that, but at least, he smirked, the leg was waterproof.

Not surprising for a Friday afternoon, Pet Stop's parking lot was crowded. Reid ignored the blue and white marked space close to the entrance and steered the Wrangler into an empty spot toward the end of the building. He held a strange belief that accepting the handicap parking lot equaled an admission of defeat. Similar to laying down his arms, forfeiting a return to normalcy. And Reid would never surrender. His mother had labeled it pride.

Reid killed the engine and lowered the windows. Yard didn't waste a second. The glass was still sliding down when he thrust his head out.

"What is it with that twitching nose of yours?" Reid laughed at the dog, shrugged out of the slicker and tossed it on the passenger seat. "You're in charge, bud. I'll be back in a few."

He neared the entrance just as the sliding glass whooshed open, and a woman carrying a 50-pound bag of dog food slammed into him. *Thump.* The bag slid and crashed to the ground. Heads turned. Great! Jade green eyes flashed and assessed.

"Dadgummit! Don't you watch where you're going, Mister?"

The strawberry-blonde appeared flustered. Reid calmly regarded her judging stare with a scrutinizing look of his own.

Corkscrew curls hung to her shoulders and loosely framed her flushed face. A shapely figure inside jeans, long-sleeve Mossy Oak shirt, and matching rain boots. That get-up was most likely to blame for the flush, but hot damn, it looked good on her.

"I'd say I'm sorry, lady, but I believe it was *you* who ran into *me*." He cocked his head. "Maybe *you* should be the one apologizing?" The woman had barely been able to peek over the bag when she crashed into him. What nerve!

"You saw me coming through that door!" Keira flung her arms up in visible frustration. "Unless you're not only rude but vision-impaired, too?"

Was she for real? Stunned, Reid slid his military-style shades on top of his head. "Excuse me?" Steel within narrow eyes sliced through the somewhat disheveled woman. He'd been accused of a lot of things, and rightfully so, but being rude to a lady wasn't one of them. His mother would have his hide. Letting his cool gaze travel from unruly curls to Mossy Oak rain boots, she didn't appear much of a lady. And he dropped that thought immediately.

"You could have stepped aside. But okay ... you made your point," Keira burst out.

"I beg your pardon?" Reid's tone didn't hide the rising temper. Keira bent to pick up the heavy sack, but Reid beat her to it. "Allow me to apologize for *your* mistake and carry this to your car," he offered, lifting the bag effortlessly in one swift motion.

Keira squinted her eyes at the annoying sarcasm in his voice but thought better than to respond in kind. "I don't need your help, *Sir*. But thank you just the same." She flashed him a broad smile and, with startling strength, grabbed the bag from his hands.

The unexpected action took Reid by surprise. What was up her craw? Freckle-face must be having a bad day, he concluded. When he answered, he met her smile with a beam of his own, amusement lacing his voice. "You're welcome, ma'am. Didn't mean to get your breeches in a bunch."

Not waiting for a response, he entered the store.

***

On any other day, Keira found it easy to connect and put a smile on even a stranger's face. What, for heaven's sake, had gotten into her? It wasn't the guy's fault she hadn't paid attention and smacked right into him as she left Pet Stop. Right?

So, why didn't she just say sorry and let him help? Because …. Keira pulled her lower lip between her teeth, because, today, for some silly reason, the mishap made her feel incompetent and stupid.

When she'd crashed into the guy, the heat from her embarrassment had scurried up her face, delivering the final push to blow her tolerance meter over the top. The slow cooker of emotions had been on simmer for most of the day, and it had felt good to let off steam. She could admit to that.

In retrospect, Keira felt sorry for the guy. He'd been polite, even showed a sense of humor, she'd give him that. But she hadn't missed the steel in his eyes or the sarcasm in his voice at her stubborn refusal of accepting his help. Neither had she missed the flex of muscles tightening the sleeve of his shirt when he'd picked up the heavy load of kibble.

CHAPTER 4

Sharp edges in an angular face softened with a grin that lifted the corners of Houston Miller's full mouth.

Alyson Shephard laughed. "You're welcome. You can thank me later." The hum of the office fax stopped with the drop of the final page into the paper tray. In one fluid motion, his dad's office manager flung a thick strand of lengthy, black hair over her shoulder and picked up the papers.

"A'ight. Dinner and dance?"

"In your dreams, Miller." Eyes that reminded him of the silky-smooth brownie he'd just wolfed, twinkled with amusement. "Forget it. We're not going on a date."

"Aw, darling. You're ripping me apart." Hand over heart, he went for a hurt expression, only a chuckle rumbled in his rich voice.

"Good. Serves you right." A smile as sweet as Blackstrap molasses. "Because before I know it, you'll march right out of here and take to the road. You'll forget my name before you even reach the end of town. Isn't that so?"

The hurt expression deepened. "Me *forgetting* you? Now you're just being silly, darling … . I'm offended." His face twisted into a comical expression. "How can I forget my heroine, who assists me in this fight of endless questions and answers? She, who battles bureaucracies with grace and charm and the power of her keyboard?"

"Oh, stuff it, Miller." Alyson laughed.

When Houston accepted the stack of papers she'd inserted into a large manila envelope, his fingers drummed with nervous energy across the paper's smooth surface. Inside was the application for his non-profit organization, Heroes Rise.

"Isn't it obvious, how?" Alyson's gaze skipped to the envelope in his hands, and she challenged, "Tell me what's racing through your head right at this moment?"

"Darling, what are you talking about?"

Alyson held up a hand. "No need for words, Miller. You're an open book."

"And what, might I ask, did you learn by reading the most interesting, bestselling volume of the brilliant Houston?"

Tongue-in-cheek, Alyson laid her index finger over her lips and studied his face. "Your mind just skipped into the future. Not just into next week, but *years* ahead."

"Oh?" The sound carried curiosity.

Squinting, Alyson tilted her head and pretended to think.

"Hmm … I imagine you just met at the mayor's office where you discussed the location of the new veteran's sanctuary you're building. From there you're heading straight to the key ceremony of that mortgage-free house y'all built for the paraplegic vet with a wife and five kids. A demanding day, and yet, you still go the office building and poke your head into the finance seminar. But you find it had been rescheduled for the next day, so you pop in on the music therapy instead, pick a guitar and play with the guys. Because that's really your thing. That's the heart of the matter. Hanging with the guys, being part of what makes them heal. Being one of them. Hah, Miller. You're a busy man."

A mischievous look stole across her pixie face. "But not too busy for a little R&R with a cute little blonde who barely reaches your chest on 4-inch heels."

"You're hilarious, darling!"

He'd chuckled, but Alyson's guess had grabbed the bull by the horns. Indeed, his vision for Heroes Rise was a grand one. He could see it. The veterans, the families, the programs that would give hope and meaning to those whose wounds weren't visible. Therapy animals, art in all its forms—they'd utilize it. And the challenges they'd create for those whose confidence blew into smithereens when their limbs did—physical activities such as hiking, climbing mountains, playing ball, would restore faith. And the partnerships they'd forge along the way. At the center of it, a place amid nature to calm the mind.

Houston leaned against the metal filing cabinet, crossing his arms. The manila envelope dangled from his hand. "So, now you read minds, too?" The quip a reference to the tarot card reading he'd stumbled into as she laid cards for his sister, Tessa.

His sister called her Raven. A nod to her midnight black hair? Maybe. But more than likely he suspected the "gift" Tessa gushed about had sealed the nickname. And that was just nonsense. To him, she was Alyson—a person of exceptional perception, an unconventionally attractive style, and a face untouched by make-up that was beautiful to his eyes. But, he conceded, the combination held a magic all of its own.

Alyson pursed her lips, and eyes narrowed to laser beams, drilled into his. "Yep, it's how it will be."

The force with which she'd spoken took him by surprise. Frown lines across his forehead deepened with the lift of brows, but he didn't drop the gaze.

"Hey ... !" Houston shoved away from the cabinet, but the moment had passed; the strange electricity had left the room.

A burst of air surged from Alyson's lungs, clearing the daze from her head.

"Sometimes, though, it comes in handy." Lightness and a hint of amusement were back in her tone. Had she startled him? God, she hoped not. On rare occasions, a vision surged sudden and with incredible clarity, making it impossible to suppress.

"What comes in handy?" The second the words had left his mouth Houston could've slapped himself. Too late.

"It's difficult to explain. It's a vision. Knowing something before it happens …"

"Yeah, right."

Alyson spun around, the colorful skirt brushing in a smooth swirl against black lace-up boots. "You've already forgotten about me." Striding to her desk, she peered over her shoulder. "And you haven't even left yet."

"Slap … slap." Houston smacked the envelope against his thigh. What could he say? She was right, Heroes Rise was his baby. It consumed his every waking thought, had taken residence in his brain on the day he'd watched that documentary in Afghanistan.

"Relax, Miller. You're registered with the Attorney General. Now we wait."

Alyson shut off her computer and slung a cloth-bag over her shoulder. "Since you insist on charming me with food, you can order lunch tomorrow." Her white teeth gleamed. "That new place on Main is supposed to have Old World-style pizza and out-of-this-world desserts. My taste buds wouldn't mind judging for themselves."

"Date. I mean, deal." Houston pushed off the cabinet and sauntered to the window. Outside, a vehicle pulled into the parking lot. In two strides, he'd reached the door and flung it open. Mack had made it. A Jeep door slammed open, and a dog gave two short barks.

"About time, man!" Long legs crossed the parking lot in a few hurried strides.

You've already forgotten, Alyson thought as she dashed to her car. The men were locked in an intense bear hug that seemed to last and last.

***

Reid and Houston didn't need words to express what hung like lead in the air. Their lips, curled inward and pressed into tight lines, said all that needed to be said.

Another shoulder slap. "Great to see you, Mack. It's been a long time ... too fucking long, man." Emotion showed in the ticking nerve under Houston's eye.

"You got that right, bud." Reid turned to the Jeep, hiding the sudden dampness in his eyes. He needed to get back on neutral ground and opening the back door did precisely that.

"Hey, Tex," Reid used the old nickname, "Say hello to the mutt."

Black-and-white fur leaped out. "Some woman just dumped him at your place?" And Houston's eyes grew wide. "I'll be damned—"

Reid nodded, anticipating the reaction. People couldn't help it, and it ticked him off. But in all fairness, he'd never brought up the dog being 3-legged when he said Yard would be going on the road with them.

"This is Yard ... like in three feet," he repeated the same words the anonymous woman had left in her note.

Unruffled, Yard closed the distance just as he would without the missing limb. His tail's long hair flapped in excitement as he sniffed Houston's outstretched hand.

"Cool name. You come up with that?" Houston looked up from petting the animal.

"Nope. Can't take credit for it. But I named that one."

Now, Houston could hear it: the whimper. Yard scampered to the open vehicle, making a noise that landed between a yawn and a bark as he stuck his head into the interior.

Houston followed Yard and peered inside. "What the hell, Mack?" He wasn't easily stunned, but here he was, knocked for six a second time in fifteen minutes.

***

Reid followed Houston to his parents' place just outside the city limits.

The genuine warmth of Helen Miller's welcome came unexpectedly. "What's with that handshake, young man?" She shook her head and threw her arms wide open. "Houston talked about you; so it's as if I know you already," she said, embracing him in a great big hug.

Houston's face split into a grin. It was so like his mother, whose Southern charm and hugs went hand in hand. When his eyes met Reid's, he lifted his shoulders in a gesture of "what can you do?"

Now, Reid politely declined Helen Miller's dinner invitation, but the matron of the house wouldn't take no for an answer. Fist on hip, she stood looking up at him. With the tilt of her head, a delicate, open-leaf earring followed the sway of her silver bob's sharp angle.

"That's just nonsense, young man. Harold and I have been looking forward to meeting you." Sharp eyes cut to Houston, commanding support. "And now that you're here, you want to deprive us of the pleasure?"

Houston shot Reid an amused look that said *Give it up, man. You're no match.*

"You don't want to upset an old lady, now, do you?"

"No, ma'am, I wouldn't dare. Your grace and charm make that impossible." No muscles twitched, but humor twinkled in his eyes. He'd heard the tease in Helen's tone that reminded him so much of his own mom.

"I'm happy to join you for dinner."

Helen's face softened. "You're spending a whole year with my son, trekking across America. I want to get to know the person that's as crazy as he is."

"Yes, ma'am. I understand. I appreciate your kindness."

"Good. Now that we're clear, Houston, why don't you get the key and show Reid the way to the cabin and help him unpack?" Not a question, Houston knew, but a gently phrased instruction.

"Yes, ma'am."

Bones lay in a kitchen corner on an old blanket, sleeping the sleep of exhaustion. Helen had been sickened by the sad appearance of the dog and insisted on Reid bringing him inside. She had checked the cut on his paws and fed him ice chips. Neither of the two animal rescue shelters had returned Reid's phone call yet. "Great, it's been over two hours," he mumbled under his breath and questioned if he'd still be hearing from anyone today.

"Reid, you can leave Bones here for now; let the poor thing rest a little more."

"Thank you, ma'am. If it's not an inconvenience."

"Young man, would I have offered if it was? Now you two get out of here; I've got dinner to cook." Houston and Reid exchanged a look.

Yard, who'd kept his eyes peeled on Bones, scampered to his feet when Reid called his name.

Helen selected a frying pan from the large rack over the island. "Oh, and dinner's at 7:00," she called over her shoulder as the guys headed out.

"Dismissed." Reid followed Houston, cracking a smile. "I see who's the general in your family."

Houston shrugged. "She can be bossy; a real pain in the ass sometimes. Other times she's soft as a cotton ball. It's how she is. She means well, though. You'll get used to it. Okay, let's go. Ready to get settled?"

Houston scooted into the passenger seat of the Jeep. About a mile along the country road he had Reid turn into a wooded section of the Miller property. The paved road turned into dirt tracks winding along with dogwoods and redbuds blooming under the spring canopy of giant trees. Here and there, boulders rose from the lush undergrowth of shrubs, bushes, woodland ferns, poison ivy, and wildflowers.

Ahead, a clearing came into sight and there stood the cabin, its rustic charm blending with the backdrop of the woods. "Home, sweet home for you, buddy. Park over there," Houston pointed to a graveled section beside the cabin.

"Wow, Tex. This is great! Hard to believe you're this close to town." Thumb and index finger indicated the space of an inch. Reid filled his lungs with the scent of rich earth, a fungal mix of moisture and sunshine. A few feet away, Yard did the same, scampering around the house with his nose to the ground.

"Well, I certainly appreciate your parents' offering up the cabin." Reid's hand glided along the porch railing, smoothing over knots and gnarls, feeling the imperfections of the wood while Houston unlocked the front door. "Thanks for making this happen, man."

"Don't worry. It's a great place to accommodate the occasional overflow of houseguests. Family reunions, Christmas parties, you name it."

Houston threw open the door, and smirked. "And for now, it'll be home base for operation Heroes Rise. So, don't give it a second thought."

They entered a short hallway which flowed into a spacious room, revealing a cozy and comfortable looking set-up. A deep-seated sofa faced an impressive fieldstone fireplace to the left. "You'll need those," Houston indicated the hearthside holder stacked with logs.

But at the moment, Reid didn't care about firewood. "Man, look at that!" Straight ahead, top to floor windows revealed an astonishing view.

"Tex ... this is freaking awesome! Why the hell aren't you staying here, man?"

"Nah, I'm good. The apartment's got everything I need. It's quite ideal living over the old man's workshop. Especially since dad's office manager did a ton of research to get the application paperwork filed just right."

"With your level of patience for paperwork? I bet it was."

It teased a sly grin from Houston. "I just had to skip down a few steps. How convenient is that?" Houston went to the tiny kitchen to the right and grabbing a couple of bottlenecks from a fridge crammed full of beer, he held them up. "This one still your favorite?"

Reid's gaze shifted from the outside view to the open fridge. "How can I say no to that?"

"Cool." Popping the tops, Houston beamed, and handed Reid an open bottle while Yard checked out the rest of the cabin. "I've got us covered."

"Bedroom's upstairs?" Reid gazed at the steep wooden stairs to the loft.

"Yeah, there are beds upstairs. No bathroom, though, just chamber pots," Houston said without a single nerve twitching on his face. At Reid's bewildered expression, he roared. "Just kidding, man," he said, opening the door next to the steps. "Care to check out *your* chambers?"

The queen-size bed, imposing and inviting with its creamy white duvet and luxurious damask pillows leaning against a black metal frame, drew Reid's eyes first. Silently he gawked at the walls, covered in rustic wood from a barn, before his eyes fixed on the large red rug. Atop lighter shaded floor planks it offered an elegant contrast to the room. In place of the expected cabin décor, the contrast provided a welcoming oasis of country chic.

Words like "country chic" didn't enter Reid's mind, but "cool" summed it up in one word. "Didn't I hear you say, 'Not a fancy dig'?"

"Would you have accepted the cabin if I'd told you otherwise? Knowing your stubborn ass, I'd say no. Your bathroom is through here." Reid had missed the door that was clad in the same barn wood as the walls.

"Jeez, Tex. What can I say? This is fucking awesome."

"Well, don't get too cozy." Houston tipped the bottle, took a deep pull. "Tomorrow we'll set up shop." He tilted his head towards the dining table. "Heroes Rise home base … right over there."

Bottles clinked. "To Heroes Rise."

CHAPTER 5

SEATED IN A DELICATE SILK-COVERED chair at Mona's Bridal Creations, Keira half-heartedly listened to Mona and Emily discussing the veil selection.

"This one, you'll attach to the back of your head—just like this." Mona tugged and took a step back, assessing the sheer veil. "Oh, this is perfect for a backless dress," she purred, clasping her hands together.

During the past two hours, as Emily tried on dress after dress, a sadness had snuck up on her. The aspirin had done its job, but she could swear the tension had left her head only to move south and settle over her heart.

"Ah! Em, yes ... this is it!" She'd admired and cheered at the classy statement of Emily's final dress choice. "It's spot on!" The floor-length mirror displayed the stunned surprise on Emily's face as she stepped out of the dressing room, and Keira saw the glow of happiness on her friend's face. *Glow of happiness?* Where had that sappy thought come from?

But she knew. She'd watched Emily discuss things such as too much lace, long sleeves vs. short sleeves, a low-cut back and other things a bride concerned herself with. She saw the hue of excitement staining Emily's cheeks, and couldn't help but wonder what those stars in her eyes felt like. To experience this kind of buzz. The longing in the thought had startled

Keira. *Well, that means you'd have to start dating the right guy,* her conscious mind chided, and wasn't off base. Or was it mom's nagging to "find a nice man" that had festered somewhere in her brain? Jace had been fun to be with, but she'd known all along he didn't fit the "forever" category.

Stretching out her legs in front of her, she sipped air and debated why dating was such a chore. The ache she couldn't name spread inside her ribcage.

How does it feel to love someone who loved you back so much that if he wrote a love letter he'd run out of space?

Keira envied her friend, but she also remembered Emily's horrific accident after her aunt's funeral. Sole heir to her aunt's estate, and the new owner of Millie's Newfoundland dog, Bentley, a pickup truck muscled her 4-Runner off the road. Emily lost control, and the vehicle flipped as it tumbled down an embankment.

Had it been luck that Ryan and a friend witnessed the incident and provided first aid? Keira mused. And that Ryan's friend knew Emily? Had fate just rolled the dice and won?

Ryan, keeping the injured woman calm, promised to take care of Bentley until her release from the hospital. Yep, this had jumpstarted their tumultuous love affair. Keira grinned. *Leashed by a dog,* she thought.

Keira's friendship with Emily began when word reached the rescue and she'd visited the lonely woman together with the shelter director.

Ryan had cared for Bentley. He'd picked Emily up from the hospital, took her out, and he cooked for her. Emily fell hard for this considerate man. But she couldn't know of the demons that hid deep inside Ryan's soul; of the vow to remain a lifelong bachelor.

Her sweet friend. How she'd suffered. Ryan's break-up had come without a reason or sensible explanation.

Dumbass. If only he'd given voice to his fears. But men ... why couldn't they just talk it out? Why were they so difficult to understand?

He left the country to assist a friend with a documentary. Fled was more like it, Keira thought.

While she watched Mona fussing with the veil, she smiled, but her thoughts returned to Ryan and the day he'd run into her.

While away, something had happened that made him confront his demons. Returning to Oak Creek, he'd begged Keira's help in re-connecting with Emily. Because her friend had cut him off—she'd changed her phone number, deleted him from her social media contacts, rejected his emails, and pretended to be away when he knocked on her door. But she hadn't deleted him from her heart.

Would Keira have been more sympathetic when he'd asked for her help in re-connecting with Emily, had she known of his struggles? *Probably.*

Jeez, but she'd taken a chance by convincing Emily to accept Ryan's invitation to meet.

Yeah. She's crazy in love, Keira thought. *And he's crazy about her.* And his beach proposal in October? Her throat tightened with emotion just thinking about it—it had been perfect.

Emily would be finished soon with trying on and making decisions. She'd chosen her dress, and apparently this was the veil that pulled it all together.

Keira's gaze fastened on a spot behind Emily and she bit her lip, the pros and cons of different veil styles fading into the background. She wasn't opposed to dating, it's just that she kept so busy all the time. And why was that? *Because you're too picky,* echoed back at her. *No, not picky,* Keira corrected herself. *Why waste my time?*

Keira's mom, bless her heart, had invited the bachelor son of a business friend to their dinner party just a few short weeks ago. A man who Keira found immensely boring and a little creepy. The way his eyes kept dipping to her chest and his hands found a thousand excuses to touch her back, her arm. Yuck. No thank you.

And the disastrous date with the guy she'd been chatting with on a dating site? A major creep! His profile described a laid-back personality with a live-and-let-live philosophy. The fact that he was a writer intrigued her. She could go for smart and intelligent with a dash of imagination.

She'd agreed to meet him and now she shuddered as she mulled over the evening in question. No matter how many times she rubbed her eyes, it couldn't be unseen; the image was branded on her brain.

She'd picked a bar in Louisville where the bar manager was a friend. Safety first.

A guy with a handsome face, and a smile that showcased a row of perfect teeth showed up to the date. His profile picture hadn't lied. *Nice,* she'd thought as she smiled back. But what was up with the kilt?

With a curve of her lip she asked, "So, you're a Scot?"

Gentlemanlike he pulled a barstool out for Keira before flopping onto his own. "Nay," he grinned. "Just like feeling a breeze." And to Keira's amazement he winked and leaned into her. "Your family's Irish, you know what I mean."

What did he just say? Stunned, a quick comeback got stuck in her throat. By no means was she a prude, but besides the information they'd exchanged online, he didn't know her. Had she mentioned her parents emigrating from Ireland as a young couple? She must have.

It got worse from there. After downing a pitcher of beer as if he was going for the *Guinness Book of World Records,* he'd presented her with a book. "My most recent published novel," but Keira had missed the smirk replacing the easy smile he'd worn earlier. "Autographed with a special note."

The dark cover was difficult to make out in the diffuse light of the bar, but the ink of his penned note jumped off the pages. Heat crept up Keira's neck and burned her face. The message had scorched her eyes. Smut! Did he seriously pick up women this way?

"Does it satisfy your curiosity?" His speech held just a hint of a slur and his hand landed on her thigh.

"Keep your paws to yourself, perv; we're done." Smacking his hand away, she jumped off the bar stool, drawing the attention of her friend, the bar manager. She threw the book in his lap. OMG. Her eyes bulged. Was that what she thought it was?

Embarrassed, she whispered to the manager, and five seconds later a burly guy mingling with guest approached. Kilt-man didn't protest when the bouncer strong-armed him to settle his bill and move on.

***

Mona stood behind Emily, placing the gorgeous veil just so, when Keira's phone belted out. Startled, she reached for her purse. At the rude interruption of discussing veil length, Mona raised a neatly trimmed eyebrow and gave Keira a poignant look.

"Sorry," Keira mouthed and silenced the ringer. And grinned when she looked at her friend. Emily had stuck out her tongue sideways, and the exaggerated eye roll caused Emily's chuckle. The phone call and her beautiful friend's goofiness pulled Keira out of pointless musings.

At 8:30, Emily and Keira finally stepped out of the boutique. Emily bubbled and gushed about the dress she'd chosen. In the next moment she tugged on her lips. "What about the back? Do you think it is cut too low?"

"Em, it's exquisite, don't worry so much. Who cares if it barely covers your butt? It looks magnificent on you. So much so that I hope Ryan won't be speechless at the altar. That would be a shame."

"Oh, sweetie. Thanks for coming." Emily squeezed her friend into a tight hug. "I'm sorry you had such crappy day."

Oh, hon, you have no idea!

The women reached their cars, which were parked next to each other. "Temps are dropping." Keira shivered, crossing her arms. "My coat's in the car." A hint to get going. She didn't want to talk. Not tonight.

Emily didn't take the hint, or maybe she just ignored it. Inside her happy wedding bubble, she ran a hand up Keira's arm. "Sweetie, it's going to happen for you, too. You *know* it will."

Keira bent her head. One Mossy Creek rain boot scratched the weed that had the audacity to push through the concrete of Mona's parking lot.

"And how do you propose I meet a guy who doesn't turn into creepy weirdo?"

"Well," Emily's voice toned down. "For starters, maybe get out every once in a while. Try singles night, test the waters. Date a few guys, and so what if you don't click? You just move on. But taking cover behind work all the time—school, the rescue, assisting your mom with the news magazine? Nope, it won't work. And before you say anything … hanging out at Pat's on Thursday night doesn't qualify. Same guys, same ole thing."

"I don't know, Em—"

"Take Alyson, or Cori, or both, and head to Louisville. Have some fun."

It was true. At the end of the school day Keira went home, and after taking care of her two mutts Diesel and Boomer, she helped out at Barkville rescue. A volunteer job, but it's where she was needed.

"I'll think about it." Affection showed in Keira's smile. Her sweet but clueless friend meant well and tonight she wouldn't burst her happy bubble.

"I wish you would, but I have a feeling you won't." Emily hugged her friend, running a hand up and down Keira's back. "Love you, sweetie. Thanks for coming."

"Love you, Em. Good night."

Keira flopped into the driver's seat, pulled that offensive phone from her bag, turned up the volume, and listened to the voicemail. It was Haley, Barkville's assistant director.

"Hey, Keira. Sorry to bother you this evening. Phew, what a day. I've been out since lunch and just got around to listening to all our voice mails. Had a guy calling who found a little brown dog on the edge of town. Said he was in pretty bad shape, like malnourished with a bleeding paw. Sounds like a stray, but you just never know. Tyler and I are going to be out of town for the weekend."

Keira could hear the smile in Haley's voice. *Everyone's so damn happy today!*

"An early anniversary getaway." Haley's voice droned on.

Aha. That's why. The sharp blade of jealousy instantly pierced her gut.

"So, this puts me in a jam, Keira. Would you give this guy a call, see what's going on? Please? His name is Reid McCabe. Oh, and he's a friend of the Millers. Helen's already called, too. Apparently, she didn't trust us to call back on our own without dangling the donation carrot. I'll text you his phone number."

"But the shelter is full," Keira mumbled to herself.

As if on cue, Haley confirmed. "You already know we are at max capacity. We cannot take another single animal. Not even a small one. We can't quarantine him."

"Uh-huh."

"Please, Keira. See if he's willing to foster for us? Oh, and can you get the dog over to the vet's office? Have them charge it to our account. Better yet," Haley paused for effect, "maybe you can persuade him to adopt. Use your charm, girl."

Yeah, sure, Keira thought. Right now, she felt as charming as an ice bath on a cold day.

"Okay, you know what to do if he agrees to foster," Haley's voice carried on, animated and unaware. "You know how to reach me if you need me. *Muah.* Thank you! Love you … and good luck."

"Yep, and that's why, sweet Emily, I don't have time to date," Keira uttered, chucked the phone into her purse, and started the car. She'd make the call from home.

***

The headlights' bright beam cut through the midnight-dark forest as the Jeep bounced toward the cabin. It had gotten late and now with a belly full of Helen Miller's country cooking and a couple of cold ones after dinner, Reid could barely suppress a yawn. Around him, the occasional eerie glow of nocturnal life reflected from the low brush. Except for the small lantern dowsing the front porch with a weak beam, darkness surrounded.

Reid got out of the vehicle ... and froze. His neck vein throbbed an erratic beat as he listened, letting his eyes adjust. Yard, who'd sauntered ahead, lifted his leg and released. As Reid's feet remained rooted to the damp path, his hearing tuned to the rustle of small creatures scurrying. No threat.

His breath turned shallow as his eyes darted through weak shafts of moonlight filtering through the light canopy of trees. Night vision allowed them to penetrate past a few feet. No shapes or outlines stood out. No threat.

But darkness equated danger. Couldn't trust. He waited—a dazed and noiseless silhouette, transported from the coolness of a Kentucky night to the heat of a desert that scorched his mind.

A paw on his leg, a whimper, and his surroundings rushed back into focus. Reid shuddered, and a harsh breath surged from his lungs. "Hey, bud, did I scare you?"

Yard gently leaned against Reid's leg. A stranger may have observed a man supporting his dog. But it was he, Reid, who leaned on the dog for emotional support. No judgment, just acceptance and wisdom behind the gentle eyes; the canine sensed and chased away Reid's anxieties. Reid straightened his back and took control of his breathing.

"Hell, Yard, whatever did I do before you showed up on my doorsteps?" A warm tongue flicked against a clammy palm, the blow of his cheeks, similar to a reassurance that the dog somehow had his back. Strange, how in less than three weeks he'd bonded with the dog he didn't know he needed.

"Okay, bud. What do you say we get Bones inside, and call it a night?" Reid grabbed his phone from the console. "Damn rescues," he muttered and picked up the blanket with the dog inside. He'd been waiting on a return call all evening, but when the phone rang, it had been his parents. Since then his phone had stayed silent. "Hell of a way to run a business," he kept grumbling as he carried the bundle into the cabin.

As his gaze skipped across the great room he wondered where to put the dog and decided on the kitchen. It was tight in there, but close to the bedroom. If he left the door open, he'd hear the dog if something wasn't right. Reid filled a small bowl with water and placed it on the floor.

The cabin had a chill to it. After turning up the split unit, and too bushed to turn on the TV, he sunk into the sofa. The firebox's black hole gaped. *Tomorrow*, he thought, *I'll make a fire.*

Reid opened his phone one last time, and that's when he saw the missed call. "How the hell did I miss that?" From the floor, Yard looked up and lifted his ears.

He pressed play and listened to a woman's apology for the late return call. "Hi, this is Keira from Barkville Rescue returning your call. I'm sorry I've missed you. I'll call again tomorrow."

Heck, yeah. What took so long? But at least someone had returned his call.

***

Reid rubbed the corners of his eyes, chasing the sleep from them. No time to mess with the prosthesis, he had to hit the bathroom. He grabbed a set of crutches leaning within reach.

"Yard?" The dog had the habit of sneaking into bed at some point during the night, but he wasn't there now. Reid stretched and yawned, his chest expanding with the drag of air. Last night, when he crawled under the down comforter, he'd closed his eyes and collapsed into a dreamless sleep. A first, the door to his mind had remained shut to the ghosts of foreign nightmares. But at the moment he had a more pressing issue.

Reid came out of the bathroom to find Yard stretched out on the bed. Plopping next to him, the mutt rolled onto his back, stretching all fours into the air. "You're such a spoiled brat, you know that? But all right." Reid laughed and indulged his dog with a terrific belly rub.

Lifting the phone from the charger, he checked the home screen. "Thirty-nine degrees and afternoon storms. A great day for a fire, wouldn't you say?"

After Reid went through the ritual of fastening the prosthesis, he dressed in a pair of jeans, a T-shirt, and a flannel shirt.

"Now, let's check on Bones." He sauntered into the kitchen and found pieces of chewed gauze, but no Bones. Yard skidded into the great room. There, in a corner, a brown tail thumped an animated rhythm against the hardwood, before the mutt wriggled to his feet.

Yard shoved his nose into Bones' fur, nudging him. The little guy yipped, licked, and rolled on his back as if saying, "Hey, you're the boss."

"Yard," Reid called out. "Stop that!" He scooped up the smaller animal. Once again, he felt the bones in the palms of his hand and cringed. Reid flipped a switch and the patch of grass in the back glittered silver in the shaft of the deck light.

Opening the patio door, Yard ambled down a few steps, followed by Reid. "Hold on, and quit squirming," he told the tail-wagging dog. Ice crystals crunched underfoot as Reid stomped out a spot for Bones. The dog was more energetic than yesterday, he realized. Out of nowhere, it hit him that he talked to the animals as if they understood. *Maybe they do,* he pondered. Only, they didn't talk back, and that suited him just fine.

Back inside, he made a pot of coffee and considered the fridge's contents. Inside the meat drawer he found bacon, and the shelf held a dozen eggs and hash browns. Except for the beer Houston stocked, Helen had thought of everything. Bless her good sense! He'd fix a good breakfast later.

As he did each morning, Reid took his coffee, checked emails, and his social media pages. Yard, sprawled with his head between his paws next to Reid, yawned, got to his feet, and trudged to Bones, who was dead to the world. The morning romp had worn him out. Yard plopped beside Bones and began licking the little guy's matted fur. The animal's eyes opened with a lazy tug, then closed in contentment.

Outside, dawn slid open a curtain of gray. Reid stood and stretched. "Come on Yard, let's build a fire." Open-mouthed and tongue lolling, the dog followed Reid's every move as he placed chunks of wood onto the fireplace grate.

Just as he'd finished building the fire, his phone rang. The woman from the rescue; he recognized the number.

"Hello. This is Keira. I'm with Barkville Rescue. Did you get my voice mail from last night? I hope I'm not calling too early?" It was just before nine o'clock.

Sweetheart, you think this is early?

"I did. And no, ma'am. This is fine, he said instead."

"You called about a small dog you picked up? A stray?"

This voice. Something familiar in it tickled Reid's brain. But no, he dismissed the thought. He didn't know anyone in this town, much less anyone affiliated with dog rescue.

"Yes, ma'am, I did. Yesterday afternoon."

The woman must have picked up on the impatience in his tone, because a sigh reached his ear.

"I'm sorry, long story. But everyone from the rescue was out." And, in light of the director mentioning Helen's call, she clarified. "A rescue mission. We didn't get your message until early evening. My apologies."

"All right. Hold on a sec—" Reid pulled open drawers in search of paper and pen. "So, what's your address?" He shot a look at Bones. "I can I drop him off within the hour."

"Ahem. I'm very sorry, Sir, but that won't be possible."

"Excuse me?" Confusion slid into his voice. "Didn't you say you are with a rescue group?" No way was he getting stuck with another dog. Yard lifted his ears as Reid paced the great room.

"Yes, but ... "

"But what?" Baffled, he cut her off. "Why can't I drop him off?"

Another sigh, filled with exasperation this time. "Look, I'd like to come out, assess the animal. From what I understand, the dog needs to be looked over by a veterinarian."

"Okay." Reid hesitated. A gulp of breath tempered the growing impatience. "Are you saying you're taking him to the vet's office then?"

"Mr. McCabe, can we discuss the animal's welfare in person? And yes, I'll take him to the vet."

Reid meant to deliver the dog to the shelter, but as long as she'd take him off his hands, he didn't mind her coming out. *Lady, whatever trips your trigger.* Puzzled, he slid the phone into the front pocket of his jeans. Good. It saved him a trip.

***

At nine thirty in the morning, Yard lifted his ears and cocked his head, followed by a low rumble echoing in his chest.

Reid didn't expect the rescue lady for another thirty minutes. With plenty of time, he'd just cracked two eggs into a frying pan and lifted four crisp, sizzling slices of bacon onto a double layer of paper towels when the hum of a car outside the cabin reached his ears. The engine shut off and a car door slammed shut.

"Dammit, Yard, she said ten o'clock. I guess breakfast is shot." With regret, he eyed the bacon teasing his taste buds, snatched a piece and crunched. "What woman in this universe is ever thirty minutes early for anything? Not in my world. Thirty minutes late is more likely."

Reid went to open the front door, and Yard trudged behind, managing to squeeze beside his human. Reid's hand signal kept him there. Reid stepped out onto the porch and froze in his tracks. *I'll be damned!* A slow smile lifted the corners of his mouth at the sight of the woman walking towards him. Mossy Oak fleece, a matching headband, and hair the color of strawberry wine. Freckle Face! The woman from the pet store. That's why the voice had sounded familiar. "Oh boy, this just got interesting," Reid whispered to the dog, and decided to have a little fun.

"Well, well ... and so we meet again." The corners of his eyes crinkled. Amused, he watched her breath catch in her throat as recognition dawned. "Or should I say bump into each other again?"

Did she blush or was it the bite in the air that brightened her cheeks?

"I'm Reid McCabe, and you are Keira?"

"Keira Flanigan. I'm here on behalf of Barkville Rescue." Her eyes skimmed to the dog standing next to Reid.

"This is Yard," Reid answered the question she'd undoubtedly ask. "You're early."

"I am?" Keira squinted, a puzzled look crossing her face.

Reid glanced at his wristwatch. "You're thirty minutes early."

"You must have misunderstood. I said I'd be here before ten o'clock." She thrust her chin forward, the challenge bright in her eyes, defiance strong in her voice. "It's before ten."

Her cheeky spirit from yesterday had returned, and strangely, it pleased him. Reid's mouth pulled back, baring gleaming teeth in a strong face as he brushed a hand across his unshaven chin.

"Once again, I apologize. My fault. I must have misunderstood, just as I did yesterday."

Keira sighed. "If this is about yesterday, sir—" and blinked as he interrupted.

"The name's Reid."

"All right, *Reid*. If you don't mind, can we get to the reason you called?" Keira stepped onto the porch.

Reid chuckled inwardly at the purposeful attempt to conceal her agitation.

"Of course. Bones is inside." His eyes went to the mud-spattered Mossy Oak rainboots. "Come out of the cold."

"Bones?" Keira hadn't missed his appraising look.

"Yes, the dog you're here for. He's inside. Too lazy to leave his spot by the fire, I reckon."

Keira vigorously scrubbed the soles of her rubber boots before stepping into the hallway after Reid. "I'll take these off," she said and peeled one woolen-socked foot from a boot. "I've let the dogs out at the rescue. I had help, so I finished early." Keira placed the boot on the mud tray by the door.

Behind her, Reid shut the door. Keira stooped to remove the second boot when her foot wobbled, and she started to lose balance.

"Oh, no, no." She shot her arms out, desperate to level out. Losing the battle with gravity, she stumbled backward, a punch to the already bruised ego. Keira grappled for support; her hand smashed against Reid's chest before her palm flattened against the closed door.

"Whoa. Take it easy, Mossy!" Reid grabbed her upper arm, his eyebrows arched. "Are you all right?"

He kept his hand on her until she'd steadied, but he pressed his lip into a line to suppress a smirk. She'd all but smashed right into him. Again. "Really, Mossy, we need to stop meeting like this." His lips curved into a teasing smile as her face grew hot, turning her pale complexion bright red.

Surprised, she took a quick step back, and Reid's hand dropped to his sides.

A moment ago, she'd fought for balance; now she struggled to regain composure. Reid saw it in the wide eyes, raised hands, and the heat in her cheeks as she backed away.

Annoyance flared. Jade green eyes darkened, and disbelief laced her voice. "Mossy? My name is Keira. I'd appreciate your using it."

He'd cut her some slack. If he judged the impression on her face correctly, she'd rather have her nails pulled than deal with him any longer than she needed to.

CHAPTER 6

Alarm bells rang in Keira's head. Phew. What had *that* been about? Embarrassing as it had been—toppling and grappling not to fall on her butt—she still felt the imprint of his hands flaring up her arm. A tingling reminder of the awkward moment.

Take a deep breath. Calm down. Keira couldn't afford an ill temper to take over common sense. *Focus, Keira, focus.* She visited on behalf of Barkville business, and she'd been given a challenge: The mission to get him to foster, better yet, adopt the dog. That's all she needed to concern herself with.

Reid led her into the great room. "Ah, and this must be Bones." Keira dropped her bag to the floor and knelt a couple of feet from the dog's blanket. Yard slinked up to her, and Reid looked on from behind. "Come here, baby," she coaxed, making small clucking noises with her tongue.

At first, Bones approached with suspicion slowing him. Eventually, Keira's baby-voice babble succeeded, or maybe it was the soft treat she held out, luring Bones to her. Greedily, he took the treat from Keira's fingers.

She pulled a pair of latex gloves from the bag, slipped them on, and gently ran her fingertips over the skin between his shoulder blades. When she didn't feel the tiny microchip, she ran a scanner across his neck and shoulders, and as she'd expected, came up empty. He wasn't microchipped.

He was a wretched-looking creature inside sagging skin. Keira had seen it before. The emaciation, the hunger, the matted fur. And the eyes. It was in the eyes—some were full of sadness and distrust, others hopeful, sensing the change from trouble to freedom. This one changed from suspicion to acceptance right in front of her eyes. Yard did his thing with his nose, nudging the little guy forward. And that's when she noticed for the first time Yard's missing hind leg. She hadn't been aware until he moved right in front of her.

"What happened to him?" Keira thrust her chin at Yard, while her hand glided over Bones skinny body. She dipped her hand into the fleece's pocket and dug out a few more treats.

"Don't know. He came that way," came the short answer.

"Okay? A bit touchy, aren't we?"

Reid had been leaning against the wall, observing Keira with Bones. Now, he pushed away.

"Wouldn't you? If everyone gawked at your dog, feeling sorry for him?" he asked instead. "And feeling sorry for you too? Because your 'best friend' is beautiful, but somehow defective?"

He sounded agitated as he towered over Keira. His gait wasn't perfect, the slight limp hardly noticeable, but Reid didn't fill her in on his own defectiveness.

"I'm sorry. Did I strike a nerve?" The question issued as a challenge, but when Keira noticed the pulsing neck vein, she softened her voice. "I'm just curious. Because you know what? I may only be a volunteer at Barkville Rescue, but the things I've seen, the cruelty of humans against animals? If you think a missing leg can shock me, you're dead wrong."

He gave her an intent look that lasted a few seconds. "Okay, sorry. Forget it."

Her answer must have satisfied him as he backed off. "I don't think it had anything to do with animal cruelty. Yard's only been with me for less than three weeks. All I know is he lost the leg as a pup. Your guess is as good as mine."

Unmoved, Keira began parting Bones' fur.

"I've checked him for fleas. Didn't see any." Reid offered while scratching the mutt behind his ears. A distraction to keep Yard from getting in Keira's way.

Keira kept digging through Bones' fur. "He needs a bath."

"Yeah. He's dirtier than a pig after a mud bath."

Lifting Bones' paws, she looked at the pads, removed the gauze from his feet. "I'm no expert, but you did a great job with his paws." She beamed a smile, aimed at putting him at ease. "Your dog seems to be his self-appointed guardian."

"They get along."

"Here you go. Good doggy." She patted the small animal's head and offered another treat. "Can he have one, too?" When Reid nodded, Yard softly took the treat from her fingers.

"I can see they get along great. Yard is looking out for this little guy. He's part border collie, a working dog, so he wants a job. It's in his nature."

"What are you getting at, Mossy?"

"I told you, my name is Keira." But she'd said it with a smile, needed him to keep an open mind to what she'd spring on him next.

"Bones is lucky you found him. It won't be long, and he'll be all right again. With a bath, regular food, vet care, and lots of love." This time she didn't break contact when grey eyes pierced her gaze.

"Again, what are you getting at?"

"I think you know what I'm about to say. He's the perfect companion for Yard. Just look at them." Bones was curled into a tight ball and lay nestled against Yard.

"Whoa, hold on, Mossy. No can do. I don't need another dog. Hell, I'm not a darned dog collector." Reid threw his hands in their air. "This is closed for discussion."

Well, shit. She'd thrown adoption out, first, hoping for the best. Now Keira hoped it softened him to agree to foster.

"Reid. Just look at them. Don't you think Yard would miss his companion? I know it's only been one day but look at the way they've bonded?" With gentle strokes, the big dog flicked his tongue across the little guy's fur.

"Did you not just hear me say *no?* Listen up and listen well. *No, I do not want another dog.* End of story."

Worry wormed into her gut. "Okay, okay. There is another solution, but hear me out. Please?"

Reid crossed his arm. "If this solution is anything other than you're taking him, then the answer is still no." But her nagging about Yard had hit home. His dog already had a job, and he was good at it. At times, when Reid's mind came close to plunging over a cliff, Yard pulled him out of the danger zone. But maybe the dog deserved a friend of his own species?

"Okay. Let me tell you what happens if I take Bones out of here, today. We have *zero* space at the rescue. None." Keira's voice grew thick with distress as she emphasized the dilemma. "Bones will need to be quarantined for about two weeks, but we are already beyond capacity. We simply can't do it. We'll have to take him to the county pound. They'll take him, and he can stay there. Five days." Keira held up a hand, spreading her fingers. "Five days, that's all he'll get. And you better hope someone will claim him, because if not …" She let the sentence hang in the air, allowing Reid to draw the conclusion.

"Damn," Reid hissed and felt his heart melt for the little brown dog he'd rescued just yesterday.

"But, if you're dead-set against adopting him, there is another solution. You could foster him for us. Give him a safe place for a while, let him stay until he gets adopted. We'll post pictures, description, and network with other rescues. I have a feeling he won't be listed very long. I'd like to take before and after pictures. The way he looks now, and again in a couple of weeks. By then, he'll be the cutest dog on the adoption sites. He'll find his new home in no time."

Keira sighed and mentally crossed her fingers. *Please, God. Please, let this man have a change of heart.*

"So, tell me how this foster thing works." Reid rubbed his face. "I couldn't let him die by the side of the road, and I sure as hell won't let him die in five days."

Silently, Keira congratulated herself and danced a mental jig. Another life saved. Over the next ten minutes, she explained the responsibilities of the foster parent and the rescue organization. As it happened, she had a foster application in her car.

When she came back inside—this time she'd shed her boots without fumbling—she carried a set of papers and a crate. "Here you go, the foster application." She laid the paperwork on the table where Reid's forgotten breakfast sat forgotten and wasted. "Can you fill it out by the time I bring him back from the vet?"

"That'll cost you, Mossy."

"Dammit, Reid, my name is Keira. K.E.I.R.A. Think you'll remember that?" But her words didn't hold much punch; she was too pleased with her success of converting him to a Barkville foster parent.

Reid had his back to her as he dumped the congealed breakfast into the garbage can. "You owe me breakfast."

"Say what?"

"You heard me. You owe me breakfast."

"Oh, is that so?" She kept her cool, but when he turned and braced his hands on the counter, giving her that toothy grin, something inside her chest fluttered with gossamer wings.

"Tomorrow, nine thirty, sharp."

"And if I already have plans?"

"Do you, Mossy?"

"Quit calling me, Mossy."

"Why? It suits you."

"You're impossibly rude."

"Do you?

"Do I what?"

"Have plans?"

"Hum. It's your lucky day. My social calendar happens to be open."

"Indeed, it is my lucky day."

"And where should I repay you for *your* botched breakfast?"

"I'm not choosy. You pick. Or you can fix breakfast here." He gestured behind him to the tiny kitchen. "It's got everything you'll need."

The flutter inside her chest dialed up a notch. "Hmm … I'll let you know when I get back."

"You do that, Mossy." Reid came around the counter.

Irritated, Keira shot him a narrow-eyed glare. As she bent to pick up the crate, a black container the size of a giant lipstick tube fell out and hit the wood planks with a thunk.

Bones shuffled inside the crate, Yard eyed the tube curiously, and Reid snatched it off the floor before Keira could reach the vessel.

Looking at the black tube with the gold letters and red top, Reid scratched his head. "Pepper spray! Mossy, did you think for one minute this could have saved your hide if I wasn't such a nice guy?"

And here it is again, that smirk. Of course, Reid was right, but he didn't have to know that. She held out her hand and curled her fingers.

"Hand it over." When he did, she tucked it back into the pocket of her fleece. "I didn't reach anyone to come along on short notice." She stuck her chin out, showing a bravery she didn't possess. "It's not the only defense I've got. Besides, you're friends with the Millers. I highly doubt they socialize with serial killers." She picked up the crate for a second time and headed toward the hallway. "But I don't know about you being a *nice* guy."

In a few strides, he stood next to her, taking the crate from her hand. "Here, let me show you just how nice I am. I'll take Bones. Wouldn't want you to bust your butt getting into those galoshes." Full lips expanded into that teeth-baring grin Keira found quite sexy in the stubble-covered face she'd first seen at the pet store.

The annoying heatwave assaulted her neck at the memory. *Damn you, Reid.* But he had a way of doing that to her. *Get a hold of yourself.*

"Nice guy? Did anyone ever tell you you're a ..." Keira tromped to the car and flung open the passenger door.

"You're swearing at me?" She heard him laugh.

"The extra-large version," she shot back. "I'll be back later."

"Looking forward to it, Mossy." Had he said it, or had she imagined it over the engine jumping to life?

CHAPTER 7

Keira had just taken off with Bones when Houston arrived at the cabin, carrying his laptop and a grocery bag.

"Mom insisted. She thinks we're starving." With a sheepish grin, he pushed the sack into Reid's hands. The scent of freshly baked cinnamon rolls wafted from inside; warm and mouthwatering, it teased a rolling rumble from Reid's stomach. He left Houston to peel out of his work boots and strolled into the kitchen where he slid the delicious goodness onto a dinner plate.

"Hey, who's complaining?" his words formed around a mouthful of sticky sweetness when Houston joined him. "Coffee?" Reid asked between bites and poured two cups when Houston gave him a thumbs up. Keira's showing up early had made him miss breakfast, but this definitely made up for it.

Houston leaned against the counter. Blowing the rising steam from his coffee mug, he shot a curious glance at his friend. "Was that Keira Flanigan's car I just passed?"

"If you saw a yellow bug, then yes. She picked up Bones. You know her?"

"Not well. But yes, I met her a couple of times." Grabbing a bun, Houston sunk his teeth into the soft pastry and licked his lips. "Mm-hmm. Good stuff."

"And?"

"And what?" Houston's eyebrows rose high, thrown off by Reid's question. "What are you getting at, Mack? Are you saying she caught your interest?"

"And if she did?" Reid, who'd leaned against the fridge in the tight space of the kitchen, crossed his arms with a challenge gleaming in his eyes.

A grin replaced Houston's frown. He snatched a second bun and licked the icing off the pastry. "All right, man; if you like the spirited type—"

"Meaning what?"

"Meaning, I understand she can be quite … headstrong and prickly?" Chewing the last of his roll, he washed it down with a swig of coffee.

"Hmm, you might be right." The pet store incident flashed through Reid's head.

"A'ight. We've got work to do." Houston reached for the coffee pot, topped off his mug and headed into the great room where he'd left his laptop on the dining room table earlier.

"Then let's get to it." Ready to start working on the grand plan, Reid didn't give Keira's personality another thought.

***

"A year." Houston leaned back against his chair, stretched out his legs, and hooked his long arms around the backrest.

A pot of coffee and an empty plate of cinnamon rolls later, the men had made their first significant decisions. On the map spread out on the table, X marked Oak Creek, the start and endpoint of a walk to end all walks. Yellow highlight followed a route across the country.

Yard lay on his side, a few feet from Reid. The gentle rise and fall of his chest the only sign he was alive.

Reid scrubbed his face. Outside, a gust of wind picking up a heap of leaves, spinning them in playful patterns, caught his attention. Tiny drops of water against the windowpane deceived the joyous dance. And it hit him.

"There it is. The plan." Reid rubbed his neck, and his gaze remained fixed on the window. "Six days, twenty miles a day, and one day of rest. And kick-off is the second Saturday in September."

Houston nodded. "That's it, Mack."

They'd set the route and picked the date. Coinciding with the first day of the National Suicide Prevention Awareness Week, they'd chosen the date to honor the estimated twenty veterans taking their own lives each day. And for each one of them, they'd walk one mile a day.

"Twenty vets a day," Houston said. "Now, the real work begins. This is it, Mack. It's where the idea becomes a reality. Remember the old phrase *where the rubber meets the road?* That'll be us in the most real sense. You and me, bud!"

Somber switched to excitement the moment Houston flew out of his seat. "Hell, yeah." High fives, shoulder slaps, and grins like children on Christmas morning. "This calls for a beer," he said as he grabbed the map and shook it in the air.

Yard lifted his head, grumbled his displeasure at the interruption, and flopped back to the floor.

"So, what's the status of the non-profit?" Reid twisted off the top and took a long pull.

Too wired to stand still, Houston leaned his shoulders against the wall, tapping his foot. "Application's in. I expect it to go pretty fast, though. Took a buddy of mine only six weeks, but I'm not banking on it."

"I'll drink to that," Reid tapped his bottle to Houston's. "Five months to go, with a shitload to do."

"Monday, we'll reach out to veteran organizations, like the American Legion. We'll get in front of them, make presentations, and ask for their sponsorship."

"Good idea." Reid took a slow pull from the bottle. "So, what's the goal, Tex? We've been tossing numbers, but what's the number that's going out in print?"

"Tell you what, Mack. Let's shoot for the moon. Three mil."

The number hung in the air as big as the Great Wall of China.

"Damn," Reid snorted, nearly spewing his beer. "Well, we're sure not playing for peanuts."

Houston brought back his shoulder blades, relieving the tension that had settled there. "We'll need a building; I'm thinking of buying. Paying rent makes no sense. We'll need equipment, office staff, and instruments for music therapy. We want to provide finance services like VA mortgage information, so we'll need space to set up a classroom. And wouldn't it be great if we could build a nature refuge? And grants. We'll set money aside to take care of families who've gone through the worst and give them things like college and housing grants so we can help cover what the VA doesn't. Hell, I don't know that 3 mil will even take care of it. But it's a start."

Reid drew a fist and buddy-punched Houston's arm as a wide grin spread across his face. "Slap my ass and call me Sally." Astonishment turned into booming laughter.

"Remember the motto, Mack. 'Go big or go home.'"

"Good point.

Back to serious, Reid said, "We need to start training."

Outside, trees swayed and bent to the will of assaulting winds. Fat raindrops clung to the sleek glass before sliding down in slow motion.

Houston gazed out the window and shoved the laptop in its carrier. "How about we start hiking tomorrow? I'm heading out. Looks like a storm's brewing."

***

It was only a short ride from Dr. Willow's office to the cabin, but Keira's knuckles had turned white from the death grip she kept on the steering wheel. Just outside the city limits, some asshole passed her in a souped-up monster truck at neck-breaking speed on the narrow country road. A gush of water hit the windshield, robbing her of the ability to see until the furious swish of the windshield wipers cleared the view.

"Jesus Christ! What kind of idiot does that?" She yelled, giving the speeder a single finger. Twice. Wind gusts and driving rain shook the vehicle, challenging her senses and the ability to steer straight.

From the passenger seat, Bones eyed her with suspicion. "We're okay, little guy." Keira breathed a sigh of relief. Ahead, between swishing wiper blades, she spotted the turn to the cabin. "Almost there, Bones. Hang tight."

Woods enclosed, and trees loomed intimidating and scary. With their crowns whipping, and branches shrieking, the trees appeared like bullies in a school-yard. Clouds the color of burned coal turned her surroundings into something dark and foreboding. Goosebumps raced up Keira's back, and she mouthed a silent *thank you* when the outlines of the cabin appeared.

Taking Bones to the vet's office had turned into a marathon waiting session. Dr. Willows, she'd been informed, was tied up in emergency surgery. But, finally, it had been their turn to see the vet.

Keira did a mental jig when doc confirmed the dreaded heartworm test had been negative. Thank you, Jesus! No issues other than being underweight and filthy, with paws indicating extended exposure to the elements. The dog's true temper meant he had belonged to someone. Perhaps he ran away? Or had that someone dumped him?

Bones, freshly vaccinated, bathed, and with his matted fur trimmed, laid in the crate on the passenger seat. Thankful to return the dog to Reid with good news, Keira looked forward to going home, slipping into comfy yoga pants and sweats, and snuggling on the sofa with her own dogs. Maybe later she'd order a chick flick and pop a bag of buttery popcorn. It's what days like these were made for.

She shut off the engine and dug into the driver's door side pocket and—against better judgment—searched for an umbrella. Notepad, fast-food napkins, and gum wrappers were all she found. Well, no umbrella small enough to fit in the tiny space would be a match against the pouring rain, anyway.

Keira mentally braced herself for what would be an icy shower, hesitated for just a second, and flung open the driver's door. She rushed to the passenger side. "Come, Bones." She retrieved the dog from inside the cage and cradled him in her arms. Already, the rain had slicked her hair and soaked her fleece. *At least my feet are dry,* Keira thought and slammed the car door shut. The soles of her rain boots gave excellent traction, but five feet from the stairs her left heel hit a slick spot and she plopped right into a puddle of mud.

At the precise moment her butt hit the ground, the front door opened. Reid, stunned at the woman sprawled in a patch of mud, still gripping Bones to her chest, rushed down the stairs. "Mossy, what the hell are you doing?" He lifted the dog from her clutch and offered his hand.

Embarrassed, Keira stared daggers. "Thank you, I'm capable of getting up myself." Humiliation brought a quiver to her voice, but digging deep for a sliver of dignity, she ignored his hand and hoisted herself upright.

Why did this keep happening? Disgrace dampened her eyes, and shame lashed her insides with the ferocity of the roaring wind whipping the treetops around them.

Rain pelted without mercy. "Take Bones inside, I'll call you later." Keira hollered over the howl of the gusting wind.

She turned into the blasting air and felt him grabbing her arm. "Hell no. You're not going back out in this. Come inside."

"You're telling me what to do?" A fire had replaced the moisture in her eyes.

His eyes softened as he fixed his gaze on hers. "Mossy. Please come inside; Channel 11 just announced we're under a severe thunderstorm warning. This," his eyes scanned the sky, "may get worse before it gets better. Don't be stubborn."

The concern in his voice cushioned her bruised ego. Maybe he wasn't such an arrogant ass—at least not *all* the time.

Her teeth chattered, and her body shook as she hunched against the rain. "All right," she said, shoving wind-whipped hair from her face.

Holding a wiggling Bones in one hand, Reid grabbed Keira's with the other. "Come on, let's get inside."

CHAPTER 8

Reid strode into the great room, carrying Bones. Tail swooshing circles, Yard pranced along with that teeth-baring, tongue-lolling kind of doggy grin. Bones' tail flapped, with his skinny body squirming in apparent joy. A flowery scent itched Reid's nose. He lifted the dog, took a whiff. "Phew ... what's with that funky smell?" He wrinkled his nose at the perfumed fur.

"Doesn't he smell great? Doggy cologne. The groomer in Dr. Willow's office had time to give him a bath." Keira, who'd stripped off her boots and soaked fleece, entered the room.

Reid sat Bones onto his bed of folded towels and stood. His eyes fixed on Keira standing by the fireplace, warming her back. Reid's gaze poured from head to toe, grazed her curves, and wasn't the least bit subtle in his appraisal of Keira's mud-splattered appearance. Reid did his doggone best to suppress a smirk, but the raised brows and wicked smile defied his good intentions.

His eyes crinkled at the corners as he burst into a short laugh. Dirt streaked across her cheeks, clung to her hair. Mud splattered her rain-soaked clothes. She shivered; her full lips appeared a purplish shade of blue.

Annoyance flashed, and Keira wrapped her arms around herself. "What's so funny?"

"Not a thing." But Reid's smirk widened when he said, "You could use a bath, too, Mossy. You look like a wet cat."

Keira flinched as renewed humiliation shot flames up her neck. "Oh, really? Evidently, it's not enough I gave you an entertaining show with my mud splash, but you seem to take some perverse pleasure by rubbing it in."

"Not at all, Mossy. But you've got to admit, it's kind of funny." *Wrong thing to say, Reid.* Her glowering face left no doubt how much she wanted to throttle him.

"Jeez, I'm out of here." With the agility of a caged animal, she spun on her heels, headed for the entryway. "How about growing some manners?" she spat in passing.

Houston's words echoed in Reid's head. Not warm and sweet, but a wildcat. And Reid never backed down from a challenge.

Once again, he grabbed her arm as she darted past. "I'm sorry, Keira. I'm just messing with you. It was rude; I apologize." His deep voice persuasive, his hands on her arms drove ripples of nervousness all the way to her fingertips.

"Humph."

"I didn't mean to razz you about the spill." He lifted a finger to her face, traced a mud streak, "But, it may make you feel better to clean this off."

Keira's anger simmered, anxiety eased, and the fire left her eyes. But the imprint of his finger on her skin lingered, skipped to her chest and pulsed in her stomach. How was it possible he drew such opposing emotions from her?

"Your teeth are chattering. Let's get you out of the wet, and into some dry clothes. I'll show you to the bathroom."

He tossed her a towel, grabbed one for himself, and sauntered into the kitchen. Reid wiped his head and face, and slung the towel over his shoulder. He'd been drenched to the skin, too.

***

Keira came back wearing dry clothes—clothes that belonged to Reid. She'd pulled the drawstring tight, but the sports pants ballooned and swallowed her hips. Luckily the long sleeve shirt covered it. Her face scrubbed clean and wet hair pulled into a loose ponytail, she carried her soiled clothes in a plastic sack and dropped it on a chair.

Reid cracked a smile, which immediately earned him a scowl. "Don't go there, tough guy." The firm tone and index finger aimed a direct warning.

His grin widened as he threw up his hands in mock surrender. "I was just going to say, I like your style."

"Uh-huh. I bet." Keira, still freezing, folded her arms around herself and scanned the kitchen.

Reid noticed the shivers and thrust his chin in the direction of the coffee maker. "Help yourself. I'll go change."

The corners of her mouth pulled up. "Thanks."

"Well, in any case, the coffee's fresh." Reid slid the towel from his shoulder and headed towards the bedroom door. "Be right back. Make yourself at home."

And she did. When he returned with a steaming mug in his hand, she'd wrapped herself in a plaid blanket, sat with stretched-out legs on the sofa, and cradled a mug in her hands. Bones nestled against her, and Yard sprawled on the floor.

"Traitors," Reid said with a sideways glance eyeing the space on the sofa. Keira pulled her knees up to her chest, Bones scooted closer. "Sit down," she smiled, patting the seat beside her. "I only bite if you misbehave."

Wood popped like gunfire. Reid placed his coffee on the table, moved to the fireplace instead, stoked the flames, and added more logs. Gold and orange burnished tawny skin, threw light and shadows across his face. He felt her eyes on him, and instantly, the fire's pops rose to a roar. Attraction settled as a mild pain near his heart.

He'd considered it—the reaction to his physical appearance from the woman who'd caught his interest. Pulling on the leg of his jeans, he made sure the leg stayed covered. He'd seen his ex-girlfriend's response to the mutilation when she came to Walter Reed—the conflict and pity before she averted her eyes. With the visit painfully strained, he'd ended the relationship before she left town, sparing her the disgrace while preserving a measure of dignity for himself.

Would Keira react similarly to his imperfection? Reid had to admit, she wasn't the type he usually felt attracted to, but this beautiful, curvaceous woman with the sassy attitude had caught his attention and interest.

The bothersome self-doubt didn't stop him from flashing her a roguish smile. "Storm's still going strong. Looks like you're stuck here with me for a while. No better time to find out just how nice a guy I am."

Keira took a sip, peered at him from over the rim. "We'll see."

"Or how nice *you* really are, Mossy."

"Oh?"

And that's when it happened. Pop, pop, pop ... *Gunfire?* Reid moved at a fast clip, knocking Keira flat on her back. *Where's my gun?* Bones yelped. Yard sprung to his feet, barking frantically.

He'd pinned her with his body, and hovered. "What the hell?" Keira yelled as her hands shoved against him. Reid's eyes were flat and hard. The punch to his chest hadn't fazed him.

He lifted a finger to his mouth, shushing her. He would protect her. Reid turned his ear, listening. How close were the shooters?

Jammed between the back of the sofa and his body holding her down, she dug her fingernails into his arms. Much good it did. She might as well have dug her nails into bars of steel.

"Get off me," she shouted, landing shallow punches, to no avail. She wriggled and struggled to slide out from under him. "Now!"

"Be quiet." Reid half-whispered, raising his head. Yard pawed Reid's leg and pushed his nose into him—his moves firm, yet gentle. Keira thrashed beneath Reid, clamped her teeth onto his forearm, digging through the fabric of his shirt.

"Let go of me!" She screamed. Reid stared at the window over the sofa's backrest, assessing the threat. He blinked. The window wobbled before his eyes, steadied, and realization slammed into him—not gunfire. Instead, the rapid-fire sound hitting the glass panes were gigantic balls of hail.

"Jesus, Keira." Reid pulled back, eyes wide with distress. He buried his head in his hands. "I'm sorry," he mumbled into his hands. "I'm so sorry."

"What in the hell just happened?" Keira jumped off the sofa. Skin flushed and heart pounding, she lifted Bones off the floor.

"What is wrong with you? Scaring the shit out of me like this ... and him!" Keira backed away from the sofa. Yard sat on his haunches, his head resting on Reid's leg. Dark, liquid eyes stared fixedly.

Reid grabbed the back of his neck, lifting his eyes to the ceiling. "Jesus, Keira. I scared you, and for that I'm sorry. I'm okay now. Really, I'm okay." He patted Yard, murmuring,

"Good boy," got to his feet, picked up the knocked-over mug, and turned to the kitchen.

"You jumped on me like a freaking mad man. You scared the living crap out of me, Reid! Don't you think you owe me a little more than just 'I'm sorry?'" As if she needed to hold on to something, she crushed the little dog to her chest.

With a roll of paper towels in his hand, he stared at her. "It sounded like a gun going off, Keira; I thought someone was shooting at us." Reid bent, wiping spilled coffee from the wooden planks.

"That's all you have to say? You thought a gun went off? Dammit, Reid, do you care to explain?"

"No, Mossy. I don't. Not now. Let it go, okay? I wouldn't have hurt you, just shielded you. That's all. Let it go."

In response, Keira opened her mouth and shut it again. Her gaze flicked to the window. The hail had stopped. Clouds that just a few minutes ago plunged afternoon into night now gradually receded. Like a child in the throes of a temper tantrum, the storm had lost its energy as sudden as it started.

"I'm getting out of here. I'll leave Bones and expect he'll be all right. The shelter director will follow up with the foster agreement on Monday."

"Keira, you don't need to be afraid. Please stay." *Jeez*, Reid thought, *she's terrified. I fucking scared the daylights out of her.*

Keira grabbed the bag containing her wet clothes, leaving no room for discussion. "I'm going."

She reached the front door. "And Reid?"

He cocked his head. "Yes?"

"That breakfast you claim I owe you?"

"Uh-huh." Hope welled.

"Screw you."

***

The door clicked, the engine revved; she'd left. Reid's vision shimmered, his muscles tensed, palms turned sweaty. *Fuck!*

She'd panicked. He'd wanted her to stay, wanted to explain. Too embarrassed, he couldn't find the words. It had been easier to let her storm out.

His fist shot out in rage, striking the solid oak of the front door. The impact throbbed from fingers to shoulder, but he welcomed the pain. It eased the numbness, the shame, and settled the anguish.

After the first signs of PTSD, he'd done the therapy. One-on-one talks, aided by medication, and he'd conducted his own research. Therapy had helped, his outlook turned from bleak to positive, and meds gradually phased out.

Besides the therapist, his mom, and sole confidant, had helped ease the heavy load. At first difficult and awkward, Reid had been astonished at his mom's inner strength. And now, moving to Oak Creek, planning the walk across America, and starting to train for it with Houston had put him back on top of his emotional game. The chance of *this* lasting was excellent. Moving to Oak Creek had been a terrific choice.

But now it had happened again. The flashback. Embarrassing. He didn't have to imagine what had fired in Keira's brain; the bite mark on his arm told him. Hadn't she joked about the Miller's not associating with criminals? No, Reid sneered, not a criminal, just a raving madman. But damn, the cheeky woman sporting Mossy Oak clothes like it was the trendiest fashion statement had grabbed his attention.

Yard moaned and shoved his muzzle into Reid's leg. "Yeah, bud, you're right. I need to clear my mind. Let's get out of here."

CHAPTER 9

Houston arrived at his place just before the storm broke. His instincts screamed the moment he'd partially opened the front door, and before he stepped into the apartment, he caught a shadow, and a faint rustle. He yanked the door shut, and with his side pressed against the metal, he used it as a shield.

"Houston, it's me."

His sister's voice. He sucked in air; his nostrils flared. A slow count to five and he flung open the door. Tessa lounged in the comfy chair, grinning from ear to ear at her surprise.

"Dammit, Tessa! Not cool," Houston thundered. His features darkened as his eyes scanned the room with a frosty look. He slammed the door shut and threw the keys onto the small table by the door.

"Howdy, bro. Good to see you, too."

"I've told you once before—don't *ever* sneak into my place. Do I look like a freaking tape recorder?"

Unfazed, Tessa got out of the chair. Tight chestnut curls bounced with the movement, accenting her melon-pink sweatshirt.

"Take it easy, will ya?" She picked up a parcel from the floor. "Here." Tessa held out the package. "This came to the house. Since mom and dad are in the city, I'm designated courier. Blame them. Besides, this is technically *their* place."

The tick under Houston's eyes faded as she threw her arms around him. "I'm just so happy my big brother is home. And for good this time."

"Well, for a few months, anyway." Frustration calmed in the face of Tessa's good-natured temperament. Smiling, Houston scooted her up and swung her around.

Four deployments to war-torn regions had changed him. Tessa didn't understand his heightened vigilance to his surroundings; he realized that.

Houston held her at arms-length. "Seriously, Tessa, don't pull this shit again. It could get you killed."

Ruefully, she lowered her eyes. "I'm sorry. Next time, I'll remember to call first."

"A'ight, that's what I want to hear." Houston eyed the package and recognized the logo—it had to be the GoPro he'd ordered online.

As he ripped open the box, huge raindrops began splattering the window with a clattering noise. "You might want to wait this out, sis. Want to grab us a Corona? Lime's in the fridge."

Tessa skipped to the galley kitchen, got the beer, handed him a bottle, and flopped down beside him.

"Nice camera, bro. So, when you start walking, you'll be recording every day?"

Houston slid the camera off the package's mounting base, nodded, and dropped her a smile. "Yep. Every. Single. Day. We'll invite everyone in America—and beyond—to join the journey. Let them walk with us from the comfort of their chairs. We'll share all of it—the towns, their people, the meetings with vets, the good stuff, and the shitty stuff, too. We'll live stream."

"Download the app, and you can share directly online."

"No kidding—" Houston lowered the camera and widened his eyes in a fake look of astonishment. "Tessa, my baby sister. When and how did you become so smart?"

Tessa punched his arm. "Smartass. You know, I have massive respect for what you're about to do. It's pretty amazing when you consider the miles you'll be clocking."

"Yep, twenty miles a day, six days a week."

"Hmm. Not an easy thing for anyone ... under the best of circumstances." Tessa fell silent while Houston kept fiddling with the camera.

"What's with the brooding, sis?"

"Just curious." She picked on the condensation-moist label of her bottle. "You reckon Reid will be okay doing this?"

Houston looked up, studied her. "What do you mean?" And it dawned on him. "You mean because of the leg?"

"Mm-hmm. I mean, isn't that torture?"

Houston shook his head. He didn't skip a beat sliding the battery into the camera. "Why should it be? Obviously, you haven't seen the amazing things some amputees accomplish every day. Peel your nose out of books on occasion, sis, and if you look in the right spots, you'll see that the real world is an awesome place."

"Houston?"

The serious look puzzled. "Yup?"

"I want to walk with you, too. I can meet up with you and Reid." Tessa bounced with excitement. "During school breaks and holidays, I can drive to wherever you are. Yes, I'll definitely walk with you during the holidays. Maybe even a long weekend?"

Stumped, Houston searched Tessa's face and saw tenacity in pursed lips and gleaming eyes. His little sister. He'd always admired the strength of character in her. He draped his arm around Tessa's shoulder, drew her in. "I'd love that."

Tessa grabbed her phone, jumped out of her seat and aimed the screen at her brother. "Keep messing with your new toy, and give me your best smile, bro. Your first live segment is coming up."

***

Keira drove away from the cabin, feeling troubled about what just happened. Reid had attacked her. His distress was troubling, but his refusal to explain ticked her off. Ahead, a broken tree limb blocked the wooded lane, causing her to stop and get out of the car. Heaving the unyielding thing did nothing to improve her mood. Water brimmed in her eyes as the knot in her throat grew. *Hell, Reid. I just started to like your smart-ass attitude. But you scared the crap out of me.* Keira wouldn't cry; she swiped the back of her hand across her eyes. Didn't she deserve a little more than an apology? The doggone limb didn't want to budge, but she'd rather walk back to town in the lingering drizzle than turn around and ask Reid's help. Adamant about moving the rigid obstacle, she dug deep for strength and finally hauled the limb aside far enough to pass through.

It felt good to come home to her house and her dogs. The tail-thumping, paw-clawing excitement of her mutts' greetings never failed to coax out a smile.

"Good, boys," she praised when they sat, patting each in turn. "Mommy is so glad to be home," she went on in that silly high-pitched tone one reserved for babies and dogs. Two sets of shiny eyes leveled on her.

"Want to play?" The question stirred renewed frenzy, and two stout bodies bumped and slid to the back door. She laughed at the sheer display of joy.

"All right, let's go, boys." By now, the rain had stopped, and Keira grabbed the balls from the basket the dogs hadn't chewed to bits and pieces yet. In the backyard, she engaged them in a vigorous game of fetch.

After a while, she called the dogs and went inside. She needed a shower. Tired and sore, she felt the sharp pressure of the showerhead massaging the aches from her muscles. Hot, and long, it never failed to swirl the tension down the drain.

She changed into her own comfortable sweats; Reid's clothes lay in a heap on the bathroom floor. Why she gave them an evil eye, and a kick for good measure, she couldn't say. She'd clean them and leave them at the rescue. And if he wanted them back? Well, for all she cared, he could pick them up there. Or not.

In the kitchen, she'd put on the tea kettle. The whistle shrilled, and she poured hot water over the owl-shaped tea infuser holding a fragrant berry mix. Witches' brew, her favorite. On the stove, she heated up a bowl of soup, toasted a piece of bread, and maneuvered everything on a tray to the living room. A late lunch, early dinner, it didn't matter. The rich scent of the broth caused Keira's mouth to pucker, and the rumble in her stomach reminded her she hadn't eaten since the crack of dawn.

Spooning soup and sipping tea, she flipped through the TV channels. Re-runs, harebrained reality-shows, or movies she didn't care for; she turned it off, finished her meal, and called her friend Emily.

"Hey, Keira. Where the heck are you? I left a couple messages."

"Yes, you did. Did you miss my sweet voice, or do you have an emergency? Like having second thoughts on that dress?" *Dial it down,* she thought as the bite in her words reached her ears.

"Dang! Aren't we a little condescending, today? Maybe I just wanted to see if you're free to share a bottle of wine? But maybe I've changed my mind."

"Ah, Emmy. I'm sorry. I'm leaning towards bitchy right now. To sum it up, another shitty day." Keira gave a mirthless laugh. "For the second day in a row; isn't that just great?"

"Hmm. I think an excellent bitching session over a bottle of wine is in order. Feel like company?"

"Sure. Come on over. And don't forget to bring the wine—or we'll have to bitch over tea. And that's no fun."

Thirty minutes later, Emily pulled into Keira's driveway. Keira's two dogs danced around Emily as if she'd been lost and now found. "Hold up, boys." Emily pulled a treat from her purse, and soon they trotted off with a homemade dog biscuit dangling from their lips. Spoiled brats!

"Guess what? I brought two bottles of this lovely Merlot." At home in Keira's kitchen, she sat the bottles on the counter, and pulled the corkscrew from a drawer, while Keira wiped out two glasses.

"Oh, boy. Are you trying to get me drunk?"

"Now, there's a thought. It's been a while," Emily said with a smirk. "Keep the second one for later; in case you want to get buzzed tonight."

Keira glanced at her friend and laughed. "Look at you. Blonde, and tall, smart and confident, hair pulled up, oh so casual, in that perfect messy bun, and about to get married. And to top it off, so very wise." Keira squinted. "You know if I didn't love you so much, I'd have to hate you."

"Uh-oh. It's pretty bad, huh? So, tell me. What happened?"

Keira poured and sniffed the fruity flavors of the wine. "Excellent." Her bones ached; the wine would loosen her up. She skated into the living room, followed by Emily.

Nestled against the cushions of the deep-seated sofa, Emily slowly circled her goblet, watched as the ruby-red liquid swirled inside. "What's got you tighter than a coiled spring, Keira?"

"So, get this ... "

Keira recounted everything from Haley's phone call last night to Reid's light-speed rush thrusting himself onto her.

"Jeez, Keira. I'm so sorry. I would have panicked, too. But did you say he acted as if there was some kind of imminent threat? What spooked him?"

"I know! Emily, I had no freaking clue what was happening. I was so mad, because, you know ... he'd just said he was going to show me how nice a guy he was. Next thing, he's pinning me down with no way to escape. What was I supposed to think? I mean, first he makes that comment, and then this?"

"More wine?" Keira filled near-empty glasses, took a swill. "I haven't got the foggiest about *what* the fuck went on inside his head. I was terrified, couldn't breathe. I fought, but ... he was too strong."

"So, what happened next?"

"Well, his swagger returned. He kept saying he wouldn't have hurt me, only protected me. From what? Some imaginary threat? Heck, if I know. But Emily," Keira threw her hands up. "Call me crazy. As bizarre as it sounds, I believed him. The anguish, remorse, the shame—you could see the emotions on his face, and the water in his eyes."

Keira thought of Bones, and how gentle Reid had treated the dog. "You know, he looked like this stray puppy he found, so sad and in need of some loving care. I couldn't help it, but I felt sorry for him."

"Keira, I bet something terrible happened while he was in the military. Didn't you say he'd been in the Army? Got out less than two years ago?"

"That's what he said in the foster interview."

Emily took a thoughtful sip. "My guess, Keira? He's been to the war zone, probably Afghanistan. And saw things that haunt his mind. Ryan's uncle doesn't care to speak of some of the stuff from his time in Iraq, either. But it's just a guess. Could be something different, though."

"I have no idea, Emily. He didn't say, didn't want to talk. Only said that it had sounded like gunfire."

"PTSD maybe? I bet that's it. Or something like it. Every single day you hear or read something about it."

"Hmm."

Keira drained her glass; her body felt warm and weightless. The wine had painted her cheeks red.

"But what's worse, Em? You could say the guy is quite handsome in that rough kind of way. And his attitude? Provoking at best, with an ego the size of a country—and sexy as hell. All rolled into one giant badass. But I kind of liked him."

Emily shook her head. "Uh-uh, sweet friend. There's no *kind of.* You do or you don't. Like him."

"I was at the cabin for only a short time, but from the time I got out of the car, he kept at it, pushing my buttons, so cock-sure of himself." Fist balled, she pounded her thigh with short bursts. "I could have choked him."

Keira winced, remembering the assault on her insides as Reid had brushed the dirt from her face. "I shouldn't have been attracted, but I was." Unable to sit still, she squirmed, the shade of red on her cheeks deepening. "Until this happened."

Keira stood, her head feeling a tiny bit fuzzy.

"I'm sorry, my friend. I don't know what to say to make you feel better." Emily rose, carried her glass to the kitchen. "I hope you won't keep bumping into him," she said, giving her friend a tight hug.

"I hope you're right," Keira agreed. "That could be awkward."

CHAPTER 10

THE STORM HAD WASHED THE town and scrubbed the streets. Wet brick-paved sidewalks and remnants of puddles glistened under the whitish glare of streetlights when Houston and Reid entered Pat's Place. The tavern, as usual on Saturday night, a cacophony of various noises. Conversations rattled and shouted over the band's tuning of instruments.

Houston and Reid headed to the bar, with Houston greeting, waiving and high-fiving, and Reid receiving curious glances.

Behind the bar, Pat bustled between tapping beer and dispensing mixed drinks. When he spotted Houston, he raised his chin and smiled his acknowledgment.

"Full house tonight." Houston greeted, leaning in for a fist-bump.

"What can I say? A blessing."

Pat's gaze slid beside Houston. "Let me guess ... you are Reid?" He swiped his hands on a bar towel and extended his hand.

"And you know that how?" Reid grinned, knowing damn well how the man had guessed.

"Our lady friend, here," Pat jerked his chin to Houston, and bared powerful teeth, "spilled the beans."

Reid roared. The affection that Pat and Houston held for each other was evident in that teasing remark. He already liked the bald-headed bartender with the intricate tattoos decorating both arms.

"Call me Mack," Reid said, shaking Pat's hand.

"Sure thing. First round is on the house. What will it be?"

While Pat filled two glasses with the local brew, he asked, "You guys ready to make the announcement tonight?"

Houston removed the GoPro from his pocket, handing it to Pat. "Darling," he mocked, "you're taping it."

"Nice!" Pat accepted the device, admired it. "I'll let you have the stage after the band finishes their first set. Will ten minutes be enough time?"

"Plenty. I appreciate you, man." Houston lifted his glass in salute.

While Tessa had used her phone to video his playing with the GoPro, the idea of announcing their walk tonight when the bar would be jam-packed took root. Why hold off? No better time than now to start posting and spreading the news of the walk. Maybe even take in a few dollars in donations? A short call to Pat had cemented it.

They'd finished the beer, and when the band stopped playing, and Pat took the stage, snagging the mic, Houston and Reid joined him.

"Hey, all! Can I have everyone's attention for a moment?" Curious what was happening, and except for a few voices, the room quieted.

"Everyone, please," Pat prompted again. When he was sure to have all eyes on him, he went on.

"Folks, first of all, you're the greatest. Thank you, everyone, for coming out and supporting BCBB every week. Second, I have two special guys here with me, Houston Miller, who most of you know." Cheers and whistles interrupted. "And Reid McCabe."

From the audience, speculative glances flitted between Houston and Reid.

"But I need to get back to filling your glasses, keeping you hydrated," he quipped. "So instead of me blabbering on, I let these guys tell you what either is a really, really stupid idea or a mind-blowing venture."

Instead of working the beer taps, Pat worked the GoPro as Houston gave an outline of the Heroes Rise vision, and Reid shared rough details of their planned walking route.

"So, folks," Houston took back the mic to close it out. "I am so damn lucky to call this guy"—he glanced warm and affectionately at Reid—"a friend and partner."

Houston paused, searched faces, and locked eyes. In the corner of the bar, he noticed a guy with a ball cap sporting the Wildcat emblem. Eyebrows drawn tight, and mouth puckered, he glowered at Reid. Houston was too cheerful to consider what the look meant and continued. "Now that you know what we're planning, I want to give you something else to think about. You wouldn't guess it, but my buddy, Mack, here," Houston paused again and turned to Reid, "will be the first to take on a monumental journey like this as an amputee."

Stifled intakes of breath rose from the crowd. Houston held up his hand, commanding attention.

"You see, during this last Afghanistan tour we served together? Well, he didn't just *leave* the service as he made it sound like. Courtesy of an IED, he retired on a medical. Because, when our convoy stopped, he was in charge of securing his vehicle. He never saw it coming. The bomb hit the truck, injuring him severely, killing two others."

Gasps, less subtle now, sounded. Someone clapped, and Reid, embarrassed at this sort of attention, scratched his neck. A few second later the room erupted in an explosion of appreciative whistles and applause.

***

In the corner seat, Bill Schuster did not put his hands together or show his appreciation any other way. He'd watched Reid, or *Mack,* and wanted to knock that smile from the asshole's face. What was the son-of-a-mother goat doing in this town? Yes, he was very much familiar with the name Reid McCabe.

Sergeant Reid McCabe, charged with securing his truck, and the lives of the comrades within, had walked away from the blast.

The man loathed Reid. Acid churned. A prosthesis. Huh. It was *nothing.* Had McCabe not missed the incoming threat, his son would be alive. No, losing a leg wasn't the worst. The Sergeant lived, unlike his son, who'd lost his life that fateful day. It was this bastard's fault his son was dead. *Damn you, McCabe,* his tortured mind screamed.

Sickened, he settled his tab and left the tavern.

When he got home, William Schuster gave the front door a swift kick, slanting the picture over the hallway table, and rattling the change in his pocket. The steel-enforced toe of his work boot only left a slight impression skittering up his chin. Behind him, Mandy, the tabby, flattened her ears and hissed from a crouch.

"Hissss." The man stooped and stared. The animal retreated, spun around and vanished. "That's right, you good-for-nothing scaredy-cat," he smirked and stomped to the fridge. "Can't even catch a little mouse." It still irked him having to pay for the exterminator last week.

William Schuster was an angry man, but this evening, he felt close to bursting out of his skin. The color in his ruddy face had climbed a few notches, and for good measure, he gave the refrigerator a shove with his boot, too.

"Bill," his wife, Carol, called from the back. "Is that you?"

"No, it's the goddamn neighbor," he yelled back. "Who else do you think it is?"

Carol, a woman in her fifties, waddled into the kitchen. "Bill, honey. What's wrong?" One look at her husband and the ugly anger twisting his face told her not to push it.

He hadn't always been like this. A quick temper? Yes. But not like this. As much as Carol wanted to shake sense into him, scream at him, she related to the pain consuming her husband.

Since Bill Jr. had lost his life in Afghanistan during an attack on his convoy, Bill hadn't been the same. No one had. She'd kept it locked away, the agony, or she wouldn't be able to bear it. Despite an iron will to keep the hurt at bay, from time to time it seared. Especially when Bill got this way.

But Carol had her ways of calming him; it just took a little finesse and lots of patience.

"Now, Bill. You know I don't like it when you cuss like that," Carol pouted.

Bill eyed her, took a healthy swig from the bottle.

"How was your day, hon?" She didn't have to ask; the storm in his eyes had darkened them to near black. And he'd been at Pat's, drinking. "Let me have a sip." She held out her hand, keeping Bill from guzzling the entire bottle at once.

"Sit down, hon. I'll heat up your dinner."

"I saw him. In town. At Pat's." Bill's fist smashed the table.

"Saw who, hon?" Carol asked, setting the re-heated dinner on the placemat.

"I fucking saw him."

A sharp intake of breath. "Bill!"

"Sorry." He shoved his fork into the mashed potatoes.

"I saw the guy responsible for Billy."

"You mean, his Sergeant?"

"I mean the asshole that killed our son."

"Bill." Her tone went to mild. "Sergeant McCabe didn't kill our baby. You *know* that. The Afghan insurgents did. *They* killed him and the other soldier. Cowards with bombs did it. Didn't the Sergeant lose his leg in the explosion, too?"

"The Sergeant is alive. Billy is dead."

Carol laid her hand on her husband's arm. It would be a troublesome night for him. Many a night she'd gotten out of bed to find him at the computer, scrolling through picture after picture—Billy, filled with an insatiable appetite for life. The spotlight at family gatherings, mountain climbing with friends, with his girlfriend at the beach. And tandem jumping from an airplane—Carol had died a thousand little deaths watching him sailing to earth. It had been an unfounded fear.

"A whole life unlived. The wife he'd never had a chance to propose to, the grandkids we'll never have. Had McCabe done his job, Billy would be alive."

It didn't matter that, under no circumstances, Sergeant McCabe could have prevented the attack, nor did it matter that he'd come within a frog's hair breadth of losing his own life. The twisted mind of William Schuster needed someone to blame. And now that the SOB was in town, he'd avenge his son.

CHAPTER 11

THE NEXT DAY, KEIRA FELT spaced out, her body low on energy. Too much wine last night, she chided herself. Or not enough sleep. On cue, her mouth gaped wide open with an impressive yawn. Every other weekend, she volunteered at the rescue, and this weekend her name was on the schedule. Keira groaned thinking of the thirty-plus wildly energetic animals waiting to go outside for a little playtime.

Short on volunteer staff, today only Keira and only one other volunteer would be tackling the demanding morning chores. *Face the barks, and get on with it,* she gave herself a little pep-talk. *Get it done, go home, and go back to bed.*

Despite the early morning hour, she usually enjoyed working with the dogs. It gave her a sense of purpose—that warm and fuzzy feeling that came with the knowledge of helping the animals and her community.

"Keira, all kennels are clean. Let the stampede begin," Tracy called out after two hours of intense work of alternating between keeping an eye on the dogs in the play yard and cleaning kennels. Bringing the animals inside, the mutts pushed and shoved each other in a race to their designated bowls.

While Keira went through all motions of the chores, her memory recalled the volumes of stories she'd read about PTSD last night.

From every article, she gathered compassion, support, and understanding as to the most critical influences in recovery. Conflict tugged on the inside. Her head ached, and she questioned her hurried retreat after yesterday's incident. Did she overreact? *Nope.* Keira latched a kennel and moved to the next. Reid could have helped her understand. But did he? *Nope, again.* Just like a bullheaded male, he clammed up, didn't want to talk. So, did she have an option? Keira puffed air through closed lips. Pffft. Reid had withdrawn into his inner man-cave. Not her fault. Or her problem. Like spoiled milk, she had no desire to have a second taste of it.

"Hello, Keira. Are you still here, or am I talking to myself?"

"Huh? Yes, of course. I'm sorry, Tracy. Let's get them inside."

With every dog accounted for, kibble crunching and noisy slurps of water rang from behind locked kennels. "Thanks, Tracy," Keira said as she locked up. "You were terrific." A glance to the wall clock confirmed they'd finished in just over two hours.

Cobwebs had cleared from her head, but now, Keira craved only the solitude of her home and the company of her dogs.

"Hey, Keira!" Tracy, who'd stepped outside while Keira locked the office door, swung the door open and stuck her head back inside. "There's a guy in the parking lot, with a dog. Looks like he wants to drop him off. Will you talk to him?"

"What?" She snapped her head to look at Tracy. The animals loved the shy woman, but Keira knew Tracy was reluctant to deal with visitors to the rescue.

"No worries. I'll talk to him. The shelter is full, but I'll give him the number to the Humane Society. And if he wants to dump the animal for no good reason, he can have a piece of my mind too," Keira huffed. *Stay professional,* her inner voice warned. She'd gotten carried away a time or two, clashing with dog owners when they dropped off their animals for no valid reason other than their cute puppies had turned into inconveniences. "Sunday morning, to top it off. Selfish schmuck," Keira muttered under her breath.

"I'll be right there, Tracy."

Keira stomped to the entrance and stopped in her tracks with a gasp. She was surprised, but not entirely displeased to see Reid and Yard walking toward her.

"You know him?" Tracy cut in.

"You could say that. He's not dropping off this dog."

But Bones. He didn't have Bones with him. Was something wrong? The animal had seemed all right when she left yesterday. No, she decided at the smug grin he wore on his lips. He would have called. Reid coming to the rescue building had nothing to do with Bones.

"Hey!" Reid lifted a hand in greeting.

"You sure?" Keira noted Tracy's eyes flitting between Reid, the three-legged dog and herself, and would have loved to be privy to her thoughts. What's his motive? And why was he showing up here at precisely this time?

"We're closed." Keira turned her back to lock the hefty metal door. When the lock caught, she spun around, shut her eyes to the sky before her gaze bored into him.

"Or is something wrong with Bones?"

Reid shook his head. "Nope. Bones is great."

"Then what do you need?"

Reid gave her a dazzling smile, ignoring the question. "And a good morning to you, Mossy," he teased and turned his smile to Tracy. "Is she always this delightful in the morning?" Warm breath formed little clouds of fog on the chilly morning air.

"Uh, Keira?" Tracy didn't want to get caught up in whatever inexplicable vibe radiated between Keira and this visitor. Not an alarming feel, more charming in that brittle exchange of words, but Tracy felt like an intruder to that barbed greeting.

Keira opened and shut her mouth, then answered Reid with as radiant a smile she could muster. "Why, thank you. And yes, I'll have you know, I'm an all-around delightful person."

Keira tugged on Tracy's arm. "Come on; we're leaving." Yard, who shoved his nose into Keira's leg, lifted his head, stared at her with intense brown eyes and stopped her from moving. Tail speed-fanning from side to side, tongue sticking out, and lips stretched wide, he gave a joyous expression at recognizing her.

"Aw. He's gorgeous," Tracy offered, smiling back at Reid for the first time.

"By gorgeous, I hope you mean the dog." Keira crouched to pet Yard. She looked up and saw Tracy's face burn a bright red. Damn, why did she have to say that? She should have guessed it would bring high heat to her shy friend's cheeks.

Reid scoffed. "Ah, Mossy. Such a subtle way to boost a man's ego," he said in a tone that didn't match the downward slant of his mouth.

Tracy shuffled her feet, drawing back Keira's attention. Keira gave the dog a final gentle pat on his head, straightened her back, and slanted a questioning look at Reid. "We need to get going. What do you need?"

Reid's hand stroked the back of his dog. He tilted his head, eyebrows lifted, and the teasing smirk had left his eyes. "A moment, Keira. In private?"

Keira pursed her lips, studied, and considered the pros and cons. He'd come to see her. Why? Had he come to explain? How had he known she'd be at the rescue building? She must have mentioned it. Yesterday. He'd mocked her for showing up early to their appointment. Maybe then? Thoughts of yesterday's incident—his body pinning, the fear pounding—caused jitters.

But he was here to see her now. Handsome. Unshaven. Rough, with a roguish smile. Thoughts fumbled irrationally. Safe. Would she feel safe? Alone with him, out here at the fringe of town? *Compassion and understanding,* the screen in her mind flashed. And Keira settled on yes.

"Keira?" Tracy's voice broke through the jumbled mess of her mind.

Keira flinched; shoving her hands into the pockets of her fleece, she locked eyes with her friend. Assurance passed in a silent message, saying it was all right for Tracy to leave.

"Okay, I'm heading out of here. Be careful." Tracy shot another look at Reid, patted Yard on his rump, and closed the distance to her car.

***

Reid watched the exchange of glances between Keira and Tracy and blew out a breath of relief when Tracy trudged to her car. Keira thrust her chin out, giving him a challenging look. "So, what's up? What the heck are you doing here, if not for Bones?"

As Reid figured, his unexplained appearance at the rescue had rattled her. She'd covered it with curt words and brusque movement, but it had been there. He'd seen it.

After Keira stomped out yesterday, more ticked-off than scared, he'd taken Yard and hiked into the woods. After the storm, the heavy scent of decaying matter, the sounds of buzzing, chirping, croaking, and the rustling treetops, and the crunch of leaves under his feet renewed the calm. Each breath of the wet, fresh earth, of pines and spring blossoms, and each step on the narrow woodland trail stilled his thoughts and calmed his spirit. That's when the notion to surprise her had popped into his mind.

Now he wasn't so sure about it anymore. "I must say you look as if you could use some coffee." Reid tilted his head, assessing the gray circles under her eyes, and the messy hair she'd pulled into a ponytail.

"Gee, thanks. I'm flattered." Keira lifted her fingertips to her eye and rubbed across the lid. "But you have a point. Two-plus hours working with the dogs can do that to you. So, make it quick."

"Okay." Before she could utter the first word of objection, Reid grabbed her hand. "You'll need to eat fast, then," he said and pulled her around the corner to a break area, where a picnic table stood.

He caught the catch in her breath. A tiny sound, but he'd heard it, and it made him smile. Paper plates, napkins weighed down with ceramic mugs, and a thermos filled with coffee; he'd laid it all out. To the side, an insulated bag sat with the restaurant's logo promising delicious country food stamped across.

Keira stared from the table to Reid, pulled her hand away and crossed her arms in a shiver. "What the heck is this, Reid?"

"I figured you might get cold. So, there's a blanket. On the bench." A camouflage poncho liner blanket, lightweight and smooth to the touch, lay folded on the seat. "Breakfast. We are going to have breakfast."

"Breakfast?" Keira stammered, brushing back a strand of hair in a gesture of uncertainty and surprise, and her lips curled into a tentative smile.

"Breakfast," Reid confirmed. "The one you owe me. Remember? I got a little of everything, but I assume bacon and eggs will hit the spot?" The corners of his eyes crinkled with an infectious grin.

For one speechless instant, Keira blinked. "What is it with you and the damn notion I owe you a breakfast?"

A sting, but it didn't put him off. He wanted time with her. Not in public, but away from eavesdroppers. And if he'd placed a blind bet, he'd wager against her coming to the cabin. But, as Houston liked to say, "You can't be late if you don't show up." Even if it meant showing up in the chilly mist of a Kentucky morning.

Reid tugged on her arm and drew her beside the table. "About yesterday. I want to set things right." His voice dipped to somber. The aroma of bacon drifted from the warming bag as he tore open the Velcro closure.

"I hope you'll stay, have a bite, and let me humiliate myself. But I won't force you. I'd never, ever force you. So, you choose. Sit down, wrap this blanket around you, and warm your inside with hot coffee? Or we'll stop this right now. I'll leave, and you can take this"—Reid gestured to the food he'd pulled from the bag—"and feed it to the animals."

"Good Lord, Reid." Keira's face went slack with surprise. She took a tentative step toward the bench.

Reid recognized the conflict in her voice, in her eyes, how she hugged herself and offered a lopsided grin.

At the smell of food, Yard sidled up, his nose twitching in anticipation. "Down," Reid gave the command, and the dog dropped to the ground with a quiet grumble.

The way he saw it, he didn't have to explain to anyone. But what compelled him to tell this stranger? Not a stranger, he reasoned, and a smile tugged at a memory.

Yesterday, when she stumbled backward in the cabin's entryway, he'd held onto her for an instant longer than necessary, and at that moment she'd touched his soul. And if he'd read the signs, he'd left an imprint, too.

Reid snagged the blanket, shook it out and wrapped it around Keira's shoulders. "That'll keep you warm. As I said, you look like you could use some coffee."

***

Keira had been quiet during most of the impromptu al fresco breakfast, listening, asking few questions. For that, Reid was glad, because one thing off-limits for discussion was the loss of his leg.

He'd sketched a rough picture of his three tours to Afghanistan, but he offered no details. Just enough to give her a glimpse of the ugly, deciding she didn't need to hear of the carnage he'd experienced. Reid described the attack on the convoy but left out details of his injuries.

"Time helps mellow the bad. It doesn't happen very often, but flashbacks come when I least expect it," Reid's voice trailed off. "Like yesterday. A blasted hail shower, of all things, set off a flashback." He clenched his fist as a growl of humiliation pushed up his throat. He stood, gathered plates, cutlery, napkins, and dumped it all in a plastic sack.

It didn't bother him anymore, the partial loss of the leg. Complaining didn't solve a thing, so why bother? The silver lining? He lived; two of his teammates didn't. Then why hadn't he cleared the slate and told her about it? Because if he saw pity, he'd cut her loose.

And, he wasn't ready for that.

As he watched the straight-forward, hot-tempered woman huddled inside his blanket, Reid wondered how she'd feel cradled in his arms. He brushed a hand across his forehead, swiping at the surprising thought.

Keira pushed off the bench, shrugging the blanket from her shoulders. "Phew. I don't know what to say, except I'm sorry."

Reid searched her face, looking for signs of distress, and saw none. "The apology is all mine. I shouldn't have let you leave yesterday thinking I was a raving lunatic."

Keira folded the blanket and slanted a playful smile at him. "Oh, I wouldn't say you're not. I mean, look at this," she gestured at the leftover breakfast. "I mean, who does that? Besides a raving lunatic?"

"I didn't hear you complain, Mossy."

With quick strides, he was beside her. Had he imagined it, or had she flinched when his fingers brushed against hers as he took the blanket from her hands?

Keira shifted her eyes to the table and snatched up her keys. "Thanks for breakfast … and for shedding light on yesterday."

Yard scampered to his feet.

Reid grabbed her arm, stopping her mid-stride. Unflinching, eyes the color of unpolished jade stared into his.

"You're welcome." He paused a beat, touched a finger to the gray shadows under her eyes. "You're tired."

"Yes, I am. I need to get going." Keira broke eye contact, and she took a step back. Reid slid his hands into his pockets, cocked his head.

"Have dinner with me?"

Her eyes flitted back. "Hmm? Why should I?" she asked in a voice as cool and smooth as glass, but her eyes presented a challenge.

"Because I'm a *fascinating* lunatic? And because you know you want to?"

She laughed, petted Yard, and headed to her car. "And you're just a little full of yourself, too. Aren't you?"

Reid gathered the plastic sack and thermos, signaled for Yard to come, and hollered back.

"Yep. But you know you like it."

CHAPTER 12

Reid drove back to the cabin, crooning to the country hit belting from the radio. He thought of the band Houston, he, and another guy from the company had formed in the Army. And the Saturday night gigs they'd had, if they were not on duty. Before Afghanistan. Mostly dive bars, he mused, though it had been an intoxicating thrill when their band got booked. God, he missed it—the energy strumming through his veins, from the sound check to taking the mic.

At the cabin, Reid cut the engine and opened the door for Yard to get out. Breakfast with Keira had put him in an optimistic mood. "That was a brilliant idea, boy," he told Yard and gave himself a mental pat on the back.

She'd been reluctant, at first. Reid had seen that. Remarkable how his spirit had spiked when she took the blanket and swung a leg over the picnic bench.

"Why the hell did the explanation matter, Yard?" The dog gave him an inquisitive look. "Ah, wait. We're in a small town, and we don't need the word of a crazy dude staying at the Miller cabin getting around. Particularly a crazy dude who'll soon be soliciting donations. That's why."

Yard lifted his ears, slanted his head as if saying, "If you say so? But *I* say you're full of it."

"Ha! You're funny, boy. It's what she'd said, too. Well, maybe you have a point. Maybe we want to see Mossy again. And well ... scaring the crap out of her is not the way to do that. We'll need to fix it. Think she'll come back here for dinner?" he asked Yard as they skipped up the porch steps together.

Whistling, he kept going in a great mood. After being medevac'd from Afghanistan, battered and immobilized, he'd felt weak and powerless. And when he broke up with his girlfriend, intimacy had not taken a front position in his mind. But, while recovering at Walter Reed, he couldn't help the suspicion of what impact the loss of his leg would have on him this way.

As soon as physical therapy gave the okay, and in a crazy need to prove he was still active, independent and most of all able to live his life any way he damn chose, he hit the gym. And weight-trained within a hair's breadth of collapse. Endurance and strength—he aimed for both—and regained what had leaked out of him in that hospital bed. A work in progress, he kept steeling his body.

As muscles strengthened and his body recovered, the vacuum inside expanded. Since getting out of rehab, weird reactions to his shiny new amputee status had kicked him in the teeth and twisted his temper. The gray edged into his mind and darkened his thoughts. Had the IED not only butchered his leg but cut off the likelihood of having a family one day? Or would he have a go at meeting someone who'd see beyond the prosthesis and the crutches? What would it be like? The questions had ricocheted through his mind and gnawed on the inside.

It had been on his mind a lot—sex, and how his injuries might mess it up for him. But he needn't have feared. Okay, his lower leg was gone, but all other parts were intact and functioning. And he didn't stop having needs. Hell no. He was still a red-blooded male.

Meanwhile, encounters during the past months had been little more than emotionless sex, detached and lacking passion, because on the inside Reid was as hollow as the roadside crater the bomb had ripped. His pleasure hopeless and dull, tarnished like the brass medals he'd shoved in a box and stowed in the basement of his parent's house.

Reid wanted the whole package—not just a pretty face but a physical and emotional connection. A caring partner with humor and intelligence, but most importantly, someone who accepted the scuffles with the ghost of the past. He wanted a relationship, and with muscles regaining strength, fresh confidence returned.

Keira had provoked his attention. But how do you catch a cloud and pin it down? Or rather, how do you hold on to "Freckle Face" when she nearly falls into your arms?

Reid unlocked the front door and found Bones tail-thumping in the hallway. "Hey," he scooped up the little guy. "Dude, this is entirely your fault," he said. "Friday, she smacks into me, and yesterday she happens to be the one coming here to check on you. A rescue volunteer. Hmm." In the kitchen, he set down Bones and pulled a treat for both dogs from the counter.

"Do you believe in coincidence?" Reid hollered at Yard as he strolled to his bedroom. "Yeah, I don't either, buddy."

From the closet, Reid pulled a military rucksack and began stuffing it with a pair of hiking boots, blanket, a set of clothes, first aid kit, water—things he'd also carry on the walk. Guessing at twenty-five pounds, he zipped it up, slung it over his back, and tested the fit. That'll do for the first week of training.

He still had thirty minutes before meeting Houston. Reid hauled the rucksack to the kitchen where he thumped it on the floor. At the dull thud, both dogs pushed to their feet.

"No reason to get excited, boys, I'm not ready. And, Bones, you're staying, anyways."

Printed pages, shoved together on the table, caught his attention. The signed foster application. Crap. Reid snatched up the documents he'd forgotten this morning and rubbed his chin rifling through the pages. He considered swinging by the rescue to leave it in the dropbox, but he changed his mind and threw the papers back on the table. Nope. He'd call Mossy later, letting her know the signed documents were ready for pick-up.

***

"Here goes day one of training up to the big event," Houston spoke as he swung the GoPro from the downtown view ahead to Reid and to Yard. "The mutt is incredible," he remarked, zooming in on the dog. Walking in unison with Reid, Yard showed no signs of slowing down.

"He was trained; it's the only way to explain this," Reid said, when Houston turned off the camera,

For the first week of training, they're walking goal was set to a relaxed pace. Houston drew his phone from the jacket pocket, checked the running stopwatch, and announced, "One mile, seventeen minutes."

"According to military standards, we just failed," Reid grinned. "But who's rating?"

"Right now, we're covering a flat ground," Houston brought up the phone's calculator app. "With that, it'll take roughly six hours to walk twenty miles. But terrain will change. And so will the weather."

"And that has ever made a difference how?"

"We'll have to hump it."

Reid scoffed, thinking of the many ruck marches of the past. In particular, he thought of the blistered feet after his first twelve-mile march. Too green and cocky, he'd ignored the older guys' recommendation of donning two pairs of socks. An inexperienced wise ass, he'd laughed. Before he'd finished, Reid walked in torture, skin on heels and toes chafed and bleeding. Yep, his dogs had been barking, and the laugh had been on him. After that, a pair of thin polyester socks with a tight fit under another pair of woolen socks had prevented blisters while marching in Army boots. Reid suddenly laughed out loud.

"What's so funny?" Houston asked.

"You remember the double-socks thing, Tex?" Reid glanced at Houston's hiking boots. Both men wore ultra-lightweight footwear with a manufacturer promise of a minimal break-in period.

"Affirmative." Houston raised his hand, returning someone's wave. Despite the stores being closed, restaurants in Oak Creek were open and bustling.

"And do you remember First Sergeant wearing his wife's knee-highs under his socks?"

"Dude, how can you forget that picture?" Houston, too, laughed at the memory.

"Hey, Mack." Houston punched Reid's arm. "Last night, at Pat's? We stirred a buzz."

"Oh yeah? How so?" Reid looked expectantly at Houston.

"Got a phone call from one of the radio station's D.J.'s. They sponsored the band, so the D.J. was at the bar, meeting them." He paused, a knowing grin spreading across his face.

Yard stopped, lifted his leg at a parking meter, slowing the men for a moment.

"And? Did he say anything good or are you just grinning for shits and giggles?"

"Mack, this dude ... let's just say the listeners love his show. And he was impressed. So much, in fact, that he invited us to the studio one day next week. He'll call with a date and time."

Houston and Reid turned to each other, grinning like two ten-year-olds who snuck a peek into a copy of *Playboy*. "That's what I'm talking about, my man!" Reid clapped his palm to Houston's in a thwacking high-five.

"We need to set up a Heroes Rise account A.S.A.P. We'll have the number on hand during the interview," Houston said as they passed one of the town's three banks. "For donations."

"Roger that. Let's not forget to mention the support vehicle. We need to lock it in pretty quickly. A van and a driver." Reid whistled to Yard, who'd fallen back into a trot. "I don't know about him walking twenty miles a day. He'll probably need to get off his paws and ride part of the way. Which reminds me, I need to have a chat with the vet about that."

With five miles clocked, one-hundred minutes had passed in the blink of an eye. About mid-point, Reid had slowed down. Still, they'd averaged twenty minutes per mile. An impressive feat for a man walking with a prosthesis.

CHAPTER 13

"Hey, Mossy."

Keira cringed. Why did he insist on infuriating her? Mossy Oak was her style, not her blasted name. It didn't define her. Or did it? Because she lived in a rural town, and fairy dust and unicorns weren't part of her world, did he see her as a country bumpkin? What did it matter that she wasn't a girly girl? *Never mind,* she thought. *I don't care if he pegs me for Honey Boo Boo's cousin.* She swallowed the sharp retort ready to roll off her tongue and remembered the reason why she was returning his call.

"You called about the foster agreement. I'm sorry," Keira said, "I won't be able to come out today. Or any day this week. Can you take it to the office? Any time before five o'clock today or tomorrow will be fine."

"Sure, no problem. I presumed you'd stop by to get them. I'll drop off the paperwork later."

That was quick, Keira thought, and it rankled. Had she expected his resistance? Keira lowered her head with a twinge of disappointment at the obliging response.

"I know Bones is receiving excellent care. How is he?" Keeping her tone light, she paced, fixing her gaze on the gray floor tiles in-between the desk and door. Tiny wings fluttering in her chest were not to be ignored. Chewing the inside of her cheek, Keira kept the conversation going, half-expecting Reid to follow up on the mentioned dinner invitation.

"Bones is getting better every day. His pads are healing; he looks as if he's packing on some meat, too."

"That's great." It sounded lame, even to herself. "Thanks for fostering. Oh, and would you send picture updates? Maybe once a week? You can forward them to me or message Barkville Rescue."

"Will do." Reid agreed too easily. The outcome of the phone call should have satisfied Keira; he had solved the problem. But why had it flattened her mood?

***

Reid gulped. What the hell kept Mossy so busy she couldn't come by for the damn paperwork? Reid's forehead furrowed as he rubbed across the stump. He'd only agreed to drop off the papers because asking her to come today was like inviting her to a date with Murphy. If it could go wrong, it would. The morning had already proven that, and his mood was on the downswing.

Reid snatched the remote lying next to him on the sofa and shut off the TV with one swift stab to the off button. The panel of experts discussing the Afghan government grated on his nerves. "No fucking clue," he said aloud, flinging the remote onto the table, an outward sign of annoyance.

The stump was red and hot, and damn if he didn't have to cut today's march short. That, he admitted, was the real cause of aggravation. Two days of five-mile walks through the town proved too much. It stung.

He'd experienced low points before, in the early days, when getting used to the prosthesis. Reid had admitted to being pissed at his own weakness. *Stop it. You know the difference between try and triumph?* The therapist's voice echoed in his mind, as precise as if he stood next to him. *You know what to do.* And Reid understood he needed to find a little "umph."

He dropped his hand, grabbed the crutches leaning against the sofa, and thumped to the bathroom. The mutts followed behind, with Bones growling at the crutches with every step. "Stop yapping; you'll get used to it."

At the sink, he filled a tumbler with cold water, reached for an amber bottle inside the medicine cabinet, and shook out a prescription pill. From the over-the-counter bottle, he jiggled a second pill into his palm and washed both down in one huge gulp. The antibiotic would keep a lid on infection, and the acetaminophen helped with pain.

Back in the great room, he thrust aside crutches, dropped to the floor, and worked off frustration with push-ups and sit-ups. The dogs laid next to him; two pair of eyes following the repetitions with fascinating curiosity, until Bones got up and licked his face. "Move, boy." Reid shoved the dog away with a firm hand and without breaking stride. Every push and stretch of muscles drove out stress, and confidence returned.

Tomorrow I'll bench the leg—Push.

Give it a day of rest—Lower.

After that—Push.

We'll see—Lower.

Shorten the walking distance—Push.

Work up to five miles—Lower.

Ten miles—Push.

Then twenty—Lower.

Reid finished and rolled onto his back. He'd decided. Dropping off the paperwork could wait till tomorrow, too. For now, the workout had drenched him in sweat.

He headed to the bathroom in need of a hot shower. The water pelted and rushed over his body, washing away the lingering thoughts of self-doubt.

Refreshed in mind and body, Reid slumped onto the sofa and ordered a large, all-meat pie for delivery. He scrolled through phone calls, found Keira's number, and assigned it to his contact list. From there, Reid opened the messenger app and began tapping the keyboard. Half-way through his message, he stopped, read, and erased everything. Keeping it short and light, he retyped *Cookout on Saturday. Sound good?*

It wasn't until after eight o'clock in the evening when the ping of an incoming message pierced through the noise of the basketball game on TV. Three more seconds, crucial to the game's outcome, he ignored the intrusion. He shouted, his body tensed, and he laced hands behind his neck. Bones jumped off the sofa, slinked up to Yard, who snoozed on the floor. Had Bones interrupted an animated dream of chasing a squirrel? Because Yard's paws stopped twitching, jaw opened wide, and a pink tongue rolled out in a lazy yawn before he dropped his head back down.

As the last shot made the basket, Reid pumped a fist into the air and exhaled relief at the win. He picked up the phone lying next to him on the sofa, relaxed his shoulders, and checked Keira's return message. A smile tugged at the corners of his mouth as he read, *What's on the menu?*

Thumbs flew over keys. *Are you afraid of steaks and potatoes?*

My idea of a dinner. The answer pinged right back.

Yes! A wide grin spread across his face. *Five o'clock. Beer or wine?*

Beer, or wine. Either is fine. A smiling emoji. *Rhyming. Not intentional.*

***

On Wednesday, Reid and Houston resumed rucking, keeping it to three miles. Antibiotics and mild pain killers had calmed the leg.

"Dude, don't beat yourself up." They'd driven the short distance to a nearby conservation and research forest, where Houston led along a narrow hiking path. The soft surface of the dirt was easier on joints—and the stump—than the town's unyielding concrete sidewalks.

Reid responded with a curt nod, swatted at an insect, and kept walking. "Damn bugs are back." He sounded gruff. Shorting Sunday's walk still irked.

"The thing to remember? We're not in the Army anymore. No one's pushing; there's no time limit to meet. Give yourself a break, brother."

"Failure is not an option," Reid said, as if Houston had read his mind. Their motto in Afghanistan, and a mindset that impacted combat. "I'm not giving in, bro. Not until I run with the bucks."

CHAPTER 14

Stay on both feet this time, Keira told herself as she pulled up to Reid's cabin and wished to forget last week's embarrassing slip and fall. Just then the front door opened, and Reid stepped out with a smile and an amused expression on his face.

"Mossy. Right on time, I'm impressed."

"And hello to you, too. I see nothing's changed. Rude as ever." But when she looked up, a disarming smile negated her blunt words.

Yard and Bones scampered down the stairs and rushed over to Keira. "You could take a cue from them," Keira leaned forward, using her free hand to pet them. "They're happy to see me."

With one hand holding the bottle, she dug in her purse with the other, pulled out two dog bones of different sizes, and treated the dogs.

"You have dog bones in there?" Reid raised his brows, staring at her with astonishment.

"It's how you make friends. In case you didn't know." The mutts raced to the porch and Keira came up behind, holding the bottle out to Reid.

"Thanks." He took the wine, and he gave the label an appreciative glance. "I get it. You want to be friends with me, too," he grinned and touched his lips to her cheek.

"That remains to be seen." Keira smiled and followed Reid into the great room, where the dogs had taken their chews and now chomped side by side.

"Well, maybe my superior grill-master talents will convince you." Reid's gaze bounced to the smoking grill on the deck and back to Keira.

She gave him the thumbs-up with an impish smile on her lips. "We'll see; I love a perfectly cooked steak."

"You look nice."

"Thanks, I clean up. Occasionally." Uneasy with compliments, she slung her purse over a chair and changed the topic. "Are you going to open that bottle, or am I supposed to help myself?"

"Why, the lady is impatient. I like it." He flashed a smile.

The nerve-tickling feathers were back again.

"I'll dig for a corkscrew." Reid strolled around the counter and pulled the opener from a drawer. Opening one cabinet after another, he didn't find a single wine glass on the shelves. He held up a tall water glass. "Will that do?" He slanted a boyish grin. "I guess I should have checked before now. But wait, here's a straw."

Keira laughed out loud. "Unprepared, soldier? But yeah. That's fine, minus the straw."

The moment his eyebrows shot up, she held up her hand. "Yep, *soldier* fits."

Awareness glinted on steel gray eyes. "I see, *Mossy*."

"Stop, stop," Keira waved a hand up and down as Reid poured. "Slow down."

"Why? There's more. Got a couple different bottles since I had no idea of your taste."

"Uh-huh. Two bottles of wine and a straw. Nice try!"

"Not a terrible idea, Mossy. Might loosen you up some."

"Excuse me?" She crossed her arms. "What's *that* supposed to mean?"

"It means there are two sides to everything. Life can be full of intense shit, like what we talked about Sunday, but there's fun stuff, too. You gotta take time to relax and enjoy."

"Are you saying I'm too serious?"

"Maybe. 'Tense' might be a better word."

Keira unfolded her arms, accepted the glass, and sniffed. "I had a demanding week."

"Hmm." Reid poured another, touched his glass to Keira's, and peered at her. "A tasty steak, mellow wine, and a laid-back guy like myself make relaxing easy."

His piercing eyes made her squirm. Unsure of what to do with herself, she leaned against the counter, and far from relaxed, took tiny sips.

"All right. Time to take this to the next level." Reid carried the marinated steaks to the deck, and Keira exhaled. While Reid grilled, she played with the dogs. That and sips of wine calmed her nerves.

When Reid brought in the filets, cooked to perfection, he arranged them on plates, added foil-wrapped potatoes, fished out a salad and condiments from the fridge, and plopped everything unceremoniously in the middle of the table.

Keira had to smile at that. So much like a man. "It smells great," she said, taking her seat, and noticed for the first time the tiny flowers nestled inside a super small mercury vase sitting next to her plate. Charming. Where did he get this from?

Her fingers ran across the pink blooms. "This is nice. Thank you."

"You're welcome. More wine?"

Keira looked up, brushed away the curls that kept falling into her face, and nodded. "Just a little."

The dogs, smelling the meat, sauntered to the table, salivating and licking their lips. "Yard, Bones, go to your place." Reid pointed to the new dog beds sitting next to each other. "No begging."

"No table food for the kiddos?" Keira tilted her head. Even she, who should know better, didn't restrict her dogs to kibble only. "Not even a little?"

"Well. I've cooked one just for them." Reid admitted. "But, later."

"Enjoy." He forked a chunk of meat, chewed, and watched Keira squint as she ate. Behind him, the sun's setting rays slanted across her face.

"The sun is in your eyes," he stated the obvious, pushed back his chair, and got up to close the drapes. As the room plunged into shades of gray, Keira's butterflies returned. A few seconds later he'd switched on the table lamp by the sofa, picked up a multi-wicked candle pot, and brought it to the dining table. When the flames licked, an intimate atmosphere radiated through the room.

Seemingly at ease, he sat, unwrapped his spud, and slathered butter into it. "I've told you my skeletons, tell me yours."

Green eyes fastened on his. "I don't have secrets. My life's busy but uneventful."

"So, tell me about it."

By the time they'd finished dinner, Keira rambled of growing up in Oak Creek, her parents, friends, teaching, and volunteer work.

"That's great, Mossy. What I learned is that you're a teacher, a volunteer, and a damn good daughter to your parents. But I still don't know your secrets. I want to hear what makes you happy, what causes you to be sad, and what drives you so mad you'd like to smash someone's face in."

Keira swallowed and gave him a crooked smile. *Why?* Her insides quivered, shook, and crashed against self-imposed barriers. She'd wired herself to believe it was *just* a dinner, but her gut had known the real reason she'd accepted his invitation.

Reid scooted out of his chair and stacked their plates. "But hold that thought. Are you good with pie and ice cream? Coffee?"

"Yes, please. Sounds great." Coffee would ground her, clear her muddled head. Keira's face was flushed from wine and talk, and candlelight had caused more flutters. Far better at listening, revealing herself wasn't something she enjoyed.

The dog's eyes danced, and tongues lapped as Reid cut up the third steak. He fed Yard and Bones before letting them outside to follow the call of nature.

After calling the mutts back inside and they'd settled into their beds, he heated pie in the microwave, added a huge scoop of ice cream, and filled two mugs with coffee. Seated back at the table, he polished off his slice while Keira nibbled.

"Back to you," he leaned back in his chair, stretched his legs, and crossed his ankles.

Keira pushed her half-eaten pie aside. She smiled as she studied him. She liked his unshakable confidence spread across high cheekbones, eyes the color of storm clouds, and the little cowlick above his forehead. And the quirky personality. Her gaze flicked to the tattoo she'd noticed that day at the pet store. Only the bottom part sneaked from under the T-shirt, and she wondered what hid beneath the sleeve.

Bracing her elbows on the table and cradling her face inside her palms, she asked, "What is this? An interrogation?"

"Do you think of this like that?"

"I do."

Gray eyes bore into hers. Keira didn't flinch.

"Fair enough, Mossy. Tell you what. I'll ask you a question, you respond."

Folding her arms at the edge of the dinner table, she leaned forward. "And if I don't want to answer?"

"Then it's a dare."

"Hmm. I see. Sounds a bit like Truth or Dare. I haven't played that since I was a teenager." Keira paused and fidgeted, propping her chin up with a fist.

"I can ask questions?"

"Anything you want, Mossy."

She drew air, breathed a sigh. "No kinky dares."

"Depends on how you define kinky."

Her heart skipped a beat, and her face warmed. "Okay, I trust you know what I mean. So, shoot."

Reid shifted his weight, leaned forward. "I'll be gentle."

Keira swallowed. Damn if the heat didn't increase.

"I want to know if you dance crazy when no one is looking?"

Keira laughed. "That's easy enough. No, I don't dance crazy. I don't dance much at all. But I belt out a tune when no one's listening."

"Hmm. Interesting. Well, that wasn't horrible, was it?" Teeth gleamed in the candlelight. "Your turn."

"Okay. I'm curious. What's the last thing you searched on your phone?"

"Well, this is top secret," Reid teased. But if I must, I've looked up a hiking boot manufacturer."

"Oh?"

"Nope. My turn to question."

After a while, the questions became more personal. The next one took Keira by surprise.

"What does your boyfriend think of marriage?"

"My boyfriend? What the hell, Reid? If I had a boyfriend, would I be here, having dinner with you?"

"Okay. Don't get your hackles up, Mossy. Just checking."

"And while we're at it, why do you keep calling me Mossy?"

"I told you before, it suits you." His gaze flicked to her T-shirt. "And I like it."

"Uh-uh." She opened her mouth, peered at the tattoo, but Reid leaned across the table and pressed a finger to her lips. "Nope. My turn. Again."

"I'll dare," Keira said, fearing his next question.

"You're sure?"

"Yes. Hey, what's with that grin?" Keira debated. "Wait. No. Ask your question."

"Okay. If you're sure."

Keira nodded. "Yeah, go ahead."

Reid leveled his gaze on her, reached, and took her hand. "What did you do today to get yourself so sexy?"

Heat rushed to her face, the blood pounded in her ears, her body tingled. "Oh no, you don't."

The pressure on her fingers increased, and Keira fought the urge to jump from her seat. No way would she let him see the effect the question had on the wings batting inside her stomach.

Reid's eyes blazed. "You know there's a punishment for not answering a question." He held on to her hand, and when he pushed to his feet, he pulled her up with him.

Keira's eyes widened and her mouth gaped in surprise.

"Close your eyes."

She shrunk back. "Hell, no."

"Close your eyes, Mossy." His tone turned soft, his gaze bore into hers, pinning her. "It won't hurt; I promise."

At a loss for words, Keira's eyelids fluttered, as did her insides. She hesitated. But Reid's low voice rushed ripples over her back, and she closed them. Her heart hammered with anticipation; her head felt like on a caffeine buzz.

Reid's questions had become dangerously intimate. She detected his movement, but his crisp scent of ocean and citrus stayed close while he kept her hand in his.

With the tip of her tongue she moistened dry lips, half-expecting the touch of his mouth. Instead, he moved a strand of curls from her face. At the touch, goosebumps raced across her back. Keira sensed him taking a step, still holding her hand, and flinched when a finger touched her cheek, leaving a frosty, sticky substance. Ice cream. Keira breathed vanilla; her eyes flickered open and her free hand shot upward, but Reid stopped her mid-motion, and lowered her arm to her side.

"Keep your eyes closed." Warm breath tickled her ear.

The dogs' snoring faded from her senses, as did everything else. The strength of his arm, the rising heat, it became the focus of her concentration.

Unhurried and tender, Reid touched a finger to the sticky mess, drawing slow circles until he dragged the damp sweetness across her lips. Keira swallowed. The air crackled with tension as his free hand cradled her head. The tip of his tongue brushed against her cheek, swirling ice cream in lazy strokes, and with one agonizing slow lap after another moved to the corner of her mouth. Sensual and gentle. When his tongue flicked across her lips, Keira's knees turned wobbly, and butterflies left her stomach and migrated south. On a whimper she leaned into him, but when his mouth took hers and parted her lips, the kiss was deep and demanding, and just a little rough. It took her breath.

"Do you have a hidden agenda, soldier?" A shaky exhale when he released her mouth.

"Nope, not hidden at all." Wine infused breath feathered across her lips as Reid drew her into him.

Keira gasped; her pulse jumped. "I'm not sleeping with you."

"Not today, Mossy, but I look forward to it." Low and scratchy, his voice vibrated through her system.

"Damn you, and your arrogance. Why are you so sure I'll sleep with you?" She pressed her palm against his chest, her eyes sparked fire, but her voice was soft.

"I'm not." Reid's hands braced her face. "But I hope you will." His lips closed over hers, drowning any objection. Soft and gentle this time, he took his time exploring her mouth.

When the kiss ended, he held her eyes. "One last question, Mossy?"

"Really, soldier?" Spoken softly, her words hummed on a warm breath.

"Yes. The most important one of this evening." His pulse throbbed, the teasing left his eyes, and nerves turned to bowstrings.

"If I told you that I need a prosthesis and crutches to walk, would you still want to date?"

The silence stretched, and neither paid attention to yapping dogs as Reid awaited her answer.

CHAPTER 15

Dammit, was she going to say something? Anything? A vein popped out in Reid's neck; his face turned blank.

Keira's hand flew up to cover her mouth. Her gaze bounced to his legs, skipping from left to right. While he wore jeans, the mangled one was impossible to detect. Tears shimmered, but she didn't speak; she squeezed her eyes shut instead. Fingers raked through curls, held them back, and released with a small intake of breath. "Reid." The sound a low moan. "No, no. This can't be true."

Eyebrows knitted, and her nostrils flared.

He dropped his arms, stepped back, and saw shock in wide eyes. Hesitation, tears, a few mournfully uttered words, and it was all he needed to know she was backing out. Should have known. Message received.

An instant kick to the gut, but he should have expected this. It had happened before.

A storm gathered in gray pupils while a throbbing ache tightened his chest. He'd accepted his fate and the damage beyond repair. War had branded him, but rejection, judgment, and pity was the branding iron that seared his pride. How would he ever deal with this? His hands curled into fists, a harsh breath left his lungs as he resisted the urge to smash the wall, because this particular sting he could handle.

Only one thing could make the situation even more awkward, adding insult to injury. And that was the pathetic excuse of an apology. That's how it went, and Reid saw it coming now. With no intentions to let this happen, he was hell-bent on denying Keira the chance to humiliate him—or herself—any further. He'd push her away; a dependable mechanism to hang on to his dignity.

Breath.

He unclenched his fists. Reid's voice was void of emotion, his tone as sharp as broken glass. "Look. I'm sorry. I should have told you before. Springing this on you like this wasn't fair. I'm sorry." He ran a hand over his close crop. Aw, shit! Why did *he* apologize now?

"No, no. Reid," Keira shook her head, held up her palm. Under the freckles, skin had turned paper white. With the line forming between her brows, the throat working to keep tears from flooding, she looked as miserable as he felt.

Despite the crashing waves against shored-up pride, a strange impulse to reach out, fold his arms around her in comfort, arose. But he didn't, because it would undo him. He rubbed the back of his neck, cutting Keira off before she could speak.

"Stop. Just stop. No need to say more. All right? I enjoyed dinner and your company, and I had a great time. But the kiss was a mistake. Forget it. Blame it on the wine; I'm not used to drinking it."

"Reid, I'm so sorry. It's not … let me explain." Keira stepped forward.

"Don't apologize; I understand." He turned, lifted Keira's purse from the counter, and thrust it at her. "You should go now."

"Reid, please." Keira's lips quivered; her tears spilled out. He shook his head, a hard stare cut through the water in her eyes. She swallowed, and words died.

"Goodnight, Keira."

Reid's gut tightened as she straightened her shoulders, grabbed her bag, and fled.

***

She'd left, not paying attention to the dogs rushing after her. At the evening's abrupt ending, sadness and distress had stared back at Reid with dazed and mascara-smudged eyes—when it was *he* who'd been kicked in the teeth? And yet, under the armor of self-protection smothering his chest, ambers of longing refused to be choked out.

Sweet Mother of Jesus. What had possessed him to invite her to the cabin? From the moment she came into the door, he'd imagined kissing her.

Dishes clattered as Reid cleared the table; the flowers caught his eyes. When was the last time he bought flowers—even if it was just a tiny arrangement—for a woman, other than his mother? He couldn't remember.

Unlike Yard, who lay watching Reid's movements from a distance, Bones kept getting under his feet when he ditched the left-over food. Yeah, you're still a skinny dude, but that's enough for today. Reid shooed the mutt away.

Frustration gave way to a hollow feeling of disappointment. Reid scrubbed plates under running water; he needed to stay busy, keep his hands occupied while his mind circled back to Keira.

For one unguarded moment, Reid let himself dream of the impossible—finding a loving partner, building a relationship; it hadn't seemed so crazy anymore. Right.

Keira's package of sassy and bold, smart and attractive, inside that tortoise-hard shell, had lit a flame brighter than he'd ever expected. And maybe one day it would turn the self-doubt into ashes and make him whole again. Yeah, he'd have a better chance of running a one-legged marathon.

Reid piled the dishes on the drying rack, while the kiss replayed in his head. Damn. Her response and the thirst for more heated his blood. And damn it to hell, but he'd sensed that same heat burning inside her, too. The tiny sweat beads above her lip, the pulse drumming in her neck, her body going limp.

Reid grabbed a beer from the fridge, popped the top, and ambled into the great room. Yard, who'd followed, dropped to the floor with a huff while Reid collapsed onto the sofa. Bones' attempted to jump and missed.

"Hey, bud, on the battlefield, dropping your defenses will get you killed," he said, lifting the dog to the seat. "Out here? Well, it just fucks with your dreams. Doesn't it?"

He took a long pull from the bottle, and as the cold beer hit his stomach, the icy ball of bitterness spread inside his chest. "She hasn't even seen the goddam leg, but can I blame her?"

Soulful black eyes seemed to understand. "I've lost my head, boy. It won't happen again."

The evening had ended on a rocky note but, flipping through the TV channels and settling on a basketball game, he cheered. The fridge was stocked with long-necks and the dogs were perfect company. Was there anything more a man needed? Well, Reid thought, throwing a line, catching bass at the first flush of the morning wasn't such a bad thing, either.

With the ballgame over, Reid trekked to the fridge for another beer, then flipped through TV channels and chanced upon a country music station. *Beer never broke my heart,* the musician's throaty voice reverberated. "You got that right, buddy!" Reid grinned and twisted another cap. "Cheers, man."

That song was written for him. Humph. It could have been written *by* him, he pondered while reflecting on gigs of the past. The band, the performances, and the fun—they should pick it back up.

While traveling on foot for a year, in their mission for awareness and funds, they intended to meet with veterans, listen to their stories, and offer support. Reid envisioned himself strumming and crooning in the relaxed environment of bars and American Legion Posts, lighting up the atmosphere as he had before heading to Afghanistan. Yeah, he could see it. Why not have a little fun while at it? A signature song, he mused, with lyrics that held meaning to the mission.

A few more icy ones, and the soft edges of a buzz mellowed his brain.

He'd chew it over. Tomorrow.

***

Was it only seven thirty? Distraught and overwhelmed by the need to vent, Keira pulled into the gas station's parking space and cut the engine. A glance into the rearview mirror confirmed a mess—red, puffy eyes, a wet trail underneath, and mascara smeared across her cheek.

Keira drew a napkin with a fast-food restaurant's logo from the glove compartment and wiped away the black marks, only to leave red and blotchy skin in its place.

U up 4 company? She typed into her phone and waited. The horrible weight of a colossal misunderstanding made it difficult to breathe.

Sure. Date over?

Yes. I'll be there in five.

Keira started the engine. A few minutes later she pulled into Emily's driveway, counting on her friend's impartial opinion.

Emily threw open the front door, and her dog lurched out, hauling his bulk against Keira's leg. "Hey, there Bentley," she dug her fingers into the heavy fur, kneading the thick muscles of his neck.

"What's wrong, Keira?"

She'd cleaned off the mascara, but Emily's voice buzzed alarm at the red eyes and puffy skin. Keira drew air deep into her lungs and exhaled with a huff.

"Please tell me he didn't flashback and attack again?"

"Oh." Keira hadn't even considered her friend drawing this conclusion. "No, it's nothing like that." She shivered, pulled the cardigan across her chest, and followed Emily into the house. "I could use a glass of water and a bottle of wine." A warped smile twisted her lips.

"I'll get the wine," Emily disappeared to emerge a few seconds later with their favorite Merlot. In the great room, Keira sunk into the soft leather of the oversized sofa, kicked off her shoes, and tucked her legs under. She hugged a pillow to her chest as if it were a life vest.

"You've been crying. That's not like you. Why?" Emily plummeted on a cushion next to Keira, while Bentley plunked his bulk on the lush rug in front of them.

"Well, I screwed up. Royally." Eyes shimmered as Keira tucked the throw pillow closer to her chest and lifted her shoulders. "I should have known, but never in a million years would've expected."

Emily raised her hand, patting the air. "Hey, slow down. Expected what?"

Keira mashed her face into the pillow, but when she lifted her head again, her chin squared, and irritation flicked in dried eyes. "He asked if I knew he needed a prosthesis or crutches to walk, would I want to date."

"Oh, wow." Emily gasped, fingers touching parted lips.

A moment passed in which neither woman spoke. Both reached for their wine; Keira gulped, and Emily sipped. When Emily put her glass on the table and asked, her tone was mild. "Whoa. First, how did dating come up? And second, what did you say?"

Letting her friend in on the details of the dinner, Keira's face turned bright red as she admitted to the kiss. As expected, Emily raised an eyebrow with a smirk on her lips, and Keira's usual feistiness returned.

"Don't smirk. Yes, it was hot, and yes, I kissed him back. There. Satisfied?" Keira realized she'd cradled the smooth bowl of the glass just a little too hard, took another sip, and set down the glass.

"I would be—if you wouldn't be sitting here in obvious distress. So, what happened?"

Keira uttered a sigh as if the biscuits had burned. But, hey, they had. Hadn't they? With an angry motion, she shoved unruly curls from her face. "I froze. A million things raced through my head, and yep ... the ball of crap rolled downhill from there."

"Okay?" Emily tilted her head. "I'm listening."

"I just stood there like an idiot, thinking how I hadn't noticed. How could it be? Reid's gait is near perfect; he walks just fine. No indication there. Maybe a set of crutches leaning against a bedroom wall should have been a hint?"

"Bedroom? Want to tell me something?"

"Hey! Keep your mind clean. His bathroom is through there."

"Okay, so you didn't notice a limp, or off gait, and his surprise revelation shocked. Did you reject him?"

"Emily … ! It shocked, of course. But all these despicable things he'd experienced in Afghanistan crashed through my mind. And the terrible things you see on TV—soldiers coming home with their limbs cut off. It was as if an iron fist reached inside my heart, squeezed and suspended time. Pictures of how horrific it must have been flashed through my head, and it took my breath. I never had the chance to ask, and he didn't say, but it must have been one of those sickening roadside bomb attacks that injured him. And I cried. Argh."

"Sweetie." Emily embraced her friend. "You care about him." A statement Keira didn't deny. "I ask again, why are you sitting here with puffy eyes and not drinking wine with him?"

Keira put her face into her hands, the slithering snake of anxiety curled in her stomach. "Because when I found my tongue again, it was too late. Reid completely misjudged my reaction; he read my stupid, hypersensitive emotions for rejection. Emily, he cut me off each time I started explaining. He couldn't throw me out fast enough." Keira buried her head in her hands. "Reid refused to listen; he must think I'm a monster."

"Keira, don't do this. You're not a monster. You are the kindest, most caring, and most helpful woman in Oak Creek. So, stop it."

"My new record," Keira sniffled. "Relationship over before it had a chance to begin. What did you say about dating again? I'll be sticking to these guys, thank you very much." Keira leaned forward and stroked Bentley's broad back.

"Well, sweetie. Crow is not a tasty dish, but one you must eat to put things right. Approach him and open a dialog."

"How? He didn't give me a chance this evening, why should he want to hear me out later?"

Emily angled her head as if she'd just thought of it. "Bones?"

"Doubtful." Keira shook her head. "He'll send pictures and report Bones' progress to Haley."

"You'll make it happen. Reach out. Make him see the real you. Find a way. Because, sweet friend, from what I'm hearing, he might struggle with acceptance. He's expected the worst; your loss of words screamed rejection, and pushing you away saved face."

Startled at the revelation, Keira's mouth slackened, and her eyes opened wide as she stared at Emily. "Damn. When did you become so wise?"

CHAPTER 16

Sunday morning Reid awoke with a dry throat, a buzz inside his head, and Yard staring at him from the side of the bed. His bladder urged. Pushing back the covers, he crutched into the bathroom first before gulping a tall glass of ice water. Shit. How many long necks had he killed last night?

It was still dark when he took the dogs to the backyard; at five thirty, he'd slept longer than usual. Two sets of furry legs romped and bodies quivered with every sniff of a night visitor's trail, the nip in the breezy morning air cleared the cobwebs in Reid's brain, and for the briefest moment the image of a certain red-head stole inside. *Damn you, Mossy. I read you wrong ... didn't peg you for a snob, or the pitying type. Yeah, well. Whatever.* He shook his head, shook her from his mind. Coffee. He could use a strong cup of coffee right now.

At seven o'clock, the thought of a savory country breakfast watered his mouth. Reid drove into town and wasn't surprised by the number of cars and trucks already in the restaurant's parking lot on a Sunday morning. Early birds and travelers, he guessed.

While polishing off the fried country ham, eggs over easy, and buttery biscuits, he'd caught the glowering glare of an older guy from the corner of his eye. *What's with the stare?*

Reid wondered, acknowledging him by tipping his head when the unfriendly gaze fastened once again.

Reid finished his breakfast, and crumbling the napkin on his plate, he signaled for his check. Beaming a flirtatious smile at the cheerful waitress, he cracked a joke about coming back tomorrow to pay. From a couple of tables away, hostile eyes in a ruddy face burned into him. The woman at the fellow's table twisted, gave Reid an once-over, and when she turned back, she whispered across the table. Something was off about this conversation that seemed so blatantly about him, and although Reid strained his ear, the chatter in the dining room made it impossible to tune in.

Reid left a generous tip on the table, grabbed the ticket, and when he passed by the couple, he noticed the man's balled fist, his crimson face, and the sharp intake of breath. A miserable stick-in-the-mud, Reid decided. Had he imagined it, or had the man sputtered, "I can't stand the sight of him?"

"Bill. Let it go," the woman's voice urged.

What had that been all about? The crotchety old man's stare shot darts as Reid passed by their table. He must have mistaken him for someone else.

After returning to the cabin, and with no definite plans for the day, Reid made a fresh pot of coffee. He brought his cup to the sofa, and balancing the laptop on his thighs, sipped from the steaming brew. They'd need sponsors for the walk, like hiking boot manufacturers. How many boots would they even go through on their route? Clothing, rain jackets, cold-weather gear, and outdoor gear for nights they wouldn't make it to a town. How many high-protein energy bars would they put away?

Not ready to submit formal requests to corporations yet, Reid made lists, searched for contacts and phone numbers. At noon, Houston phoned.

"Hey, bro. How's it going?"

"All right. What's up?"

"Not much. I'm just checking on how *dinner* went last night." A low chuckle carried across the airwaves. Somehow it sat wrong with Reid. He could see it in his mind's eye, that smirk crossing Houston's face, and it irked.

"Do me a favor and wipe that fucking grin off your face, okay?" He sounded gruff.

"Oh. No offense, but from the sound of your loving expression, I guess it didn't go too well. Someone has his boxers in a bunch."

"Let's just say our expectations differ. That's it. Game over."

The tone said it all, and Houston understood when to shut up. "Sorry, man. But keep your head up, because we will get busy. Ready to pump up tomorrow's walk?"

"Yep. The stump gives his thumbs up."

"A'ight. Come to the office at nine, Alyson's got a couple of brochure designs for us to look at. First drafts, but it's happening now."

"Roger. I've been getting together a list of contacts. We can go over it tomorrow and add others."

"Okay. Mom wants you to come for supper."

Reid groaned. "I appreciate the invite, man. Please tell her I'll be missing out on her out-of-this-world cooking, but I've made plans."

"Uh-huh. Plans. Got it. Want some company with your *plans?*"

Today, the well-meaning dinner banter and fuss of Houston's family would grind on his nerves. Reid was grateful for the Millers warm embrace, but some days he just preferred solitude. And as he suspected, Houston had picked up on his mood.

Reid grinned into the phone. "Cool, man. Bring your guitar."

***

The afternoon sun had bathed the room in an ocean of warmth, soothing canines and man into a relaxing sleep.

Bones woke first from a deep nap and yawned. Yard lifted his eyelids, stretched his legs and lazily eyed the little dog. On the sofa, Reid dozed with the laptop on his thighs. Had the dogs snored, or had he woken himself? Jesus, his mouth felt as dry as the desert with his tongue sticking to the roof. Just like the furry ones, he stretched, yawned, and got up to down a tall glass of water.

In the bathroom, he splashed his face with cold water, brushed his teeth, and instantly felt refreshed. "Eh, guys. How about going into the woods?" Yard was by his side before he finished the question, and Bones wiggled right behind.

Reid grabbed a leash, snapped it to the small dog's collar. "Let's see how you'll do, exploring these woods."

The animal had gained weight, his fur filled in, and a playful personality developed a little more each day. He'd make an excellent pet for someone—a wonderful companion for a kid. Maybe soon. After the nap, Reid had checked emails to find one from Barkville Rescue's director. She'd informed him of an inquiry on Bones.

Reid should be excited, but wasn't it too soon? The mutt needed additional time to fill out loose skin. He'd gotten used to the little guy, and before giving him up, Reid didn't mind having him around a little longer.

Outside, he chose the path into the woods away from the street and cabin. Yard dashed ahead, his tail a big, wagging question mark, while Bones pulled on the leash, straining after Yard. Soon, the trail narrowed. Brush exploded undisturbed into a lush blanket, dotted with yellow, purple and white. Dust motes floated on sunny spears, penetrating a canopy of green; the air smelled earthy and mossy and clean.

Mossy. He thought of her, but he pushed it off.

He didn't know what kind of birds chirped and sang overhead; didn't need to. Their pitches and tones let his thoughts stray to the lyrics he'd been messing with earlier until his eyes had grown heavy and he'd dozed off.

Two-hundred more yards and Bones slowed down. Whistling for Yard who had roamed ahead, Reid turned back. The short walk in nature's perfection had restored his mood and inspired his mind.

***

Hunched over at the dining table, Reid scribbled, scratched out, and rewrote lyrics on a legal pad. In bold letters, twice underlined, followed by a large question mark, he'd written a title on top of the page. Since coming back from the walk in the woods, time raced as he wrote the lyrics to a song.

When Houston bounced through the door with the guitar case slung over his back, he balanced a covered plate. "Mom said you need to eat."

Reid shook his head, taking the food from Houston. "She's a sweetheart. Smack a kiss on her cheek for me, will you?" Reid crossed to the kitchen, deposited the dish on the counter, but thought better of it, and grabbed a fork from the drawer. "Want a beer?" When Houston confirmed, he lifted two longnecks from the fridge. Yeah, a cold beer sounded good again.

"I've had this idea." Reid moved to the dining table and made room to eat by shoving together loose pages that were scattered all across its top.

"You've been writing; that's why you need a guitar." A statement, not a question. Houston shrugged the instrument off his back, leaned it against the wall. While Reid loaded his fork with mashed potatoes and green beans, Houston lifted the notepad, studying the scribbles.

"'Boots?'"

"Yep. Haven't gotten far, but it's a start." Putting down the fork, Reid pushed aside the plate. "This tune's been buzzing around my head. Listen …" He hummed a short melody.

Houston reread the lines.

There's a whisper in the breeze

Reminding me of home

That whisper builds

That whisper cries

Blasts in the morning skies

But that ain't no way to lead a life

Step by step, take a walk in my boots …

"It's been a long time," Houston said, flicking a finger to the notepad. "Jeez, Mack. This is deep. But, hell to the yes, I like it—"

"Damn, straight, Tex. It's been a long time. Too long, if you ask me. Don't you miss it? We were living it up on Saturday nights, singing in dives, for shits and giggles and a few cold ones." Reid lifted the bottle, took a pull. "Because most times, it didn't pay for the gas to get there. But I wouldn't trade it; we had a hell of a time."

"Sure did, bud." Houston laced his fingers behind his head and leaned back, his eyes taking on a far-away look. "I still have a tote full of CD's floating around. Somewhere."

"Dig it out. We're going on tour."

Houston dropped his hands, laughed. "You forgot we're going on the road in four months, dude."

"Exactly. So, listen." Reid peeled the guitar from its case, strummed a few chords, and tuned. "This song has meaning. For you, and me, and all the boots that ever touched hostile ground *anywhere*. We'll be going through villages, small towns, cities, and at every place, we'll meet with brothers who wore the boots. In bars, veteran's halls and, hell, parks for all we care. We'll do a few songs, smooth the path, break the ice, or whatever you want to call it. And this," Reid plucked a few more chords, "will be our signature song."

Houston's eyebrows shot sky-high as he flung an astonished look at Reid. "Damn, Mack," he scratches his head, "you might just be onto something." Excitement crossed his face. "*Boots,* huh?"

"It has a ring to it." Reid grinned as they slapped palms together in a high-five.

Excitement pumped. "We rocked it," Reid puffed out a heavy breath as the guitar's sound faded. Line by line lyrics fused with melody into a kick-ass song—a song that was meant to grab the listener by the heart.

***

Across town, while Houston and Reid replayed, adjusted, and edited, William Schuster pulled a container from his dead son's closet and hauled the box to the desk opposite the bed—two filing cabinets with a countertop serving as desktop.

There, the computer's screen sat unblinkingly. Models of tanks, jeeps, and personnel carriers were lined up with military precision and outdated Army magazines remained neatly stacked on the countertop.

Nothing had changed in Billy's room since he'd left home to join the Army because Bill forbade his wife to pack away a single item. Because here, Bill felt close to his son, sensed his spirit in everything—unlike the vast cemetery filled with monuments and headstones. Sometimes, when he spoke to Billy, he swore he'd hear his son answer in his head. Bill wanted to touch Junior's things, connect with him, run his fingers over the medals the Army had awarded his dead son, but it wouldn't temper the malice living in his heart.

That smug SOB. The guy responsible for Billy's death, tipping his head with a shit-eating grin at breakfast this morning, had launched Bill's blood pressure into the danger zone, tempting Bill to smash that smile off his face right then and there.

Bill's temples throbbed recalling the incident as he lifted the satin-lined box holding the Purple Heart out of the container. With thick, stubby fingers, he opened the lid, brushed across George Washington's raised profile, and smoothed the white-edged purple ribbon. Moisture collected in the corner of his eyes as the familiar thought burned his mind, and scorched his heart—*Why Billy?* But no matter how many times he questioned, there simply wasn't an answer. Cradling the precious medal in the palm of his hand, Bill studied every detail as if for the first time.

"Billy," the burly man whispered, "he won't get away with it."

CHAPTER 17

Just before eight on Monday morning, Reid's phone buzzed. "Hey, man. What's up?"

"Change of plans, Mack." Houston led straight in when Reid answered the call.

"Okay?" Reid didn't have a clue to what could have come up in the few hours since midnight when he and Houston had finished writing their song. And at ten o'clock they'd meet again for distance training.

"Just got a call from the radio station. A scheduled guest canceled because of an emergency. The spot is ours, if we want it."

"If we want it? Hell yeah, we want it." Heightened attention straightened his back as Reid clutched the phone to his ear. "What time do we need to be there?"

"The show starts at nine. Buck wants to meet with us, go over a few things first. Can you be at the station by eight thirty? WOXG is around the courthouse, you won't miss it."

"Roger that."

"Hurry up, boys," Reid rushed the dogs outside while guzzling coffee from a travel mug, jumped into his walking gear, snatched the car keys, and arrived at the station with time to spare.

Ten minutes before going live, Houston and Reid perched atop tall wooden stools, adjusting microphones and chatting with host Buck Freeman while a country hit rode the airwaves.

As the top of the hour approached, bold numbers flashed on Buck's large computer screen, counting back seconds, and three—two—one.

"Morning, Folks! This is Buck Freeman, and you are listening to 'According to Buck.' Today I have two exceptional guests with me in the studio. I'm privileged to welcome Army veterans Houston Miller—who grew up in Oak Creek—and Reid McCabe, who moved to our town from Florence, Kentucky."

"Thank you for inviting us to your show; we appreciate being here," Houston answered.

"Gentleman, thank you for your service!"

Humbled, and with an air of unease, Houston and Reid scooted in their seats, heads nodding at once.

Why does everyone thank us for our service? Reid thought. No one forced us to sign up for this; we just did our jobs.

"You're welcome. Thank you for your support, Houston said."

"Houston ... Reid, before we get started, why don't you tell our listeners a little about yourselves? When did you know you wanted to join the Armed Forces? How long did you serve?"

Buck eased into the questions. When he came back on air after playing a patriotic country tune, he went straight to the heart of the program's topic.

"You established the nonprofit corporation, Heroes Rise. Its mission is to raise awareness to the staggering number of veteran suicides." Paper rustled as Buck consulted his notes. "Every day, roughly twenty veterans end their lives, according to data from the Department of Veterans Affairs. What does your organization hope to change?"

Houston launched into it with rising passion. "You know Buck, if we can make a difference for only one man, one woman, or one child, the mission will have been a success."

The listeners couldn't see Reid nodding, but they could hear the zeal in his tone as he followed Houston's statement.

"A daughter walking down the aisle without her father, a son growing up without his mother, a wife or husband left behind, struggling for answers." The mic screeched, and Reid adjusted. "Not because these men and women were killed in action, but because the side of war that's so horrific that it erodes minds—and we won't get into that—claimed their lives *after* they came home. It's difficult to think about, and in reality, much more complex than this, but in a nutshell, this is what it comes down to."

"Indeed, challenging to think of it in these terms, to envision the faces of real people behind these numbers. Twenty veterans a day, folks." Buck let it hang for impact.

"Reid, we've also just learned of your injury. You've lost part of your leg in a roadside explosion, and you just adopted a three-legged dog. How will you both tackle this year-long walk across America?"

"That's a good question, Buck. And real easy to answer. My dog, Yard, and I are going to take it step by step. Because, that's the only way. Think along the line of, 'How do you eat an elephant?'"

"Definitely. An ambitious goal, and a challenging mission you tasked yourselves with, gentlemen.

The show raced toward its end as Buck led Houston and Reid through the interview.

"We have time for a couple more questions," Buck said. "Please share with our listeners how you intend to raise funds, and how donations can be made."

"Yes, fundraising is a huge part of our campaign and ultimate success," Reid said. "We're counting on donations from national and local corporations, and support from veteran's organizations. But make no mistake, we appreciate *every* donation, and *no* amount is too small; every dollar counts."

Reid read the P.O. Box address he'd jotted on a piece of paper, repeating it as he detailed the various ways people could make a donation.

"And if you stop in at Pat's Place," he said, "you'll notice a pair of black military boots sitting in the corner of the bar-top bearing the Heroes Rise logo. And yes, let me assure you, they're brand-new. So, don't hesitate to fill 'em up by throwing your pocket change into them." And with a grin that could quite possibly be heard on the radio, he added, "More boots will be coming to a store near you."

Buck gave a thumbs up and closed out the program. "Gentleman, it was my pleasure having you in the studio. We have about one minute left. Do you have anything you would like to add?"

Houston nodded and spoke up. "Thanks for having us, Buck. It was a real pleasure. We have one more thing for anyone who's listening—every Thursday afternoon at five o'clock we plan to be at Pat's Place, and we want to meet you. Whether you're a veteran, spouse, child, or sibling of a veteran, we're standing by to hear your stories. Come see us."

"Thanks, guys. And thank you folks for listening to 'According to Buck.' Until tomorrow. And, as always, be safe."

"Great interview, guys." Buck came around his booth and shook hands with Houston and Reid after the show. "You're welcome to come back any time. Let me know if you've got something you want to get out, and we'll schedule it."

The men left the studio, and once outside, Reid let out a breath and rubbed across tight neck muscles. "Wow, this was intense but amazing."

"Buck's been doing this for as long as I remember; folks listen to him."

"Well, let's see how well they listened to his call for donations." Reid lightly punched Houston's arm. "Let's go rucking now."

***

Around noon, the guys returned from their hike in the forest and decided to head into town for pizza.

While crossing over the busy traffic circle around the courthouse, Houston pulled his cell phone out and called the office of Miller's Construction. The office manager answered on the second ring.

"Alyson, darling. Something came up; we couldn't make it to the office earlier."

"I know, big guy. Congrats on the fantastic interview."

"You know, huh?"

"Well, of course, I do. I'm clairvoyant, remember?" Alyson chuckled; she loved to tease him and could imagine the eye roll. "You better stop rolling those eyes, or you'll lose them to my marble collection."

"Ha, you think that's funny, Aly? I didn't know you're listening to Buck's show."

"Lots of things you don't know, big guy."

"Enlighten me. Reid and I are heading to the new pizza joint. It's lunchtime; if dad doesn't keep you chained to the desk, haul your butt over here and bring those brochures. We're looking at it over pizza."

"Yes, sir, Houston."

***

Alyson bent her head to peek inside her shoulder bag, unsure whether she'd picked up the brochure samples or left them on her desk. She'd just crossed from the other side of the road and was paying little attention to her surroundings when she accidentally brushed against one of the two utility workers walking next to each other on the sidewalk.

"I'm sorry," she mumbled, shocked at the hostile vibe skidding up her arm. She clamped a hand around the prickling sensation and rubbed. *Phew*, she thought, *that's one angry fellow.*

It had happened again, at the mere touch—that sudden flash of clarity that gave her goosebumps and a glimpse of a person's energy or future. Sometimes it was both. She never wanted it to happen, and she never wanted to get used to it. Alyson shivered at the lingering negative energy and knew without a doubt, this man was a hairsbreadth away from a heart attack.

The vision took on an aura of sadness. Yet, relieved not having to spend the next hour in the same establishment, she watched the two men entering the diner next to The Thin Crust pizza restaurant. She wished that bike accident at age ten had never happened. When she awoke from a two-day coma, Alyson was physically unscathed, but she'd woken with a strange case of heightened perception. Shaking off the negative thoughts, Alyson entered the restaurant.

Reid, who met Alyson for the first time as she stepped up to the table, flicked his eyes to Houston in an "are you kidding me" kind of look. From the corners of his eyes, he'd glimpsed a black-haired woman leaving the office of Miller's

Construction the day he'd arrived in Oak Creek. Reid had paid little attention, but he noticed her now.

"Alyson," he smiled, stood and pulled out a chair. "Great to meet you." After a few words of small talk, Alyson laid the printed papers on the table. By the time the pizza came, Reid and Houston could visualize the black-and-white print in full color. A tri-fold brochure, a flyer-sized announcement containing contact information, and a tear-off section for donations. A few minor changes and they'd send the order to the print company.

"Houston didn't lie. I see why he's been bragging about you." Reid lifted his glass, peered across the rim. "Excellent work."

Houston had described Alyson as striking, humorous, and sometimes a little strange. Reid didn't see strange, but definitely striking.

***

Next door, in the diner, Bill Schuster's face turned beet-red as his co-worker, Carl, sang the praises of the two Army veterans on Buck's radio show this morning.

"Good for them, I'll say. Damn, if I were twenty years younger, I'd join them, walk with them." He looked at Bill, took a bite of his burger. "Since I'm not, I'll take the guys up on their offer to meet. Might stop at Pat's on Thursday if I can tear my nephew out of his house. He could use some help."

He noticed Bill's expression, the creased forehead, and narrowed eyes. "What's up, Bill? Your meat turn sour, or what?"

Bill's mouth pinched as he swiped the back of his hand across his lips. "Don't trust them; that's all," he mumbled.

"Now, why would you say something like that? Those boys seemed honest in wanting to help and make a difference. Some of our vets coming back from *over there* are having a hard time; my nephew's one of them. A wife and three boys." The man adjusted the ball cap with the company logo, a sheepish look on his face. "To tell the truth, I'd say he's come close to ending it for himself a time or two. It might do him good to meet these guys. You should meet them, too." The man's voice went gentle, the reference to Bill's state of mind after Billy's death remained unspoken. He couldn't know Reid McCabe was the reason for the mounting pressure in Bill's heart.

"I might do that."

CHAPTER 18

On Thursday afternoon, not knowing what to expect, Reid and Houston had pushed together a couple of tables for the veteran meet-and-greet.

"Think anyone will come?" Reid just asked as a hefty man, wearing a work-shirt and cargo pants, came into Pat's Place.

"Howdy." The man seemed skeptical as he approached the table, fiddling with his hat, lifting and adjusting the black ball cap with the utility company's embroidered logo. "You the guys with Heroes Rise?"

"Yep. That's us." Reid pushed to his feet. "I'm Reid McCabe, and you are Tim?" Reid scanned the name above the shirt pocket.

The man's eyes flitted, scoping out the taproom, but it was early, and only a couple of guys at the bar were watching a ballgame, while others occupied tables in the dining room. "I'm Timothy Cox—Tim." He pumped Reid's hand. "I heard you on the radio the other day."

"That's great, Tim. Glad you could come." Reid's smile aimed at putting the man at ease. "Why don't you have a seat?"

"I'm not a veteran." Tim shuffled his feet. A thick, calloused hand lifted to his neck, scratching and lifting the hat, again. "But I wanted to meet you guys, shake your hands. I've told Matt, my nephew, about what you said in the interview.

That you want to meet veterans from this town. I'll expect he'll come."

"That's fantastic, Tim." Houston introduced himself, indicating again for the man to sit. Scooting into his seat, Tim seemed relieved when the waiter came to take his drink order.

"So, your nephew served?" Reid asked.

"Army. He got out after twelve years; he's had a hell of a time since … PTSD. What you said about that suicide rate? I can't be sure, but I heard it from his dad, my brother. Matt's wife's been talking to him. As my brother put it, she thinks he'll be doing something stupid. He has depression. She says he's got nightmares, can't sleep, and the slightest thing irritates the crap out of him. He's having a hard time adjusting at work. And flashbacks. I guess that's the worst of it. His wife asked him straight up if he wants to kill himself. And you know what he said?" Tim's nostrils flared; he was getting angry. He said, "Yes. Every damn day."

Shit, Reid thought. *Tim's the first guy to meet us, and he brings it home with a sledgehammer.* But he could relate. Hadn't he gone through some of the same? Not that he'd ever considered to take his own life, not even after the leg came off. But this was precisely why he'd signed up to do this walk with Houston. To make a splash in this ocean of sorrow and distress. The edge must have shown on Reid's face because Houston spoke up.

"I'm sorry, Tim. I know this is tough on everyone. What's your email address? I'll send you a list of excellent resources for Matt and for his wife. Pass it on to Matt or your brother. You're a good man, Tim. Thanks for talking to us."

Houston jotted down Tim's email while Reid watched the shadow of despair cross Tim's face. He laid his hand on the beefy man's shoulder. "Tim, I know what it's like." I'm here, and I'll listen whenever he's ready. Tell him that."

By the time the karaoke band set up at eight, four more vets had sought out Reid and Houston. They'd come because the radio interview had resonated, and curiosity motivated.

Now, with a bucket of beer between them, Reid and Houston watched the band get ready to perform. Alyson, who'd joined them at the table a few minutes earlier, took a chair between them. Since Pat had hired the karaoke band, Thursday nights were immensely popular, and this evening was no exception, as the growing crowd proved.

"What do you say?" Reid shouted above the noise, tilting his head to the stage. Houston's lips stretched into a wide smirk as he gave a thumbs-up. It would be fun. Not as much as commanding the stage with their own band and their own songs, but it would give them a fantastic way to practice before performing "Boots" the following Thursday.

Reid had selected his song. When he took the stage and lifted the microphone from the stand, the familiar excitement hummed in his chest. The band started up, he cleared his throat, and his amplified voice roared.

Halfway through the song, to the tune of "Friends in Low Places," and as his gaze swept the audience, he caught her leaning against the bar. Upturned green eyes drew his. With a slight lift of the Miller Light in her hand, she acknowledged him. Reid turned his eyes back to the small crowd thundering along and firing him on. *Yeah, Mossy, I do have friends in low places.*

Reid didn't catch another glimpse of Keira; elbowing his way to the back end of the bar room, patrons fist-bumped and high-fived him until he reached the bathrooms.

He'd just zipped up and soaped his hands when an elbow rammed into his back. What the fuck? With the speed of a bullet, he shot around, his mind exploding with scenarios, but he wasn't prepared when the fist connected with his face, momentarily stunning him.

"'Hero,' my hairy ass; a goddamn murderer is more like it," the slurred voice spat venom.

With no intention of getting into a brawl with a tanked-up patron, Reid grabbed the man by his shirt. Disgusted by the alcohol emanating and the animosity in his eyes, Reid shoved the brawny man aside just as the bathroom door opened, knocking him back into the unsuspecting new arrival.

"Hey, watch it asshole," the newcomer yelled as the drunk crashed into him, but the assailant pushed him out of the way with unexpected strength.

"Murderer!" He spewed out once more and disappeared into the cover of the crowd.

Reid reached up to examining the sore jaw. The hook could have been worst. At least nothing's broken, he brooded, probably just black and blue by morning.

"You all right, man?" The stranger asked.

"Yeah. Goddam drunk," Reid said as a way of explanation.

What had *that* been all about? Why had this man called him a *murderer*, not once, but twice? Who was he? He looked familiar, but Reid didn't know him. Besides Houston's circle of friends, he didn't know anyone in Oak Creek. Reid breathed in; a drunken mix-up, he suspected.

A clatter similar to someone hitting the jackpot at a nickel machine reached Reid's ears when he stepped back into the barroom. Coins rolled on the floor, howling and shrieking voices turned the air heavy with tension. The asshole had swiped the donation boots off the counter. As crowded as Pat's

Place was, that had to be the stupidest thing to do. Three men were on him, pushing and pummeling, when security swiftly ended the brawl, dragging the inebriated man to the door and throwing him outside.

The band had stopped playing. Pat stepped up to the podium, took the mic, and ran a steady hand over his bald head. "Folks, drunk or not, what just happened is reprehensible, and disappointing in more ways than one."

Someone had returned the boots to the bar top, and Pat pointed to the pair now. "Thank you, everyone, for collecting and returning the change to where it belongs. We're here to have a good time. If you happen to know this bonehead, be sure to pass on that he can make amends by dropping a few bills in here or stay the hell away from our place."

"Yeah, I'd like to meet him on the other end of *this*," a patron shouted, throwing his fist in a punch, and was quickly joined by others.

Pat ignored the comment and secured the microphone back to its stand. The band started playing, the noise level rose and soon, shouting was the way to be heard.

Reid made his way back to the table when he felt a tap on his shoulder from behind. He turned. He shouldn't have been surprised, but he was when his eyes connected with Keira's.

"Hey, Reid." She raised her voice above the noise.

Reid lifted his hand. "Hey."

At the level of sound, a conversation had to be pared down to a few words.

"Nice vocals."

"Yeah. Thanks." Jaw muscles twitched; he forced a smile.

"Reid—"

"Got to go. Have a great time," Reid pushed through clenched teeth. When he'd glimpsed Keira earlier, standing by the bar, he'd credited the rush of blood to the thrill of playing with a band. Standing face to face with her, he wasn't so sure anymore; a convincing reason to put some distance between them.

Reid sauntered back to the table, pulled a chair, and dropped into his seat. "Ugh, woman. Stop it!" He cringed at the thirty-something brunette sounding like a frog with a sore throat, belting with an enthusiasm that made up for the lack of talent. From the bucket, Reid picked up an iced bottle and held it to his jaw.

Alyson, who'd studied the song sheet, smiled and bumped Reid with her elbow to get his attention. He leaned over, squinted and shook his head, mouthing "I'll pass," while pointing to his jaw. Alyson's mouth opened, "Oh." Startled, she touched tender fingers to the swelling. "What happened?" She brought her mouth to his ear, but Reid just shook his head. He was fine. "Later, he mouthed back."

A band member called Houston's name. With a swagger, he stepped onto the platform and took the mic from the stand. He didn't need the lyrics; they were engraved on his brain. "I Don't Dance" was a slow number.

At the table, Reid held out a hand and cocked his head. Unspoken words exchanged, Alyson nodded, and together they stepped onto the dancefloor. Alyson's head barely reached Reid's shoulders, long tresses flowed where he held her, slender fingers curled around his neck. Bodies moved to Houston's voice, left little space in-between, touched, and moved apart again.

Keira glided from the barstool, flushed. She skirted the dancefloor to add her name to the singer sign-up sheet.

The song ended, Reid released his hand from her back, and as he stepped out, Alyson's eyes broke away from Houston.

And it became clear; the attraction in the glint didn't need interpretation. *I'll be damned,* he mused. How had he missed it?

A damn good thing there hadn't been a spark between them as he held this attractive woman in his arms. Strange as *that* was.

"I need to ice this thing," Reid excused himself when Houston returned to the table. His lip wasn't cracked, and he counted himself lucky for not having any loose teeth, but the swelling was getting worse and the throbbing needed to stop.

The notes of a new song had sounded, and he stopped, turned, and just stared. Damn, that voice!

Mossy?

***

"For crying out loud, Bill. You've been to Pat's, drinking. Again," Carol's tone accused as he stumbled into the living room. She marked a page in the book on her lap and closed it with a thwack.

She didn't need detective's eyes to make out the bloodshot eyes, the unhealthy red face, and identify the whiff of breath that smelled like roadkill.

Carol had gotten tired waiting for Bill and had changed into her nightgown and robe. Today was his birthday, and this morning she'd splurged to make it a special evening at home. She'd vowed to make it a happy occasion for both.

This morning, she'd gone to the beauty salon with the intentions of a trim and had walked out with a stylish cut and highlights blending with her own silver strands. The new look made her feel frivolous and just a little sexy. Bubbling inside, she decided this was an occasion for a new dress. Bill would like it, she hoped.

She'd bought a bottle of sparkling grape juice in anticipation of a small celebration. After that, she hoped to re-create the spark that had been missing in the bedroom for too long. In truth, the anguish of Billy's death, the heartache, and the gray had paralyzed them. It had put their marriage on a slide, while her husband's flight to alcohol had been on the rise. Today, Carol aimed to change this. Bill's birthday would be the moon changing the emotional low-tide. It didn't mean to let go of Billy's memory. Never. But it was time to celebrate life again.

Carol slapped the book onto the table and thrust an envelope at Bill. "Happy Birthday, Bill—if you even remember. I hope you enjoyed your evening drinking with ghosts." Gone was the excitement she'd felt earlier. Now only anger welled.

Bill swayed as he stared at Carol through a haze. His face seemed to turn a shade darker if that was even possible. "Bitch," he uttered and collapsed into a chair. But the slamming of the bedroom door drowned the slur.

Elbows propped on knees, Bill buried his face in his hands. His shoulders shook, and tears trickled through calloused fingers.

CHAPTER 19

The next morning, Reid groaned at the color palette of his jaw. Swollen and with shades of purple, he concluded it looked worse than it felt. He wiggled his jaw and winced. Shaving was off; thankfully, he didn't have to. The bruise wouldn't be visible under growing scruff, and this, Reid counted as a bonus.

At first light, he opened the patio door to let the dogs out. And, as every morning, they rushed down the deck stairs ahead of Reid. The air still held a chill, but bursts of orange and pink on the horizon promised a pleasantly warm day. Travel mug of hot coffee in hand, Reid flopped onto a tread at the bottom of the stairs and watched the mutts follow their morning ritual. Bones dashed over, darted up, dropped his butt beside him, and without fail, nosedived into the pocket of Reid's hoodie.

Since when had he started hauling dog treats in his pockets? Just a quirky habit he'd adopted since Keira had shown up with a treat in *her* pocket.

"Easy, boy." Reid scratched the little dog's ears, but he caved, and pulled out a small biscuit. "Don't get yourself too comfortable, ole boy. Today's a big day for us; some family wants to meet you. If you're lucky, you'll be adopted."

Two weeks ago—had it already been two weeks?—and on his way to Oak Creek, he'd rescued the brown dog after nearly running him over. A bag of bones no more, the animal had put some meat on his ribs since.

"You're starting to look like a real dog," Reid muttered, stroking the smooth, furry head. "I can't imagine why they wouldn't want you."

Bones tilted his head with a puzzled look.

"You'll have a little girl to play with." Reid kept stroking, but his mind went to the woman who'd convinced him to foster, and the image of gentle hands handling an emaciated Bones burst into his head. Mossy. She'd been remarkably trusting with both dogs, and in return, they'd trusted her. She hadn't treated Yard differently or pitied him for missing a hind leg. It was *him* she pitied. *Get your head out of your butt and move on,* Reid berated himself.

With his mind preoccupied, he followed Yard, who trailed a scent along the tree lines. The call from Barkville Rescue for Bones had come yesterday in the early afternoon. Reid should have been happy for the little guy, but what was with that scratch in his chest when he spoke of adoption? He'd gotten accustomed to having the mutt around. Yard did, too, as was evident in the way he fussed over, bossed around, and played with him.

"Well, you can't stay here, buddy," Reid pushed to his feet. He'd be crazy to even consider keeping Bones; he hadn't signed up for that in the first place. Not with the walk coming up in September.

Reid had Yard. And in just little over a month, the dumped animal had become his buddy. Not just a faithful friend, but a boulder against the undercurrents of stress in a bubbling river of unwelcome memories. And he didn't care about Reid's missing leg. Heck, the dog didn't even know *he* was short of a limb. On the year-long walk, he'd be his and Houston's companion.

A visit to the vet had assured Reid it was okay to take Yard on this venture. Doc had mentioned service dogs and the missions they accomplished, which were short of miraculous. Of course. Yard would be fine. "With periods of rest," the vet said, "he can handle it. Or, you can get a carrying harness."

"I suppose," Reid said, warming up to the idea. "I'll look into it."

Yes, Yard would rule the road, but a peanut like Bones? Not a chance.

Liquid eyes the color of dark chocolate looked up to Reid. "Okay. One more cookie." The dog gently took the treat from Reid's fingers.

***

Later that morning, Reid and Houston met for their daily walk, switching it from the soft underground of woodland paths to the pavers and concrete sidewalks of down-town.

"Hey, Tex." Reid pulled into Miller's Construction's parking lot just as Houston stepped from his apartment above the office and sauntered down the stairs. "Man, you look like something that needs warming up. Did you get loaded at Pat's last night? Or what?"

Houston eyes narrowed as he zoomed in on Reid's blooming bruise. "Spoken by the man who looks like an eye-catching piece of crap himself. And that's a description, not an insult. How'd you manage to get your pretty face spanked, anyway?"

"Shut up and do me a favor—Go jump into a lake, bud."

"A'ight. Anything else, or can we go now?"

Done with the good-natured ego jabs, Houston shot Reid a grin while both strapped on their backpacks and started walking.

"You left early. What happened?"

"No clue. I've never met the guy. I'm in the privy washing my hands, next thing I know he rams me in the back. I turn around, and wham, his fist is in my face, and he spits 'murderer.' Lucky for him he was a dud-grenade—three sheets to the wind, and a sissy-punch. It was the same guy who swiped the boots of the bar.

Houston's eyes bulged to the size of golf balls. "You're kidding. Tell me you're fricking kidding, Mack."

You know him?"

Houston opened his mouth to answer but pulled behind Reid as three mature women toting shopping bags stepped out of a store and onto the sidewalk.

"Yard, heel." Reid shortened the leash to let the ladies pass.

"Oh, my ... how well-trained." The petite, gray-haired woman said, offering a sweet smile.

"Thank you, ma'am." Reid gave a courteous nod.

"So, do you know the guy?" After the shoppers had passed, Reid asked a second time.

"Kind of," pressed through tight lips.

"Kind of. That's it? I'm not buying it. My gut says there's more."

Houston lifted his gaze to the sky with a sharp intake of breath; he scanned Reid's face, unsure of how to break the news.

"Yes, I met him. Once. Huh," he scoffed. "What about the odds of us living in the same town?" Houston mused, sounding as if he'd just revealed an incredulous piece of information to himself. "I did what I had to and went to his home—to show my respect, extend my condolences, and offered to share memories. The toughest thing I've ever had to do."

At the somber tone, Reid turned his head and searched his friend's face. "Want to clue me into what you're talking about?"

"I should have guessed it might come to this; should have told you. Kick my ass, man, but I didn't think. I didn't fucking *think!*"

"Tex. Calm down. What the hell are you talking about?"

Houston had turned into an alley, where it was just the two of them. He stopped in his tracks, threw his hands behind his neck, and flung his head skyward.

"Billy ... PFC William F. Schuster. The man that decked you last night? That's his dad."

Stunned silence.

"Jesus, Tex. What are you saying?"

"Schuster is mad with pain. Losing his only kid broke him. It didn't take a psychology degree to see that. I can't blame him for that. But—I guess he's looking for a scapegoat, a body he can pin his son's death on. He didn't blame me, but it sure as hell sounds like he's looking at you: Billy's section leader."

"Billy." Reid's head spun, he stumbled and braced a hand against the wall of the building. *Murderer* echoed in his head as the scene of the fateful day played in his head.

The convoy stop. It had been his job to provide security. The wail, the flash, the hit, followed by darkness, until he woke in a hospital where he learned that two of his men were killed in the attack. One of them PFC Schuster. Had there been more he could have done to prevent their deaths? Countless times the question had tormented him. But there hadn't been a single thing he could have done differently. And yet ...

He squatted and dropped his head between his knees. Nausea took his breath. Breathe. Just breathe—the way counseling had taught.

"Billy," Reid croaked, wiped a sleeve across his mouth, and fumbled for a bottle of water. When he found it, he gulped until the last drop, frantically washing down the acrid taste in his mouth. "Twenty-one-year-old Billy, who lived and breathed Army. And who was pumped-up about going on his first deployment."

For most it would be a cliché, Reid accepted that, but everyone who'd ever met Billy would agree he'd died doing what he loved most. Last night's incident at Pat's Place had made it clear Billy's father didn't see it that way. Was Bill Schuster out for revenge?

Next to Reid, Yard whined and scratched his human's leg. Reid draped an arm around the dog and buried his face in the animal's fur. *Murderer.*

The shock passed, and the men did what they had to do—train. Stepping up and stepping out, they walked.

"You okay?" Houston asked an hour later as they returned to where they'd started. "Come into the office. If Alyson's made the changes to the print material, we could get it to the printer today." He twisted the office doorknob, the jingle of the entry bell announcing visitors.

"Sure," Reid said. "But let's make it fast. I need to get back to the cabin."

"What's the rush?" Houston glanced over his shoulder as Reid shut the door, and Alyson looked up from her keyboard.

"I'm taking Bones to Barkville—someone wants to meet him. Fingers crossed he'll get adopted."

Behind her desk, the corners of Alyson's mouth lifted at Reid's last comment. "He will. Greetings, guys. What brings you in?" She'd propped her elbows on the desktop, leaning her chin on top of clasped hands.

"Darling." Houston huffed. "We're too tired to beg. Please, tell me you've made those changes we discussed?"

"Ah, I see. The changes we discussed only yesterday. Your patience is outstanding, Miller." Alyson's eyes twinkled as she tapped the stack of papers on her desk. "What would your dad say if I put your needs before these invoices and estimates?"

Houston scratched his head, pretended to think. "Now that you mention it, I'm sure he said to make me your top priority."

Reid pressed his lips together, clenched his jaw, and winced. Trying to keep a straight face, he'd forgotten about the bruise. Tension shimmered underneath teasing, but despite laying the charm on Alyson, his idiot friend seemed oblivious to it.

***

The Jeep rumbled into the parking lot of Barkville Rescue. He'd left Yard at the cabin, but Bones made the trip secure in his crate. "You don't need to be *that* happy," Reid muttered as the mutt bounced on his leash into the building.

"Hey, Reid." As if on cue, the director stepped from her office. "Why do they do this?" Reid asked himself when Haley squatted, and baby-talked to Bones, but leveling a smile at her, he returned the greeting.

"Haley. How's it going?"

"The adopters will be here any minute," the director babbled on, picking up a wiggling Bones. "They want a small dog for their three-year-old. The mother said the little girl fell in love with Bones' picture online. And he's just perfect for a family with small children—playful, energetic, and friendly."

When the building door opened, Reid's eyes scanned over a yuppie couple with the child holding onto her mother's hand. A Disney princess came to mind as he took in the girl's frilly dress.

"Keep your fingers crossed," Haley whispered as she sat Bones onto the floor and greeted the visitors with her brightest smile.

"Mommy ..." The girl shrieked, clapped her hands, and tore from her mother's side. It terrified Bones, who scooted as close to Reid as his leash let him. Haley picked him up again.

"Voice, honey." The mother touched a finger to her lips in a shushing gesture. "We don't want to scare him, do we?" With a glance at Haley, she lifted perfectly groomed eyebrows in an apologetic look.

Haley kept smiling as she opened the door across her office, a comfortable space set up for adopters and animals to interact on their own terms. "Please, come in."

Dad was the last to enter, and the director closed the door. The mother bent and held her girl tight against her thighs, both keeping an eye on Bones as Haley sat him down and released the leash. Dad stood a couple of steps away, stance wide, unsmiling, and with arms crossed over his chest.

Reid leaned against a tall shelf. He, too, had his arms crossed with his eyes glued to Bones closing in on the girl. Scared? Like an overprotective dad, Reid held his breath, hoping the girl wouldn't startle him again. Wishful thinking. The animal's cold nose brushed against bare legs, and an ear-piercing squeal erupted as Disney princess pulled from her mother's embrace, dropped to the floor, reaching for the dog. His paw got caught between the girl's leg and arm.

"Don't," Haley rushed in as Reid pushed away from the shelf. And Princess screamed. When a frightened Bones pulled back his paw, his nails had left marks. Two red welts bloomed on her thigh.

"Damn, Liz. I told you coming here was a waste of time." The dad spouted at his wife after springing forward, picking up little Princess, and examining the scratches on her leg. His wife padded her chest; the girl wailed with her head buried in his shoulder.

"No pedigree, and with no idea where these mutts come from? Find a breeder," he spat. "Vicious mongrel." But he wasn't finished yet. Red-faced, he pointed the finger at Haley. "Count yourself lucky we're not taking action against you."

"Shh, Princess. We're getting you a *nice* doggy." Hiccups interrupted sobs. Dad shot a final glare at Haley. "We're leaving."

Haley had picked up a shivering Bones, while Reid, with a mockingly gallant flourish, held open the office door for the couple's exit.

"You have a real nice day now." Reid's exaggerated drawl added to the mockery, but he doubted the couple paid attention. He let the door slam behind them.

"Holy shit." Haley drew a relieved breath. She didn't usually swear, but this had been too much. "What were the parents thinking?"

"They didn't. In a way, I'm sorry for the girl growing up like this. Pampered and spoiled. And one day, when reality crashes castles in the sky? But hey, that's my two cents."

Haley kissed the top of the dog's head before setting him onto the ground. "They wouldn't be happy with a rescue dog, anyway. Thanks for bringing Bones in, Reid. It didn't work out this time, but, trust me, he won't stay on the adoption list very long."

Reid took the leash. "All right, mutt. We're stuck together for a while longer. Let's go home."

By the time Reid drove out of Barkville's parking lot, the gloom had crept inside like a toxic mist and dropped a sick feeling into his chest. Murky shadows clouded his mind, nixing the trip he'd planned earlier in the day to visit his parents in Florence. His chest hollowed as his mind's eye conjured up Billy, and he thought of the young soldier's gung-ho attitude.

Murderer whirled and bounced inside Reid's skull, and he felt the overwhelming need to be alone.

Turn the Jeep around, he told himself. *Call Houston.* But swerving the Jeep into a parking space in front of the liquor store, Reid slayed the nagging for moral backing and shut off the engine. "Stay," he ordered Bones, as if the dog, tucked inside his crate, had a choice.

Damn, he was tough, hard, and gutsy, not a sniveling, weak-kneed milksop. Reid went inside the store, beer needed replenishing. He grabbed a bottle sealed with red wax. Why not? It had been ages since he'd tasted a full-flavored bourbon.

Next stop was the drive-through at the place with the golden arches. Fast food wasn't Reid's normal thing, eating well was. As it stood, he was neither in the mood to fire up the grill nor was he hungry. Rocks filled his stomach, but it had been early morning since he'd had that slice of toast. Fast food would do. He ordered, and deciding the dogs deserved a treat, he added five plain burgers. Tap, tap. The gloom deepened, fingers drummed an impatient staccato against the steering wheel. What the hell was taking so long?

Back at the cabin—finally—Reid kicked the door shut with his heel. The dogs greeted each other as if they'd been separated a year and not just a few hours. "Dinner," he said in a tone as low and dull as the thwack the paper bags made when he dumped them on the kitchen counter. Two furry rumps hit the floor, and two pink tongues licked their chops respectively. Responsibilities.

"Catch." Reid flung a hamburger patty that Yard caught in mid-air "Good catch." He tore four patties and tossed the pieces onto the kibble in two bowls. His meal remained untouched inside the sack; he wasn't hungry after all.

The waxed bottle beckoned.

A pull of the tab, a twist, and he poured the amber liquid. The water glass reminded Reid of sloshing red wine, and the redhead who'd teased him about it Saturday evening. Chemistry had been thick, but the date ended in a mess; his fault. Had he leveled with Keira about his amputation before fast-tracking to hot and seductive, would her reaction have been different? Useless speculation, but damn if it didn't sting.

Reid took a huge gulp, hissed, and relished the burn in his throat. He carried the glass and bottle to the dining table, where he slumped into a chair.

Frustration had grown deeper with bumping into Keira at Pat's bar last night. And again, today as he passed the yellow bug driving away from the rescue. For Pete's sake, why did it still pester him? He'd misread her—hard feelings and tears were the only results of this mistake. Bad enough, but no one had died.

Unlike on that unscheduled convoy stop in the remote Afghan mountain range. That day, had he made a deadly error? Misjudged the situation?

Reid's phone shrilled. He shut off the ringer.

A second gulp and he sucked air through clenched teeth.

You're not responsible, they had said—his platoon sergeant and friend, SFC Houston Miller, his chain of command, doctors, nurses, his parents. How did they know he wasn't at fault?

Murderer.

Bill Schuster's angry, red face blazed into his mind.

Reid emptied his glass with a chug, filled it up again. Another swallow; Bourbon slid smoothly now, melting the icy ball in his gut. The mobile vibrated on the table, but his attention wasn't with the phone.

What could he have done differently? What had he missed?

He dropped his blurred gaze from the wall he'd been staring at and shut his eyes. Slumping forward, he braced his forehead with the heel of his hands.

At once, a blinding light flashed behind closed eyelids, and the deafening explosion rung his ears. After the attack, darkness had enveloped him, but right now, the claws of guilt dug into him and tore. It should have been his body inside a flag-draped coffin, and not one of the men he was supposed to secure inside the vehicle.

Secure. Reid sneered.

He took pride in his leadership skills, and his men had followed him, trusted him, but he'd let them down. A great leader he was; one that took two of his men straight to the bowels of hell.

Thoughts became tumbleweeds, twisting and rushing in a battling stream of guilt—could have done more—not your fault—you're not alone in this.

CHAPTER 20

THE SOUND OF THE DETONATION kept playing on a loop in Reid's head. Boom ... or was it bang? And why were the dogs behaving like the hounds of Hades? Snarling and barking. Not snarling, just barking their heads off. Something crashed: the noise. He covered his ears.

And out of nowhere, Houston was there.

"Mack. What the fuck are you doing, man?"

Houston bristled. Nostrils flared, face red and contorted with suppressed anger, he capped the open bottle and put it out of Reid's reach.

"Hey ... gimme that." Reid reached, but his hand fell to the table. "What do you want?" The words came slurred.

"What the hell is going on, man?" Houston planted his hands on the table, and his temples throbbed as he stared into his friend's agitated eyes. "You're punishing yourself, or is there another reason to get smashed on hard liquor? Thought you gave that up. Isn't that what you said? It sure as shit doesn't look like it to me."

Reid lurched up straight. Bloodshot eyes shifted and focused with great effort. "*They fucking died,*" Reid slammed a fist on the table, "because I failed ... not doing my job ... should have done more."

"Uh-huh. My gut was on-target. Lost count on how many times I called and texted, but no answer." Houston ran a hand through his hair. "Mack. If there's a corner of your brain that's not drowned in bourbon, I want you to listen—IT WAS NOT YOUR FAULT! You *know* that. Not *your* fault, or mine, or Schuster's. No one's fault but the goddamn Taliban's. Got that?"

"Piss off."

Houston went to the kitchen, leaving Reid slumped over the table. A few seconds later he returned with a tumbler of ice-water. "Here, guzzle this. And go sleep it off."

Reid pushed to his feet, stumbled, and grasped the edge of the table. Houston grabbed him by the arm, but Reid shook him off. "No."

"Okay, then. I'll be sleeping in the loft. We'll talk when you're sober."

***

"Morning." Reid shuffled into the kitchen and went straight to the refrigerator where he dismissed the urge to guzzle the O-Juice directly from the carton.

"And he's alive," Houston spoke to the dogs, who'd taken up a corner of the tiny kitchen, their eyes intent on sizzling slices of the bacon Houston dropped into a frying pan.

"Shut-up." Reid leaned against the counter, opened his mouth in a humongous yawn, and ran both hands over his face. The scruff covering his face hid the bruise.

He craved coffee. Ratatat, the woodpecker living inside his skull drilled, and took it up a notch when he bent to pet the dogs. Not a good move. The drilling hadn't stopped since he'd opened his eyes. Houston had made coffee; hot, black, and pungent. Reid shuddered.

"You call this coffee?" At the first taste of it, Reid pulled down the corner of his mouth. "Tastes like tar." He took another sip and got used to it.

A smirk plastered across Houston's face, masking understanding and empathy. "Man, how's that hang-over? Hand me the eggs." Pouring the scrambled mass into a second pan, he said, "You can thank me later."

"Hmm." Reid realized the last time he ate was yesterday morning; a slice of toast and nothing more. If a hearty breakfast didn't kill the hairy gremlins in his stomach, Houston's coffee would. "I'll live. Did you have a reason for coming here and crashing my party?"

"I told you: a gut-feeling. Blowing the whistle on Schuster Sr. shook you. It put the monkey on your back again, but I didn't pay attention."

"I was shocked, yes—but I was all right. Don't know what changed, bud." Reid tensed at the tightness coming into his chest. "But all of a sudden, here I was with a bottle of Maker's for company."

"Honestly, if Alyson hadn't jabbered on for receiving scary vibes from you, I would have shelved it, because who pays attention to that kind of thing, right? But it nagged, and I came to check on you."

With breakfast cooked, the guys carried their plates and coffee to the table. Aspirin taken earlier eased rough edges, and working on his second cup of tar, Reid's head cleared.

Houston chewed on a piece of toast loaded with scrambled eggs. "Wanna talk about yesterday?"

Reid focused on the mug, setting it down with exaggerated care. "Nope; but I know you won't quit badgering. So—" His eyes went hard as he fixed his gaze on Houston.

"Someone calls you a 'murderer,' it messes with your mind. Particularly if that someone is the father of the man whose life you're supposed to defend."

Staring back at Reid, Houston's jaw worked back and forth at the grief that shadowed his friend's face.

"Schuster." An exasperated statement punctuated with resentment and disapproval. "For Christ's sakes, Mack— Billy's dad *wasn't* there. How he justifies his anger at you escapes me. Billy was his only kid; I guess he needs a face to pin the blame on. Stuck in a rut of grief."

A bitter sound squeezed past the golf-ball-sized lump in Reid's throat.

"You did what you were trained to do. Okay? And it cost you, too."

Reid shoved back the chair and stood. "Hell, Tex. But, I'm still here, and Billy's not."

"Yes. So, honor him, and all the others." Houston got up, too. Not knowing what to do with his hands, he pushed them into the front pockets of his jeans.

"That's why we're doing this, Mack. Wetting sorrows with booze won't solve anything. It wasn't anything you did or didn't do. Not your fault. Engrave it on your brain." Houston cocked his head with a sudden thought. "You're not backing out?"

Reid stopped pacing. "What would I do if you hadn't hassled me into doing this thing with you?" A start of a smile tugged at the corners of his mouth. "Hell, no. I'm not backing out."

Houston had broken through the soul-crushing, self-inflicting pain of accepting useless blame. He'd been a good soldier. Wrong. He had been an *outstanding* soldier, having his men's backs, as they had his. There hadn't been a thing he could have done about the explosion. And Houston's willpower in building the corporation had strengthened Reid's purpose.

Try not to think about it. That was well-meaning advice others dispensed so freely. What did they know? Well, Reid had tried, and it didn't work. He *needed* to think about it: his men, the bonds, the little things that made them smile.

"Remember Billy's 21st birthday?" Reid asked. Still raw, he smiled and recalled the celebration.

"One hell of a way to celebrate your twenty-first."

"No shit, but Billy loved it. The squares of pound cake from an MRE kit. We all had a piece. Someone put a candle on his. I don't remember who did, or where it came from. When he blew out the candle, no fancy decorated cake could have put more shine in his eyes."

Good memories. Reid needed to hold on to those. *One day,* he thought, *I may get a chance to tell his old man.*

***

Keira pulled the duvet over her head and groaned. Another Saturday shopping with Emily. The wedding was in August, just three-and-a-half months away. A small event, consisting only of Ryan's uncle and a few of their friends. Ryan, like Emily, was an only child. His dad had passed away while servicing overseas, and he hadn't seen his mother since she'd abandoned his dad and him while he was still a child.

And today Keira would meet Emily and three other bridesmaids at Mona's Bridal Creations for their bridesmaid's dresses. *Please, don't turn us into Barbie Dolls,* Keira sent a silent prayer.

Mossy.

Keira startled at Reid's voice echoing in her mind, prompting her to push to her feet and call the dogs. Squinting against the rising sun, she squashed the awakening memories of a kiss that warmed her insides and heated her cheeks. And rejection. The horrible misunderstanding of rejection.

"Reach out, show him the real you. Find a way," Emily had said.

Hadn't it been Reid who'd rejected *her?* He'd cut her off, dismissed her without a sliver of a chance to set the record straight. And on Thursday, at Pat's, she'd attempted to make small talk, but did he have to distance himself as if in a hurry?

Damn it, Reid. Did he think of her as so shallow and callous to only concern herself with looks? Alas, he was on the wrong track. Not even close. But dadgummit, if it didn't rankle.

CHAPTER 21

"Get in." In the driveway of his parents' home, Reid signaled Yard to jump into the Jeep. On a whim, he'd left Oak Creek at the break of dawn and had driven to Florence. Bones, buckled into the backseat, thumped his tail as Yard settled beside him.

"You're sure you don't want to keep him, Mom?" Reid, grinning at Bones, hugged Amanda, and kissed her cheek.

"Trust me, hon, he's all yours. Right Bones?" She leaned into the Jeep and petted the dog. Smiling at Yard, she gave him a pat, too. "You keep watching my boy, okay?"

"And you," Amanda poked Reid in his chest, eyes swimming. "You just stop collecting animals, you hear?"

Her boy—tough and thick-skinned—showed his heart by taking in these animals. When Reid had shown up unannounced this morning, trailed by two dogs, Amanda's heart leapt, her face a mirror of pride and joy, although he'd only moved a couple of hours south. Catching up on details of his time in Oak Creek, time had hurried along.

Another quick hug and a "Hey, I'll be back soon." Reid needed to get going.

"You got your guitars, boy?" Dad asked, laying his hand on Reid's shoulder. A question he'd already asked a couple of times.

"Yep. I'm good." Sliding behind the wheel he started the engine and rolled down the window. "Let me know if you change your mind about Bones."

Amanda shook her head and waved. "Text when you get home."

Shortly after nine o'clock Reid turned onto the path to the cabin. He was still a distance away when the Jeep's headlights picked out the paper fluttering on the front door.

Had Houston left him a note? Tacked to the door? Unlikely. Reid's trip had been at the spur of the moment with no notice to Houston. Why explain? Houston was his friend, not his keeper. They didn't clock in and out with each other.

Reid slowed the Jeep, pulled into the parking space, and shut off the engine. His eyes, hard and narrow, surveilled the surroundings, peered into the dark; ears strained to listen. Instinct and training taught him to be cautious.

Detecting nothing out of the ordinary, he got out of the Jeep and released the dogs.

A few long strides, up a few porch steps, and he ripped the sheet of paper from the door. A tack flew out, bounced, and fell through a crack in the planks.

I know what you are. Murderer! Get out of our town.

Hatred, scribbled on a sheet of yellow lined notepad paper, dripped off these few words.

"Goddamn!" Reid's fist smashed against the door. His breath came in shallow bursts, his heart slammed against his ribs.

Steady. Breathe.

Who, other than Schuster, would have done such malicious thing? Who else had any interest in getting him out of town? No one he could picture but Bill Schuster. Resentment and bitterness, Reid thought, were vipers nursing in the man's bosom.

It wasn't your fault. Houston's refrain buzzed in his head as clear as if he stood beside Reid.

Reid went inside the cabin, threw the paper he'd torn off and wadded into a ball onto the table, and leaned the guitars against a wall in the great room.

Should he call the police? He pondered it while unpacking the bag of leftovers his mother had pushed into his hand.

No. Reid decided against it. A police report wouldn't serve anything or resolve Bill's anger. A note. It was just a note; a desperate attempt by a shattered man. Nothing Reid couldn't handle. He just needed to be alert and extra cautious.

***

Monday morning, rucksacks strapped, Reid and Houston walked at a steady clip through town. This week's walking goal was to increase the previous week's distance by two miles.

Neither man broached Reid's free-fall into an alcoholic stupor on Friday night or their Saturday heart-to-heart. They didn't have to. A tight bond and complete trust formed in combat situations held firm. It was done and over.

"I've been debating whether to mention this or not." Reid's sideways glance met with Houston's. "Last night, I'm getting back from Florence to find a piece of paper tacked to the door with a nasty threat," Reid said, and repeated the scribbled words on the note. "And since this is your parents' property, I've decided you should know."

Houston snapped his head to his friend and slowed his steps. "You've got to be kidding me." Deep lines creased his forehead, and the knuckles of his hands curling around the straps of his backhand turned white.

"Schuster?" Reid asked, lifted a hand in question, and adjusted his stride. "How did he know where to find me?"

Houston's laugh came low and harsh. "Buddy, have you noticed this is a small town? People talk. A neighbor, a co-worker, or he might have overheard someone at Pat's. The non-profit, our walk—it's gaining traction, and people are curious. They talk about it, and they ask questions."

"Good point. I reckon it wasn't too difficult for him to figure out."

For a minute, neither man spoke.

"Mack, considering Bill's aggression, I'm leaning towards him, too. You're going to report it?"

"Nah. I'll let it ride. When I feel the moment's right, I'll pay him a visit, and my respect."

"Yeah. Good luck, buddy. I went to see him. Remember?"

"Understood. But I've got to try. Maybe he'll regain a sliver of peace by hearing *me* talk about Billy."

"Okay but be careful. Anything else comes up, you let me know. We're in it together. And don't you forget it."

"Appreciated. But do you see the irony of what's happening here? He, the father of a veteran, has experienced the worst kind of loss— his kid. And now his mind is screwing with him. Bill Schuster needs help; precisely what Heroes Rise wants to accomplish—provide services and resources to veterans *and* family members."

"Good point, Mack. But don't dismiss his grudge against you. Empathy is one thing, but there's no tolerance for personal attacks."

"Mm-hmm."

Reid and Houston stepped it up in amicable silence, stopping only at crosswalks or pausing long enough for Yard to lift a leg.

At the edge of town, the men passed Oak Creek Middle School at the same time as two adults—teachers?—honed their drone-flying-skills on the school lawn.

"Check this out." Houston's gaze followed Reid's outstretched hand at the drone's straight upward lift.

"Yep, we're a small town with city-sized ambitions. It's an after-school program in its first year. Wish we would have had a sharp club like this back then."

Their eyes trailing the device, the display of dips and arches grabbed their attention, and the men stopped walking to watch its smooth flight pattern.

"He'll crash that thing," Houston predicted, keeping his eyes on the drone as it changed direction and plunged. The operator adjusted, circled, and flew the drone into the parking lot where he maneuvered the contraption into a flawless landing on the asphalt behind a bright yellow Volkswagen beetle.

"Show off," he mumbled, but appreciation softened the gruff in Houston's tone.

Getting back to walking, the men left the school building behind.

"Damn, for a second I thought he'd hit that car. I bet Keira would have been royally pissed."

A bait, Reid knew, cast in a flat tone. Houston was fishing, but he let it hang. A monster truck screeched by, music blasting out loud through open windows, and Yard's barking put off a response. Besides, what was there to say? Yes, she'd be pissed. He could just see it—heat springing into her eyes, temper flaring. And he realized the pleasure he'd taken in teasing her and setting them ablaze.

Reid's eyes fastened to the horizon. His face appeared void of emotion as the memory of a heat-packed kiss flashed through his mind. But that was before the big leg-reveal. No use in hitting the mental refresh-button; her message had come through pretty damn clear.

Houston must have picked up on Reid's internal monologue because when he shot a glance at his friend, his eyebrows raised.

"Mack, you with me? Slow down, man. We're not in a race."

Reid and Houston had veered off the main street and rucked at a steady pace along a narrow, paved country road, flanked by open fields and gently rising hills.

"Huh. Yeah." Reid flinched. "Just got a little distracted," he said, slowing his pace.

"I'd say." Houston thumped over his shoulder and grinned. "That yellow bug back there have anything to do with it?"

Eyes shifted from Houston to Yard, and Reid's cheek needed scratching. "What the heck makes you think that?"

"Just a hunch."

"Well, get your gut checked. Your hunch is feeding you bull."

"My gut is just fine. Matter of fact, it tells me it's you who's serving up bull."

"Is that so?"

"Look, Mack. It's none of my business, I get that. Last week? You made it pretty damn clear your one date with Keira was a whopping failure. But …"

"There's no 'but' man."

"Okay. If you say so." Houston raised his hand, stopping Reid. "It's just an observation, but I've gotta tell ya, the vibe I caught on Thursday at Pat's? It says differently."

"No clue what you're talking about, Tex."

"I guess not. You were too busy flirting with Alyson."

Reid grinned.

"I'm curious, Mack. I only know Keira through my mother's work with the rescue, but I have a hard time pegging her for a snob. Did she turn down dating *because* of the leg?"

"She didn't *say*, Tex. And didn't have to. She teared up, mumbled sorry, but not before regret slid over her face as clear as Saran Wrap. Well, I'm sorry too. But that doesn't buy me a new leg, does it?"

"Hmm."

"This …" Reid stabbed his forefinger to the prosthesis, "rattled my cage, but to hell if I let it define me. I'm still the same guy, only tougher now than before. And, in more than one way, I've got my eyes firmly set on the road ahead. So, she can't accept me the way I am? Well, then she needs to stay the hell out of my way."

"A'ight. So, to cut through the chase, she didn't *say*. But okay. If you're sure."

***

Keira's students became distracted by the drone flying outside the classroom window. While scribbling a math problem onto the whiteboard, she turned at the disturbance taking place behind her back. Well, did the science teacher not have *any* common sense? Hands on hips, she marched to the window, joining students who'd jumped out of their seats to watch the outside display.

She'd have to address this flying nuisance with him. Two weeks left until summer break and the kids were already twitchy. As was she.

"Hey, guys, who wants no homework today?" The cheers answering her question brought a smile to her face. "I tell you what … how about you get back into your chairs, and if we finish our lesson early we'll have a pop quiz instead of homework—sound good?" she called out, eying the gadget's plunge and change of course, until she recognized Houston and Reid on the sidewalk, following the drone's direction.

For a brief moment, everything faded into white noise as the men walked by, drawing Keira's gaze to the dark, skinny pylon of Reid's prosthesis below the khaki shorts. Touching a hand to her throat, she blinked, and her heart skipped a beat as she watched him call to Yard and march away.

A hitch of breath and she drew away from the window. Grief snagged against her breastbone—torment, pain, agony—the physical and emotional tortures he'd undergone she couldn't imagine, but the surgical tool of empathy sliced a piece of her soul with the same intensity as it had at the night of the dinner.

Blowing her cheeks out, she slowly released the air. Amidst a classroom full of students, Keira felt his caress on her cheek, strong hands against her back, and relived a toe-curling kiss. And how she could see herself fall for this man with the rough exterior and smart-ass attitude.

She'd blown it. What if she'd just curled her arms around him and kissed him with fire dancing on the tip of her tongue instead of reacting like a tranced rabbit? For one thing, it would have put a lid on the idiotic question of rejecting him because of the injury.

Dadgummit, McCabe. Cutting me off without hearing me out? What are you afraid of? Nope, we're not finished, she thought. *Not until I have my say.*

CHAPTER 22

Keira found her answer later that afternoon when she went to her parents' home. Pitching in with mom's online publication, *Oak Creek Weekly,* she often was reporter, photographer, and proofreader all at once.

A short drive and Keira pulled into the driveway.

After her mother greeted her with a warm hug and gave the dogs homemade biscuits, she kissed mom's cheek and followed her inside. "Hmm." Keira sniffed the garlic-infused air.

In the kitchen, she lifted the lid to a simmering blend of meat, tomatoes, and spices, inhaled the spicy fragrance, and sighed. "You're making spaghetti? Smells great. Be sure to save some for me."

From the cabinet, she pulled out a box of Oreo's and snagged two. "Barkville volunteer meeting is in twenty, finalizing the Mutt Strut."

"The event write-up is ready to go, love. Any updates we'll add tonight," Caitlin said, tucking a red-gold curl, streaked with silver, behind her ear.

"Oh, and in a couple of weeks I want to spotlight Houston Miller and the friend he's got roped into crossing our country by foot. Shoot, I forgot his name."

"Reid McCabe, Mom."

Caitlin shook her head as she stirred the sauce. "Isn't that the wildest thing you've ever heard? This boy is a little more than crazy hiking across the States with a prosthetic leg."

"I heard." Caitlin had captured Keira's full attention. "Buck interviewed them a few days ago." Leaning against the counter, she nibbled on a cookie while the wheels started spinning in her head. Keira's eyes widened and a little smirk played at the corners of her mouth. *Find a way* had just turned the corner.

"Crazy, but he sure has my respect." Keira split open a cookie and swept the tip of her tongue over the sugary cream.

"Right. Good for him and Houston." Caitlin shot Keira a sideways glance as she placed the lid on the pot. "Besides, what's the point of not living your dream? I'll want a series of features on both of them until they take off at the end of summer, then I'll give them monthly follow ups."

"Yes," Keira nodded, but her mother's words faded into the background. Suppressing a completely inappropriate grin, she said, "If you can set up an interview for late afternoon, or early evening, I'll get that for you."

"Aye, lass. You're an angel. With the intern on vacation, I'm up to my ears."

"My pleasure," Keira beamed, giving Caitlin a quick hug. And was grateful mom couldn't hear her heart thumping against her ribs. The answer had been right in front of her—interviewing Reid and Houston, representing *Oak Creek Weekly*. He'd have to talk to her then. Well, he didn't, but it was free advertising. Why would he object? A start. Why hadn't she thought of it?

"Okay. Gotta go." Boomer bumped his nose against Caitlin's leg and sat. Hopeful eyes ignored Keira as he begged for another treat. "Traitor," she laughed and gave each of her mutts a peck on the head.

***

Keira rolled into Emily's at the same time as the director. Haley's assistant and seven Barkville volunteers were already mingling when they came through the back door. Offering her spacious home as a meeting place and inviting the jumble of mixed personalities had been a great move, Keira thought.

In its third year, the tensions of planning the perfect event had eased from stress-snapping to something close to a social occasion. Edges of agitation were smoothed with a glass of wine, and finger snacks tempered hungry bellies before the meeting began.

"Helen! So glad you could make it," Emily greeted the new arrival. Helen Miller, board member, and financial supporter attended meetings whenever possible. "Pour yourself some," Emily indicated the open bottles on the island.

And it was all business.

"This year's Mutt Strut will be bigger and better than last year. The park is the ideal location for our growing event. It's powering up, and we're expecting donations to exceed last year by at least twenty percent." Haley smiled at the interrupting cheers.

"Entrance fees for our 5K Mutt Strut are streaming in, and since it's an all-day event, income from vendor fees alone have doubled."

"That might be so, Haley, but Carter Nash & his band are not playing for free," the accountant pointed out. He hadn't been in favor of throwing money away on a live band, but he'd been outvoted. The eyebrows pulling together showed it still piqued.

"True." Keira piped in, saving Haley from uttering a snarly comment. "They did give us an awesome discount, though. They're local, if you consider Louisville that, but their name draws a decent crowd."

"Never heard of them," the accountant mumbled loud enough to make his displeasure known.

"People will show up to get autographs and pictures."

"Keira's right," Haley picked up. "Mutt Strut leads off with a 5k walk, but the police dog demo, the best-dressed dog competition, the kiddie games, vendors, the band, and let's not forget our adoptable pets—they will draw folks. And the people will donate."

"We need donation buckets on shepherd hooks between vendors, by the bandstand, and in volunteers' hands. Harold has plenty of plain white ones we can use. I've ordered decals with the Barkville Rescue logo to go on it. At my expense." Helen shot a pointed look at the accountant.

"It's coming together, except we need more volunteers." Haley twisted the top of a water bottle and sipped. "We need folks to sell raffle tickets, handlers for our adoptable pets, and we should have a few eyes on the donation buckets. Please everyone—ask, plead, beg, or whatever you need to do to get your friends, neighbors, or co-workers to donate a few hours of their time."

"Hey, mom is running another piece on the Mutt Strut on Friday. I'll ask her to put out a volunteer call." Keira glanced at her phone, checking the time, and caught Emily's eyes.

"Great meeting, everyone, but I've got to go," Keira excused herself and stood. Emily, escorting her friend, whispered, "Hey, I bet Helen will badger Houston into volunteering—and she can bug his sidekick, too." Emily blinked an innocent look that made Keira smile. "Or you could ask him yourself."

"Troublemaker," Keira said, but the thought had already bypassed *maybe* and docked on *hell, yes.*

***

As Emily predicted, Helen Miller did not sit on it. Barkville needed volunteers, and Helen had two guys in mind. The next day she called Houston, asking him and Reid to come by the office that afternoon.

At four o'clock, Houston and Reid filed into the office, only to find Helen studying hardwood samples Alyson had picked up from the flooring store. Fingertip pressed to her chin, she squinted and turned, a bright smile replacing frown lines of indecision.

"Oh, good, you're both here. Come, and let me know what you think," Helen motioned them over. Although she chose all interior materials for Harold's construction projects, today she couldn't make up her mind. "Which one?" She gestured between two finalists similar in woodgrain and hue.

"I don't know. Both of those look good; just pick one. Or ask Alyson." In a show of indifference, his eyes shot to the ceiling. "Where is she, anyway?"

"She's off to the post office, dear. Why? You miss her?" In place of an answer, her teasing tone just earned her another eyeroll.

Reid watched the exchange between mother and son with an amused smile on his lips.

"Okay, Mom. Surely you didn't call us over for my expert opinion on the flooring." The corners of his eyes crinkled with the smart-alecky smile.

Helen gave his arm a playful slap, her gaze going to Reid. "I have a favor to ask. I'm on the board of Barkville Rescue," she explained. "And a week from Saturday, we'll have one of our largest fundraisers for the year."

She gestured to the visitor chairs, "Let's have a seat." Helen lowered herself into the seat cushion and crossed her legs.

"What can we do?" Reid asked.

Helen's hands lay folded in her lap as she drew in a long breath, slowly rotating her ankle. "We need more volunteers, Reid. I'm hoping you're free and available to lend a hand with our cause?"

Unfolding her legs, and smoothing her skirt, her eyes twinkled as she fastened her eyes to her son's. "I know Houston will be there." It wasn't a question, but a statement, delivered with a disarming smile.

Well-played, Reid thought. His lips twitched as his friend answered Helen's smile in kind. "Of course, Mom. Anything for you," he said, holding up his hands in a conceding gesture.

Her gaze skipped back to Reid.

"It's my pleasure. Just let me know what to do."

Helen's face lit up. "You could bring Bones; it'll give him an excellent chance at adoption."

"Consider it done, ma'am. We nonprofits have to have each other's six," Reid smiled.

Helen blinked. "Each other's *what?*"

"Back, Mom. It means we have each other's back. Army slang," Houston clarified.

"Thanks, boys. I knew you two wouldn't dash my hopes."

When Helen pushed to her feet, Houston laid his arm around her shoulder and kissed her cheek. "Bye, Mom. Let us know when and where."

On the way out of the office, Houston punched Reid's arm. "Smooth move, man." Grinning, he made the okay sign.

"What was?"

"As if you don't know. The perfect aw-shucks moment."

Reid punched back. "Never hurts to score points. Not when you're staying at your pal's mother's place, and she feeds you, on top of it."

The phone buzzed in Houston's jeans pocket. "Hold on." He answered while Reid followed him up the stairs and into the apartment.

"Yes, ma'am … That's fantastic …" At the top of the stairs, Houston turned, giving Reid a thumbs-up as he listened. "Yes, that should be fine, but let me check with my partner. Yes, ma'am, I'll call back to confirm."

"Whoa. This has been one heck of a day already, and it's still early." Houston unlocked the door, dropped the keys and phone on the entry table, strolled to the kitchenette, and opened the fridge. "*Oak Creek Magazine* wants to run a feature on us." Grabbing two beers, he handed one to Reid.

"Cool. I'll drink to that." Reid took a pull, flopped onto a chair, and stretched his legs.

"Front cover pics, double-sided spread." Too energized to sit, Houston paced the room.

"How big is this outfit?" Reid wondered. "It's a community mag, correct?"

"Right. It's free to subscribe; it's the place to go to for local news and events. How many subscribers? Hell, I have no idea. The way I see it? It's another outlet to get the word out about Heroes Rise. And not just a single feature. She'll run scheduled updates until we're ready to head out on the road."

"Sounds great. Speaking of updates, have you checked social media today? Holy crap!"

"A'ight. Eyes cast to the phone's screen, Houston sounded distracted.

"Okay, Tex, spit it out. I can see your wheels turning."

"Social media," Houston said thoughtfully, and finally sat. "We should set up the Go-Pro, record the interview, and upload to our page. In segments."

"Who's the show-off now, bro?" Reid quipped, pointing the bottleneck at his friend.

Houston clasped his hands behind the head and leaning against the back, he angled a sheepish look at Reid. "The editor is Caitlin Flanigan."

"Okay? With a blank expression Reid drew out the question, wondering why he should be impressed by the name. "Who—?" He cut off when it suddenly clicked, and his brows shot up high. "Wait. You mean as in relation to *Keira* Flanigan?"

Houston's lips curved in a smug grin, and his brows mirrored Reid's.

"I take this as a yes." Scrutinizing his friend with narrowed eyes, he took another swig from the bottle. "You're not kidding."

"Can't say I am."

Tipping back the bottle, Reid finished his beer and stood. "Well, it's unimportant. Set it up."

CHAPTER 23

KEIRA HAD DRIVEN HOME FROM work with no problems, but now less than an hour later, her car engine wouldn't start. She was supposed to meet Emily to pick out her wedding flowers and bridal bouquet, at five o'clock. To the tail-wagging delight of her dogs, she went back inside, dug the phone from her purse, and called Emily.

Keira huffed and explained the dilemma when Emily answered on the second ring.

"Yeah, it's not budging, Em. I can't meet you at the flower store on time. I'm sorry."

"Ah, Keira, that bites. Maybe it's just the battery? We can try jumper cables," Emily offered, but hearing the disappointment in her friend's voice, Keira declined her offer.

"It could be the battery, but who knows? Go to the flower store, I'll call my garage and ask Tony to come out or send a mechanic. Call me later and tell me all about the arrangements and your bouquet?"

Having phoned Tony, he came as soon as he'd finished his current job. After several failed jumping attempts, he now pulled his shoulders out from under the hood, pressed his lips into a thin line, and shook his head. "I suspect the starter," he said, wiping roughened and cracked fingers with an already dirty rag. "But I'll have to take a look at it at the garage."

Keira sighed, making mental notes of the things she needed to do this week.

"Well, it doesn't sound like I have a choice."

Emily drove up Keira's street just as the tow-truck pulled out of her driveway. Taken by surprise, she waited for Emily to park. When the driver's door opened, Keira glanced at the screen of her phone, checking the time.

"You're finished picking flowers? Already? Wow, I'm impressed."

In response to the snide comments, Emily got out of the car, threw Keira a glowing smile, tilted her head, and said, "I re-scheduled. Get your purse, we're going out to dinner."

"Emily! Why did you do that?" Keira placed a fist on her hip, but the smile tugging at the corners of her mouth overrode the firm tone. *Yes,* she thought, Emily's simple gesture was an instant pick-me-up after dealing with the stress of being without her car for a few days.

"Pizza and a red?" The favorite combination cheered, as Emily knew it would, although chocolate with the wine was a toss-up on their list of comfort foods. "I thought we'd check out the new place on Main."

"Yes. Give me just a second," Keira sprinted inside the home, grabbed her keys, and for the second time this afternoon, assured her dogs she'd be back soon.

Ten minutes later, the friends stepped into the rustic, Old World-inspired atmosphere of The Thin Crust, where the hostess showed them to a corner table, placing napkin-wrapped silverware and menus on top. "Your waiter will be right with you." She smiled and left the friends to scan over the list of options.

"Great choice, Em; this is a cool place." As Keira complimented her friend, her eyes traveled across the interior, admiring the artful decorations, the bulky cases displaying various wines, infused olive oils, and bottles of vinegar.

That's when she saw Reid sitting in the back room at the bar, a half-eaten pizza and a tall glass of beer in front of him. Her pulse skipped a beat as she reached for her friend's hand. Emily, aware of a change of vibe, looked up just as the waitress introduced herself, placing two glasses of water and straws on the table, and asked to take their order.

"We'll have a half-carafe of your house merlot." Emily smiled at the waitress and asked for a few more minutes to look over the menus.

"Take your time; I'll bring a basket of bread and a couple of dipping oils. They are to die for." Three fingers extended as she touched the tips of forefinger and thumbs together in an approving gesture.

"You were saying?" Emily prompted.

Keira couldn't help it. Her gaze kept skipping to Reid, who had neither paid attention to new arrivals nor felt her eyes skimming over him in the lively surroundings of the busy restaurant. Unaware, he bit into a slice of pizza. While chewing, he let his eyes skip to his phone and washed the pie down with a healthy swallow of beer. Clearly occupied with eating and reading, he didn't take notice.

"Reid's here." Excitement filled her as she fiddled with the clasp holding her curls at the nape of her neck. In a nervous motion of energy, Keira pulled off the clip, let her hair fan out, scooped the strand back up, and pinned her hair again.

Emily lowered the menu; her lips parted with surprise as she scanned the room. The waitress drew near, balancing a tray with bread, oils, and wine. Unloading everything onto the table, her eyes flicked to the open menus. "Enjoy, ladies. I'll check back with you in a moment." And she left.

Keira lifted her glass, touched it to Emily's, and closed her eyes as she took the first sip. "Mmm ..." She followed with a satisfied lip-smack.

"Thanks, Em. I love you for doing this, changing your appointment, I mean, and dinner." Tiny wrinkles between slanted brows changed her expression to serious. "I *wanted* to go with you today, because it's the most important thing in your life right now—and wedding flowers are huge. Who knew my car would pick this day to crap out on me? Just know that you'll have my support until I hear Ryan promise to love you to the end of the world, until the last shoe is kicked off, and the music stops playing." And the smirk came back when she said, "After that, you're on your own."

Stunned at her friend's emotional speech, Emily reached across the table and grasped one of Keira's hands in both of hers. "Wow, girlfriend! Thank you."

"You're welcome. But you know, I still get a kick out of aggravating the 'you know what' out of you."

"What you said—if it was your goal to make me cry, well, you did it ... Great job!" Emily smiled and blinked away the moisture at the corner of her eyes. "There's no measure tall enough for what this means to me, aggravation included. Though I'd be worried if my friend unexpectedly turned into a sugar baby, 'cause, you know ... I'd miss my sour patch."

"Aw. You don't need to hold your breath on sugar baby," Keira teased in a dry tone. "But, hey, enough with the goop, this is a great place to end a crappy day. Thanks, marshmallow."

"Ah, don't mention it." Emily twirled her glass, swishing the Merlot in lazy circles. "So, back to Reid. You were saying?"

Keira took a large gulp of red. Carefully setting down her glass, she glanced up at Emily through lowered lashes and tipped her head in the direction of the bar. "I'll just go and say hi; mind if I invite him to our table?"

Emily threw a glance over her shoulder. "Oh," she mouthed as she turned back to Keira with a fanning motion and leaned across the table. In a low voice, she uttered, "Do I mind? Heck, girl, I'd be disappointed if you didn't. What, for heaven's sake, are you waiting for?" Emily chuckled as she gave her friend's arm a playful shove. "Can't wait to meet him."

***

Across the room, Reid looked up as Keira neared the bar with a confident smile on her face, and flapping wings inside her chest.

"Hey, I thought that was you." Heart thumping, and hyperaware of herself, she lifted a hand in greeting.

"Hey, you."

Steel gray eyes assessed as he raised his beer and finished it with one gulp.

Keira tensed, and her cheeks warmed under the intense stare that made her stupidly lightheaded. Her heart ached as she realized at once he wouldn't make smooth talk, but had she expected him to?

Her gaze swept over his laid-back appearance. His buzz cut was growing out, she noticed and wondered how it would feel to run her hand through his hair. The gruff on his face was getting fuller, too.

Placing a hand on his arm, she leaned over the pie, inhaled. "Yum, smells delish."

The feel of his arms was imprinted on her brain, as was the faint scent of the ocean-fresh cologne tickling her nose. Her thumb twitched, and she came close to tracing the lower edge of his tattoo showing under his shirt sleeve. She'd noticed it before, the first time at the pet store, and again when he'd invited her to dinner at the cabin. She was curious, all right, but she hadn't asked about it. It hadn't even crossed her mind when, after dinner, all questions had been fair game.

Keira expected him to draw back at her touch, and when he didn't, she took it as a favorable sign. But he hadn't reacted at all— if one overlooked the tightening of his jaw.

"It is."

Short and curt. Keira swallowed a smart remark that had jumped from the brain to the tip of her tongue. Instead, she leaned against the vacant barstool next to his. Her grip tightened around the edges of the seat, hiding her trembling fingers until her knuckles turned white. Aloof, yes, she reasoned, but not unfriendly.

Even though his attitude bordered on gruff, being so close to him, feeling his warm skin under her fingers caused the wings inside her chest to beat furiously. Pushing back the wave of attraction for this jarringly rugged, and most unsettling man was as pointless as stopping a tidal wave with a sand bucket.

And clearly, he'd mastered in unsettling. Given that the curious magnetic pull didn't blind Keira to his closed expression, she felt his casual gaze and attitude flick over her, and a tiny flame of annoyance brightened the green in her eyes. Flustered, she bit her lip and shifted position and made an effort to keep her voice soft.

"Hey, someone at Barkville mentioned you volunteering at *Barks in the Park*. Truth or rumor?"

"You heard it right. I offered, Mossy."

Casually, Reid wiped his mouth, and crumbled the napkin onto the plate, pivoted on the stool, and faced her. When he leaned so close that she could make out tiny golden flecks in the oceans of his gray eyes, she held her breath.

"Can you think of a reason why I shouldn't?"

The color drained from her face. He'd called her *Mossy*, but the frost in his tone made her wince. Keira's pulse sped as she clearly understood the question as a poignant reference to his leg—or the part that was missing. What was *that* supposed to mean? Was he goading to expose her as ignorant and somehow prove something to himself? She wondered. How could she handle this with grace and not lose her temper?

"No reason."

Appearing unruffled, she shrugged her shoulders. Fast and deliberate, her gaze flicked from Reid's eyes to the prosthesis and back, letting him know she'd gotten his hint.

"I'm impressed you offered; Barkville needs more volunteers for this event. Are you bringing the dogs? How's the little guy?" Keira babbled, had to slow down, but found it challenging to remain calm under his steady gaze.

She felt the tension ease and herself relax when Reid's expression softened at the mentioning of the dogs. *Small talk,* she thought; a start.

"Of course," he said. "I'm hoping Bones will get adopted."

Keira's face lit up, yet, a moment later, her eyebrows rose in question. "He's a sweet boy, and *you* saved him. He and Yard get along so great—won't you miss him? Maybe just a little?" Tilting her head sideways, she gave a questioning smile. "By any chance, have you considered adopting him?" And she saw the flicker in his eyes, but when she looked again, she only stared into the gray of polished steel.

"He needs a home. I've agreed to keep him until he gets adopted, and that's only because you roped me into it. Do you remember?" Reid's face darkened, and his voice took a firm and uncompromising tone. "I haven't changed my mind, Mossy, so don't push the subject."

Keira blinked once, twice; the harsh tone in his voice a tear to her pride. What was happening here? This was not just about the dogs, was it? Her heart thundered as she reached out once again and put a hand on his arm—and let it fall to her side when she felt the muscles tense.

Her pale face turned scarlet, but there was no detour. She wasn't prepared for this when she came to invite Reid to the table and meet her friend Emily. But was there ever a moment that would be the *right* one? With no clear answer rushing to the rescue, she forged ahead.

"I'm sorry, Reid. I didn't mean to upset you." And it occurred to her that, once again, she found herself expressing regret. "Bones will find his home. I'm sure of it. I came over to invite you to our table, meet my friend, but I don't know. I feel like … like a pesky fly you keep swatting at. I'd be interested in hearing the reason for it."

"My apologies. No offense, Mossy, but I'm not in the talking mood." Softly spoken, his tone was even. The bartender offered another beer, but Reid shook his head and asked for the bill.

What? He wasn't in a flippin' *talking mood?* Jeez. But she had something to say, and she needed to get it out now before the rocks in her stomach grew in size.

Reid drew a bank card from the wallet, laid it on the bar top.

Agitation swirled. Frozen with indecision, Keira thrust away from the stool, pushing a stray curl behind her ear. Her gaze bounced from Reid to the bartender whose turned back assured a degree of privacy.

"Fine. Don't talk, just listen. I recognize I've hurt your feelings, or pride, or dignity, you know, when, um … a couple of weeks ago." Pressing a hand to her heart, she hurried on, "Whatever I've said—or didn't say—I realized it tapped on a bruise. But I want you to know, it's not what you were thinking."

Keira jolted when Reid jerked up his hands, cutting in. "Please, Mossy, don't presume to know *what* I've been thinking. Look, it's all good. Don't give it another thought, okay? *I'm* not."

If Keira's face could have gotten any redder, it would have jumped off the color wheel. Anger flared fast. She wanted to throttle him. Despite his chilly attitude—or *because* of it, she'd sensed his feelings for her were alive under that Kevlar shielding his emotions. Or would he have called her Mossy?

As much grief as she'd given him, now she'd be thrilled to hear the tease in his voice again as he used the nickname. Despite his maddening refusal to listen, she longed to be close to him still and just *knew* he felt the same.

"Dadgummit, Reid … why don't you get out of your head and listen just once instead of cutting me off every time I'm humiliating myself, trying to explain?" Keira forced herself to speak low. After all, this was not the place for a scene.

His forehead creased as he studied her face with concentration, and his voice softened at the glistening lashes. "Not now, Mossy."

"When, Reid?" Her voice thickened, and the words threatened to choke her. *Never* was the most likely answer, but feeling like she'd been on a fool's errand, she didn't wait for an answer. Taking a few steps before looking back, her eyes met his. "For what it's worth," she swallowed around the hard knot sticking in her throat, "this is driving me nuts. In case you've wondered," and stalked away on rubber legs.

When she returned to the table and dropped into her seat, Emily took one look and started pouring more wine from the carafe into her glass. "Oh, dear," Emily said. "You're looking a little pale around the gills. What happened?"

Keira shot a glance at the bar, but Reid must have left by way of the backdoor.

"Argh. He's such a stubborn, rude, and cocky—in short, infuriating …" Keira stopped mid-sentence when the waitress stepped to the table with a steaming pie, sliding the plate on the pizza serving stand.

"Uh-huh. Did you mean to finish with *hunk?*" Emily's voice carried a sweet and innocent quality, which promptly earned her a blazing glare. Sliding a piping hot triangle onto her plate, she flashed an unconcerned smile. "Hope you don't mind me ordering while you two were busy chatting it up."

"Not funny." Keira followed suit loading her plate, but not before taking a large swallow of wine. "Crap," she said, setting the glass down. "If it weren't for picking up dad's truck, I wouldn't mind a happy, little buzz."

At the remark, Emily just raised a brow. "Well? Do I need to ask for pliers?"

"Sorry, friend. There's not that much to tell. He was close-lipped, not much of a talker. It was I who needed pliers. Imagine, he actually told me he didn't feel like talking. Jeez. I don't know if he left his sense of humor in his truck, or if he buried it in those woods he lives in. But he sure didn't carry it with him today."

"It went that bad, huh?" Emily savored the bite of pepperoni pizza, flagged down the waitress, and ordered a second half carafe of Merlot. She expected to be at the restaurant for a while, mulling over Reid's words, tone of voice, gesture, and anything else that came up.

Keira's appetite hadn't suffered from the rude encounter, so when they'd polished off their pie, the waitress came and cleared empty plates from the table. She returned with the check and a pleasant smile on her lips, her eyes skimming the half-empty wine glasses. "No rush, ladies. Take your time," she said, handing Emily the bill.

When she was out of earshot, Keira blew out her cheeks. "I can't believe the attraction to this guy. It can't be real. I mean, we see each other a handful of times, and we go on one date. Well, kind of a date. We kiss, and bam, the butterflies are going south?" A deep intake of air and she puffed through pursed lips. "Only now, he's an insufferable gasbag who treats me like an annoying nuisance. Pfft."

"Hmm, sounds familiar." Emily touched her forefinger to the rim of her glass, circling in slow motion. Her eyes followed the sensual play of her finger. "I don't think there's a written rule for how long you need to know someone before you realize the butterflies have come to stay. Did you know the first time Ryan kissed me, I initiated it?" Emily smiled as she brought the glass to her eyes and studied the red as if it held the wisdom to this ancient law of attraction.

"You did? No way."

Emily's eyes glittered as she recalled the moment, a wicked smile curving her lips. "Yes, way. Sometimes you just have to go after what you want, *Mossy*."

Keira just about spewed wine across the table, covered her mouth, and coughed. "Hmm, did you just say what I think you said?"

Elbows braced on table, Emily's smile held as she rested her chin atop folded hands and locked eyes with Keira. "You got it, girlfriend. Remember the day we shopped for my dress and how we tossed around the dating scene? And I predicted *it* would happen for you, too. But you wouldn't stumble over it inside your comfort zone? Tell me, this strange buzzing in your gut when you see Reid, talk about him, think of him ... When was the last time you felt this way with anyone?

"Uh-huh, I thought so," she said when Keira gave a half-shrug. "Look. What happened at your date night, or dinner, or whatever, it meant something. What came later was an unfortunate misunderstanding. That's it. You know it, I know it, and it's time he knew it, too."

Keira swallowed, her head buzzed, and she had a smidgen of suspicion that the conversation headed into a lecture. "Nice advice, Mom. Did you even listen to what I said? I made an effort to talk to him earlier. And you heard me say his glare could have frozen a penguin, right?"

"Babe, I'd say that's one heck of an emotion. But as long as neither of you makes a real move towards clearing the air, whatever it is between you? Sooner or later, it will die. Simple as that. And I don't see him making the first move."

"Oh, Em."

Emily's lips curved when she dropped her elbows to the table and played with her wineglass, circling the stem between thumb and forefinger, moving the base around and around. "Keira, sweetie. Remember the kiss, hot, and exciting, and mind-boggling. Hold that feeling, and tell me if this here," Emily waved her hand in a sweeping gesture, the smile on her lips slipping into sly, "is where you want to make up?" She let it hang long enough to sink in. "Trust me; you don't."

Keira kept fidgeting with her glass in embarrassment, mortified at Emily's blunt reasoning.

"Woman, you're confident, fierce, and sweet. Well ... you can be." Emily gave her a teeth-bearing grin. "And right now, you're a little bit pissed off. Two words—girl power. So, you go to him." Emily didn't skip a beat. "Go to him and make him listen. And take it from there. If he's an asshole about it, well, at least you'll know. But if he isn't ..."

Emily reached for her purse, drew her credit card from the wallet, placed it in the bill holder, and signaled the waitress.

On the ride to her parents' house, Keira was exceptionally quiet, but it wasn't the wine she blamed for her buzzing head. As Emily parked in the driveway, Keira slipped off the seatbelt and turned in her seat with an impish smile crossing her face.

"So, you made him kiss you, huh?"

Emily just laughed, leaned over, and kissed her friend on the cheek.

"Goodnight. Sweet dreams."

CHAPTER 24

GOD, HE'D BEEN AN ASS.
Under the rolling steam of the shower, Reid lifted his face into the pelting force of the hot spray and owned up to it.

After leaving Houston, he'd debated whether to go home or get a pizza in town. The pizza had won. Seated at the restaurant's bar, he turned his head at the chime of the door, a reflex since he hadn't expected anyone to join him.

Mossy?

He'd been caught by surprise, seeing her walk into the restaurant, chatting with a friend. But why should he? At this time of day, folks came in to relax after a busy workday, grab a drink, and dinner. And the Thin Crust offered hands-down the best pizza in town. It shouldn't come as a shock that she had the same idea of coming here to grab a bite to eat. Seeing her unexpectedly had jolted him. For Pete's sake, why? He'd averted his gaze, didn't want her attention, and dove into a bulletin he'd come across on his phone.

This story had grabbed his interest, a story that read much like his own. An Iraq vet and amputee like himself had just adopted a three-legged dog who was found wandering in the woods. Scraggly, emaciated, and hurt, this wretched mutt had been taken in by a rescue. *He's the perfect dog for me,* the piece quoted the veteran, *and we'll teach each other to live life to the max.* Hot damn. The same applied to Yard and him. The article took Reid's eyes and thoughts off the strawberry-blonde distraction sitting at a table across the room, facing him.

True to the red-head label, the freckle-faced spitfire swaggered up to him before he'd finished his pizza and beer. He had restrained himself from acknowledging her purposeful stride and bubbly smile until she stood right next to him.

Reid lathered up, vigorously scrubbing his head, neck, and the spot on his arm where the palm of her hand had seared his skin with a feather-light touch. At the brush of her fingertips, his traitorous heart went from stop to overdrive in two seconds flat, not that his impassive expression had given away any of it. Or the impulse to grab that hand and yank her into him. Common sense kicked in, and a mask of indifference slid over his face, sending confusing feelings into retreat.

He'd antagonized her, and taunted Keira when she asked about his volunteering, measuring her reaction. He had to hand it to her; she'd held her own, staying composed under his hawkish stare when she flicked her gaze from his face to his leg and back to him, locking eyes as she responded.

In the jade of her pupils, he'd searched for revulsion, aversion, or pity. When he saw none of those, he softened. What had she seen when she'd lowered her eyes to the prosthesis? Nothing less than an enabling device, and nothing more? He wondered what thoughts hid behind that poker face. For a moment, he hoped she'd seen him for the man he was – vigorous, tough, and courageous.

She wanted to talk about Bones. Would he miss him if he got adopted? The little guy and Yard had wasted no time in becoming buddies. And if he was truthful with himself, he had gotten used to having the brown fur ball around. So, yes, he'd miss him.

Would he have stopped and cared for the dog on that rainy afternoon if he was a cold-hearted son-of-a-mother-goat? The question sat wrong, but he presumed she was making small talk and saw no need for discussing his thoughts or feelings on the subject.

Her next question proved he had been right to keep these things to himself. Would he consider adopting him? Always the rescue worker, she had an agenda after all. His blood heated.

As it did now.

Annoyed at the crisscrossing emotions of longing pulsing inside his chest, countered by rejection radiating through his veins, Reid adjusted the shower knob with a sharp twist. The punishing drop in water temperature prickled his skin as it cooled the heat but did little to straighten his wound-up frame of mind.

Especially when he recalled the one passionate, bone-shattering, demanding kiss they'd shared. The memory of it wasn't like data on a hard-drive, easily erased if no longer needed. One kiss. So what? He'd kissed lots of lips. Only this one had reached deep and touched his soul.

He'd shared his living nightmare—the amputation—and she had balked. Ice formed in his stomach as he recalled the moment. What was there to talk about? The humiliation was best struck from his brain. And excuse the hell out of him if he was in no mood to talk.

One. Single. Kiss.

How could he keep the memory from bouncing around his head, knocking reasonable sense into a lightheaded daze? Like it did right now.

Shuddering under the icy spray, Reid shut off the water and shuffled out of the shower with the issue at hand resolved.

It had burned him to injure Keira's feelings, to burst that shimmering bubble of expectation with scorn. Yet it had been the dead-on right thing to do. Because rehashing the awkward matter would be akin to pulling a grenade pin, but *this* grenade was not his friend. Considering he'd leave Oak Creek in a few short weeks to follow a dream and walk across the country, what was the point?

With the bath towel wrapped around his waist, Reid grabbed hold of his crutches, thumped into the bedroom, and dropped onto the edge of the bed. A few feet away, Yard flopped down with a heavy sigh.

Clean and dry, and with the stump resting on the other knee, Reid inspected the skin for redness and bruising. The socket's fit had loosened, and since morning he had managed to ignore an irritating rubbing sensation.

"Shit!" Yard's ears pricked with attention, and Bones looked as if he was trying to figure out the annoyance Reid hurled through clenched teeth. "Damn, this blows."

The friction of the socket against the protecting sock had chafed raw spots, like an ill-fitting shoe rubbing against the heel of a foot, only there wasn't a blister.

He must have lost weight, daily rucking did that thing to a body, and Reid figured the stump had shrunk. Maybe it explained the increased phantom pain, too. He just hadn't expected it to happen so quickly.

For fuck's sake! Just when he'd gotten into the groove of increasing the daily walking distance, the blasted socket needed adjustment. And what if this thing caused a dreaded infection? How long would that set back his training? A week? Two? Longer?

His skin tingled as sweat formed.

First thing in the morning, he'd call Derby City Prosthetics, set up an appointment, and move on. Ruck it, as they'd called in the military. Putting things in perspective, it was no more than an annoying inconvenience.

The gray veil of anxiety had lifted, and the tension leaked from tight muscles. A cooling gel pad covered the sore, and after slipping into jogging pants and a T-shirt, he cleaned the prosthesis socket. Recharged, and once again in high spirits, he tossed the device onto the bedroom chair. He wouldn't need it tonight.

On crutches he went to the backdoor to let the dogs go out. Leaning against the open doorframe, Reid filled his lungs with the woodsy scent, carried by a gentle evening breeze. An unexpected peace seeped into his bones and cleansed lingering doubts. In this rare moment of tranquility, Reid understood that this place in time was exactly where he was supposed to be. Something inside of him shifted. Everything was right. Or would be.

As if he needed convincing, Yard and Bones bounced up the deck-stairs. Quickly, their bottoms dropped to the ground and two sets of shimmering eyes stared up to him. Maybe they too were in the zone, but if Reid had to put money on it, he'd say it was because of the training treats he carried inside his jeans pocket.

Bringing the good vibes inside, Reid hobbled to the fridge for a beer, carried it to the sofa, and picked up the guitar. It felt right to hold the instrument, brushing the strings, picking, creating a melody.

Boots. The new song. It wasn't finished after all—not ready to make its debut at Pat's tomorrow. Reid played around, adjusted, listening to the chords with closed eyes.

There's a whisper in the breeze

Reminding me of home ...

And like a Polaroid picture, the image of a freckled face, framed by strawberry-blonde curls, slowly developed behind closed lids.

***

Reid had called the Louisville VA partner for prosthetics yesterday morning, explained his situation, and like a miracle, they'd worked him in for a device inspection today.

Sitting in the waiting room, he scrolled through his phone with an occasional glance at the TV hung high at the wall when his phone vibrated.

"Hey, our print stuff's ready, brother," Houston launched right in when Reid answered.

Reid shook his head. Only Houston could get excited over brochures and posters.

"Tex, you're killing me. Right now, you sound as patient as a three-year-old with a birthday present."

"Hell, yeah. After yesterday's negative? I'll take it."

"Roger that."

Rejections. Of course, they'd expected them. Still, the first ones felt a little like burst soap bubbles.

A response from a hiking boot manufacturer Reid had contacted was a polite denial letter. The decline for sponsorship or donation came couched in admiration for the mission. In a nutshell, donation funds for the year were already allocated. So sorry. Try again next year. Good Luck. Damn. Couldn't they see there was a marketing opportunity in this for them?

"Enclosing a pretty color package with our donation request might make a difference," Houston said. "I count on it. So, hell yeah, I'm excited to get this going."

"All right, man. Want me to pick them up on the way back?"

"Thanks, but no. Alyson is on her way to get them now. Just thought I'd be a good kid and share my birthday present."

"Share your present, huh? One more thing, Tex. We talked about treating your personal assistant to a fancy dinner? What do you say we do it tonight?"

Houston scoffed. "Personal Assistant. Don't let my dad hear that."

Reid imagined the grin and pushed. "Okay. *Darling* sounds much better, anyway."

"Hey, what's that supposed to mean, man? Alyson is a friend, okay? I intend to keep it that way."

"Uh-huh," Reid said. "Ask her if she's free this evening."

"What if I'm not?"

Reid smirked at the sly tone in Houston's voice. "Then you won't mind if *I* ask her. Right?"

"Strictly business speaking—keep your paws off. Got that?"

At Houston's growl, a knowing smile spread across Reid's face. "Gotcha, brother—strictly business speaking."

"Subject change." Teasing left Reid's voice. "I've got no clue how long I'll be here so that meeting with the Legion Commander? I'll probably won't make it. But you go ahead."

"Mack, we can reschedule. No biggie. What's a couple of days?"

"Appreciate it, man. But this is a key meeting. Rescheduling won't look good; we could lose momentum. You handle it. Whatever you'll decide, I've got your back."

"A'ight. I'll head over there soon. Break a leg, my man."

To a stranger, this odd way of wishing Reid luck would have sounded cruel. But strangers would never know of the ingredients of the glue that bonded them like brothers.

"I already did," he sneered, adding, "I'll pop in at the office later."

"Don't you ... "

Just then, Reid heard his name called. "Hey, gotta go. Later." Reid said, cutting the line. He chuckled at knowing precisely what Houston was getting at. On his way home, he'd stop at the office and pick up some brochures.

***

"Strike two." Houston swiveled in the chair behind the other desk at the office of Miller's Construction. His knee bounced with nervous energy.

"Miller—Stop. Bouncing. You're making me nervous," Alyson glared at Houston.

The doorbell chimed, and Reid caught the last part of her words as he entered. His gaze swept over Houston before settling on Alyson.

"You need me to take care of him, *darling?*" Accentuating Houston's pet-name, Reid flashed a wide smile. He was in a terrific mood. Getting a rise out of his friend, in the way guys teased each other, felt just right.

Houston's eyes blitzed an unmistakable warning sign. *Back off.* "How did it go?" he growled.

Reid tapped his leg. "I'm getting a new one; socket that is." When Alyson's eyes went wide, and Houston's brows raised, he added, "Yep. Newest technology."

A slow grin lit his face. "Speaking of birthday presents, this is mine. Now show me yours."

"Reid, that's fantastic." Alyson clapped her hands.

Houston slid a portfolio across the desk. "Check for yourself."

Reid picked a brochure, unfolded the pages. "Nice!"

"Meets your approval?" Houston asked, shaking posters from a cardboard tube. "Then you will like these."

"Son of a gun. Happy Birthday to us." Reid slapped Houston's palm, and in one swoop, turned the corner of Alyson's desk, and smooched a kiss on her cheek. "Thank you, Aly. Consider yourself officially crowned as the fairy godmother of Heroes Rise."

Alyson laughed and slapped his arm. "Reid McCabe, you are too much."

"That he is." Houston jumped from his seat, agreeing with a rumbling voice, "But he's right, *darling*." He flicked his gaze to Reid, gave him a hard stare. Returning his gaze to Alyson, he said, "Your fairy dust creates magic." And thought he'd spew. Where the hell had this come from?

"Stop it, both of you. Before I die laughing." The satisfaction of a job well done shone in her eyes. "My pleasure. And you're welcome. But it's still *no* for dinner. Plans," she added, grabbed her purse, and pushed to her feet. "I'm heading out. Make it an A-mazing weekend. See you on Monday."

When she was gone, Houston grunted. "Jesus, Mack. Can you lay it on just a little heavier? The syrup isn't quite covering it."

"Well, we'll have to practice. I hear it makes things perfect." Reid winked and slapped a hand to Houston's shoulder. "I also hear payback is a bitch."

Houston understood it as a nod to his mentioning of Keira. Only he hadn't been teasing.

"Smartass."

"So," Reid said. "What's strike two? Anything to do with the American Legion?"

Houston grabbed the office keys. "Let's get out of here. Feel like a burger and a beer? I'll fill you in."

"Sounds good to me." Reid picked up a box of brochures and a tube of posters.

"See you at Pat's in five minutes." Houston locked the door and grinned at his partner. "You're buying."

***

"Not what we hoped for." Reid picked a fry and slathered it in the massive mound of mayonnaise squeezed next to his fries. "But I'll take it the meeting was still a success?"

"Yeah, it went great—they're a fantastic group of guys, and gals. They offered to support us in whatever capacity they can. It just won't be in the shape of a support vehicle."

"Damn."

"I hate to cut this short." Houston crumpled his napkin onto his plate. "I have instructions to build a kissing booth. I want to get a start on it tonight," he said when Reid gave him a quizzical look.

"A what?" In tandem with his head, Reid's eyebrows snapped up.

"You've never heard of a kissing booth? Where people kiss for money? Only this one is for dogs to slop people in exchange for money." Houston's curled lips held amusement. "Puppy kisses, they're calling it. My mother. What can I say? She's volunteered to donate a kissing booth to the dog fest. Dad's too busy, so that leaves me. And she wants something *cute*."

"Oh, brother." Reid chewed, regarding his friend with a suspicious eye. "You need help?"

"Tess is coming home this weekend for summer break. I thought I'd put her degree in construction management to the test," Houston said with a teeth-baring grin. "You know—test her *cute* skills. But you're welcome to come over if you're bored."

Reid laughed. "I may do that. See if your project passes kissing regulations."

When Houston left, Reid moved to the bar.

"How's it going? Is this seat taken?" He asked, sliding onto the barstool when the guy shook his head.

Behind the bar, Pat looked up while keeping busy cleaning glasses.

"The usual," Reid answered the unspoken question. While Pat tapped his favorite, Reid looked up to the row of TV's above, then skimmed his gaze over the guy next to him and turned on his stool.

"You served?" A stupid question, in light of the ink on the guy's arm, but a conversation starter. *SAPPER* ran along the man's forearm in bold letters.

"You're a combat engineer," Reid acknowledged the design with a thrust of his chin.

"Was." The man finished his beer, eyed Reid, and extended his hand. "Name's Matt Cox."

Reid shook with a firm grasp. "Reid McCabe, nice meeting you, Matt."

"Got out about a year ago," Matt offered. How about you? You a vet?"

"Yep, nine years before getting out on a medical about a-year-and-a-half ago."

Two beers into the conversation, and swapping info on time-in-service, rank, and duty station, the surface talk turned deeper. But something kept nipping at the back of Reid's mind. Matt Cox—the guy's name sounded familiar.

Holy crap, he thought, when it finally clicked. On the day of the radio interview, the first person who'd stopped by had been worried about his brother's son. What was his first name again? Tim Cox, yes. And the guy next to him was Tim's nephew.

Reid thought fast. How to get him to talk about what pushed him to the edge of sanity? He glanced around the room. This bar— not a place to wake the demons who'd crawled into the caverns of Matt's mind. Reid had had his dance with the devil, but the private hell of this man threatened to destroy his family.

He faced Matt and speculated. What he saw was an ordinary man. Late thirties, he figured. Hard lines in a thin face, a testimony to his suffering? Would he open up to him? Tough to say. In spite of having made a connection, it wasn't something one would casually weave into conversation. Dammit.

Like the neon sign on the wall behind the bar, Heroes Rise flashed through Reid's mind. There was one possible way. And when Matt asked about Reid's medical discharge, it gave him the opening. Reid swallowed hard at what he was about to do. Had Matt noticed the prosthesis? When Reid twisted on the barstool, it brought Matt's attention to the mangled leg.

"Shit, man; what happened?" Not surprise, but resignation marred Matt's voice.

The blood sped through Reid's veins and suddenly the room grew hot as the memory of that fateful day in Afghanistan flashed before his eyes.

"Courtesy of a convoy attack," he said, "and the reason for the medical."

Hostility gleamed in Matt's dark, sunken eyes, and Reid saw the lack of sleep and scorn in the weary expression. Somehow Reid noticed Matt's grip tightening on his glass. "Damn, man. I'm sorry."

"No sweat, it's all right now. Though, at first, I wanted to kill the S.O.B. who did this with my bare hands. The rage I carried inside, it's all I could think of. My leg had been blown off from under me, and if this wasn't messed up enough, the head-screw that came with it?" Reid paused. "I've never really left the battle zone."

He reached for his glass and drank deeply to cool the flares inside his stomach. Sharing his combat-related PTSD with this man, who, in a twisted way, was no stranger, was something he'd never once contemplated before.

"I hear you, brother," Matt mumbled. With his gaze fixed on some point behind the bar, it appeared to Reid as if he'd retreated to a different place and time.

"But," Reid continued, "The hard fact is, life goes on. Thanks to my therapist—a tough-love kind of guy—I've figured it out. Let me tell you something, if someone had told me back then I'd be hoofing it across the US for a year, I would have said he was out of his fucking mind."

Matt's gaze snapped back to Reid with his eyes wide. "Say that again?"

Reid kept it on the low when he brought up the organization, the mission, the hike. He didn't push, didn't preach. Just a friendly conversation between brothers-in-arms about life after the Army. Matt said little—giving no clue of having heard about Heroes Rise from his uncle, Tim. Every now and then, he fiddled with the bill of his ball cap. Occasionally his eyes flicked to Reid, but mostly he leaned against the backrest with his arms crossed and his gaze on something else. But he kept listening.

When Reid finished, he rapped a knuckle against the socket's hard shell. "Most people think I'm crazy to attempt a walk cross-country with this."

"Most people," Matt sneered, "don't give a crap."

Reid regarded Matt with a tilt of his head. "The brotherhood. You miss it, don't you?"

"I do." Two words that held too much weight.

"Tomorrow," Reid paused. Once he'd push, there was no taking back. "You'd be interested in going rucking with me tomorrow?" And though Matt didn't answer right away, there'd been a flash of confidence piercing through the fatigue.

A grin spread across Matt's face, eyes lit, a sudden vigor smoothing out the wrinkle of despair.

"Hell, yeah. Brother."

***

Red heat, the color of an angry sunburn, blotched Bill's face as he stood by the kitchen counter, listening to the voice mail a second time. Carol wasn't coming home.

She'd called twice—this morning, and again in the afternoon, which he'd ignored both times. Bill saw no reason to call her back; she hadn't bothered to leave a voicemail.

Did she not get it through the wooden block of a head that he didn't have time for petty crap while on the job? A man's work was important, and he didn't need interruptions and the nagging about some meaningless crap. She gave him plenty of that when he was at home. Carol knew to leave a message if it was something urgent. But it never was. Besides, she was coming home today; she'd yak his ear off tonight.

When Bill pulled into his driveway after a stop at Pat's, Carol's car wasn't parked in the garage. What the … ? He couldn't shake the uneasy feeling rising from his gut when he called her name a second time. Carol? You home?

Her sister only lived a two-hour drive away. What the hell took so long? After a rough day at work, he expected to come home to Carol waiting on him, with supper on the table. A whole week of heating TV dinners and ordering take-out, and she couldn't make it back in time to fix a decent meal?

A few minutes ago, she'd called again. Just when he had taken a piss. This time she did leave a voice mail. Carol wasn't coming home today. Or next week. She wasn't sure *when* she'd be coming back, that it depended on him. No longer the peacemaker, defiance spiked her mild tone.

She'd given him an ultimatum. Bill grunted and slammed the phone on the kitchen counter. Counseling. She said he needed help. So, he could come to terms with Billy's death. She wanted him to see a goddam grief counselor! *He* had a problem? Bill could feel his blood pressure rising. Would that bring Billy back? Hell no. So, there is your answer, *Carol*.

He stomped to the fridge and tore open the door—that damn sister of hers. Bill grabbed a beer. He just knew she'd fed Carol a bunch of horse manure. Just knew it. Bitch! He popped the top, gulped.

Rage churned inside his gut and the need for confrontation roiled just under his skin, eager for release.

After work, he'd stopped in at Pat's—it was about time to meet that asshole McCabe head-on. He'd keep his wits about him and only have a couple of pints, or so he'd told himself.

Perched on a barstool, Bill kept vigil from his corner spot with his ball cap turned low. Where the hell was McCabe? Turning and craning his neck, his glazed eyes had scanned the bar and dining room. When Reid finally came into the bar, Bill sensed more than saw him enter. Somehow the air grew into a thick haze, and a fiery blaze set Bill's chest on fire. Much as he wanted to kick the crap out the traitor, he was at a disadvantage. Bill was sloshed, hadn't stuck to the two pints he'd promised himself. And he wasn't a fool. He didn't need a repeat from last time, and he needed to get a hold of McCabe away from his sidekick, Miller. Seeing the cocky punk strutting around so self-assured had kept the fire burning.

Now Bill plunked his butt into a kitchen chair, and the beer can onto the table. He rubbed his fist. The itch to smash McCabe's face was powerful; he could all but feel the cartilage smash into matchsticks under the weight of his punch. He could see the rush of blood, could smell it like a shark three miles away. Bill's eyes latched onto the phone, laying on the kitchen counter.

She had given *him* a fucking ultimatum.

CHAPTER 25

"This is Yard," Reid introduced Matt to his dog when the mutt jumped out of the Jeep.

It was Saturday morning, and cars and trucks filled nearly every spot of the smaller parking lot of the town's park—although it appeared devoid of people.

Matt stretched his arm and opened his palm to Yard. Bending down to the dog, his T-shirt hung loose on his tall, skinny frame. Yard sniffed Matt's hiking boots and jean-clad legs up and down and sideways. Another sniff, and he lost interest, wandered into a brushy area, and marked a fallen tree branch.

"He's handling it well," Matt said as his eyes followed Yard, his fingers raking back dark blonde strands of hair that had fallen over his forehead. "Getting around on three legs."

"Yard doesn't care. He doesn't know he should have four legs."

"Lucky for him." Matt hoisted his old Army rucksack. Stuffed away with the rest of his military things, he'd pulled the bag from a corner of the basement last night. Despite little sleep, Matt had gotten out of bed with a refreshed mental attitude. Morning stubble covered his hard-edged chin and hollowed cheeks, but his grey-blue pupils shone clear.

"You ready?" Reid whistled, and Yard fell in beside him. A pat on the dog's head and the men were off.

Hiking five miles around the lake, mostly through a wooded area, Reid hoped for the calm surroundings to work against the darkness within Matt.

Reid drew in the wood-scented air. "Ah, man, this is great."

"I haven't been out here in ages," Matt confessed. "A crying shame, considering I live just a couple of miles down the road. We used to bring the kids here." Matt pointed to the pavilion on the other side of the lake and the playground next to it. "Let them run around and let off steam. And on the rare occasion we were without the kids, Shelly and I would come out here to walk, talk, and clear our heads." Matt paused. "But that was before …"

Reid wouldn't push Matt to reveal his past trauma, maybe nudge. Definitely nudge, but not push. "There's no better place for that than nature." He only knew this too well. "It's where I pull myself together when shit gets tough."

Skirting a muddy section with a protruding rock, Reid continued. "Not so long ago I felt as if I'd never hike in the woods again. But now? Life is good once more." A crumb on the road Reid hoped that Matt would follow.

A mile-and-a-half into the trail, woods flanked on the left, and the lake shimmered through trees on the right. The air felt warm and smelled of water and vegetation. Soft ground cushioned the men's footfalls. At the restrained silence from Matt, Reid shot a quick glance at his hard-set face. "You all right, man?"

Matt opened his lips as if to speak but pinched them together again. A sharp look at Reid, a moment of hesitation and a stunning confession burst from his mouth.

"You know, my family's worried I'll blow my brains out."

For a moment, the words hovered in the air. The statement rattled through Reid's bones. Tim had said that much. But hearing the confirmation directly from Matt? He turned around and trained his eyes on Matt's blank expression.

"And sometimes I think it would be for the best. You ever feel that way?" Strangely, Matt's voice held no emotion. Just a matter-of-fact statement, uttered in the same vein as "pass the butter, please."

There it was—laid open, raw, and rotten. Suicidal thoughts. A grunt broke through pressed lips as Reid failed to answer. His chest was a drum, banging wild and loud against his ribs.

"You want to talk about it, brother." Reid felt at a loss of words.

Without losing the momentum of stride, eyes forward-facing, the men kept walking while Matt kept talking. As if on a military mission, they kept pushing. There was no room for weakness.

While they walked side-by-side, Reid met the devil riding Matt's back. He showed himself in the form of dead bodies, forced to endure things beyond human imagination. The tapestry of the evil feats tortured Matt's mind. Because the bodies weren't dead—they lived, begged, and shrieked in Matt's head.

Reid saw tears shimmer in the corners of Matt's eyes when he recalled his first night back at home. How his wife had been scared for her life. After touching him in his sleep, he'd clamped his hands around her neck in a fit of perceived danger.

Sleep. Would he ever sleep again without nightmares and medication?

And Matt had spoken of his suicidal thoughts of last summer.

After his wife and boys left for the city pool, he'd grabbed his gun and slunk into the basement. The details were shocking and vivid as he described himself seated in the ugly, red chair, its fabric torn by his wife's neurotic, little dog.

Reid could smell the stale air—impregnated with sweat, fear, and hopelessness. He could feel the cold steel of the handgun weighing in his lap as perspiration dripped and mingled with tears. And he heard the voices of despair begging for an end to the torture.

"Shit, man," Reid uttered. This summed it up. Nothing else needed to be said.

As they continued walking side-by-side, Reid shot a gaze at Matt. He had been in Matt's boots and experienced the same horrors, and wanted to believe that opening up, recalling the ghosts of the past with someone like him had cleared Matt's head. At least for now, because Matt raised little objections to Reid's advocating professional counseling. A small victory. Understanding that Heroes Rise would stand for Matt and everyone like him settled over Reid in a wash of gratification.

Back in the parking lot, Reid shrugged the straps of his rucksack down his arm. "As I said, you're welcome to hit the road with us on Monday, brother. Think about it."

Yard hopped into the car, and Reid slid behind the wheel. "Oh, man." Filling his lungs with a deep breath, he felt the weight of Matt's admission with unexpected force. And gray slithered into his soul.

***

At Barkville Rescue, the phone rang just as Keira stepped into Haley's office.

The director seemed frazzled. "Keira, this is amazing. This phone has been ringing all morning like crazy." In a dramatic gesture, Haley flattened her palms to her cheeks, her mouth forming a silent scream.

When she dropped her hands, she smiled. "No, complaints, though. Everyone wants to visit today to look at our kids."

Keira smiled back. "I hope it's a happy day for the furry ones."

"Your mom dedicating a whole page of *Oak Creek Magazine* to Barkville?" Remarkable. It's beyond generous. Thanks for making it happen."

"No problem. I have a hunch she'll keep it up."

Keira had bugged her mom into doing a free monthly ad. This week's issue had showcased the organization, a handful of selected dogs, and offered an adoption discount. A significant boost to a struggling non-profit group that couldn't afford costly advertising fees.

As Haley answered the phone, Keira stepped over to the coffee pot and sloshed the hot brew into a Mossy Oak tumbler. After letting out the dogs and spending plenty of time with their newest rescue, she wanted to catch up with Haley before heading home. At the mentioning of Bones, her ears perked up.

"Yes, I am going to contact the person fostering him now. Uh-huh. It's short notice, but I'll call you as soon as he confirms he's available to bring the dog in. Yes, ma'am. I'll call you back." Haley ended the call.

"Bones?" A hollow feeling plunged into Keira's stomach. "He wasn't a featured dog." The words busting through her lips sounded sharp. The moment she'd said it, she realized the undertone of disappointment. When Haley sent her a puzzled look, Keira quickly covered her words, "She must have seen him on our website. Good to know folks are clicking the link."

"Yes, ma'am," Haley said, tearing the woman's number from a sticky pad and tacking it to her keyboard.

Keira hadn't given it any thought before, but suddenly realized Bones was her only actual link to Reid. Because of this pitiful stray, and her volunteer work at Barkville, she'd stumbled onto this man whose cocky attitude maddened her to no end but intrigued at the same time.

Bones' adoption was undoubtedly going to bust that link. The interview she'd wrangled from her mother? Keira couldn't remember what she had hoped to gain from it. Or, for that matter, from the "Barks in the Park" event.

But Reid was bringing Bones to the shelter today. Keira was sure of it. Why wouldn't he? At a glance, she noticed immunization records and unprocessed adoption applications sitting in a bin on top of Haley's desk and decided to hang around a little longer.

"Need help with that?"

Haley pushed a stream of air through pursed lips. "Girl, do I ever. Are you sure you can spare a little more time?"

"Got nothing else going on today," Keira said as she picked up the tray and went to work.

For the next hour, Keira filed reports and called prospective adopters from her mobile phone while Haley left two messages for Reid. "This is urgent. Please call me back."

Both voicemails remained unreturned.

"Last try," Haley picked up the handset.

A few seconds later, her forehead bunched with frustration. "Ugh. I can't reach him," she said, sticking out her lower lip in a gigantic pout.

"The lady wanting to see Bones? She fell in love with him on our website—said she felt as if his eyes had looked straight into her heart. Hmm."

At the filing cabinet, Keira stuffed a sheet of paper into a folder and shut the drawer. Emotions spun her insides. Turning to Haley, she reached for a wayward strand of hair, and twisting and twirling, she wrapped the piece around her index finger. Conflicting thoughts tumbled through her head.

For a moment, she pictured Bones with Yard and Reid, together in the cabin's great room, and felt a twinge of guilt for hoping Reid wouldn't return Haley's call. And that Bones wouldn't get adopted today by a lady already in love with a little dog she'd only seen on the internet.

Keira made up her mind: Bones' deserved this shot at a permanent home—and she would drive out to the cabin and pick him up. Reid had probably just shut off his ringer, she reasoned.

She snatched her tumbler from the top of the cabinet, went to the volunteers-designated closet, and retrieved her truck keys. Dad's truck keys. The bug was still in the shop. "I'll take a ride out to his place, see if he's there. This is Bones' chance."

Keira braced herself to meet Reid's scorn for showing up uninvited and unexpected. But she'd suck in her cheeks, zip her mouth, and swallow her pride. She could do it.

CHAPTER 26

EMOTIONS CHURNED INSIDE HIS GUT as Reid guided the Jeep from the parking lot into the flow of traffic.

"You ever feel like ending it all?" Matt's question had caught him off guard. Hell no. Except for the time in the hospital when he'd learned of the blast's consequences. That's when he had wished the IED would have taken all of him. Not just a part.

Having one's leg blown right from under him was one mind-shattering thing, but for two of his men, life had ended in hostile terrain—on a fucking dirt-road, framed by craggy mountains. They were dead.

Above and beyond the call of duty, Reid would have taken their place without a second thought. That's how it was. Each one of the brothers knew the hazards of war and willingly accepted what they'd signed up for. But never did that knowledge stave off the pain and guilt in dealing with the loss. Never. Not for comrades, and definitely not for the families.

He thought of Billy's dad. Despite his hateful anger, Reid possessed empathy for this man. A man could understand another's particular kind of torment in the face of losing an only son, the way Schuster had lost Billy. From thousands of miles away, the blast had torn a crater where there used to be a heart. Reid understood the hollowness of Bill's future, bereft of grandchildren, and everything in-between, even so, Schuster had pissed him off. Suffering or not, the man was a snake. Face me, man-to-man—take your swipe at me then. "Wuss," he muttered under his breath. If there were a sliver of a chance in facing Bill, he'd welcome that. It would mean to tackle his own demons. Maybe it would take the edge off the terrible guilt that Billy had died under his watch.

But Heroes Rise, the walk for awareness, to prevent just one person from drowning in the river of darkness, it was something good and worthwhile, and it alleviated the pressure.

As the Jeep turned from the paved road to gravel, the phone's screen flashed with an incoming call. While being with Matt, he had turned off the ringer. Seeing it was Houston, he answered.

"Hey, Tex. What's up?"

"You still with Matt?"

"No. I'm heading back right now."

When gravel met dirt, Reid saw the truck. "Hey, you're calling to tell me someone's at the cabin?"

"Uh. No," Houston denied. "You must have a visitor."

Reid slowed the Jeep. "It looks like an F-250. White. Any friend of yours?"

"Hmm. Off the top of my head, I can't think of anyone driving a white one."

"Okay. I'll call you back." Reid cut the line. Something wasn't right. This truck? It wasn't supposed to be here—not a friend of Houston's. And he sure as hell hadn't given anyone this address.

A buzzer went off inside his head. The note from a few days ago, tacked to the front door, zipped into his mind. On sudden alert, Reid pulled the Jeep to the forest's edge.

This couldn't be good. A fog of suspicion rolled over him, and his voice dropped to low when he ordered Yard to stay.

Reid kept his eyes on the truck as he slid out of the Jeep, shoving the phone into the front pocket of his jeans.

Detecting no movement, he approached with caution, the black T-shirt and beanie blending with the dappled shade of trees and brush. As Reid got closer to the vehicle, his muscles tightened. The truck's cabin was empty.

Eyes darting, he quietly surveyed the cabin and its surroundings on stealthy footsteps. Hyperactive barks came from inside the house. Bones.

Reid turned his head, squinted, and listened—birdsongs, hums, the whisper of trees, but he didn't pick up the signs of a human presence.

Swirling fog enveloped his senses, and his mind leapt back in time, and into hostile territory.

***

What was that?

Keira stopped walking and tilted her head, trying to make sense of what she'd just heard. Snapping deadwood had caught her attention. The soft rustling between the trees, had it come from a deer? Her pulse thudded as she listened, straining her ears. With her gaze cutting over brush and skipping from one tree-trunk to the next, she was certain to have caught an out-of-place shadow. But shadows moved all around her, and when she looked again, it was gone. The light filtering through the canopy of trees must have tricked her eyes.

Just a small critter, Keira assured herself.

She hadn't given it any thought when she strolled into the woods without the Millers' permission, but this was private property, and suddenly she worried that someone might find her trespassing. Keira slunk off the wooden path, throwing furtive glances over her shoulder. Despite carefully picking her way forward, the surrounding stillness amplified the cracking of dried leaves, bark, and branches with each step. Not that she was sneaking, but dadgummit, she had no business wandering around the property. She should have just waited on the porch.

After arriving at the cabin, and finding Reid's Jeep gone, she'd knocked on the front door anyhow. When only Bones' hyper barks greeted her from inside, Keira opted to wait for Reid. She gave herself fifteen minutes before heading back to town. Catching a good whiff of the forest's somewhat damp scent, she declared the day too gorgeous to wait in her truck. On impulse, Keira decided to pass the time with a short stroll down the path into the forest—it would settle her nerves for meeting Reid, she reasoned. Zipping up the hoodie with the trademark Mossy Oak pattern, she donned a ball cap with the same design.

Along the wooded trail, her soul flushed as she sipped the perfume of wild rhododendron, woodland ferns, and of wildflowers she couldn't name.

There. She'd heard it again—the odd disturbance that didn't seem to fit. A critter would seek refuge by crashing through the ground cover. Wouldn't it?

Usually not easily frightened, Keira's pulse notched up, and the fine hairs on her neck raised. All at once the air's atmosphere thickened.

Not a critter.

Keira picked up speed as she headed back to the truck. Was someone near? Prickles crawling up her back flashed warnings of someone's presence. Throwing quick glances over her shoulder and into the woods, she picked up a broken branch mid-stride. Not too heavy, but sturdy—just in case.

Her heart galloped out of her chest as she stumbled forward. Ahead, she could see the cabin and her truck. Reid's Jeep was still not there. She wouldn't panic; if someone was stalking her, yelling out in hopes to scare him made no sense. Better to remain quiet and make it to the safety of her truck.

Blood thundered in Keira's ears as she rushed ahead.

Almost there.

The uneven terrain was difficult to navigate in cowboy boots; brambles scratched her jeans and tore at her shirt. A branch whipped her face, slowing her down. She felt her cheek sting and a trickle of blood, but *adrenalin* kept her moving.

Someone was behind her.

God, oh God, oh God. Don't turn.

A second later it happened. She screamed as shock crashed her system. Hard and fast, one arm clutched around her waist while the forearm of the other snaked against her neck with a firm grip. Rage surged, and her heart wanted to explode. His forearm squeezed so tight, her screams came muffled. Oh God, was he going to choke her? Who wanted to hurt her? Why?

"Let go." Air pushed with great effort, but her voice was little more than a rasp. In a rage of fury, Keira twisted, whirled, and bucked, fighting to get out from under this powerful grip, and realized she had zero chance. Arms of steel bound her to his hard body in a tight lock.

"Drop your weapon." The words garbled in her ears.

"Fuck you." The stick. Though one of his arms immobilized both of hers, Keira hadn't let go of the branch. Her lifeline. Letting go would mean surrender. She swung her foot backward— and connected with air.

"I said, drop your weapon."

Deep, calm, and dangerous. Through the blood thundering through her ears, Keira detected something familiar in the voice.

Something she'd heard once rushed through her mind. Using every bit of strength and wit, she turned her muscles to Jell-O and went slack. Adrenalin gave her the extra boost, but to no avail—his surprise lasted less than a second.

The maneuver took both of them to the ground. Going down, Keira released the branch on instinct as her arms slipped underneath his grip. Her body slammed to the woodland floor and although, it cushioned her fall, a dull pain shot up her hip. Now she greedily gulped air, but his weight pressing down her back was suffocating. Her cheek pressed into moist dirt and leaves. Keira knew her fight was over. Still, she wriggled and squirmed, too pumped-up to cry.

As he rolled her over, fear paralyzed her. Keira squeezed her eyes shut—her last measure of control. Partly because she wasn't going to give him the satisfaction of seeing the panic in it, in another because she was terrified of what she'd see. Straddling her, he held her in place while fists, solid as iron vices, clamped around her wrists.

"Get your hands off me. What do you want?" She spat, unable to move. Her pulse hammered, and with fear rushing through her veins, she finally opened her eyelids. And froze.

Holy shit!

Keira felt a hesitation, a subtle shift of his body. Steel-gray eyes, dark and hard, stared into her face. His neck vein pulsed fiercely, matching the banging drum inside her chest. Did he not see it was her? Keira? From the glacial glare in his eyes, she imagined his mind locked in battle, fighting an unseen enemy in a remote part of the world.

She wanted to shout and scream, make him hear, and see. The afternoon of the rainstorm flashed in front of her eyes. Thoughts scurried like tumbleweed. No—the wrong move. With utter determination and grit, Keira forced the tension from her body and stopped fighting. Offering no resistance, her wrist slackened, and her body went lax and still beneath him.

"Reid. It's me!"

He squinted. Tension eased from high cheekbones. Still, he hesitated.

Keira's eyes didn't leave his. "Reid, it's me. Mossy." Soft and low, her voice pierced through the hazy veil of anxiety. In the depths of gray, Keira glimpsed shock and disbelief as the mist lifted and the light of awareness came back.

Trapped beneath Reid, Keira felt his body turn rigid.

"Mossy."

A weary grunt, spiked with agony and distress, Reid closed his eyes and shook his head.

Denial or flinging off the last of the cobwebs? She couldn't tell, but did it matter? Her panic was gone, he didn't frighten her anymore.

A cross between a snarl and a cry gathered and roared into Reid's throat, reminding her of a trapped animal. The pressure on her wrist ceased as his fingers curled into hers. Keira's insides were still in turmoil, but when Reid opened his eyes again, grief and sorrow burrowed into her, and an aching tenderness spread inside.

A shift. And his face came so close that for a moment, Keira thought he was about to kiss her. But Reid dropped his forehead to the ground beside her head as another strangled sound left his throat.

Adrenalin left her body, and with earthquake-like tremors shaking her system, it was difficult for Keira to think. For what seemed an eternity, they lay on a bed of leaves, entangled in a mountain of emotions.

***

Surprised at Yard tugging on his arm, the world rapidly shifted back into focus. Sharp and assertive, Yard barked wild and frenzied. His powerful jaw gripped firm yet gentle as he pulled Reid out of bewilderment. As he lifted his face from Keira's tangled mess of hair, her body felt soft underneath his weight

He shook his head and angled his face toward the cabin. Frenetic barking rung out from there, too, mingling in a cacophony of barks and yaps. He turned his head back to Keira, who shoved against his chest.

"Your phone," she said, as if it was the most natural thing to say in a situation like this. "It's buzzing against my hip. Get off, or it'll give me a giant bruise."

With a groan, Reid rolled onto his back, releasing Keira from this surreal grasp they had on each other. *Keira— not an attack,* his mind raced. How had this happened?

Calm now, a strange sense of emptiness cut through his core as fingers detangled and their bodies separated. The sensation of her frame under him as he held her down, the heat rolling off her back after this deceptive chase, the weird embrace on the soft forest floor, it flooded his system and imprinted on his brain. It surged into every cell of his being, and it marked him.

Reid pulled the dog to him, and their bond tightened with every rough scrape of Yard's tongue against Reid's chin. "You knew I was in trouble," he muttered and ruffled his fur. A burst of alarm and Reid jumped to his feet "How did you get out?" But then he remembered; he'd left the Jeep's windows open.

Keira's legs shook as she stood. With trembling hands, she brushed clumps of dirt and other debris from her clothes, her hair a tangled mess. Reid stepped close as she finger-brushed her curls. Eyes met, and in a blaze of jade-green he did not detect blame or pity; instead, he read uncertainty and courage and daring.

"Keira. God. I don't know what to say, except … this is what it's like to be me. I'm so sorry."

Goddam. For the second time, she'd seen his lapse. He kept his eyes on her as she calmly brushed leaves and dirt from her clothes and straightened her back. And the look in her eyes—not horror or disgust of the crazed lunatic he'd morphed into. Just trust and faith. Faith in what?

Reid only hesitated for one second. "Mossy," he whispered, and tugged her into his arms. The smell of forest floor clung to her, damp and musty, mixed with the lemongrass scent that was uniquely Keira. It was an embrace meant to comfort. As she buried her face into his shoulder, he all at once recognized how right it felt. How right *she* felt, and he tightened his arms around her.

"I shouldn't have come unannounced." Keira's voice strengthened as she stepped out of the embrace. "Or stayed around, uninvited."

Reid's arms dropped to his side. "It's not your fault."

He rubbed his neck, couldn't stay in place. The unsettling incident churned his gut. A few feet away, Yard stood on guard. Reid shoved his hands into his pockets, paced three steps, and turned. He blew out a breath; annoyance fumed. He kept pacing. "I saw the truck with no one inside, and no one around, and it flipped a switch. When this happens, it scares the crap even out of me."

She didn't know about Bill Schuster's threats, and so he didn't share his suspicion of Bill sneaking around the property had triggered his PTSD. Or that having failed to recognize her, shredded his insides. Reid turned back to Keira and his tone went mild. "I don't expect you to understand."

"You're right, I don't." Keira closed the distance. "It scared the living shit out of me, too."

Seconds ticked. "Jeez." Reid raised his eyes to the sky. How had he fucked this up?

Keira touched a hand to his arm, "But I'm still here. So, try me. I'm great at listening."

He shoved his hands deeper into his pockets, curiosity stood in his eyes as he leveled his gaze on her. "Why did you come here?"

A deflection. She pursed her lips. "You know, I almost forgot the reason for coming here. Bones. There's an adopter who wanted to see him, and Haley couldn't get a hold of you." Her mouth twisted into a warbled smile. "I thought you'd just turned off your phone. I came to pick up Bones."

"Yeah, I've turned off the ringer." Another pause. Reid didn't offer any explanation as he swung around and started toward the cabin.

"This isn't his day to be adopted. I'll call Haley," Keira said, but he'd already turned his back.

"Your call." All of a sudden, he sounded gruff.

What the hell had he been thinking, wanting to date her? She was the kind of woman—self-assured, quirky, gentle, and kind—who deserved more than falling in love with a man whose ghosts would pop up at any time, any place. The prosthesis, had it been an excuse to push her away? To spare her precisely from what happened, back there in the woods? Hell if he knew.

Keira followed Reid into the clearing, catching up with him. He'd stopped at her truck, expecting her to leave. Instead, he saw the hesitation, the speeding pulse in the vein below her ear. Nerves. He anticipated her questioning. Was this what riled him? The questions, the prying?

"Reid? Don't shut me out again. Please?" Uttered as a soft plead, she crossed her arms and leaned against the tailgate. "Something is happening that you say I don't understand. Why don't you explain it to me?"

In one fluid motion, Reid braced his hands against the truck to each side of her head, his frame trapping her. Reid's face was inches from Keira's, his smile dark. "You want to get to know me? Really get to know me? Figure out what makes me flip a lid? Is that it?"

Yard's ears perked, his low growl barely audible.

Keira's mouth went dry as dust, and she swallowed hard as Reid stared at her, blades of steel slicing through jade. And she nodded.

"Yes. All of that."

"You don't know what you're getting yourself into." Jaw tightening, Reid's stare didn't waver as he pinned her gaze.

"Then tell me." Bold and unafraid, her eyes challenged.

For an endless moment, his gaze lingered as he regarded her thoughtfully. "There is something you need to know about me, Mossy." He'd used her nickname, but his tone was flat. "There's the leg—but you know about that." Reid huffed a laugh, low and murky. His breath slid hot across her cheek as his face closed in. "But that's not all. Know what we called someone like me in the Army?"

When Keira just shook her head, his gaze skipped to the wildly pulsing vein in her neck. "We called him 'messed up like a soup sandwich.'" With a flick of a wrist, his hand cupped the back of Keira's head. Fisting hair, he crushed his mouth to hers. Lips, rough and ready, parted her mouth, his tongue exploring hard and demanding. And Keira matched his rough caresses in a dance bearing the marks of lingering darkness.

His hips pinned her against the truck, his erection pressed into her stomach. Locked in the tidal wave of this kiss, his free hand tore down her side, pulled and tucked in a white-hot frenzy, slipped under her shirt, and cupped her breast.

"No. Hold it." Keira's heart galloped when she shoved her hands against his chest.

Yard barked. A warning?

Wide-eyed, she panted, gasping for air. Unlike the forest encounter, Reid stopped cold. Releasing her from his grasp, he willed himself to step away. His breath, too, came in ragged bursts, a volcano under pressure. "You still want to get to know me, Mossy?" he sneered, his hand rubbing at the tension in the back of his neck.

Green eyes measured. Keira smoothed her shirt and stalked to the driver's side of the truck. Her lips were puffy, and the scruff on his chin had scratched her cheeks, turning her pale skin a hot pink.

"Color me crazy. I do—but not like this, soldier." Keira spoke quietly, using the name she'd called him on their first date. Her pulse still stuttering, but deceptively calm, she climbed into the truck's cabin. With an air of indifference, she kept her dignity intact.

Through the open driver's window, she lowered her eyes to him. "You ask me out on a date, and I mean a date that includes dinner and a show, I may say yes."

Gravel crunched under her wheels as she slowly backed out the vehicle.

His phone buzzed inside his pocket. Staring after the disappearing red lights of the F-250, he pulled it from his pocket.

Jesus Christ. This woman. Surprisingly, she hadn't driven away like a bat out of hell. Messed up like a soup sandwich, and it didn't seem to faze her.

***

"Mack. What the fuck? About time you answered the damn phone. Where are you, and what in the hell is going on?" Houston's deep tone boomed through the speaker after Reid answered the call.

"Whoa, take it easy, man." Reid climbed the steps to the front porch. From inside, Bones kept barking. He could just see the dog pushing up on his hind legs, scratching on the door. "I seem to recall telling you I was heading for the cabin. So, what's your problem?"

An exasperated huff reached his ear. "What's *my* problem? Let me see. I get a call from your number, but all I hear are disturbing sounds—frantic movement, rustling noises, and you're yelling, 'Drop your weapon.' The chill in your voice, man … it raised the hair on my back. And then the line went dead. So, *you* tell *me*."

Reid opened the front door, Yard pushed inside while Bones jumped for attention. With the chase now a hazy blur, talking about it was the last thing Reid wanted to do. What a rollercoaster to come down from. Clamping the phone between shoulder and ear, he picked up Bones, shuffled into the great room, and sunk onto the sofa.

Bracing an elbow on his knee, Reid dropped his head into his hand and took a jagged breath. His friend deserved the truth, but he stalled. "Butt dial. Damn phone," he said.

Bones scooted to his side, sniffing and licking with great curiosity at the scents clinging to Reid's clothes and skin.

"No kidding, Sherlock. I figured that much. I only called back a thousand times without an answer. So, what happened? What about that truck you asked me about? Was it Schuster's? He came by to make trouble?"

Reid's gaze went to the ceiling. "That was my first thought. But nope, not Schuster. I wish it had been."

Houston must have heard something in Reid's voice that gave him pause, because a second passed before he asked, "So, what happened?"

"Shit, man. You don't want to know."

"A flashback?" Empathy vibrated in Houston's voice.

A groan. "Yeah." Defeated, Reid rubbed across his forehead as if it could clear the shredded veil behind. "It happened again. Keira came over to pick up Bones. I wasn't there, so she waited, took the trail into the woods. When I got to the cabin, there was a truck, but you know that. Only there wasn't anyone. Schuster, I thought. And shit happened, the fog rolled in."

"Jesus, Mack. Where's Keira? Is she all right … are you all right?"

"She's heading home right now. And before you ask, she's okay." Reid swallowed. The kiss, possessive and with a measure of aggression—well, it had turned his insides. And her response to it, deep and intense, had cemented a need. His throat felt dry as sandpaper. Getting up from the sofa, he went into the kitchen and grabbed a bottle of water. He felt as thirsty as a man stranded in a desert. Reid guzzled the chilled water, but his thirst went soul deep.

"Mack. I'm about to leave Louisville; I'll be over later."

Reid ran a hand through his hair. Jeez. The day had stirred a stew of emotions. Compassion for Matt, a rush of perceived danger, and feelings for a woman who'd kindled a bonfire in his blood—he needed to get out of here. And do something to rid himself of this restless energy twisting his insides. Maybe the gym. His eyes fell on the cardboard tubes containing posters and folders bulging with brochures and information on Heroes Rise, and he had a better idea.

"No worries," he told Houston. "I'm okay now. I'll be out of here for a while. Text me when you get back? I'll meet you in town."

Reid ended the call and after taking a shower, he pulled a lightweight shirt over his head and stepped into a clean pair of jeans. Picking up the phone from the bed, he gazed at the screen, contemplating whether to call or text Keira and settled on texting. There was no hesitation in his thumb as he typed, *are you okay?*

The answer pinged as he got into his hiking boots, *yes, are you?*

Despite this horrible experience today, she'd answered right away, so he made up his mind and went for it. *About that dinner and a show, are you free tomorrow?* Why wait?

I'll have to get back with you. That little smiley face she'd tacked on? For some reason, it made him grin. *You do that, Mossy.*

CHAPTER 27

TEN MINUTES LATER, REID CIRCLED Main Street. Downtown bustled with shoppers and diners and out of town folk, and parking places were in high demand. "Here we go, boy," he said when a spot opened up. Yard yawned and lifted his ears as Reid backed the Jeep into the vacant spot. He'd wanted to bring Bones but decided it was too soon.

Getting out of the Jeep, he released and leashed Yard, and picked up the cardboard tube containing Heroes Rise posters from the passenger seat. There were bubbles in the air. The kind that transformed grumpy to cheerful the way only a sunny spring day could do. The kind that charged his spirit and breathed energy into his core.

"You smell that?" From the coffeehouse behind him, the aroma of dark roast wafted through the open door, challenging his taste buds. "Let's have some of that before we get going, bud." The dog just tilted his head as if saying, "What are you talking about?"

Next to the coffee shop's entrance, he ordered Yard to stay. "I'll be right back," Reid said in the same manner as he would tell a small child to wait.

He returned with a large to-go cup and dropped into one of the bistro chairs sitting on the bricked sidewalk in front of the store. He placed the tube on the table and stretched his legs. A voluptuous middle-aged woman stepped outside, her smile friendly and warm, her attitude solicitous. It appeared to Reid the woman was about to strike a conversation, and right on target, she proved him to be correct.

"This is a good day."

"Yes, ma'am," he answered respectfully, placing her accent somewhere in the Balkans. She touched her gaze to Yard, who laid next to Reid's chair. "And your dog, he is good, too."

"Yes, ma'am, he's the best." Reid, who'd been slouching in the chair, straightened his frame. When waiting for his coffee in line, he'd observed her talking with the barista. Hands flying up in the air, giving off the vibe of someone in charge, he'd pegged her as the owner.

"I'm Tanya."

"Tanya's Beans," Reid smiled, stood, and extended his hand in greeting. "Of course. I'm Reid McCabe. May I talk to you about something?"

"Ah. The perks of being the owner." She waved to a passerby across the street in answer to her greeting. "I can take a break," she said, directing her attention back to Reid.

He'd picked up on the hesitation, the way *solicitation* stood written across her face. It occurred to him that Main Street businesses were prime targets for donation requests.

"Please, won't you join me for a minute?"

"Hmm. Reid McCabe. I know your name. But I don't know how." Tanya's lips pursed as she sat.

"May I," she asked when Yard's head popped up. Reid nodded, and she stroked the dog' back, crooning how soft and pretty he was.

"Perhaps, Heroes Rise sounds familiar?"

The question brought her attention back to Reid. "Yes, yes. Of course." Tanya injected, and that warm smile returned. "You're the fella who talked with Buck. On the radio."

Tanya's eyes skipped over Reid from head to toe, brazen and unapologetically blunt, and he perceived what she'd ask before it came over her lips.

"That's me." On the inside, Reid cringed. It's how it always would be. How people would differentiate between Houston and him—the guy with the missing leg. Unlucky bastard is what he wanted to say, but that would not be polite. Would it? Not when he was about to ask her to become a sponsor. Or to place a donation box inside her store.

In place of a rebuke, he gave her a dazzling smile. "May I talk to you about our sponsorship levels?"

Seeing the cloud coming over her face again, he pitched, smiled, and told Matt's story without naming him. When he finished, Tanya didn't sign up for a monthly sponsorship, but she donated a grand.

Self-satisfaction spiked at the first success, but it made his day. "Of course," he said. "Just as soon as our Tax ID comes in, your donation will be tax-deductible. In the meantime, I'll leave you this colorful poster to place inside the store or window display. Would that be all right?"

Tanya stood, and Reid pushed to his feet as well. "I'm happy to help," she said. "Bring your hand-out sheets, and I'll put them on the counter."

Tanya extended a hand, they shook, and he saw the surprise glint in her eyes when he turned over her hand and placed a kiss on top. "You are very generous, Tanya. Thank you." He kept his eyes on hers just a bit longer than necessary.

"Oh, you are welcome." He'd cranked up the charm, and it had put a blush into her cheeks.

Reid took Yard's leash and disposed of his to-go cup. "You're my lucky charm, boy," he said. "Let's go and pound these pavers." And on fickle wings of first success, he sat out to make a pitch for Heroes Rise with store owners along Main Street.

An hour had passed when Reid's phone buzzed in his pocket. He was inside a western store, listening to the entertaining stories of the owner's life as a cattle hand on a large-scale Wyoming ranch. Fascinating as they were, it was time to move on. Jim, the owner, had taped the Heroes Rise poster to the glass of the entrance door, but hadn't committed to a donation yet. Reid excused himself and answered Houston's call.

"Hey. You back in town?"

"Yep. What are you up to?"

"I'm downtown, hitting up some stores for our cause. Tanya's Beans is donating a grand—how do you like those beans, Tex?" Reid chuckled and kept talking while he headed from the side street toward Main. "I spoke to a few others, and we've got some posters up in store windows now. I'll fill you in later."

"Cool, man. Come over to my place. Unless you still want to meet in town?"

"Yeah, let's meet at Pat's? Give me thirty minutes?"

"A'ight. I'll see you around five o'clock."

Reid tugged on Yard's leash. "Okay, boy. Let's get you back to the cabin."

By now, a few of the novelty stores were closing for the evening; three-story buildings shadowed the side street, and traffic had slowed.

His phone pinged. A message this time. Keira. *About tomorrow. What time will you pick me up?*

Reid grinned. The no-frills, straight-forward message a reflection of Keira's nature. And it was precisely that. The absence of ruffles and lace around the edges of Keira's personality, linked with warm-heartedness, affection, and one hell of a lot of strength, had stirred an attraction unlike any before. Jeez. What depth of character she'd revealed this morning after the attack. It hadn't killed her compassion.

Reid started typing out a message but changed his mind and pressed the green phone icon instead. Ahead, at the pedestrian crossing, the light flashed down seconds. The Jeep parked curbside on the other side of Main Street, and he hotfooted it.

***

Easing his truck onto Main Street, Bill felt hot, dizzy, and nauseated from the all-you-can-eat buffet. He needed an antacid. It would help; it always did. Traffic moved at a steady pace. In just a few minutes, he'd be home.

Closing in on the center of town, Bill squinted against the setting sun, blinked, and squinted again. And he felt his blood pressure rise. There he was—McCabe. Strutting towards Main Street with that mongrel next to him, his phone pressed to his head. No effing care in the world. His resentment was a burning ulcer in the pit of his gut. Bill felt sick. Acid washed into his throat, and red spots danced before his eyes as he swallowed the burning bile.

Ahead the traffic light changed from yellow to red, but Bill didn't see. It took all his attention to focus on that smile spreading across the bastard's face as he spoke into his phone. Loathing churned in his gut. His vision blurred, the blood roared through his veins, his damp shirt clung. Bill couldn't breathe.

A thud against the fender. Iron bands squeezed his chest, choked him. A last coherent thought sprinted through Bill's head—stop the truck. Oh, God. This was it. A heart attack. Would his life end on Main Street, a public spectacle?

Overwhelming regret surged—for losing Billy, having failed Carol, and for letting hate shade his soul and blot out empathy. Maybe it was a survival instinct, or perhaps the resurgence of scruples, but with single-minded focus, Bill stomped on the breaks. Aware of metal screeching against metal, he slumped and folded like a wet towel.

***

Thwack.

While Reid hadn't been struck full force, the truck's fender grazed his hip from behind. The impact pitched Reid to the sidewalk, his body knocked onto the brick pavers, and the prosthesis' socket crushed against the concrete curb. Numb and dazed, he didn't feel any pain. A terrible screech cut through his disorientation as the vehicle lurched forward, smashed into an SUV parked curbside, and finally came to a halt.

Behind Reid, people spilled out of stores and rushed to him. A group gathered around. Kneeling, standing, lips moving. He couldn't make out what they were yelling. They looked like they were yelling.

"Oh, my God. Are you okay? Someone's calling 911," he understood through the roaring ocean receding in his ears. Yard stood over him, licking his face.

Yard! Reid sat and groaned. "Buddy, are you all right?" Adrenalin left, and now the entire side of his body screamed—his leg screamed louder.

Reid scrambled to his feet; the prosthesis damaged but still in place.

"You should sit down," someone said. An old man with a neatly trimmed goatee offered help, but Reid declined and hobbled to the bench on the sidewalk a few feet away. He didn't have to look to see the prosthesis was damaged, the socket cracked. He'd known that the moment he'd kissed the sidewalk. Yard, seemingly unharmed, sauntered along.

A slender woman in athletic wear came up, holding out a phone. "Sir, I believe this is yours?"

His phone. Cracks zig-zagged across the thin film of the screensaver, but otherwise, it had fared much better than he. Reid thanked her with a warm smile.

"I'm terrified about what happened to you. I hope you're okay." She withdrew a card from her bag. "I've witnessed the entire incident and will make my statement to the police. I'll be glad to answer any questions you or your insurance may have. Call me at any time."

Call. He needed to call back Keira. And reach Houston.

His gaze flew to a separate group of people gathered around the black Silverado to his right. The driver's door stood wide open, but that's as far as he could see. Traffic on Main Street started to back up.

"Are you all right, son?" the nice old man asked, and Reid nodded.

"I had worse. Getting run over by a truck? Piece of cake."

Reid needed to crack a joke to keep his self-control. His body ached, and his prosthesis was shot. Anger surged. No doubt, this had been no accident. Had Bill gone nuts and targeted him? But in that micro-second of a glimpse, he'd seen fear casting a shadow over loathing. Had it been an accident? Reid wasn't sure. In any case, he felt like knocking Schuster into the middle of next week, but he also felt a measure of pity for him.

The old man with the Colonel Sanders goatee lifted his eyebrows; empathy flickered in watery eyes when he nodded toward Yard. "Your guardian angel," the man stroked the dog's head, "he saved you from worse."

It sobered him. "He did." Reid lifted his chin in the direction of to the Silverado. "I wonder what conditions he's in."

The woman spoke up. "Some guys got him out of the truck, and one of them happens to be an EMT. Sounds like he may have had a heart attack."

Reid nodded silently. How much had Keira overheard before the line went dead?

Sirens wailed as he punched in her number.

CHAPTER 28

Reid rejected a ride in the ambulance and had no inclination to visit the ER. "I'm all right, scraped and bruised, but all right." He only agreed—and with great reluctance at that—when Keira and Houston convinced him to get himself checked out. After all, he'd wrestled with a pick-up truck. Just a clip, he'd insisted, but now, here he was—at the emergency room.

They'd just taken a few x-rays. Keira, perched on the blue plastic chair placed against the wall, stood and stepped aside when a technician wheeled Reid back into the tiny space of the emergency cubicle.

"Hey," Reid said with a lopsided grin spreading across his face.

"Hey, yourself," she answered with a tentative smile.

An IV line protruded from the front of his elbow, and a clear bag hanging above his head dispersed a steady drip of saline and pain meds into it. A pulse oximeter extended from the tip of his forefinger.

From nearby, a baby cried, its wail cutting above the hum of a buzzing ER.

The tech locked the wheels to the bed, saying he'd check back in a few, pulling the curtain closed as he stepped out of the cubicle.

Keira seemed oddly self-conscious as she brushed her fingertips along the back of Reid's hand. Was it the environment of the ER, or the horrible awareness of what could have been?

"How are you feeling?" she asked, softly curling her fingers around his hand.

When the curtain swooshed back again, Keira dropped her hand to her side and turned her head, a light blush slithering up her neck. Beside the tech, Houston's frame loomed large in the opening of the cubicle.

"How is Yard?" Keira and Reid asked simultaneously.

Houston, who'd been on his way to the pub at the time of the incident, arrived at the accident site just a few minutes before Keira did. Keira drove him to the ER while Houston took Yard to Reid's cabin.

"The mutt has settled down; he's doing great. When I checked him over, he didn't give any signs of being injured. He's not just smart, but lucky, too."

Keira exhaled a sigh of relief.

"Thanks man," Reid nodded.

"And that's more than I can say for you." Houston broke into a stupid grin. "I've gotta say, Mack ... Hollywood won't be calling any time soon. You look like shit."

"Screw Hollywood. But you're welcome to take my part, Cinderella."

"That's the spirit, soldier." Houston laughed, and Reid cringed. Soldier. It's what Keira had called him. And what a symbol of a soldier he was. Yeah ... a far cry from this morning's shrewd tracker, he was a freaking poster child for this job.

The air in the cubicle grew heavy, replacing the light banter. As if reading Reid's mood and his need to safeguard his dignity, Keira fixed her gaze to Reid while tipping her head to Houston.

"Jeez, Reid. Does he know what he's talking about? Let me just say that for someone who just went toe to toe with a pickup truck, you don't look anything like minced meat to me. As a matter of fact," she smiled, "I think you look pretty damn good. But I'm glad you decided to get checked out."

"Damn right about that," Houston agreed. "He wouldn't listen to me. So, thanks for making him understand."

It brought Reid back onto neutral ground. Or was it the mellowing effect of the medicine coursing through his veins? Reid reached for Keira's hand; a tender gesture that flushed her cheeks again. "A bump to the hip, that's all, Mossy. But thanks for insisting on bringing me here."

"You're welcome, Reid. I was going freaking nuts until you called back. Hearing the sirens when the phone went dead, and not knowing what happened? Well, I'm glad you're okay."

Houston shifted and cleared his throat.

A knock on the outside wall and the attending doctor entered, carrying papers and a tablet. Keira and Houston stepped outside.

"The X-rays are clear, with no broken bones," the doctor said without preamble. "Your ribs will be sore, so take it easy for a few days. I'll give you a prescription for pain meds. You know how to treat the stump, clean the scrapes, and keep it dressed for a couple of days. Do you have any questions?"

The doctor left, and Reid was getting ready to dress. Keira finally went home, knowing Houston was going to drive Reid to his cabin.

"I brought your crutches," Houston said. "They're in the car." Reid's eye flicked to the prosthesis propped against a corner of the cubicle, the hard shell of the socket fractured. A deep inhale, and his lungs expelled air in a great burst. "Thanks, bud."

Houston's gaze followed Reid's, lingered on the socket. "That had to be one hell of a slam for getting a crack like this."

"Yep." Reid pulled the thin ER blanket covering him aside, "Just ask the stump." It was wrapped in gauze, but underneath the pristine dressing, the skin was blistered and scraped, and something under the suture line pulsed as if it had a life of its own."

"Jesus. You think Schuster had you in his crosshairs? Snapped when he saw you crossing Main Street?"

"I don't know, Tex. But I sure as hell would like to find out. You know how he's doing?"

"They won't say, only that he's in ICU."

A short time later, the tech brought a wheelchair and rolled Reid to the pick-up door where Houston had been instructed to wait. Bone-tired, Reid slumped groggily into the passenger seat. It had gotten late, and by now, stars punctured through the inky blackness. "Your Jeep's still in town. We'll get it back here tomorrow," Houston said, pulling up to the cabin.

"Thanks, brother." Reid got out, grabbed the crutches, and thumped to the front porch after Houston.

Reid gritted his teeth. The pain shot he'd gotten in the ER had started to wear off. With each step, his muscles tensed as crutches pressed into his armpits, and it felt as if fists pummeled his ribs.

"Ah. Shit, Tex."

"You okay, bud?"

"As okay as Muhammad Ali's punching bag. Jog my memory, man. Did I leave here this morning to meet with Matt, or was that a month ago? Jeez, what a whacked-up day."

Scars Of the Past: Book 3 In The Oak Creek Series

***

"A'ight. You need anything before I leave?" At close to midnight, Houston had stayed just long enough to feed the mutts while Reid hobbled to the bathroom to freshen up and pop a couple of Tylenol.

With Yard and Bones curled into tight balls at the foot of the bed, Reid laid sprawled out with his hands clasped behind his head, appreciating the peace of the cabin.

After the accident, he'd called Keira before calling Houston. "Oh, my God, Reid." Relief rode through air. "I was worried out of my head. Thank God, you're calling." She'd sounded breathless and a little freaked out. "Are you okay? I'm hearing sirens. What happened?"

"I'm all right," he'd said and gave her quick run-down. "It was an accident. He just clipped me," assuring her of no major injuries.

As he laid on the bed replaying the events of the evening in his head, he smiled. Keira had been worried about him. When the leaded hoods of his eyes closed, memories of the day chased each other, merged, and morphed into one.

The forest. A Silverado, agile as a black panther, slithers between trees—chasing, lights bouncing, advancing. He's running, evading, his lungs are burning. He throws a look over his shoulder, assesses. The pick-up looms. Schuster—his mouth is agape, and he's clutching his chest. Tanya is riding shotgun. She extends her arm out of the window, fisting a bundle of dollar bills. A few slip out of her hand and billow on a gust of wind. Red lips part, Tanya throws her head back and laughs out loud as she opens her fist. Bills flutter—unrestrained and weightless, they engage in a strange dance, kept up by lemongrass-scented air. He stops running. This panther-truck is closing in, its purr a hypnotizing sound, and he's too tired to keep running. He resigns himself to give in. He turns, opens his arms, and embraces the unavoidable. The collision is soft, molding around him, much like a curvaceous woman, and it tosses him to the ground. The air swooshes out of him, but he's unharmed. He should be crushed to powder. Why is he not dead? He raises his lids and stares into a pair of jade green eyes.

Already, smidges of gray slipped between the gaps of drapes when Reid's eyes flew open. Jesus. His heart raced, his sheets were drenched, the memory of the dream vividly alive.

What the hell had this been about? Gritting his teeth, Reid fought against nausea brought on by a sudden sharp pain as he sat up and shifted to get out of bed. Rotating his trunk, he tested the level of pain and decided to fight back with Tylenol. It would have to do.

Too early for the dogs, Bones dug deeper into the blankets, and Yard just lifted his head, watching Reid wearily getting out of bed before flopping his head back down.

Reid's forehead creased as he hobbled one painful step after another into the kitchen. "A truck morphing from a big cat into a woman. Keira," he muttered under his breath. Could this get any weirder?

"Must have been the drugs," Reid blamed it on the pain shot he'd gotten at the ER. His mentality, clear-cut and based on facts, wasn't prone to interpret the meaning of dreams, but his mind kept skipping to the panther-morphing pick-up truck.

Filling water into the coffee pot, he pondered it. Reid convinced himself that last night had been an accident. Whacked by a vehicle, but not mowed over—unlike the dream—and he briefly wondered about its meaning. If it had any.

One scoop of coffee grounds, two ... did the panther-truck, and by extension, Bill Shuster, represent a darker force determined to knock him down?

Hell, no. This royal mind-screw would fade away with no power to smash his goals. He pressed the machine's on-switch and dismissed the whole dream as a bunch of B.S.

While he sat, waiting for the coffee to brew, Yard slunk out of the bedroom. Immense gratitude for the black-and-white dog who shared the same physical challenge as himself washed over Reid. "Hey, boy. Come here." The dog positioned himself with his back to Reid in apparent expectation of a back rub. "Spoiled brat," Reid obliged and smiled, despite the punishing bruises.

This dog. Yard blissfully wallowed under the strokes of Reid's hands. He deserved the mother of all backrubs. Reid reflected if he would have woken at the cabin this morning if not for Yard's incredible instinct jerking him backward so forcefully? "Bud, I'll get you the biggest, juiciest steak I can get my hands on. Just give me a couple of days. Okay?"

Nails clicked on the floor as Bones bounced around the corner, ears flopping. "Morning rabbit," he laughed at the joyful mutt and felt a pang of regret at knowing he'd be adopted soon. What if ... ? No way. An old lady already had her heart set on this silly little dog. That's why Keira had come by yesterday.

Reid gave Yard a final pat, Bones a few strokes of affection, and thumped to the double doors in the great room to let them out.

Reid's eyes followed the dogs. He had no worries about Yard wandering off, but Bones was a little explorer.

His thoughts circled back to Bill Schuster, and he found himself speculating on how Bill was doing this morning. Had it been a heart attack? How severe? Would he survive his ordeal?

Had Bill aimed the truck at him, or had he lost control of the vehicle as his heart seized? Although Reid wanted to believe this had been an unfortunate accident—as the saying goes— the wrong place at the wrong time. But Schuster's mind had made him, Reid, responsible for Billy's death. So, was it, in fact, a coincidence? Absentmindedly, Reid's fingers slipped beneath the T-shirt sleeve and clasped around the tattoo covering his bicep. He considered visiting Bill, once he was out of the hospital, but dismissed it as a terrible idea. Oil to fire.

Out of the corner of his eye, a motion caught Reid's attention. What was that dumb dog doing? "Bones. Hey! Stop that!" His voice carried loud and forceful. With apparent delight, Bones rolled from side to side but stopped when Reid yelled a second time. If he had to guess, he'd say whatever the mutt thrashed himself in would carry an obnoxious stink.

Great. Now he'd need to figure out how to give the dog a bath. *Ask Keira,* he thought, but quickly dropped the idea. He'd handle it.

Ah, Keira. He didn't want to think about her, but she had a peculiar hold on his mind. Within the twilight of sleep and waking, he'd felt himself drowning in a mesmerizing sea of jade-green eyes. An intense and strange sensation, a spellbinding effect he couldn't shake. Clearly, he reasoned, his brain had thrown Keira into the mix of distorted images. First, the forest episode, and later being on the phone with her when the accident happened. And the brief moment in the ER when they'd been alone. Had the meds dripping into his arm fogged his brain, or had she appeared shy when taking his hand? Well, shyness wasn't a trait he'd ever associate with Keira. But her bristles under that tomboyish exterior had softened; at least until Houston arrived. Of that he could be sure.

Shit, he thought, raking a hand through his hair. Last night, he found himself looking forward to taking her out today. A nice dinner. He'd planned taking her to the city, a fancy restaurant with real tablecloths, candles, and dinner music. He didn't care much about fancy, but the service had to be first-class with phenomenal steaks. Women liked that kind of thing.

Just dinner. A fresh start after yesterday's disaster. The forceful streak of sudden arousal, Reid blamed it on his state of mind, the intimacy of the chase, the need to let her see the dark in him. With that, he realized, he'd also given her a chance to ditch the idea of getting close to him. In the back of his mind, he'd known it would be a test. But, God, he'd wanted her. Right there, against the truck. Every cell of his being had known she'd wanted him, too. But Keira had pulled herself together and distanced herself. Her levelheadedness acted as an ice-bucket to his fire, but the saving grace for her frail trust. She'd hadn't hung around, but neither had she backed away without throwing him a line.

He'd be a moron to tell himself he didn't want to take her to bed. Confident that he could, he also knew how to exercise control. A pleasant dinner, flirting, and he would take her home. Kiss her good night. An old-fashioned date.

Well, dinner was off now—another casualty of the accident.

Reid emptied the travel mug and whistled to the dogs. As Bones bounded up the steps, Reid's nostrils caught a rotten whiff.

Crap. The dog definitely needed a bath.

***

Around noon, Yard lifted his ears and Bones scrambled to his feet and charged to the front door.

Reid was sitting on the deck, answering emails on his laptop. He'd been expecting Houston, who'd messaged he'd drop off Reid's Jeep. "I'm out back," he called. "And grab yourself a cold one on the way."

When Houston stepped through the patio doors, he carried a fast-food sack and a couple of long-necks. "How are you doing today?" He asked, depositing everything onto the patio table.

"I'm all right. Could be better, could be worst—thanks for bringing the Jeep."

"Hey, no problem, man. Tessa's supposed to pick me up. I figured it'll be a while, so I brought food."

While Yard flopped down in a sunny spot, Bones followed Houston on his heels, his tail fanning circles.

"He's rolled in some crap," Reid said as Houston's eyebrows pulled down and a look of disgust came over his face.

"Nice. He needs a bath."

"No kidding. Knock yourself out."

"Sorry. Can't help you there, man. But I have a better idea," Houston said. "Call the rescue, have them take care of it."

"Hm. I'll see," Reid said but thought he'd handle it himself. How difficult could it be? He closed his laptop, reached for a sandwich, and peeled it out of the wrapper. "So, Tex. Tell me, what am I going to do about Schuster?"

"You think it was deliberate? That he *wanted* to hit you?"

"I don't know, man. The split second I caught the look on his face, I saw the fear in it, of what was about to happen. But there was loathing, too."

Houston chewed, contemplating. "Because he doesn't know the whole story."

Reid agreed. "I hope he's able to recover, and I hope he'll get some help. When the time is right, I'll find a way to reach out to him."

"I know you will, Mack."

A razor-sharp pain rose within Reid. And with sudden clarity, he understood what he needed to do.

"What pisses me off the most is that training is screwed-up for at least a week," he said after a moment.

"Mack, hear me, okay? Don't worry about training. We won't go on the road for another couple of months. We'll be fine."

"Says the man who can't sit still for more than five minutes." To make a point, Reid directed his gaze to Houston's bouncing leg.

"Okay, you got me. Hey, this morning at church, the mayor told dad he'd organize a grand kick-off for us on departure day. Details to follow."

"A grand kick-off in a small town sounds impressive." Reid bumped his fist to Houston's.

"Hey, I've had an idea. You know Matt might want to ruck with us, right?" When Houston nodded, Reid took a pull from his bottle and continued. "I was thinking—maybe he wants to go on the road with us?"

"Hmm. Matt's got a family."

"I know. Still. I thought Matt could drive the Jeep for a while. A month, or however long he wants. We'll rotate drivers. And after, if it works out, he can be our wingman from back home. Coordinate with officials, book pubs ahead of arrival. This could be what he needs. Win/win."

"Hmm."

"All I'm saying, if he shows up tomorrow, feel him out," Reid said when his messenger notification sounded, and it was Keira.

Hey. How are you?
All right. Thx for asking.

"Keira," Reid said when Houston gave him a questioning look. Ping. *All right enough for company?*

"I'm a popular guy today. Keira's coming, too." Reid said and typed, *Yes.* "You mind?" He glanced over to Houston.

A smirk spread across Houston's face. "And why would I, Mack?"

CHAPTER 29

His Jeep was parked next to the cabin when Keira drove into the clearing fifteen minutes later. Getting out of the vehicle, she smiled at the excited yowls coming from the cabin. No longer a frightened, emaciated bag of Bones, she thought, but a confident little spitfire. Under Reid's care, the dog had gained pounds and shed fears. A testimony to Reid's excellent care.

Keira pulled her lips together and tugged at the hem of her Mossy Oak shirt. Under her favorite hot-pink and very blingy ball cap, an elastic band held strawberry curls together in a ponytail. Sliding the car key into the front pocket of her very much lived-in jeans, she climbed the front steps and paused. Houston flung open the front door just as she raised a hand to knock.

"Hey, Keira."

Startled, Keira's hand flew to her chest as she took a step back, but she quickly recovered. "Jeez. Miller … I'm sorry. You startled me."

"Sorry, didn't mean to give you a scare. Reid's in the back. Come on in."

The dogs competed for her attention as she stepped inside, with Bones jumping on her leg. "Eww." Keira scrunched her nose as she bent with the intent to pet him. "Bones. What did you do? You smell like a sewer ... I bet you had a ton of fun," she laughed and patted his rump. "Shew. Go."

"Reid's on the deck," Houston said and led her into the great room. "Want a beer?"

"Ah. No thanks. But I'll take a bottle of water." Memories of the last time she was inside the cabin flooded her mind, and suddenly she felt awkward. Not nervous, but just a little on edge.

Keira crossed the room, and even before she stepped through the patio doors, she saw him on the deck, standing on crutches, a daring look in his eyes. Her stomach pinched. Behind the bold stare was openness and exposure, a vulnerability that tugged on her heart. That's why he hadn't discouraged her from coming today, she thought.

Last night, she'd been at the hospital with him, but that had been different. Hospital sheets covered him up to his waist by the time the nurse called her to the ER cubicle. Today, he wanted her to see his true self, with no artificial limbs giving a false image, to have her understand what it would be like to be with him and the gauze-wrapped stump.

Keira swallowed around the knot in her throat. "Reid," she said, her voice a low croak. Doubt and uncertainty stared back at her, his vulnerability a blunt contrast to his athletic frame.

"Hey." In quick strides she went to him. Warmth crept over her face as she touched her lips to his cheeks. And was sure he could hear her thundering heart.

"Hey, yourself."

Weariness had slid into his voice, or had it been pride? "Look at you," Keira said, taking a step back. "If you told someone you went toe to toe with a truck, they'd think you're taking them for a ride." She smiled. "You look a hell of a lot better than last night. I'm glad you're okay." And it broke the spell.

"That makes two of us, Mossy." Reid's eyes warmed with his smile, putting her at ease. Houston, who'd watched the exchange from the patio door, gave him a nod and a grin.

"Sit down, stay a while." Reid's expression changed to serious as he shifted against the deck's rail, scrubbing his hand across his chin. "In case I didn't tell you last night," his gaze skipped from Houston and Keira, "All I can say is ... thanks for being there when I needed you."

"Of course. Don't mention it." Keira, feeling unnerved under Reid's piercing gaze, rolled the bottle of water between her hands.

Reid crutched to the table without taking his eyes off her.

A chair scraped, Houston sat, and the moment broke.

"You're welcome, man. Any time," Houston's voice cut in. "But next time you feel the need for a little excitement, just join me at Pat's." The affectionate smile Houston threw Reid was as wide as the Grand Canyon, and Keira laughed.

"I didn't understand what had happened." Back to her confident self, Keira unscrewed the water bottle and took a sip. "I just heard screeching tires, and you're yelling, 'Shit.' And then a clatter like you dropped the phone, followed by dead air. I called back to back, getting your voice mail each time." Her heart still stammered at the panic that had gripped her chest. "I didn't know what to do but to call Houston. But—" Keira raised her brows and opened her palms. "He didn't answer either."

Jeez, Keira shook her head when Houston gave her a sheepish look and mouthed, "Sorry."

"A thousand things tumbled through my head," she continued, "each one more horrific than the last. I had to find out for myself. But I'd just gotten into the truck when you called back."

Houston's ringtone blared the theme song to *Top Gun*. "Tessa's calling," he said, and scrambled to his feet to go inside.

Reid crossed his arms and shook his head. "Tsk. In his defense, I doubt he ignored your call. I kept him a little busy, you know?"

"Hmm." Keira brought the water bottle to her lips.

Both looked at Houston as he returned to the deck, huffing, "Damn, Tessa. You were supposed to be here by now. We had a deal," Houston snapped and ended the call.

"She's running late. It'll be another hour before she gets here," he said, shaking his head.

Keira pushed back her chair and rose to her feet. "Well, I won't keep you guys. I just wanted to drop by to see if you need anything, Reid. But this guy here," she pointed to Bones, who had settled next to Reid's chair, "definitely needs a bath."

"No argument here," Houston chimed in.

Reid reached for his crutches and stood, too. "Stay a while. What's the rush?" He cocked his head, skimming his gaze over her face. "I'll take him into the shower with me. Later."

Keira laughed. "I don't know whom I should feel sorrier for. The dog trapped in the shower stall, or you, trapped in rotten-smelling steam. I feel sorry for both of you. Besides, what about infection?" Keira's eyes skipped to the bandaged leg.

"Nay. It's no problem." At the doubtful lines etching into her forehead, he gave a thin smile, and explained: "Plenty of experience and a watertight cover. But the smell? Yeah, that might be an issue."

"Phew." Houston raised a hand, fanning his nose.

Two grown men stumped by a little dog, Keira thought, and her lips twitched with amusement. "Tell you what, Pet Stop has a washing station, I'll take him and bring him back later."

In a dramatic gesture, Reid sighed and raised his eyes to the sky. "You're rock 'n roll fabulous, Mossy. I'll be endlessly grateful."

"Okay. I'll do it. Where's his crate?"

A few minutes later, Keira leashed Bones, then beamed Reid a wide smile. "We'll be back in a couple of hours," she said and was thankful he couldn't hear her heart skip a beat.

Her eyes darted to Houston, who hung back with a silly grin on his face. "See you, Miller."

"I owe you," Reid said, crutching to the front door behind Keira and Bones. The flippant tease from a few minutes ago had left his voice.

***

Crutches thumped on the hardwood as Reid made his way to the deck, where Houston crumpled sandwich wrappers into a paper bag and snatched empty bottles from the table. His mood had flipped to somber.

Reid saw Bones' trust in Keira and, as he trudged next to her and out the door, something else became clear. Keira had bridged the terrible moment of vulnerability with ease. And the attention she'd paid to his account of the accident, her concern for his well-being? His bullshit meter had detected no pity. Every word, gesture, and action rang honest and real. When he said he owed her, a dog-bath had not crossed his mind.

She'd left no room for doubt in his mind. Reid couldn't be more decisive, and he wanted to learn everything there was to know about this woman. As the realization sunk in, a cloud slid over his consciousness.

An earlier unspoken thought flooded his mind and soul with urgent need. Was it to knit this hole in his stomach and smother the licks of internal pain? He didn't know if peace would ever find an opening, but Reid knew what he had to do. Someone he needed to show his respect to. It was past due, and it was payable now.

"Tex."

Houston stopped mid-motion at the somber tone. "What's up?" There was tension in the air as he glanced at his friend with a puzzled look on his face.

"I need you to do something for me."

"Sure, man. What is it?"

"Take me to the cemetery."

Houston squinted, a muscle under his eye twitched. As he studied his friend's eyes, he saw the emotion, recognized the sorrow in the glint of steel. Reid didn't have to say it. Houston knew whose grave Reid wanted to visit. Had known all along this day would come—it had just been a matter of time. He nodded.

"Let's go."

***

The Jeep crawled between ancient graves and memorials for those who used to walk among the living but now lived among the dead. When they reached the new section of Oak Creek's mid-town cemetery, Houston pulled aside and stopped the vehicle.

Odd, Reid thought as he climbed out, *how traffic fades into silence in the face of tombstones and markers.* Trees as old as the gentle slopes of the land gently dispensed shade over time-worn and new graves alike.

Houston removed his ball cap and led the way. Since returning home, he too, had paid his respects to this soldier. The men moved silently, each hanging on to their thoughts, Reid's face a granite mask. He suspected this visit to be as difficult for Houston as it was for himself.

When Houston stopped in front of a gray headstone, Reid's gaze fell to the simple inscription. William F. Schuster, II, glared in large letters. Reid swallowed hard. A picture of Billy in uniform on the left side of the stone drew his eye, and overwhelming grief punched him in the gut.

Houston's fingers curled into Reid's shoulder. "I'll wait in the Jeep," he said when a cutting sob pushed past Reid's throat. Hunched over on crutches, Reid nodded, unable to speak through the onslaught of piercing pain and guilt. The trill of birds seemed wrong and utterly out of place as memories and images of the young soldier rushed through his mind.

Reid brought a fist against his mouth. Unashamed, he let the tears stream as he talked to Billy. As he riled Billy over his collection of comics he'd stashed in his duffel, as he begged his forgiveness of being unable to save him from enemy fire. Time ceased to exist, and Reid stayed at Billy's grave until he felt drained of emotions.

Unaware of the faltering steps of a heavy-set, middle-aged woman, Reid pulled something from his pocket and placed it on the headstone. "You should have this—my military challenge coin. You, my brother, deserve it more than me." He patted the headstone, straightened his body, and gave a salute. "You've passed the ultimate challenge."

The knots in his stomach were still there, although the pressure receded. When he turned and crutched away without another backward glance, he didn't see the woman at Billy's headstone or the bewildered look as her fingers touched the coin.

"You all right, Mack?" Reid heard the concern in Houston's voice as he climbed into the Jeep. And he appreciated it. Only a few would understand the bond of the brotherhood.

Reid squared his chin. "Thanks, man. I needed to do this. But, yeah. I'm all right."

***

Reid lay on the sofa, staring at the ceiling. With his hands tucked behind his neck, his mind was on that fateful day on the Afghan mountainside. He could almost smell it—the acrid stench that had lodged in his nasal passages, the stench of explosives, charred metal, dirt, and destruction. Could he have done anything different to influence the outcome? To save his men? He'd asked himself the same question a thousand times, and like a thousand times before, it was as fruitless as pushing noodles up a hill. Today the weight crushed like a ton of bricks.

The scenario of the explosion played on auto-repeat until his phone pinged, and a message finally stopped the endless loop. *We're back. Please don't get up for us. Bones and I are coming inside.*

Keira must have returned and been on the porch because immediately the door opened. Reid swung into a sitting position, and Yard jumped to his feet. "Hey, boy. Sleeping through guard duty?" He ruffled the fur on the dog's neck and felt the rocks within his chest slowly dissolve.

A brown fluff-ball charged into the room, flew to the sofa, and bounced on hind legs, begging for Reid to pick him up.

"And who are you?" Bones promptly rolled onto his back and exposed his belly when Reid lifted him to the seat.

Yard slunk to Keira's side and pressed his weight against her leg. She came into the great room, scratching the dog's ears. "Hey, Yard. Is he neglecting you?" As Keira spoke to the dog, her gaze skipped to Reid. Her smile wavered at the lines that seemed to have edged deeper into his face.

Since taking Bones to the pet store, something had changed. The subdued atmosphere hanging in the room was as transparent as it was unmistakable.

"Hey, Mossy." Reid's features softened, his lips curved into a smile, instantly transforming the murky mood. "About time you came back. I'm feeling a little neglected, myself." And just like that, the playful tone was back.

The corner of her mouth quirked up, but he noticed the effect of his words in the pink flushing of her cheeks.

Keira crossed her arms. On a sideways puff of air, wavy tendrils smoothly lifted from her cheek. "Did I hear you say thank you? Well, Mister, you and Bones are welcome. It was a pleasure to scrub that stink off him. Anything else I can do for you while I'm here?"

She'd made her point with a smile on her lips. Reid plucked the crutches from the floor and pulled himself up. Jeez. Why had he said that instead thanking her for taking Bones? Because it was true. Keira coming into the room had shredded the gray, and his tease had slipped in a flippant tone.

"You're right, Mossy," he said. "It was a dumb thing to say. I appreciate you taking the mutt. Hallelujah, he smells decent again."

"You're welcome."

Keira relaxed her stance and dropped her arms at the same time Reid reached for the half-empty beer bottle on the coffee table. She lunged and reached for it, a gesture of help.

"I got it." His voice carried a clip, and Keira backed away with a mystified frown creasing her forehead.

"Oh." The word hung loaded in the air.

Reid diffused the moment with a half-shrug and a lopsided grin. "Practice. Nothing to it." Clearly, at a disadvantage, Reid hobbled on crutches carrying the bottle. Damn his pride, not accepting help.

Still holding Bones' leash, Keira drew her truck key from the front pocket of her jeans and followed Reid into the kitchen. Placing the leash on the counter, she said, "Well, I should be going, and you probably need to take it easy. Need anything before I head out?"

But Reid didn't want to hear it; he wasn't ready to let her go. He set down the bottle and turned. "Yes. There's something I'd like you to do for me."

"What's that?" She asked, raising an eyebrow and slipping him a curious glance.

In the small space of the kitchen, she was within arm's reach. Reid stepped forward. Leaning into the crutch, he ran his knuckles along her jawline with unexpected tenderness.

"I was looking forward to our date. Since it got smashed, will you stay for a glass of wine?" Reid's gaze deepened. And for a few seconds, he wasn't sure if she would—until he caught the fluttering pulse in her throat.

"Do you have a red?" Words uttered on a shaky breath.

Reid leaned closer. Soft as the gentle touch of a snowflake, he brushed her lips with his. "Merlot?

***

This man. What had happened to him? Keira wondered. A roadside bomb; this much he'd told her. But how?

He seemed more serious than she'd seen earlier, she thought as she watched Reid pull glasses and wine from a cabinet, open the bottle, and pour with crutches digging into his armpits. It did have a practiced ease to it, yet her soul felt tender at the sight. His roughened exterior was a shell. To shield his scars—the visible ones, and those he wasn't always able to hide. And to protect his stubborn pride.

"What's chasing through your mind?" His voice startled her. Keira hadn't been aware of staring into space or Reid watching her. Grabbing a piece of hair, she twirled.

"Oh, not much. I was thinking about Bones." A white lie, but that was okay. She couldn't just blurt out the many questions like discussing the flavor of a wine. Could she?

A line etched between Reid's foreheads. "He's knocked out on the sofa. What about him?"

"I meant to tell you earlier." Her finger twirled, and the strand of hair wound tight. "The adopter from yesterday—the elderly lady?" She wasn't sure why she stalled, except she hoped he'd see it as great news. She wished he'd just adopt Bones. In her opinion, the three *guys* were the perfect fit for each other. "The woman backed out. Go figure," Keira rushed on. "She was head over heels, and sold on Bones, just to come in and adopt another when she couldn't meet him."

"Hmm." Reid finished pouring.

Keira paused. Her hand dropped to her side, and hair sprung from her finger in a tight coil. "You'll be enjoying his company a little longer."

"Uh-huh. I see."

Keira tilted her head; a dazzling smile lit her face. That's all he had to say? It gave her reason to hope. For Bones. "I'm sure we'll find a home for him soon." Bait, she supposed, but Reid didn't bite.

"Mossy." Reid corked the wine bottle, and deliberately slow, set it on the counter. "I understand you'd love to see him stay here, because you say he's a good fit for Yard, and me. Under different circumstances I might consider, but—"

"But?" Keira studied Reid's profile, taking in the hollow curve of his cheekbone and the deepening creases of his forehead. His voice remained mild, yet his words left no doubt—her hopes had only been wishful thinking. "I can't adopt another dog, Keira. Remember, in a few months I'll be leaving here. Yard will be all right going on the road with me, but I just can't take responsibility for another one."

Something inside Keira's chest pinched, but she nodded; he'd made his point. Yes, he'd be leaving, and it was best if she'd remember this.

As sudden as Reid's forehead had creased, the lines smoothed out and his face settled into a look of amusement. "I don't want to talk about Bones."

Keira exhaled. "Okay. Just checking."

He leaned closer. "Instead, I want to talk about you." His breath tickled her ear. He might as well have dropped an ice-cube down her back; the quiver racing up her back raised prickles in its path.

Keira recovered quickly. Her gaze fell to the bottom line of his tattoo. "You are a far more interesting subject." She beamed a smile while curiosity nipped.

Reid ignored her statement. "Carry the glasses, Mossy? I'll take this," he said and corked the wine bottle.

In the great room, Bones had sprawled out on the sofa. Amazing how much space a little dog can take up, Keira thought and chose to sit in the smaller area between dog and armrest.

On the other side of Bones, Reid plopped into the seat cushions. Never one to be inflicted with self-consciousness, right now Keira felt a little bit on edge. Keenly aware of Reid being so close, she inhaled the clean, ocean scent she associated with him. Thank heavens for the dog between them.

He'd hardly touched her. But sweet Jesus. The slightest touch of his lips; the words breathed into her ear—both deeply intimate and seductive—were a licking flame skipping up her spine. And much like that toe-curling kiss he'd laid on her yesterday, it was hot and arousing.

The silly dog rolled onto his back, stretching his legs skyward in a rub-my-belly pose. His tongue popped out, and his eyes disappeared into his head. Keira laughed and was back on safe ground. She rubbed his tummy when Reid handed her a glass.

"Cheers. I'm glad you stayed." The corners of his eyes crinkled as he clinked his glass to hers.

Her lips curled into a warm smile. "Thank you. Cheers."

The mellow wine and warm dog against her thigh settled her tension. Keira placed the glass back on the table and shifted in her seat. Bracing her elbow against the sofa's back, she rested her head into the palm of her hand. Her free hand kept massaging Bones' belly. "So …"

Reid twisted to face her better, resting his arm along the sofa's back.

She noticed the grimace as his body turned. "Are you okay?"

"I'm fine," he nodded, and she let it go.

"So," he mirrored. "Tell me something about yourself that I don't know."

Keira's palm came up before she placed it back on Bones' underside. "You already know all there is to know." And she thought of the truth-or-dare-game a few weekends earlier. "Well, most of it."

Reid's fingers lifted a curl from her neck. He played with it, his fingertips brushing against sensitive skin as if by accident. "I know you teach math, rescue animals, and you have two dogs. Summer break's coming up. What do you do with that much free time? Vacation?"

Keira's pulse sped. With his fingers caressing her neck, she found it difficult to concentrate. "Ah, summer break. Yeah, I can't wait. Don't misunderstand, I love my kids, but ... I'm not sure I'll renew my contract for next year." She kept her eyes trained on the dog's belly.

His fingers stroked the back of her neck in slow motion. Oh, God. The smooth caress set her scalp ablaze and turned her brain to mush. Please, she thought. Don't let me drool.

"No vacation plans." Gosh, had she slurred her words?

"That must be boring."

His hand cupped her head. Strong and warm, his grip felt just right.

"My best friend is getting married in August. She keeps me busy."

Talking. It took too much energy. She leaned into his touch; a herd of wild horses stampeded across her heart. His free hand came up. Hyperaware of his fingers deftly moving across her cheek and curling into her hair, she closed her lids.

Between them, Bones got to his feet. He stretched, and stomping across Reid's stump, he jumped to the floor.

"Argh." Reid scowled and let out a harsh breath. In an accelerated motion, he pulled back and splayed his fingers over the bandage.

Keira's eyes flew open. She jumped up, sucking air through teeth at seeing Reid rubbing across the gauze. "Shit, what's wrong?" With scrunched brows and pressed lips, she asked, "Are you okay?"

"Yes. Yes." Reid rubbed the heel of his hand across the bandages a few more times. "Cute dog, my ass. Nails like daggers digging in the wrong place." He let go of the leg and raked a hand through his hair. A crooked frown replaced the strain on his face. "Saved by the dog, huh?"

"Phew." Swiping curls out of her face, she sat and made light of the moment. "He got bored hearing about me. Didn't I say you were a more interesting subject?"

With tension leaving his features, Reid leaned his back against the sofa. His fingers knitted behind his neck. "Fair enough—"

All at once she felt apprehensive. "You sure you're okay?"

"I'm good, Mossy. Don't worry about it. Okay?"

Conflicted thoughts rushed her brain. This could be a moment of revelation, but did she dare? Would he let her come into his world, or would he keep her at a distance? And she remembered mom's magazine feature. Dadgummit. With everything that's happened, she'd forgotten to mention that it was she who would lead the interview. Keira debated. But Reid's journey being a part of the monthly write-up gave her the answer to what she needed to do.

Keira lowered her eyes, but when she looked up, her gaze held steady. Gently, she placed her palm to the skin above the bandaged stump. "Will you tell me what happened?"

Underneath her fingers, she felt his muscles tense. His hand grabbed her wrist but didn't move her hand. Time stood still until he relaxed under the softest of touches. His throat clenched, and a weight settled on Keira's heart.

"It's not a pretty story, Mossy."

"It's *your* story. I want to hear it." Her palm warmed his skin, seesawing ever so softly above the bandage line.

He let go of her wrist.

"But first, I need to say something. Full disclosure."

Reid opened his mouth, but Keira cut in. "Please, Reid. Let me finish." Her hand stopped moving. "You wanted to know if I get bored during the summers. The answer is no. I don't know the meaning of 'bored.' You see, I have my rescue work with Barkville, and I also have a third job. I think of it as a second volunteer job."

Reid listened, but she could see his mind ticking, wondering where this was going.

"Teaching comes first, Barkville second, and in my spare time, I am a reporter, editor, and personal assistant to my mother."

"That's right," Reid injected. "Caitlin Flanigan is your mother. *The interview.* Are you saying you want my story for a damn magazine?" Blazing eyes left no doubt what he thought of that.

"No, Reid. I'm saying I work on my mother's magazine. And I wanted you to know this is not an interview and your story is not for sale." Keira blinked, her eyes shimmered. "Dadgummit, Reid, I'm asking because I care about you."

His mouth twitched. "'Dadgummit,' huh?" It must be her favorite swear word. Reid chuckled. "Mossy, you're a real badass, you know that? My granddad used to say that," he teased and drew her against his chest.

"I'm glad you're amused." Her words were muffled with her face pressed against his chest. The old-fashioned stand-in for any situation had broken through the layer between ease and annoyance. Breathing him in, Keira wiggled and settled into Reid with her head leaning against his shoulder.

His chin rested on top of her head. "So, you care about me?"

Dammit, was he still teasing her? His tone sure seemed to imply it. "Did I say that?"

"Hmm." He nuzzled her neck.

"Reid?"

"I'm listening."

"Tell me what happened."

She felt his muscles tighten. The nuzzling stopped, and his hands cradled her face. For an intense moment, he studied her. A haunted look pinned her eyes, and it froze her words. "I will, Mossy—because I trust you. But not today."

Keira slowly nodded as sorrow closed her throat. "I understand."

Reid's hands fell away. "Thank you."

Keira felt terrible. Her inquisitive nature had wanted to know. Well, now she did. But it had boomeranged. His memories were wrapped in barb wire, and her nosy questioning had only twisted the knot a little tighter.

But through this ache slamming against her heart, something else had become as clear as cut glass. Despite knowing of his mission with Heroes Rise and that he wouldn't stick around, she'd fallen in love with this wounded warrior. How had she let this happen when he couldn't be interested in anything more than a casual fling?

"I should go now." Keira stood. "My dogs. They need to go out."

He didn't object, didn't hold her back. "I'll walk you outside."

Yard and Bones scampered off to the forest's edge as Keira opened the driver's door to the truck. A hurricane of emotions twisted her gut. For a second, she'd peeked into his soul and seen his despair. But on the edge of anguish, sorrow, and pain, a hint of hope shimmered. A pivotal moment, she realized; she was falling in love. Inside her chest, a jumbled mess of feelings, warm as a summer breeze, heady as a wine buzz, and acid-churning as a parachute jump, crashed against her ribcage. It scared her witless.

Keira swung open the driver's door, ready to hoist herself into the vehicle when Reid closed the space behind her. In one seamless motion he leaned the crutch against the truck bed snaked his arm around her shoulders and turned her to face him. Keira's mind raced, yet, powerless to move, she stood rooted to the ground as Reid's fingers splayed into her hair. Leaning into her, he kissed her slowly, his lips soft and tender.

"Come back, Mossy." His voice sounded scratchy as he broke away.

CHAPTER 30

Carol's sensible shoes squished on soft ground as she turned into Billy's section of the graveyard. She had come here to clear her mind.

Last night, the shock came with a punch to her core when an officer from the Oak Creek P.D. had called with news that Bill was in the hospital. He'd suffered a heart attack. As shock ebbed, it left a boulder of guilt in its wake.

Tears shimmered in Carol's eyes. Oh, Bill. When did we go so wrong?

But she couldn't deny blinding herself to the signs that had stood right in front of her with his increasingly foul temper, his beer-guzzling, and his growing anguish over Billy's death. His unproven accusation against Billy's Sergeant, blaming him for their son's death, had flashed like a broken neon sign. But she'd ignored it until she could not handle one more day, and she'd left him.

Carol often came to the cemetery. Here, in Billy's quiet presence, she was able to sort her thoughts. It gave her courage and the strength to carry her grief. Today she came to pray and ask God for a way to let go of her guilt.

As she drew near Billy's resting place, she noticed a man standing hunched over on crutches by his grave. Who was he? Carol slowed her steps to observe.

In life, Billy had been blessed with lots of friends, and most had come to bid their final farewell. Few she'd been aware of had come back since that day. From a distance, the man appeared crestfallen, his grief palpable, but Carol didn't recognize him.

It pricked her heart the way his shoulders shook, the motion speaking of his grief. When he reached into his pocket and placed something on her son's headstone, she tilted her head and watched with curiosity. A sharp salute, and he turned from the grave. The hushed lull of the early afternoon amplified the thud of his crutches as he walked away.

He hadn't seen her, but Carol caught a passing glimpse of his features, and something familiar stirred her memory. Where had she seen his face before? The answer slinked around her head, slipping just out of her mind's grasp until she reached the headstone.

Still puzzled over the stranger's visit, Carol picked up the medallion. The metal felt warm to the touch and heavy in her hand. Something military, she thought, turning it around. Red and white colors, a yellow shield with a black stripe and a horse's head. Gold letter on a black rim—1st Cavalry Division. The First Team.

Bringing it up close for inspection, she squinted against the sunlight and made out two sabers crossing.

Hmm.

What is this? It must have meant something important to Billy for the man to leave it on his grave. She slipped the coin into an inside pouch of her purse. Later, when she went back to the hospital, she'd show it to Bill. He would know.

Carol bent one knee and fussed with the bouquet of artificial flowers, stuffed inside the plastic container. It didn't need arranging, but it kept her hands busy. She pulled a handheld American flag from the arrangement and repositioned it.

Oh, Bill. She thought of her husband in the hospital. She couldn't lose him, too. Last night she'd rushed from her sister's house to the hospital in under two hours. He'd been in ICU. The oxygen mask, IV drip, frequent blood draws, and monitoring tests had scared her senseless. Sitting beside his bed—she hadn't been allowed to stay the night—she'd worried, and she'd prayed.

Today, Bill had been moved to a regular room. He already looked so much better. Thank you, Jesus. For the first time, and she couldn't remember in how long, Bill had taken her hand, holding on as if he never would let go. "Carol. I'm sorry—" He'd sounded hoarse, and she believed emotions roughed his voice and brought water to his eyes.

She'd squeezed his hand. The warmth wrapping around her heart made her smile "We'll get through this, Bill. Together. Just hurry up and get better."

"The doctor thinks I may go home by Tuesday." When Carol questioned the short stay, Bill affirmed, "He sounded pretty positive about it."

The doctor had also been stern about Bill making positive lifestyle changes—to stop drinking, make a change of diet, and add exercise. But something else needed changing. And that something had to do with forgiveness and attitude. Billy was dead, but he lived in their hearts. There, he would never die.

Carol gave the flowers one last fluff and pushed to her feet.

Her husband was alive, and it was high time he respected their son's sacrifice by living his own life with honor. He wouldn't come home a changed man, she understood that. This only happened in the movies. Since she expected no miracle; she had to find the strength to be patient.

Clasping her hands in front of her, she dipped her head and prayed in silence. When she finished, a gentle breeze brushed her cheeks and joy flowed through her.

Carol lifted her eyes to heaven and smiled.

"Thank You, Billy."

***

Carol's steps bounced when she returned to the hospital in the afternoon. She entered Bill's room to find him sitting up, flipping through the channels on the wall-mounted TV. Feeling a little uncertain, Carol went to his side. A coy smile played on her lips when she stooped and kissed his stubble-roughened cheek. When was the last time even the smallest affection had passed between them? She laid a grocery bag on the bedside tray and dropped her purse into the recliner next to Bill's bed.

"I brought you a snack. Some grapes." Carol removed the Tupperware container from the bag.

Bill grunted. "You better check with that dragon who calls herself a nurse. She catches me eating something I'm not supposed to have—? I'll bet these things will shrivel into those tiny turds right in front of our eyes when she spews fire."

Carol laughed. "You mean raisins?" She'd always loved his blunt humor, and it was still there. It felt good to laugh again.

"Now, Bill, how would you know that? Did you already sneak something in?"

Bill's effort to look stern, failed when his lips curved up. "Who me? Nope. But, boy, you should have heard her when she caught the guy in the bed next to me. He went home after lunch. Couldn't get out of here fast enough."

Carol lifted her purse from the over-sized chair and lowered herself into it. Ah, the coin.

"Bill, I want to show you something." She dug her fingers inside the purse. When her tips curled around the metal, she shoved back to her feet. Carefully she perched herself at the edge of Bill's bed, extending her hand, the flat, round piece lying in the palm of her hand. "Do you know what this is?"

Bill picked up the coin and held it between his fingers. Carol's head tilted with curiosity. She saw his surprise in the widening of his eyes and the arch of his eyebrows. Bill's gaze skipped from image to the raised letters on the rim. His lids blinked rapidly. And had his breath stuttered for a second?

"Where did you get this?" Gripping the metal tighter, his breath shook.

Oh, no. Carol's pulse picked up speed. Bill seemed agitated. His heart—this was not good. The coin was causing him distress. Why? What was going on?

"Bill—what's wrong?" Carol stammered. She reached for the call button, but his hand shot out, fingers curling around her wrist.

"I don't need a nurse. Who gave this to you, Carol?"

Panic surged when the image of the man on crutches popped in her head—as he laid down the coin, as he raised his right arm and brought his hand to his brow. She felt light-headed. In her mind's eye, the stranger turned his face to her, and brain cells fired, flooding her memory.

Dear Lord. Her hand flew to her chest, balling into a fist. Billy's Sergeant. Of course. The restaurant, she remembered now. They'd gone out for breakfast, and he had been there. Bill had almost caused a scene. It was him. McCabe, wasn't it? She hadn't made the connection because, at the restaurant, he walked by their table without crutches.

Should she tell Bill? And if she did, could his heart handle it? No, she decided. She wouldn't lie, but he wouldn't need to know this. Maybe later, but not now.

"I went to see Billy before coming here," she said quietly. "This was lying on his headstone. What is it?"

Bill's fist closed around the coin. His forehead disappeared under his hairline as he raised his eyes to the ceiling and pinched his lips together. Carol looked at the closed fist raised to his chest.

"It's a military challenge coin, Carol." His Adam's apple bobbed as he swallowed hard. "The emblem belongs to Billy's organization." He paused. "It's an honor to receive one. It means if you carry this, you've proven your worth."

Carol reached out, covering his fist with her hand. Tears stood in her eyes, but Bill's voice croaked. "Someone came to pay homage to our son."

"Yes." Carol whispered. "Whoever left this must have a great deal of respect for him."

CHAPTER 31

Enough of this, Reid muttered under his breath. He shut his laptop and shoved it aside. After updating social media channels, writing e-mails, and making phone calls to potential sponsors on Monday morning, he needed to stretch some muscles. His ribs would protest, but the doctor had supported exercise to speed up healing.

As he winced at the stab of pain against his ribs, he wondered how long it would be before he'd resume training with Houston. This morning, Matt had joined Houston rucking across town. Would Matt join their team? Reid hoped so. And if his gut were right, Matt would.

Reid felt a great sense of accomplishment at his part in building a bridge to a future of hope for Matt. This was the stuff Heroes Rise was made of, and the precise reason he'd committed himself to the cause.

Reid thumped across the clearing, the breeze warm against his face. He paused, sucking in a punishing breath. He thought of Bill Schuster and wondered about his condition. Despite Bill's irrational behavior, Reid wished him well. Whether Bill acknowledged Reid or despised him until the end of time, Billy's death had linked their fates.

He followed the footpath into the forest, and regardless of the bright day, a canopy of green giants shaded the trail.

Would Bill be all right? The question loomed as massive as Mount Everest. Would Bill ever find it possible to face Reid? Would forgiveness heal Bill's heart? Reid's stomach clenched. And would *he* himself ever find the peace he so desperately craved?

"Dammit Bones—get back here!" Reid's voice boomed as the mutt vanished between trees. *We have to work on that,* he thought when the dog slunk back with his head hanging low. Teach the dummy not to run off, or he might find himself running through a fucking downpour with bleeding paws again.

Reid crutched forward, and his thoughts turned to Keira. Over there. He had taken her down like a madman on a doomed mission, his screwy mind mistaking her for an enemy. A royal mindfuck that—strangely enough—had kicked in a prison door. His heart pounded just thinking about it.

When awareness had punched through the fog, a new hope rode piggyback. In that bizarre minute, when he'd trudged through nine circles of hell, this woman, with her reddish blonde curls, freckles dotting her face, and her unafraid attitude, had thrown him a line.

He halted his steps, breathing deeply. Fuck the pain.

"Mossy," he said. "I'm coming for you."

***

The devil must have danced on his parade, because Reid didn't see Keira again until the end of the week. Though it hadn't been for lack of trying.

In the afternoon, Houston and Matt came by. "Man, I'm sorry about your luck," Matt greeted Reid. "Houston told me about it this morning."

"Thanks, bud. It's a real bitch," Reid agreed. "Come on in, guys. The beer's cold."

Three guys and a fridge full of long necks stretched the afternoon visit into late evening.

With a glance at his watch and a groan, Matt finally pushed to his feet. "Time's been flying—I better get home. Thanks for the beer."

Reid grabbed hold of his crutches. "My pleasure. I appreciate you coming, Matt."

After Houston and Matt left, Reid called Keira. He didn't get to speak to her, but he left a voice message. "When can I see you again?"

A ping, indicating a message. *Sorry. Can't talk. Busy at the rescue.*

Tuesday passed with no call from Keira. In the evening, he texted. *Are you free tonight?*

A computer emoji prefaced her answer *I'm at mom's, assisting ...*

Right.

Wednesday, she graded final papers. Her message ended with a sad emoji. Dammit. He didn't want emojis, he wanted to see her.

Thursday night, he knew where to find her. Houston picked him up for their weekly afternoon meet-and-greet at Pat's. But by the time the karaoke band had warmed up, Keira was still M.I.A. When ten o'clock rolled around, Reid realized she wouldn't show up this evening.

On Friday, he finally saw her.

***

A Garth Brooks tune rang from his phone as Reid stared into the bathroom mirror and considered whether to shave. He answered the phone, half-way expecting Keira's call, but he was wrong.

The phone call couldn't have taken more than two minutes, and like a caffeine buzz, it gave him a jolt. Damn, he smirked, he'd miss that volunteer meeting for tomorrow's event, Barks in the Park. Not that it was a big deal, but Helen Miller had asked him to attend. And Helen's asking sounded much like an order.

The call just now had changed this, and Houston would be thrilled to get out of the meeting, too.

"You're calling early" Houston stated the obvious when he answered the phone.

"Wake up, Cinderella," Reid whipped out, knowing that Houston had probably been up and about since before the crow of the rooster.

"Man, what's going on? You're sizzling like the bacon in my frying pan."

Reid chuckled. Turning down the volume on the news channel, he said: "The prosthesis is ready; the office manager called, they happen to have an opening today—"

"Oh, man," Houston cut in. "That's freaking exciting, Mack. When can you get in?"

"The appointment's at four thirty. Someone canceled on short notice."

A groan sounded from the speaker. "Crap, Mack. You know I want to be there for support; any chance you can get in earlier?"

"It's the only opening until the middle of next week. Why? You'd rather meet with the ladies? What kind of pal are you?" Reid teased—except he didn't mind having his friend at the appointment. Testing out a new prosthesis was as exciting as it was emotional. Not that he'd admit to being emotional about a carbon/fiber contraption attached to a socket.

"Shit," Houston said, dropping his tone to serious. "The volunteer meeting's not an issue, but the meeting at Planning and Zoning dad wants me to attend? Argh. I can't get out of that."

"No sweat, Tex. It's not like I can't drive myself."

"Hmm. I'm thinking you should ask Keira to the appointment."

"Hell, Tex. Are you out of your mind?"

"Listen to you. Why do you think that's so crazy?"

"Hmm, let me think ... First, for some obscure reason, she's successfully avoided me all week. Or have you forgotten our chat from last night?"

"Nope. And before you come up with more objections, I believe that's the exact reason you should ask her to the appointment."

"Sorry, Tex. I'm not following."

"A'ight. I'm no dating expert, but that thing between the two of you? You're making this more complicated than putting together your M4 rifle blindfolded."

"Meaning what?"

"Mack, on that first date with Keira, when your imagination went into overdrive because rejection flashed like a neon sign? Why did you push her away?"

"Jeez," Reid huffed. "What's that got to do with anything?"

"Everything. Because if you ask me, I'd say you recognized something in her that scared you shitless." Reid started to huff a denial when Houston cut him short.

"I know you like a brother, so let me take a stab at it. You've kept telling yourself love is nothing more than a girl in a country song—until the girl in the country song shows up on your doorstep. She's no-nonsense and perhaps a little blunt, but at the same time she's refreshing. Hidden under that tomboy exterior, she's warm and she cares. And for the first time since that blast, someone slashed through that armor of yours, stirring up something you want. But you, brother, took the easy way out, afraid of the consequences. Afraid she'd see you as encumbered and weak." Houston paused. "How am I doing so far?"

Reid, scratching a non-existing itch on his neck, forced a laugh. "So, now you're my counselor, too?"

"Want to hear something else, Mack? You pulled her in, close enough to shove her away again, and you kept her at a safe distance. After a while you realized you're a dumb-ass—and sticking to the country song analogy—she's a tune you can't get out of your head; and you want her back. But guess what? Now *she's* scared."

"Jesus, Tex." Reid squeezed the bridge of his nose. "You think she's avoiding me because she's *scared?*"

"Not in the physical sense; she's already shown that. But, yeah, bud, I bet she fears getting too close, afraid you'll decamp again. And on Sunday afternoon? If I read her correctly, she's already over her head for you. Lord, help me understand why," Houston poked lighthearted fun, defusing the intensity of his unsolicited counsel. "Don't be a dickhead, ask her to come with you to the appointment; it'll show her trust and respect. School will be out by then."

"Hmm ... you may have a point. Strange, considering I hardly know her, I do trust her," Reid admitted. "How much do I owe you, counselor?"

"As your friend, I'll settle for a pitcher of Bud."

***

As Keira drove into the clearing, she caught sight of Reid leaning against the front porch railing, waiting. Cargo shorts, and a loose-fitting khaki T-shirt did little to hide his toned frame; a ball cap worn backward completed the outfit. Tall, and on the rough side of handsome, he appeared carefree. Even a little cocky, she thought. Keira's pulse jumped into her throat, and for a moment, the drumming in her ears drowned out the sound of the engine. Emotions she'd struggled to curb since Sunday knocked against her heart.

A ripple of heat flushed through Keira just thinking about how his fingers had curled into her hair with such a sensual touch. How the slow and seductive caresses on her neck had turned her insides to Jell-O and her brain to mush; her blood rushing to her center as she anticipated their love making. *Thank God for Bones!*

Going from zero to a hundred, the stomp of the animals' paws across Reid's tender bruises changed the mood from romantic tension to yet another glimpse into his nightmares.

From the start, Reid's amputation hadn't mattered; her reaction to his revelation had been a stupid misunderstanding. At the same time, had Reid's shutting her out been a convenient excuse for him to avoid emotional involvement? Then, why now? What had changed?

She had wanted this, right? Pursued him when he'd backed off and became emotionally unavailable. Had she diluted her thinking to what her heart wanted so badly? Or was the physical act of unattached sex the balm that temporarily filled the craters on his soul and soothed the anguish in his heart? Yes, come to think of, the chase in the woods had aroused him to where he'd been ready to take her against the truck. Was sex his way of dealing with the pain of the past? It had to be.

Thankfully, the afternoon hadn't ended with lovemaking. On the same evening, in the sanctuary of her home, Keira realized she could never allow herself to be with him. A short-term, unattached and off-the-hook relationship with Reid had the potential to destroy her. This whole week she'd been an emotional mess; still was. Because any relationship with Reid would only be short term. His mind and heart focused on Heroes Rise. A short few months and he would leave Oak Creek. No matter what, she'd have to remember this. And to maintain her distance, she'd busied herself. But today he needed her, and she'd never deny him her help.

Yard and Bones scurried down the porch steps in a greeting of swooshing tails and animated barks and followed the yellow bug until it stopped next to Reid's Jeep.

"Hey boys," Keira said as she got out of the car and bent to pet the excited dogs; a welcome distraction to steady her nerves. "Pretty boy, Yard," she crooned. "And Bones, look at you—your fur's getting all fluffy and shiny." Behind her, Reid thumped down the steps as she fussed over the dogs.

"Mossy." His smile was cheerful as he kissed her cheek with a slight touch of his lips. "The boys are happy to see you … and so am I."

Although the dogs' demand for attention had bought her just enough time to calm the flapping wings inside her chest, her breath caught in her throat as his voice rippled across her skin. The mutts scampered off, and Keira adjusted her stance.

Unsure of what to do with her hands, she swiped at a strand of hair before sliding her fingers into the front pockets of her pants. Somehow, the gesture grounded her.

"I bet you're happy because your ride is here," she said, sending him a teasing smile to let him know she was kidding.

"You caught me." His lopsided smile said he was joking, too.

Keira's gaze followed Reid's as he regarded her car, so undersized and compact next to his Jeep. He'd called during lunch break, asking her to be his wing woman.

He'd asked for her moral support!

The mountain of pride she suspected he'd conquered to let her in on such important appointment, the trust he'd placed in her; it made her happy and weepy at once. Knocked for a loop, she had given no thought to the size of her Beetle.

Dang it. She should have brought the truck; she'd given the vehicle back to her dad as soon as Tony had repaired her car. *He needs a bigger space.*

As if reading her thoughts, Reid said, "What do you say we take the Jeep? I'll drive."

"Well, I ... "

"You want to drive, Mossy?" Even though his voice didn't give it away, Keira judged the question held weight as it hung suspended between them.

Gosh, she didn't mean to sound so baffled at his request to drive. The crutches had thrown her off. Of course, Reid was capable of driving himself.

Keira tilted her head as she appraised the Jeep and decided it was her turn to trust. "And feel that mighty power under my feet?" She brought her gaze back to Reid and beamed a smile. "Tempting, but I'll pass."

***

"How does it feel, bud?"

Thirty minutes into Reid's appointment, Keira followed the technician's every move as he made final adjustments to the prosthesis. Except the rhythmic tightening of Reid's jaw, his expression resembled a stone mask.

A lump of anxiety closed her throat, but when Reid took the first steps without a single wince, Keira cheered silently. His features relaxed, and he shot her a glance. Seated on a swivel stool in the corner by the door, Keira's big smile conveyed encouragement and joy as she gave him two thumbs-up.

Reid walked across the room with surprising ease. His arms dangled by his sides as he ambled, probed, and felt out the new fit. "Feels great," he said, a grin stretching across his face. "Hey, I'm ready to run a marathon."

"That's incredible, Reid." Keira clapped quietly. Despite the lump pushing up her throat, heavier this time, her smile didn't waver. This was a significant moment for Reid, and she'd cheer him on as he tested the artificial leg. The device gave him a normal lifestyle which allowed him to do whatever the heck he felt like doing. As in running a marathon ... or walking out of her life on a cross-country campaign.

The technician smiled at Reid with satisfaction. "If anything changes or you need an adjustment, come back and we'll take care of it."

"Thanks." Reid shook the man's hand. "I appreciate it."

Stepping outside the double doors and onto the sidewalk, Reid pumped a fist in the air, and in a swift motion, hugged her to his side.

"Yes! It's great to be back in business."

On the ride home Reid glanced at Keira in the passenger seat, her profile a sharp-edged silhouette against the setting sun. "Thanks for coming today, Mossy."

"Sure thing. I am thrilled everything worked out."

Keira turned in her seat, facing Reid. "You're okay? It still feels all right?"

"You mean the leg? Yeah, it feels great."

A horn bleeped as a Jeep Grand Cherokee passed to his left, and Reid raised his hand to answer the other driver's wave. "The Jeep wave," Reid said, flashing her a sheepish grin, although Keira hadn't asked. "There are rules."

"I understand," Keira laughed. "Every Jeep owner is your friend, right? I've read it somewhere."

Keira wiggled in her seat, assuming a relaxed posture. "I bet you can't wait to get back to your training routine."

Settling in, she propped her elbow against the window frame and cradled her head in her palm. "I'm curious; what makes you want to walk cross-country for a year?"

"Well, you know our mission and the goal for Heroes Rise. Since Houston brought up this crazy idea, it's become a passion … I can't explain it, but it's like a fire in the gut, a drive to do something significant. On account of sounding like a cliché, it's about being part of something bigger than yourself. And I'd lie if I didn't mention the adventure of it all; the open road and what lies ahead."

As he said this, Reid kept his attention on the heavy traffic ahead. "What about you? I imagine it takes a great deal of passion to be a teacher."

Keira filled her lungs with a deep breath, letting it out slowly. "True."

"Ah, but do I hear a hesitation? You said you're unsure if you'll renew your contract at the end of the school year."

"I don't know yet." Keira shifted, and slumped her back against the seat. To avoid the slant of the descending sun, she dipped her head to the backrest and tilted up her chin.

When the Jeep hit a rough patch of interstate, she jolted upright. "Damn these roads. When are they going to do something about this wagon trail?" A rhetorical question neither one had an answer to. Keira settled back and folded her arms across her chest. "For what it's worth, I think its kick-ass, what you're doing." She rolled her head against the backrest and took in the strong features of his profile. "About the adventure aspect of this tour … I know what you mean."

Reid turned his head long enough to give her a quizzical look before he trained his eyes back onto the rush-hour traffic.

"I realize it is lightyears apart from what you'll do, but does a summer of backpacking through Europe count?"

"You did that?" The surprise in his tone matched the arch of his eyebrows as he shot her a quick glance.

"Hey, what's that supposed to mean?"

"Nothing in particular, just didn't expect it, I suppose. A whole summer, huh? When did you go?"

"The day after I graduated from college." Keira's voice filled with pride as she talked about Dublin, where she spent the first two weeks with her Irish family, Edinburgh, where she met her two friends, and went on with to travel the Scottish Highlands, and Paris, which was nice, but in her opinion, overrated. She spoke of each country's unique villages, famous castles, and meeting the many folks along the route, most of them friendly people.

Keira could have kept talking. During the ride home, her anxiety of being near Reid had eased. She thanked her backpacking memories for that. When Oak Creek's exit flew toward her, it seemed as if she'd just blinked.

"I'm impressed, Mossy," Reid said as he slowed the vehicle and took the exit ramp. "One thing's for sure; your stay in Germany was more exciting than mine. The short time I was there, I stayed the entire time on an Air Force Base."

At the end of the ramp, Reid stopped at the red light. Behind them, the sun dipped below the horizon in a brilliant glow of fire. He pushed his sunglasses on top of his hat. "What do you say we celebrate, grab a bite to eat and have a drink?"

Keira swallowed; her hands pressed tightly into her lap. "I'd love to, but I can't," she said evenly, not giving a reason. Even though Keira had no plans for the evening, it wasn't a lie. She wanted to say yes, grab as much time with him as he offered, but each hour spent together would be a mistake.

She couldn't give in, afraid she wouldn't be able to resist his touches, his kisses. It would be a short-lived affair, and once he'd walked out of Oak Creek, each hour spent together would be a memory impossible to erase. Mere weeks ago, she thought, short-term relationships were acceptable, preferred even. But not anymore; not with Reid.

"You can't or you won't?" Reid spoke quietly. Had he picked up on the nuance of her changed mood? Certain that he had, and despite the tightening of her throat, she gave him a bright smile, hoping it came across as unforced.

"I'm sorry, Reid. But I'll see you tomorrow."

"Right. The fundraiser."

The atmosphere remained strained, but soon enough they arrived back at the cabin. As Reid cut the engine, Keira opened her door and jumped out of the vehicle. The thud of his door closing, and Reid met her at the Wrangler's rear. He touched his hand to her shoulder. "Thank you for coming to the appointment, Mossy. I'm glad you were there; it meant a lot."

And because the truth in his voice required it, she tipped her head up to him, searching his face. But in the shadows of the waning light she was unable to read his expression.

"But, of course, Reid. I'm happy you asked." Keira turned toward her car. "I'd better get going; we'll have a huge day ahead of us".

"Right. See you tomorrow, Mossy." As he had when she'd arrived, Reid kissed her cheek with a light touch of his lips.

He didn't ask her to stay.

CHAPTER 32

THE PROSPECT OF GOING TO his apartment didn't appeal to Houston. He probably should go over to his parents' house and ask his mother about the meeting, but instead, he parked the truck at his place and walked into town. He'd call her later.

Debating whether to go straight to Pat's and grab a burger or go across the street for some home-style cooking, he settled on home-style.

"Booth or table?" the young hostess asked with head-tilt and eager eyes, the menu pressed tightly against her chest.

Preferring privacy, he chose a booth. The Friday dinner crowd had not come in yet, and when she led him into the dining room, several tables and booths were still vacant.

His eyes skipped from the young hostess' slender neck to her swaying hips as he followed her. *She's new,* he thought, since he hadn't seen her before. Too young. He thought of Reid and felt a stab of—what? Not envy. No, Keira wasn't his type. A touch of loneliness, maybe. Heroes Rise didn't leave much time for romantic thoughts, but Reid? *Man,* he thought, *whatever you think you're doing? Don't mess it up.*

The waitress led Houston to a nearby booth and handed him a menu. Half-heartedly, he scanned the advertised dishes when something caught his attention at the table he'd just passed. With pulled-together brows and eyes scrunched, he trained his ears on the drifting conversation.

His attention peaked as a male voice mentioned "military challenge coin," to which a second male voice answered. What was that? Houston hadn't caught it.

The waitress came, took his order just as pieces of a disembodied female voice floated on the air, "a stranger at the grave ... his headstone."

A stranger put a coin on someone's headstone? He couldn't give a reason, but apprehension came over him. His chin squared, and he scooted to the outer edge of the seat. Curious about who was talking about military coins, he peered around the booth's corner and stared at the three guests at the table.

Shit. What was Bill Schuster doing here? This was Friday; only six days since his emergency. When did he get released from the hospital? The woman? She had to be his wife. They were talking about their son's grave. Houston knew, because he'd taken Reid there. On a scale of ten, Houston's interest shot to fifty. Apprehension dropped in his stomach. He had a feeling—

"Here you go, hon." The waitress brought his beer and water, her foghorn voice drowning out all other conversation. "Your plate will come out shortly."

She left to stop at the table behind. "How's your food? Can I get you anything else?"

"It's great ... if you're a rabbit." A grudging voice answered, and Houston figured it belonged to Bill.

The waitress retreated, and Bill spoke again. "Wait a minute, Carol. At the hospital you didn't mention anything about a man putting it down. Didn't you say it was laying there?"

Houston switched to the bench on the other side of the table. It gave him a clear view of Bill Schuster's table. The third man held the coin up to the light, inspecting it. From the short distance, Houston saw its red and white face and knew it was their unit coin—his, Reid's, and Billy's unit. He knew this because Reid had left it on the headstone. Apprehension just shot to one hundred.

The woman pressed a hand against her chest. "I didn't think it mattered."

"Hell yes, it matters, woman."

"Bill, please. Your heart," her feeble voice plead.

"My heart is fine." Bill took the coin from the other man and held it in his palm. "I'd like to know the person who did something like this. Go on, Carol. Describe the man. I wonder if it's someone we know?"

Houston's food came. "Here you go, hon." The waitress placed the plate in front of him and kept jabbering. "I'll bet my tip you will love this. The meatloaf is my absolute favorite dish on our menu." He wished she'd just stop and leave him alone. But he just nodded and smiled, "Thank you."

When he glanced over to Bill's table, Bill's face had settled into granite. Carol looked flustered, worrying her napkin. The second man's face had turned red, giving him an embarrassed look.

"It had to be McCabe. That son of a bitch," Bill's words pushed through pressed lips.

Carol's hand shot to his arm. "Bill, give me the coin. You know you're supposed to avoid stress. And if it had been his Sergeant? Wouldn't that mean he greatly respected our son? You'd said yourself that whoever the stranger was must have had a high opinion of Billy?"

Houston hadn't expected to see fire in the dowdy-looking woman's eyes—or hear the demand in her voice.

"He's the coward responsible for Billy's death, Carol, and he's coming to our son's grave to wash his black soul." Billy threw the coin on the table. The loud clang of metal against glass turned the heads of a few diners. "Get this thing out of my sight, it's got Billy's blood on it."

Without thinking, Houston dropped his fork. He pushed his untouched plate aside, unable to sit one minute longer, listening to this blockhead bash Reid. He didn't give Bill's heart attack one second of consideration when he strode to the table. "Sir, with all due respect. I couldn't help but overhear your conversation."

"Ah, Miller." If it was even possible, Bill's face hardened even more. "Always ready to cover for the Sergeant. Why? He's holding something over your head?"

Houston wanted to punch that mask and see it crumble. Instead, he pulled out a chair. He didn't ask for permission to sit, neither did he acknowledge Carol or the third person at the table. The guy looked familiar, but Houston couldn't place him. His eyes laser-beamed into Bill.

"Mr. Schuster. I'm not dignifying this with an answer. The only reason I will give you a pass is because of your recent medical emergency."

Bill opened his mouth to speak, but Houston held up his hand. His voice was firm, his tone mild; only the rapidly pulsing vein in his neck gave away the wrath inside. "No. I'm talking, and it will behoove you to listen. You've spread falsehoods and believed your own lies for some time now. This ends now."

Carol's hand covered her mouth, and Bill's chin dropped. The other man just pushed his chair back, ready to leave. And his name came to Houston's mind: Tim Cox. Matt's uncle. Son of a gun. "You might want to stay, sir, and learn the truth."

Houston turned his gaze back to Bill. The man seemed deflated; his bluster evaporated. "Mr. Schuster, do you know the full story of what happened on that day in Afghanistan? When Billy lost his life?"

Schuster swallowed. "I know McCabe told his guys to stay in the vehicle when the convoy stopped. That he jumped out, taking over security, when it had been Billy's job to secure the vehicle. Why? And why hadn't he paid attention, ending up missing the attack?"

Next to him, Bill's wife lowered her head into laced hands, bracing herself on the table, and Houston thought her cheek glistened with moisture.

"Billy was a wonderful young man, Mr. Schuster. Sharp, and always the first to volunteer for anything. But some nasty bug had been going around camp, and whatever it was, your son caught it. He was violently ill that day, but Billy also had a stubborn streak."

A whimper passed through Carol's lips. "You could say that," she uttered without looking up.

"Billy figured it would pass," Houston continued. "Instead of letting Sergeant McCabe or myself know, he kept it to himself, until he began throwing up inside the vehicle. By the time we stopped, Billy was doubled over with stomach cramps, sweat covering his face, and to say he shook like a leaf gives you an idea of how fit he was to pull security."

Tim Cox cleared his throat and shifted uncomfortably in his seat. A silent question stood in the raised brow as he shot a glance at Bill.

"Did you know that, Sir?" Houston asked, knowing the answer. He'd spare no effort to rip open the narrow mind of the unwilling listener.

Bill shifted too, resting against the chair's back, his hands clasped in his lap. Houston could tell by the puffing of his chest and the lowering of his chin that Bill wanted to hear what came next, but the bulldog of a man wouldn't cave and ask.

"Inside that vehicle, Sergeant McCabe took care of Billy as best as he could."

Mrs. Shuster's stifled a sob. Houston steeled himself against the tears that would undoubtedly break a dam.

"Under the circumstance, that meant giving him meds and keeping him hydrated. At the head of the convoy, another vehicle had broken down, forcing us to stop. To expect Billy to provide security in his condition would have been irresponsible—Sergeant McCabe relieved your son and took on his duty."

Houston paused at the memory of what followed. His leg bounced in rapid succession. To still the uncontrolled motion, he pressed a palm flat against his thigh. There was nothing he could do to stop the muscle-twitch under his eye.

The approaching waitress must have recognized the intense emotion bouncing between the parties as she retreated halfway from the table.

When Houston spoke again, his tone was flat, unreflective of the emotions churning through his gut. "No sooner had McCabe left the vehicle, they were attacked. A single missile, a hit-and-run. No one, and I mean *no one*, could have seen it coming, Mr. Schuster."

Tim lifted his ball cap and ran a hand through his hair, Carol pressed a hand to her mouth, letting her tears stream openly.

Houston crossed his arms over the table, boring his eyes into Bill's. "Do you know what it's like to come under attack by an enemy, buried in the ground like a viper?" A rhetorical question, of course. Bill didn't know and, how could he? And this was precisely Houston's point.

Carol's pain was palpable, but so was Bill's. Where her emotions ran down her cheek, Bill remained stoic. Houston wouldn't drag this out; he needed to say his piece and get out of here.

"Let me enlighten you. The whole incident takes seconds. By the time you hear the high-pitch whistle, you are already screwed. A whoosh, a bright flash, and it's over. And all you can think is, 'Holy Shit.'"

Carol flinched, but Houston didn't care. War was ugly, and it was time they understood. He owed them the truth for Billy.

"The explosives hit the vehicle, a volcano of dirt, rock, and pieces of metal dusted the air, lifting the Sergeant off the ground. When he came to, shrapnel had wedged into his leg. In the turmoil of settling dust and smell of scorched metal, he neither felt pain, nor did he hear surrounding shouts. Trauma and shock are the only explanation I have for Sergeant McCabe to have fought like a madman to crawl away from the men trying to administer aid in the aftermath. There he was: his face, neck, and hands covered in dirt and blood, his uniform hung in shreds, and his leg had twisted into something unrecognizable. Yet crawling to his vehicle with debris digging into his hands and dragging his busted leg, he refused first aid for himself. Sergeant McCabe had one single thing on his mind—and that was to rescue his men. To save Billy." Houston cleared the emotion from his throat. "By the time he reached the vehicle, he'd lost too much blood; McCabe collapsed and passed out."

Houston paused to let it sink in. Tim's mouth opened and closed on a grunt, but Houston's gaze remained focused on Bill. The mask of stone slowly transformed to a mirror of horror.

"McCabe didn't find out about the status of his men until days later—after he'd been stabilized, and part of his leg was amputated. This is how Sergeant McCabe lost his leg."

Eyes wide and red, Carol turned her blotched face from Houston to her husband. "Bill—"

Filled with heartbreak, tears, and sorrow, the single word punched against Houston's heart. "Yes. It was Sergeant McCabe who went to your son's grave. Because when he realized there wasn't a thing he could have done to save two of his men, a huge chunk inside him died with them."

Houston stood. He said what had to be said. Tim understood the impact of his words, Houston saw it in his eyes. But had Bill?

"Mr. Schuster, and Mrs. Schuster—I am deeply sorry for the loss of your son. I was Sergeant McCabe's Platoon Sergeant, and I was right there with him. So, if you want to blame someone, blame me. But know that, to this day, I trust him with my own life. He was one of the best, still is. And I am proud to call him friend."

Having lost his appetite, Houston stalked away, settling his bill.

CHAPTER 33

Saturday morning, Reid loaded Yard and Bones into his Jeep. "Guess what, buddy?" Reid muttered as he latched Bones' crate. "Today's your big day." Inside the kennel, Bones circled trice, flopped down, tilted his head, and focused black, liquid eyes on Reid. But damn if a streak of gloom didn't tug inside Reid's chest at those trustful eyes.

Driving to the city park, Reid flashed back to driving into in Oak Creek, when he rescued a worn-out bag of bones during a torrential downpour. He'd treated bleeding paws and fattened up the pooch until his ribs no longer poked through fur. Damn, he realized, he'd grown attached to the mutt. But saddling himself with another animal made zero sense. In a few weeks, he'd be hitting the road with Houston; the last thing he needed was another dog.

At the park's entrance, a humongous banner flapping with gusts of air greeted visitors with "Welcome to Barks in the Park."

Stunned by the number of folks strolling along paved lanes and grassy slopes, he leashed Bones and released him from his crate.

Low hanging banks of clouds hadn't stopped rescue dog advocates from coming to the park. Barks, yaps, and yodels sailing on a breeze affirmed a show of support. Mutts on towering legs and palm-sized canines in puppy strollers milled around with their owners, and as far as Reid could tell, most were Heinz 57's.

Reid strolled to the volunteer sign-in table with Bones trudging on crooked legs next to Yard. He passed the large pavilion where emergency services paraded their vehicles in a show of flashing lights. Reid spotted the K-9 unit who'd present a tracking demonstration later, reminding him of the dogs the Army employed.

At the table, Helen wagged a finger as he approached. "Reid, we missed you yesterday, but I heard you had an excellent excuse." Her smile seemed to excuse him from being late as she handed him a volunteer badge with the Barkville logo and his name printed in bold letters. In a conciliatory tone, she added, "I'm glad you could make it today."

"Yes, ma'am," Reid beamed his most charming smile. "Tell me what you want me to do and consider it done." With the number of volunteers milling around, he wasn't sure what he possibly could be doing.

"The mutt strut is about to kick off. After that, we'll have the first runway show of Barkville dogs."

Reid groaned. "A runway show? You've got to be kidding me."

"Yes. Our pooches will be so precious, dressed up to show off."

"Dressed up?" Reid scratched his head and pulled his earlobe. Never in his life had he heard such a ridiculous notion.

"Bones," Helen puckered her lips, smacking little kisses his way. "You will look so *cute* in a little dinner jacket and bow tie." Reid's eyes popped open. No way in hell was he parading a dog in a dinner jacket across a doggie runway.

"Oh yeah." Helen went on, oblivious to Reid's bunched eyebrows and downturned mouth. "We'll have several runway struts at different times throughout the day. Isn't that wonderful? The fur-babies will be so adorable, and adopters gobble it up."

Oh, hell, no, he thought. *Not me.* He'd tag Keira to flaunt Bones on the red mutt carpet. He searched in the crowd for her. Dammit, where was she?

Still stumped by Keira's odd mood change last night, Reid had felt a nagging in the pit of his stomach when he went to bed and it still bugged him this morning.

Reid had mulled over Houston's advice asking Keira to his appointment. He was hesitant at first; the fitting shouldn't be a big deal. Yet he'd been more nervous than a deer on a firing range. Because getting back to training was utmost on his mind?

Houston had made a solid point: Keira needed to know Reid trusted her. And while he felt safe opening up to her, admitting emotional vulnerability took a mountain of courage. On the other hand, she'd been with him at the E.R. and had experienced his shortcomings without the prosthesis. How humiliating could it be?

He shouldn't have been surprised when Keira gave her support without hesitation. As it turned out, her company calmed hidden anxieties. She'd cheered for him, congratulated him on the new device, and was happy he could move without crutches once more. Her expressions were genuine, of that he was sure.

The afternoon had gone great, Reid thought, if one considered an orthopedic appointment a good time. During the ride home, the conversation had been light and upbeat, and he'd been stunned when she revealed an unexpected passion. Reid chuckled. An image of her hiking in the Scottish Highlands interrupted his thoughts and he smiled. For one afternoon, he thought, she'd shed her bristles. Until he'd suggested dinner and a drink.

"If you're looking for Houston, he's circling the area, selling raffle tickets." Helen cut through his roaming thoughts, misinterpreting his searching gaze sweeping the crowd.

"I'll find him. See if he needs help," Reid said as he turned away from the table.

"Reid," Helen called after him. "Be sure to have Bones ready for the runway strut."

An unfavorable retort slipped to the tip of Reid's tongue, but he just lifted his hand in acknowledgment. "I can't wait," he said instead, the cynical undertone lost on the breeze.

What prompted Keira's sudden mood change? Reid couldn't wrap his head around it. When she pulled up at the cabin, he'd reined in a caveman instinct to yank her into his arms and kiss her senseless. Instead he gave her a respectfully chaste kiss on the cheek. He'd toned down on the sarcasm, too, which he contributed to her relaxed attitude. But the moment he'd mentioned celebrating with dinner and a drink, the air inside the Jeep froze. Arriving back at the cabin, he'd thought of inviting her inside, a notion he'd dismissed at the same moment her body stiffened under his touch.

Reid headed to the bandstand, the dogs trotting on leashes beside him. To his surprise, the half-pint Bones snapped and growled at some of the passing dogs, while Yard didn't seem to be bothered by the hustle and bustle.

Jeez, what had Helen roped him into, he thought as he passed the kissing booth Tessa had constructed under Houston's supervision. "Something cute," Helen Miller had said. He stopped and inspected the pink-and-white striped contraption. Decorated with painted dogs wearing hats, bow ties, necklaces, and hair bows, Tessa had delivered. In bright pink letters, *Puppy Kisses* was painted above the cut-out window.

"Looks like rain," a stranger said to her companion as they passed Reid. "Yeah," Reid overheard, "it wasn't supposed to until later. Maybe it'll hold off."

He spotted Keira taking pictures of the mayor and Haley as they launched the annual mutt strut. For her mother's magazine or Barkville Rescue? *Most likely for both*, Reid thought. Jeez, obviously her plate was filled to the brim. Why was that?

Closing the distance, Reid observed Keira shaking the mayor's hand. His attention turned to a middle-aged couple ambling from the parking lot onto the lawn.

The sight of Bill Schuster froze him to the spot. For Chrissakes.

A wave of hostility fired through Reid's cells; his pulse jumped as the accident surged through his mind. A coincidence or an intentional meeting? On impulse, Reid stepped forward and turned in the opposite direction. Sooner or later, he'd have to deal with Schuster, but this was no place for confrontation. And to face him here would undoubtedly turn into an unwanted public display of aggression.

Reid swung around and strolled up the embankment where the emergency vehicles formed a line along the edge of the parking lot. He recognized Josh, the EMT he'd talked to after the accident. With a quick nod, Reid acknowledged him and smiled at the three boys listening with curious interest at what Josh was saying. It reminded Reid of himself at that age, wavering between becoming a firefighter or ambulance driver. Instead, he became a soldier who fell right in with protecting his country and its people.

"Josh," Reid greeted the EMT when the kid's parents ushered them along and shook his hand.

"Reid," Josh clasped a hand to Reid's arm. "It's great to see you. How are you doing?"

"Great. I'm doing great. As you can see, Humpty Dumpty is put together again." He'd said it in a joking tone, but the smile left his features when someone behind him said, "Oh, look at this little guy, Bill. Isn't he the cutest thing you've ever seen?"

"Hold on, Carol," the male voice answered.

The hairs raised on Reid's neck, and his face darkened. He recognized that voice. He'd only heard it once, but he didn't need the prickles on his neck to know who it belonged to. Slowly, he turned his head and found himself in precisely the situation he'd aimed to avoid—face to face with Bill Schuster.

A bag of stones dropped into his stomach as his gaze skipped over Bill and back to Josh. "I've got to go, but thanks again for your help last Saturday. Good seeing you, Josh."

"No problem. I was just doing my job. Take care, Reid."

As Reid turned his back on Josh, his gaze bore into Bill's eyes. "Excuse me," he said and tugged on the dog's leashes, stepping away.

At the very least, Reid had expected a mean-spirited comment, a degree of hostility, or even a combative attitude. Instead, Bill's eyes shifted as if searching for something to settle on. He dropped his head, and his throat cleared with a chest-rumbling grunt as Reid stepped passed him, putting distance between them.

"Sergeant McCabe," Bill's voice came from behind.

Reid kept walking.

A hand shot out, grabbing Reid's arm. "I've got something I need to say." Yard's hackles went up, a low grow rumbled in his throat. Bill dropped his hand.

Reid swiveled around, a warning in his voice, and ice in his eyes. "You don't want to go there. Not here." But somehow Bill seemed deflated, Reid didn't see the anger and aggression he'd expected. What happened to soften him? he wondered.

"Look, Sergeant McCabe ..."

"I'm not a Sergeant anymore, Mr. Schuster. I'm a civilian. I'd appreciate you dropping the Sergeant."

Bill cleared his throat. "Very well, McCabe." And abruptly, it gushed out of him. "I owe you an apology, is what I'm trying to say."

Reid's head snapped up. What the fuck was happening here? Bill's wife had caught up, and Bill took her hand.

"I need to set something right, Mr. McCabe. For you, and my wife, but most importantly, for Billy. I didn't expect I'd run into you here, but now I want to get this off my conscience. That picnic table over there, it's vacant. Give me five minutes?"

Reid's head spun with suspicion at the sudden change of tune, but he wanted to hear where this was going.

At the table, Bill kept Carol's hand in his when he said, "McCabe, I've had my head so far up a bull's ass that I couldn't see anything but darkness. I didn't see how it ruined me and how this hurt good people." He looked at Carol, who gave him an encouraging nod.

"My grief for Billy was a horrible beast. It dug into my gut, sliced me to pieces, and began to eat me from the inside out. The more I drowned it in booze, the stronger the hate grew. And I hated your guts, McCabe. So much that I wanted to see you suffer as much as Billy did."

Reid's face hardened. Bill's words had punched a hole into Reid's chest. "Is that what happened on Saturday? You wanted to punish me?"

Bill groaned, ran a hand through thinning strands of hair. "I'd lie if I said I hadn't thought about it. But no. I couldn't do something like that. It was my heart that caused the accident. I know 'sorry' won't heal the injuries, but that's all I have."

Reid's strained facial muscles relaxed.

"I've learned the truth, McCabe. Someone finally gave me answers about what happened to Billy. It was excruciating to hear, and I fought it, tried to deny it. And I realized what I was doing was discrediting everyone on that convoy who stood in the face of terror."

Bill swallowed hard, but he kept his gaze on Reid, his voice drenched with grief. "And now I know what truly happened." The air felt saturated with sorrow. "I miss my boy so much, but there are no words for the depth of my gratitude for what you've been through trying to save him."

Bill fell silent.

Reid lowered his head and pinched the bridge of his nose between index finger and thumb. This he hadn't seen coming. He'd wanted a talk with Bill Schuster, but not here, not now. But surprisingly, it felt right—amidst a lively atmosphere and hopeful folk. Amidst life. A fresh start for many of the animals stood as a well-timed opportunity for wiping clean old debts.

"Mr. Schuster," he said when he looked up. "I only knew Billy for a little over two years; long enough to know he was an outstanding soldier and an incredible young man. I was his Sergeant, and I didn't take this responsibility lightly. I would have protected him with my own life."

Reid paused; his pulse kicked up a notch. "Believe me, there is not one day that goes by that I don't think about the two men I lost." He stood, reached across his chest and pushed up the sleeve of his T-shirt. "Do you see this?"

Bill released Carol's hand and stood, too. At first, he squinted, then his eyes popped. Tattooed on Reid's bicep was a large bald eagle's head with two dog tags hanging from its neck. Inscribed on one was Billy F. Schuster, his company, date of birth, and date of death.

Next to Bill, Carol gasped.

"He's with me all the time. Here," Reid clasped his arm. "And here." He punched a fist against his chest.

Water pooled in Bill's eyes as he rested a heavy hand on Reid's shoulders. "I don't know what to say. Except, I'm deeply sorry. For my ignorance, and the pain it added. Can you find a way to forgive me?"

Reid stared at Bill, blood pounding in his ears. Bill had forgiven him, could he do the same? Emotion welled in his eyes. In a mutual understanding, the men embraced, bonding in honor of Billy.

"One day," Reid said, stepping away so Carol could hug his neck, "I'd like to tell you everything about Billy, the soldier."

"We would like that," Carol said, smiling up at Bill.

"I've misjudged you, Mr. McCabe. But what you're doing with Heroes Rise is an excellent choice." Bill shook Reid's hand, "Best of luck to you."

***

A harrowing chance-meeting, but Reid felt light on his feet as he strode away from the picnic table. The air felt swollen with moisture, and he hoped for the sake of the event that the predicted rain would pass quickly.

The runway strut was not scheduled for another hour. By this time, the last of the mutt-strut stragglers should have been back with plenty of time in-between activities. He had to find Keira, and he spotted her waving a hand in the air.

"Reid." Her smile appeared reserved. "I was looking for Bones."

"That hurts," Reid clenched his teeth, pulling down the corners of his mouth. "I thought you were looking for me, Mossy." With playful curiosity, he tilted his head, wrapped an arm around Keira's shoulder, and kissed her temple. Had she stiffened once more under his touch?

He dropped his arm, saying, "You were looking for him because you'll take him for his runway debut? I thought it wasn't scheduled for another hour."

"Oh, no. It's too early for that. Besides, I'm not taking him to the strut." Keira shook her head. "Bones is used to you, so that's *your* job. I'm already walking a few we brought from the shelter. Your boy will get great attention at the kissing booth. Until the red-carpet prance, it's my turn there."

Reid gave her a lopsided grin. "What do you need a booth for, we can kiss right here." *To hell with chaste kisses,* he thought and cupped her head. But Keira backed up. "Reid, no."

Reid's eyebrows shot up; his questioning gaze locked with hers. Keira gave a dismissive wave of her hand. "Not with all these people. Besides, I'm on the job."

"Who cares?" he said, but let it pass. "Bones, buddy, go with Keira. She'll get you all kissed up. Okay?" Reid wiggled his eyebrows at him, handing the dog's leash to Keira. "Have you seen Houston?"

"I saw him by the bandstand earlier. No telling where he is now."

"All right, take care of my boy. I'll see you later." Mystified by Keira's coolness, Reid stalked off searching for Houston.

He found him chatting with two middle-aged women who laughed at something he'd just said.

"Hey, Mack," Houston excused himself as Reid drew near. "Where is Bones?"

"He's about to get kissed at that pink contraption you built."

Houston laughed. "The kissing booth. Yeah. It's a great fundraiser, plus the pooches get attention. But hey. You were talking to Schuster. I kept my eyes on the situation; it looked friendly enough. Everything all right?"

"Man, you wouldn't believe it. I have no idea what happened, but he did a one-eighty. He claimed to understand now what happened on that patrol; asked me to forgive him for his pigheadedness. You know anything about that?"

"Who? Me? Not a thing, bro." Changing the subject, Houston raised his eyes to the sky, studying the thickening clouds. "Man, it's going to rain. Here, take some tickets and sell, sell, sell before it comes down. Someone will win a cruise."

Reid accepted the tickets. "Later," he said, and took off toward the kissing booth. His head wasn't in the game right now. He thought of Keira and her response to his lips pressed against her temple. Had it been his imagination, or had she met his greeting with the same enthusiasm she'd welcome a migraine headache? Although he didn't have a clue what could have caused her indifference, he'd asked himself the same question a hundred times since coming back from Louisville last night.

At first, he'd shrugged it off as a woman thing, but that didn't sit right. Not for Keira. She wasn't one to hold back or to play games. And damn if he wouldn't find out what wadded her britches.

As he came up to the booth, a young girl smacked a kiss on Bones' head, and started a one-sided conversation with the dog while petting him. Bones lapped it up, and this pinched Reid's insides. Two couples were in line. Dropping bills into a jar, the first coupled took their turn and had a million questions about the brown furball. What was his name? How old was he? Was he good with kids?

Reid leaned against a tree trunk with his arms crossed, studying Keira. He'd have to give credit to his pal, he thought. Houston had been spot-on in assessing Reid's motivation where Keira was concerned.

As Reid watched her, a ball of fire answering questions with a blush of enthusiasm on her cheeks, his thoughts raced to Sunday afternoon. Keira's cheekbones had worn the same sweet blush, put there by the growing heat between them.

Keira must have felt his stare because she turned her head, peered at him with surprise, and returned her attention to the potential adopters at her booth.

Reid's gaze drew to the column of her neck above a navy-blue V-neck T-shirt. His fingertips had traced the slender line, and they remembered—the warmth of her soft skin, the prickles his touch had raised, the slump of her body under the caresses of his hands. He felt her reddish blonde locks glide through his fingers like silk. How he had wanted to hold her, kiss her, make love to her. *Damn Bones*, he thought, but he smiled. Because there was no mistaking, she'd wanted it, too. Their fuse had been set afire on their first and only dinner date, which seemed an eternity ago. Despite its hisses and fizzles, it had maintained heat. And like a superior firecracker fuse, once lit, there was no turning back.

Jesus, he thought, pushing away from the tree. This wasn't the time to imagine what making love with her would feel like.

From the kissing booth, snippets of conversation flowed Reid's way, letting him believe the second couple was taking their leave. About time, he needed a few minutes alone with Keira.

Inside his chest a tight ball of emotion expanded, seeping into his every cell. She made him feel things he didn't know existed; hadn't known before. Things that softened a man's insides and boosted his spirits. She challenged him, and the spars they'd traded? He smiled, because if his hunch was right, Keira got a kick out of teasing him, too.

She treated him as if the missing leg wasn't a sure turn-off; and under the most terrifying circumstances, she'd experienced the nightmares of PTSD. Finding herself in a scene of a horror movie would have been the breaking point for anyone else. But not Keira, he thought. She's a tough one. It was hard to explain, but her strength mixed with warmth and softness; it was the precise blend he found himself crazy about.

Reid watched the booth. The couple prepared to leave, but the woman turned back, and Keira handed her something. A Barkville flyer, maybe.

Reid drew a long breath. He wanted her—no-nonsense, bristly, spirited, yet warm, kind-hearted, and considerate, wrapped up in one package— he wanted all of it, but more than that, he wanted to steal her time. They felt strange; these fierce emotions he never knew existed, and Reid realized he was falling for her. He exhaled slowly. Jesus, if he was truthful, it scared the crap out of him.

Finally, the couple left. No one else was in line, and Reid took his chance, strutting up to the booth. "Kisses, one-dollar donation," a sign said. "I want to buy a kiss," he said and dropped a twenty into the jar.

Keira's eyes widened. "What are you doing? You don't need to buy a kiss. You can kiss him at any time." A gust of wind lifted her hair and whipped it across her face.

"Can I?" Reid crossed his arms on the window opening. "Consider it a donation." Keira held Bones up on a little ledge, but he didn't look at the dog who licked Reid's chin; his eyes bore into hers. Awareness of what was about to happen dawned, and Keira nervously swiped at the lock of hair clinging to her cheek. Reid didn't wait for an answer. Reaching through the cut-out, he took her face in both hands, and while lowering his mouth to hers, he locked her gaze. Shock mirrored in Keira's eyes as lightning zagged through the sky at the precise moment.

Thunder cracked the air, and Bones bolted. Slipping from Keira's hands, he jumped the distance from the ledge to the ground and took off like a racehorse at the starting gate.

For a split-second Keira froze, another stormy day flicked through her memory—how on that afternoon in Reid's cabin the sound of hail against the window panes had sent him into a state of alarm. Would the sudden thunder do the same?

Thank God, Reid seemed okay, with no signs of a flashback. Keira and Reid flew apart, both calling Bones at the same time. Yard yapped and strained against his leash. Did the storm scare Yard, or did he want to chase after Bones? Reid didn't know but wouldn't take a chance unleashing him.

"Bones!" Reid shouted. "Come back." His command was in vain; the rushing water dumping from the sky swallowed his yells.

"Bones!" Goddammit. He'd been afraid the dog running off would happen sooner or later. Reid's mouth set in a hard line. Since the mutt had regained his strength and confidence, the daredevil had wandered off into the woods behind the cabin on two separate occasions. Reid had ended his excursions by keeping him on the leash. Yet, Reid's jaw tightened, now it had happened.

The wind whipped, billowing his soaked T-shirt, and throwing his words back into his face. Within seconds Reid was drenched, his shorts clinging in wet folds around his thighs. He hurried after the disappearing dog. As he did, his shoes squished on patches of mud. His foot slipped. *Jesus, the prosthesis. Not again,* he thought as he stumbled, propelled forward, but lost traction and hit the ground while holding on to Yard's leash.

Keira, soaked to her bones, appeared unconcerned about the torrent washing over her as she sprinted to Reid. The sharp crack of thunder had silenced her scream to watch out when he'd stumbled. "Are you all right?" she shouted above the gusting wind, grabbing Yard's leash.

"I'm okay," he yelled back, and shook his head when Keira held out her hand to help him up. "Go after Bones, I'll need just need a minute."

"Not until I know you're all right," Keira said, and gaped as he positioned the prosthesis, rolled to his good side and took a four-point kneeling position. When he finally pushed himself off the ground, taking a few tentative steps, she exhaled. No injuries; he seemed to be all right.

Yard's muscles strained, pulling at Keira. Interpreting the dog's body language, Reid understood Yard's urge to chase after Bones, and motioned for Keira to unleash him. "Get Bones," he called out as thunder clapped, and the dog shot off the leash like a bullet.

Continuing the search, Reid veered to the right and Keira to the left. They kept a distance between them to better spot the mutt and kept calling his name.

When Reid scraped the pooch's pitiful hide off the road on the outskirts of Oak Creek, it had poured like this. By then

Bones must have wandered for days, maybe even weeks. Had he taken off during another thunderstorm? Most likely.

"We have to find him," Reid shouted.

"We'll keep searching until we do," Keira shouted back.

Word of Bones' vanishing act had spread like a flash. By now, other volunteers, alerted by the frenzied shouts, fanned out and joined the search.

"Poor thing. He's scared, but I'm sure he'll be back," Haley offered, but Reid didn't believe so. Fifteen minutes into the search, the sky lightened, and the downpour changed to a steady drizzle. Visitors to the event had fled to their cars, and while some drove off, others stuck it out. None of the volunteers had left. They took shelter insider their vehicles and huddled under the protective roofs of pavilions; the spring storm with all its bluster would fizzle out soon, and "Barks in the Park" would go on.

"Reid," Keira said. "He's gone. He took off towards the woods. He's scared to death, and he'll run. But I have an idea. Come with me." She started toward the parking lot. "Let's take your Jeep."

Reid shook his head. "I don't know. Where are we going? And what if he comes back here? He'll be searching for me."

"Haley and all the volunteers will be looking for him. They'll catch him if he comes back. But I doubt he'll return. From what you told me about how you found him? He'll keep going. Let's go. I'll fill you in as we go."

With Yard in the back and Keira in the passenger seat, Reid shoved the gear into reverse and backed out of the parking space.

"It's a long shot," Keira said. "But he went into the woods, and your place is on the other side of it. It would make sense if he tore off to a place of safety. This has been his home for the past weeks." Keira fished her phone from the front pocket of her shorts and punched a number. "I need to let Haley know we're heading out."

Ten minutes later, Reid turned the Jeep into the driveway to his cabin, and they both jumped out of the vehicle at the same time. Reid released Yard.

"Bones," they called, spreading in opposite directions. "Come here, boy," Reid took the path into the forest, Yard stuck his nose to the ground, sniffing and tracking, and Keira went to the back of the house. "Bones," she called. "It's all right, baby."

From a distance, Reid's voice thinned, "Bones …"

Having come no closer to glimpsing the dog, Keira rounded the cabin at the same time as Reid and Yard emerged from the woods. With hair plastered against their scalps and clothes fused to their bodies, they looked at each other across the clearing. Reid lifted his arms in defeat, and Keira drew a breath, shaking her head. "I'm sorry. I thought there was a chance he'd come here."

Yard raised his ears, cocked his head, and scurried to the porch with his tail swinging in frenzied circles. "Reid, look." From under the porch, a furry face stuck out, and black eyes skipped from Reid to Keira and Yard.

Keira crouched, coaxing the dog out with Yard beside her as Reid looked on. When she stood, she held a shivering Bones in her arms. Her eyes glinted with triumph. "Told ya," she said, shaking as badly as the dog.

Soreness slammed against healing ribs, but at the same time relief rolled over Reid. The dog had found his way home. Home? Reid thought. Hell yeah. Home.

Reid smiled. Yes, he'd adopt the mutt, but for now he'd keep it to himself. There was time for that later.

CHAPTER 34

"Your lips are turning blue, Mossy. You need to dry off. We all do."

Untroubled, Yard shook the water from his fur and trotted up the porch steps. Inside, Reid tossed a rag to Keira. While she dried Bones, he went to the bathroom for towels. When he strolled back into the great room, Yard was lying head-to-tail on the rug by the sofa, and Keira crouched, settling a worn-out Bones in his dog bed.

She pushed to her feet, reaching for the oversized bath towel, but Reid slung it around her shoulders and pulled her in. "I haven't thanked you for your brilliant suggestion in finding Bones." He smiled, and his eyes smiled with him.

"Reid." She grabbed the edges of the towel, twisting aside, but he pulled her closer. "I'm just relieved he came back here," she said, pressing her palms against his chest. "We found him; it's all that matters. I need to get back to the park now. Can you take me?"

The pleading look in her eyes clawed at his heart. "Why, Keira?" He wouldn't force her to stay, if that's not what she wanted, but by God, she owed him an explanation. "You're soaked to the bones, and you're cold—the shivering and that blue tint on your lips don't lie. Looks to me you could use some warming up."

He brushed his lips to hers with a soft murmur. "Yes, definitely cold. But I know how to fix that."

"Reid, no."

Deliberately slow, he draped the cloth over her shoulders, dropped his hands, and stepped back. The increasing pressure of her palms against his chest had turned the gray in his eyes to slate.

"All right, Mossy. I'm not sure what's going on here, but I'm getting the distinct feeling something is brewing inside of you. And whatever that may be, it's muddling the waters between us."

"Reid—"

"I'm listening, Mossy."

Keira fisted the towel over her chest and peeled her gaze from his face. Inside her wet clothes, her shoulders shook, and her teeth chattered uncontrollably.

"But first, you need to get into something dry; you're chattering like a rattler." There was a tenderness in his voice.

"The towel's sufficient," Keira said as Reid started toward the bedroom. "I'll be fine, if you just take me home."

Half-way to the bedroom, Reid threw an exasperated look over his shoulder. "I will, just as soon as you tell me what the hell is going on between us."

From the pile of clothes he'd slung over the back of a chair, he pulled a flannel shirt and a pair of light-weight sweat pants. When he entered the great room, he stopped mid-stride.

Keira stood leaned over, towel-drying her hair. He stared at her rubbing the tangled mess, swallowing the dust in his throat. His gaze skipped to the T-shirt clinging to her chest; had he ever seen anything sexier than a woman clad in wet clothes, standing in his great room drying her hair? Sensing him, Keira straightened and shook out her curls. Glossy and wet, they settled over her shoulders. God, he wanted her.

"Looks like you're hell-bent on wearing my clothes, Mossy." Despite being pissed at her obvious detachment, amusement laced Reid's voice as he remembered the last time he'd lent her a similar outfit. "It's becoming a trend."

The memory of his mind taking him on a bad trip right as she'd relaxed smacked against him, and the smile faded from his face.

"Not funny." Keira huffed, slung the towel around her shoulders, and accepted the dry clothes. Holding them in front of her as if shielding herself from his eyes, she marched off to the bathroom.

Reid ambled into the kitchen and took two short water tumblers from the cabinet. There was a pressure against his heart that felt bitter, and sweet, and he ached for her as he'd never ached for another woman before.

Keira came out of the bathroom to find Reid waiting for her by the dining table. She expected a smart-mouthed remark about the bunched-up sleeves of the shirt, or the too-long pants she'd rolled up to her ankles. Instead, he took in her appearance with a cool gaze and a twist of his mouth. From the table, he picked up a glass sloshing with two fingers of amber liquid in it and handed it to her. "Here, have this. It'll warm your insides."

Shifting her gaze between Reid and the glass in her hand, she raised her eyebrows. A quick sniff, and she pulled down the corners of her mouth. "What is this?" Suspicion laced her voice. "You're trying to get me drunk?"

"Wouldn't dream of it, Mossy. I'm trying to warm you up. In case you haven't looked in the bathroom mirror, your lips still wear that purplish shade that says *cold*."

Reid lifted his glass and tossed the Maker's Mark back with one great gulp. "Ah …" he sat his glass down, smacked his lips and ran the back of his hand across his mouth. "It helps. I will change now—and then we'll talk." Before she could answer, he brushed his knuckles over her cheek bones. "Drink, Mossy. You'll feel better."

The light and tender touch sent a new wave of chills along her back which he must have taken for a shudder of cold. "There's a throw on the sofa, grab it if you want."

Reid turned and left Keira shivering, holding her glass.

***

As she watched him troop out of the room, misery rolled through Keira and punched against her heart. So strong and tough, and brave, she thought as her gaze fell on the prosthesis. And handsome, intense, and heart-smashing. The soft touch of his knuckles grazing across her cheekbone. Keira curled her fingers and traced along the heat his touch had put there.

She didn't want to talk or drink or get cozy on the sofa—not with him so close to her again. *Too dangerous*, she thought, giving in to the powerful need to get lost in his touch. Or drown in his eyes, letting the storm in them take her away. And she suspected that this was exactly what was about to happen.

She breathed in his scent clinging to the shirt, a faint mix of ocean fresh and outdoors, and took a sharp breath. No, this could not be; not if she didn't want to listen to the sound of her heart crushing to dust.

As had Reid, she tossed back the bourbon with a swift swig. The liquid burned down her throat and settled in her stomach as a licking flame.

Reid, dressed in a fresh pair of cargo shorts and a faded T-shirt bearing the Army logo, sauntered into the room carrying two bottles of water. Keira huddled in the sofa's corner; a pillow pressed against her chest. Yard had taken over one of the upholstered chairs, Reid's open rucksack sat in the other.

"You're warm now?" He didn't have to ask. The bourbon had flushed her face, and she'd shrugged the throw off her shoulders. Her curls were tighter, now that her hair was drying, and he had the sudden urge to bury his hands in the glossy mess.

"Yes, thank you. You were right, the bourbon helped with that."

Mellow, he thought. She'd mellowed.

Reid handed her a bottle, and twisting the cap off his own, he sunk into the cushion next to her. With plenty of space between them, he scrunched his good leg onto the seat and swiveled his body toward her.

Downing his water, he fixed his eyes on Keira. Gray met jade in search for answers and found apprehension. Not taking his eyes off her, he capped the bottle, and without preamble he reached straight for the core of the matter.

"What's going on between us, Mossy?"

Her gaze remained steady, but she straightened her spine, and tightened her clasp on the pillow.

"Reid—"

"I've missed you," Reid cut in, suddenly afraid he wouldn't be able to tell her how he felt if she spoke first.

"All week I've missed you like crazy" he said. "Until I saw you again, yesterday." Hearing him say it out loud was a stunning revelation, but he wasn't embarrassed to admit it.

Keira dropped her head and closed her eyes as she listened.

"When I saw you driving up in that impossibly bright yellow bug of yours to go with me to Louisville? I wanted nothing more than yank you into my arms and keep you there. I still want that, Mossy."

Dropping the pillow into her lap, and her elbows onto it, Keira palmed her face.

"But it's not what you want now, or what you wanted yesterday, am I right?"

He didn't expect Keira to respond, and she didn't; she just buried her face deeper into her hands. It didn't stop him. Whatever it took, he'd go toe-to-toe with the shadow that kept her apart from him. Reid continued; he didn't move his eyes off her.

"At the appointment, your being there, and on the drive home, hearing that excitement in your voice, seeing your eyes sparkle with it, we had a great vibe going. No teasing, no B.S., just a real good connection. Until we got back. And this morning at the park, I wondered why you seemed embarrassed when I kissed you." Reid rubbed the back of his neck. "Jeez, I'm as confused as Punxsutawney Phil predicting the weather. And just now, you can't wait to get out of here ... why, Keira?"

"You're right. And I'm sorry, I'm so sorry ... It's all wrong." Spoken into her hands, the words came muffled.

"What's that supposed to mean, 'it's all wrong'—Keira, please look at me," he urged, his tone gentle.

After an endless moment, she dropped her hands and tilted her head, and he saw the moisture clinging to her lashes. It slashed at him. Damn, he wanted to cradle her, soothe whatever needled her, but suspected it would be the wrong thing to do. Instead, he reached for one of her hands, pried it from the pillow. Still cool to the touch, he clasped her hand in his, half-expecting her to withdraw.

"Care to share what's changed since Sunday?" he asked and watched the blush on her face go cardinal red.

Keira pulled back. "Sunday was a mistake." Her hand slashed the air. "I came to check on you after the accident, see if you needed anything. And you did; well, Bones did. I shouldn't have stayed after dropping him back off to you. And before you ask—yesterday, I came here to support you." Her arms crossed over the pillow as she leaned forward. "You can always count on me for that. For anything, Reid. But, it can't go beyond that; we don't have a *thing* between us."

Keira twisted the cap on her bottle, raised the container to her lips, and tilted her head. Reid couldn't tear his gaze from her neck; despite her words, his pulse ticked up. Her hand shook, her voice trembled, and Reid hadn't missed it.

"There isn't, huh?" he said, dragging his fingers through the short crop of his hair. "But you're wrong, Mossy. Because there already is." He searched her eyes. "From the first time you showed up here, it's been simmering between us. Come to think of it, it's been simmering since you plowed me over at the pet store. I know it, and you know it, too."

"I—" Green eyes flashed with denial.

His eyes challenged. "Don't say it." Despite the somber heart-to-heart, his mouth curved into a wry smile. "You know it, Mossy. There's no use denying it."

Keira looked at her hands, studying the soft pink gloss of her nails.

Forlorn and down, he'd never seen her this cheerless. He couldn't take it. Any barb, or snide remark was better than this. Reid moved with unexpected agility, unable to restrain himself any longer. He grabbed her shoulders and as she tumbled against his side, he cupped her face in his hand. "Maybe we need a refresher?" he said, smiling down at her.

Surprise widened her eyes at the unexpected move, and she stilled as his mouth suddenly hovered too close.

"Don't, Reid." Her breath fluttered across his cheeks.

"What are you afraid of, Mossy?" His hand dipped below her jawline, found the curve of her neck, and discovered her vein pulsing with erratic speed.

Keira blinked and shook her head. "It's complicated."

"It doesn't have to be." Reid sunk his gaze into the cool jade of her eyes while his own grays darkened, matching the storm within.

"But it is." Keira broke eye contact first. She scooted away from him, settling against the sofa's back, but he kept his arm around her shoulder. Light and non-threatening, it was a gesture of comfort. She didn't object.

"You don't understand, Reid." A quick shiver shook her shoulder, and she crossed her arms.

"You're damn right, Mossy. I don't. So, why don't you fill me in?"

"I've made a mess of this," she huffed. "I admit, I wanted a *thing* between us, too. Or I thought I did." Keira hesitated. "But I should have known."

Reid stilled. The admission sounded uncomfortable and resigned. "Known what, Mossy?"

"Remember when I came here the day after you rescued Bones?"

"How could I forget?"

"You were such an asshole, Reid. Your attitude all arrogance and bluster. Cocksure, and just a little intimidating."

"But I am not anymore?" Amused, his lips pulled into a one-sided smirk.

"Ha, you wish, mister. You're all that and then some," Keira shot a weak smile at him. "You rescued two dogs—adopting one, fostering the other—your caring side gave you heart, and that intrigued me. Rough and tender ... yeah, it intrigued me." She gave him a quick smile. "Jeez, I'm rambling."

"But I like it." A playful tug on her hair, and he said, "Hmm, intriguing ... don't think anyone ever called me that. Then why are you backing off?"

"You're not making this easy, you know?"

"I told you, it doesn't have to be difficult," Reid groaned. Keira had found traction, and he had a hunch he wouldn't like what came next.

"You invited me to dinner, and that's when things changed."

Reid stiffened at the memory that stood too clear in his mind. Her reaction to the amputation as painful now as it had been on that evening. A misunderstanding, she'd said, apologizing a million times. But it had torn him, more than he would admit, and it had stuck. And right now, the blood pounded in his ears. Truth or dare—he wanted truth; needed to hear her say the words.

Reid drew to the edge of his seat, dragged his injured leg into Keira's field of vision, and clasped the piston with one hand. Leaning toward her, his gaze was cool detachment, his voice deceptively calm. "Tell me right now—and I want no feel-good B.S. answer—does this contraption bother you? Is that it? Because when the intrigue wore off, and the ugliness of it hit home, you decided it was just not possible to continue what we started? And make no mistake, we started *something*." His pulsed raced as he waited for her answer.

"Reid ..." Keira shot forward in her seat. "Reid," she uttered on a soft plea. She cupped her hand to his cheek, locked her gaze to him. "No, please no. Not another misunderstanding. This contraption, as you say, doesn't bother me. Not one bit. Never has. How can I make you understand that this is my truth?"

His eyes stayed on hers for another moment and the warmth returned.

"Jesus, Reid. In hindsight, I don't blame you for throwing me out. I should have backed off then, let things go."

It was his turn to apologize. He'd made an ass of himself. Again. Hadn't he known this truth already? But caught up in this tangle of emotions, he needed to know, once and for all. Jesus. The one thing Reid had feared most, turned out to be an unfounded matter. Her answer calmed him, and until now, he didn't realize just how much this meant. At the same time, he mulled over the reason she backtracked.

"Then what changed for you that evening?"

"You kissed me." Only a whisper, she cupped his cheek for a moment longer before she jerked away as if she'd touched a scorching hot stove burner. She drew a long breath, let it out slow.

Reid stared. He swallowed hard; this he hadn't seen coming. What was tumbling through her head? What did that first kiss have to do with anything?

"Damn, Mossy, can you confuse me just a little more?" He took her face in his hands, gave it a lopsided grin, teasing her, "It was that bad, huh?" Low and seductive, his lips feathered over hers. "So, if there was anything wrong with it, we should practice more."

"No." Her breath fluttered against his lips. Her struggle was emotional, he felt the indecision in the stiffening of her body and the balling of her hands.

"No?" He breathed into her. "Tell me to stop." She didn't move, and Reid knew it to be a tipping point. His stomach tightened. He waited for a second longer; his head tilted, and his mouth closed over hers. Soft and warm, he led her into a gentle kiss. When he opened her mouth and she answered the brush of his tongue, the ball of emotions busted open inside his chest.

Keira drew away, but Reid held her, pulled her head against his chest. And missed the rapid-blinking eyelids trying to bat away tears. "I've missed you, Mossy. All week I thought of how much I want you and knew you wanted me, too. I still feel it, Mossy. Tell me, am I wrong?"

Inside his embrace, she shook her head. "I care for you; more than I'd like to admit. But I just can't be with you."

Reid groaned and released her. "It's the damn attack, isn't it? I scared the shit out of you. I should have known."

A swipe at her eyes, a shove at her hair, and Keira hugged herself. It made sense, he thought. Would she ever feel safe with him?

"No, Reid. I feel secure with you," she said, as if she'd read his mind. "Would I have agreed to go out with you the next day if I thought it was unsafe?"

"Then let's cut through the chase, Mossy. Because I don't understand. What's the real reason for backing off?"

Keira dropped her hand into her lap. In the set of her jaw, her straight posture, the clasping of hands, he could see she called upon her strength to own up.

"When I said I cared for you?" She paused, her eyes searching his. Reid waited. "I lied."

A groan rumbled from his throat, and Keira jumped to her feet. A stream of words rushed, toppled, and they made not a lick of sense to him.

"Hell yeah, I felt the attraction. Pretty much from the moment of that first kiss. No, I take that back, when you showed up at the rescue with breakfast." A quick laugh, and she went on. "Honestly, I thought it was crazy. I mean, who does something like this, but you gripped my attention. And we won't need to rehash the dreadful misunderstanding again. As I said, I should have let it go. Chalk it up as a bad mistake. But no; not me. Now I had something to prove." She threw him a poignant gaze. "Let you know I didn't care, that it made no difference."

Now Reid dropped his elbows on his knees, cradling his face in his hands, and listened. She cared for him, and that's all that mattered to him in that moment.

"The ambush in the woods. Yeah, scary as hell, but you know what? When I realized it was you chasing me, every cell of my body recognized you wouldn't harm me. But, in that moment, my heart broke for you."

Her tone was matter of fact. Heartfelt, he thought. No pity, and this was an important difference.

"But your accident; it changed things once again." She paced the length of the room with her arms crossed. From the chair, Yard lifted his head, yawned, and closed his eyes again.

"And the evening at the E.R.? Another piece of my heart shattered. When you called with news of the accident, I wept with relief—you were okay. On Sunday I came to check on you when I knew I shouldn't; but it was the right thing to do."

Reid couldn't listen to the disguised anguish in her voice and sit still. His head shot up, he pushed to his feet, and with three long strides he was next to her. Placing his hands on top of her shoulders, he tilted his head, "What exactly are you saying, Mossy?"

Keira didn't flinch as he drew her gaze to him. "I care for you, Reid. But worse, I've fallen for you—and I can't handle it. Please, will you take me home?"

He let out a ragged breath. At a loss for words he stared at her, emotions churning his gut. His throat worked at swallowing the growing lump pushing up. He didn't want to take her home. Not until he understood.

"On account of repeating myself and sounding like a dumb-ass, I don't understand, Mossy."

"Oh, for Pete's sake," she shrugged his hands from her shoulders. "Don't you understand what I just said? I'm in love with you, Reid. There, I said it." Keira turned her back, tromping off, but Reid was right behind her, snagging her shoulders, turning her back to him.

"And why is that such a goddamn problem?"

"Oh, you're a slick one, soldier. Hell, you don't know how close I came to sleeping with you. Last Sunday, I wanted to. If it hadn't been for Bones …" She shrugged a shoulder. "But it's like playing with matches; be careful not to set the house on fire."

Reid threw his hands into the air. "Damn, woman, can you repeat that in plain English? 'Cause this guy," he jerked a thumb at his chest, "doesn't get it."

"Okay. I'm sorry." She thrust her head back and gulped a lungful of air. When she spoke again, her voice had calmed. "This is a little nerve-racking for me, too. Let me try again.

"I only fell in love once before; during my backpacking trip I told you about. Ages ago. I met him two days after arriving at my aunt and uncle's place in Ireland." Keira tugged at her hair, crossed her arms, and let them fall to her side again. "It was love at first beer, if there is such a thing. He was a student, so we had that in common—studying in Dublin and bartending at the village at night. It's where we met. Since he was also on summer break, we spent much of our time together. He was a great tourist guide." Keira smiled. "I fell hard.

Reid, giving her space, leaned against the fireplace, folded his arms, and kept quiet.

"When I left Ireland to hook up with my friends, he and I made plans to meet in different places along our trip. Student travels are dirt-cheap, so he did. He loved me, or so he said, and I fell just a little harder." Keira paused, an insincere chuckle crossing her lips. She didn't pace, didn't move much at all then, just crossed her arms and shoved her hands into the sleeves of his flannel shirt.

"On the flight back to the States, I cried the entire time, but he was coming to visit. We'd see each other again at Christmas. I couldn't think of anything else, it kept me going. Long story short, he didn't. Something came up, and then something else. Well, they say love is blind, right?"

Reid pressed his lips into a thin line, keeping himself from butting in, but he nodded, unsure of where this was going.

"It never once occurred to me he'd lied." Sadness pricked her voice. "So, I made plans to go back to Ireland in the spring. I was crazy in love, wanted to see him. But when he finally called back, I learned he'd gotten engaged. To his long-time girlfriend I didn't know existed. How he swung it? I have no idea. And to be frank, I don't care anymore. But when I got off the phone that day, I had to scrape my heart off the floor. The lesson from this?" She cocked her head, her gaze a gigantic challenge. "Never ever, allow this to happen again."

The way Keira's mouth puckered to the side, and her lips pursed, Reid suspected she was trying her damned best to control emotions. He shoved away from the fireplace, closing the distance between them in a flash. This time he didn't wait to haul her into his arms. Stiff and unyielding, she let it happen

"Ah, shit. Mossy. I'm sorry. Want me to kill the bastard?" It was the right thing to say because the blue funk lightened with Keira's laugh. A short burst, but he'd made her laugh.

"It hurt like holy hell, but I got over it."

Although the mood had lifted a tiny fraction, he still felt her resistance within his arms, but he wasn't about to let her go. Reid crocked a finger under her chin. Lifting it, Keira lowered her lashes.

"I can't say I'm sorry it didn't work out. Or else you wouldn't be here with me. Enlighten me how this story relates to us?"

Keira kept her gaze lowered. "I wanted you to make love to me." Although her voice was low, she didn't tremble, and her words were clear.

Seconds ticked, the room stilled. "Mossy," Reid sounded a little hoarse.

"No, Reid. You still don't understand." This time she met his eyes, her gaze holding his, her voice strained with regret. "I can't do this again. It shredded me then, and if I sleep with you now, it will be worse than before."

"I won't hurt you, Mossy—"

"Please, don't." Keira laid a finger across his lips, silencing him. "Because I have no illusion. For you this might be a convenient distraction—it may even be more than a one-night stand, but whatever we'll start now will end in only a few weeks. For me, it's gone too deep; I won't be able to handle it. Please, if you care about me, you won't be pushing it."

"Damn, Mossy. Don't I get a say in this? Will you listen to me for one damn moment?" Reid's voice rose; he sounded conflicted. Splaying his hands into her curls, he cradled her face, his eyes plunging into hers. He needed her to look at him, to see his truth in them.

"You're making a lot of assumptions here. What the hell do you mean by being a convenient distraction to me? Did you even pause for one second and consider what I think about this, or how I feel about you?"

Her eyes widened, but gray and jade locked in an unspoken challenge.

"Hell yes, I want you. I would be an idiot if I didn't. And so you know, it's what I've been thinking about all damn week. But guess what? That's not the only thing that's been rattling my brain. I don't need you so I can get laid, Mossy." Keira blinked. Flat and deliberate, this piqued her attention.

Reid softened his tone; his thumbs stroked her cheekbones as he held her. "I have no desire to sleep with you to fill a need. As you think of a one-night stand, or an extended version of it; I crave much more than that. I want to spend time with you, and count on it, I'll take as much as you'll give. I want to spar with you, measure wits, take you to dinner, the movies, hell, whatever you want to do, Mossy. And yes, I want to hold you, feel you, taste you; I want to make love to you. There is a difference."

As Reid paused, Keira's fingers curled around his forearms. Stunned and dazed, a haze slid over jade, misting her eyes.

"Do you want to know why?" Reid asked.

Unable to say another word, Keira just nodded.

"Because as it is, I'm in love with a certain strawberry-blonde, dog-loving, infuriatingly stubborn woman who looks like an advertisement for country living in my flannel shirt. And because when she's close, she's doing something to my insides that makes me feel like my guts are flipping inside-out. But that's not all. That flush on her face? It drives me crazy. And if I don't get to kiss her soon, I know my insides will incinerate."

Reid felt her body soften. Releasing his hold on her head, he snaked one arm around her waist. The other tugged her hair at the nape, so she looked up to him. "Do you have any idea what it means to hear you say you're having these crazy, scary feelings for me? And what you mean to me, Mossy?"

He still saw it. The doubt shimmering in the corner of her eyes. "You know I don't trust easily, but I trust you. Can you trust me, too?" Her eyes were large and scrutinizing. *An implausible shade of green,* he thought, letting his gaze sink deeper. "Because, let me go on record here: My leaving Oak Creek in September won't change anything. Not a damn thing."

Keira gasped, her mouth opened. "I want to trust you … yes. I trust you," she said a second time for emphasis. A shine came into her eyes as her arms came around his waist.

"But—"

"Stop. There are no but's." He nuzzled her ear, and felt a ripple of shudders, and knew it had nothing to do with being cold. "We'll be together." A whisper against her ear, and goosebumps prickled her skin. "We'll make it happen."

"How?" Hot and sweet, her breath held a hint of bourbon "You are talking too much." His lips came down on hers, and he kissed her. Sweet and agonizingly slow, he opened her mouth to him, exploring, and tasting.

On a groan he pulled away, searching her face. His eyes were dark and filled with need, his voice a rough rasp. "God, I want you." He felt his heart jack-hammering against his ribs, waiting for her answer. And it busted wide open when her lips pulled into a lazy smile.

"Then, why are you wasting time, soldier?" She whispered on shaky breath, her eyes fluttering shut.

He took her mouth hard, his kiss fiery and greedy, stoked by the untamed mating of tongues. When they needed air, his breath came ragged. He released her mouth, trailing soft kisses across her face, her jawline, and found her sensitive spot just below her ear. He nuzzled and nipped, and when he dragged his teeth down her neck, she bucked against him, a whimpering sound coming from her throat.

There was no room for thought as his hand slid under the loose hanging shirt, her skin warm and soft under his touch. His fingers skimmed and stroked up her side, leaving goosebumps in their wake. Tracing across the edge of her damp bra, caressing the gentle swell above, his fingers slipped underneath the silky fabric, cupped her breast; and her soft moan undid him.

In a frenzy of motions, her hands were on him, stroking across his chest, along his ribcage, moving to his navel, circling, moving lower still, tracing along the top of his shorts. Skipping and tracing, her fingers were the fires that seared his flesh.

A rumbling groan, deep and thick, rose from his chest. Fisting her hair, he teased; little bites, sharp and exquisitely erotic, he kissed her collarbone, her neck, and her lips. He'd meant to take it slow, but her need matched his, and her moans and shudders echoed in his bones. He suckled her lip, plunged into her mouth, and kissed her with an urgency that left no doubt what was about to happen.

Walking her backward the short distance to the bedroom, his fingers fumbled with frustratingly tight closures. A rip, a whoosh, the sound of buttons plunking to the floor, and the shirt flaps opened. Her gasp vibrated into his mouth, the gasoline to his fire. It raced through his system, scorched his veins, and burned in his gut. There was no going back. He slid the flannel off her shoulders, pulling and tugging, and he freed her arms, dropping the garment to the floor. He felt her hands, hot and hurried, slip under the waistband of his boxer shorts, and sucked a sharp breath. Stumbling into the bedroom, he kicked the door shut.

***

Skin-slick and sated, Keira lay nestled in the crook of Reid's arm. Lazy, with the graceful moves of a cat waking from deep slumber, she stretched in the afterglow of their feverish union. In a hot frenzy, they'd urgently raced to the abyss. And when he took her over the edge, she discovered what it felt like to fly. She had touched the sun, and the heat still burned under her skin.

Warm and dreamy, she braced her elbow on the bed. Drawing random patterns across his abdomen, the tip of her fingers stroked his hips, glided over his thigh and for the tiniest moment, she registered surprise when her fingers moved lower and touched the artificial leg's socket. Only a beat of her heart, but his muscles tightening let her know it hadn't been lost on Reid. Surprised, because in that furnace of heat, the prosthesis hadn't crossed her mind. Keira smiled, doubting Reid had given it a single thought either. She let her fingers continue the journey, caressing the skin above the cup, moving back up to his chest, and felt him relax. And was supremely pleased when he pulled her into a tender kiss.

Coming up for air, she smiled. "Hmm … a girl could get used to this." In slow-motion, she scraped a fingernail across his chest and shoulders, her eyes following the path.

"Is that so?"

"With a little more practice?" Which earned her a deep-chested scowl as he grabbed her hips.

"Your words," she hummed, skimming her fingertips from shoulder to bicep. Her finger stopped at the tattoo. Power and strength stared at her through the eyes of an eagle, and with the heightened sense of looking at something important, she noted how Reid stilled when she traced its outline.

"It's stunning." Narrowing her eyes, she studied it, and grasped its significance. "A memorial tattoo." From the corner of her eye, she glimpsed him watching her as she touched her lips to the warmth of the inked skin. An understanding flashed through her mind and had a suspicion this was a decisive moment.

"These," she pressed the tip of her finger to the scroll beneath the eagle's head, "caught my eye the first time I saw you. I thought they looked like barbed wire; I've wondered what they guarded."

Keira lifted her gaze and shivered at the imprint of memories darkening his eyes. A frosty fist of sorrow squeezed her stomach—how she wanted to shield him from the shadows of the past, warm the icy gloom that followed him, but understood that only he could do that.

"Will you tell me about it?" Hope rode on warm breath. Would he open the door to his soul?

Reid's arms tightened around her back, and as she pressed her cheek against his chest, she listened to his heart beating fast and strong.

"Who are these men?" she asked in a soft voice, her heart reaching out to his. Because she had a hunch it would be a heart-breaking story to listen to.

***

Had anyone told him he'd bare his soul buck naked with a captivating woman in his arms, he'd have sent the idiot to the dentist for a new set of teeth. First, he seldom talked about the stuff that happened in Afghanistan. Second, soul bearing was overrated. And third, shop talk wasn't a smart topic of conversation in intimate moments.

But the woman stroking her cheek against his chest wasn't just any woman. It was Keira, the woman who'd broken into his heart. She had asked about the men whose names were branded on his flesh, and he'd give her the truth. Because it felt right—because she'd poured her own truth into him; trusted him. She deserved to know.

And as Reid recalled the events for the second time in one day, a calmness expanded in his chest. It was okay to let go of self-blame and guilt.

What a strange day it had been. A measure of peace delivered in a package of matted fur and bones. Rescuing the mutt had brought Keira into his life. And taking Bones to the adoption event led to a heart-to-heart with Bill, giving Reid permission to forgive himself.

"You know it's the mutt's fault," he said, stroking Keira, marveling at the sensual curves of her back.

"Hmm ... What is?"

"You, naked in my bed." He teased, cupping her cheek with a meaningful squeeze.

"I have no clue how I got this way," she slapped his arm, "and what does Bones have to do with it? They haven't budged since we found the little escape artist." Keira referred to the dogs conked out in the great room. "Under the circumstance, I'm glad he didn't get adopted today."

"Uh-huh. Did I mention he's no longer available for adoption?"

Keira's head shot up. Eyebrows raised; she cocked her head with a look of surprise on her face. "Are you saying what I'm thinking?"

"That depends. If you're thinking his new last name is McCabe, then you're thinking isn't wrong."

"Sweet Jesus. You're adopting him." Keira shot up. Flashing her teeth in a wide smile, she pummeled his chest, the surprise replaced by pure joy. "I knew you were the right match. I knew it … it's perfect. I'll get the adoption papers—"

"Wait." In a swift move, Reid grabbed her around the waist, rolled her onto her back, and leaned over her. "There's time." Gravel scraped against his throat. "Right now, we have something more important to discuss."

"Would that be our next battle strategy, soldier?" Batting her lashes, she aimed for innocent, but her voice took on smoke.

"Hmm … yes, ma'am." Smoothing the hair from her forehead, he tried not to drown in the pool of jade. "What do you say you join me on the road—with Houston, Matt, and the mutts?"

EPILOGUE

THE YELLOW BUG SNAKED ALONG the winding road to the impressive landmark, sitting atop a gentle rise. The Kentucky Castle. Keira slowed the vehicle to drink in the magical ambiance of the boutique hotel with its four corner towers and massive stone walls. Leave it up to Emily to realize every little girl's dream to get married in a castle.

But perhaps not every girl's dream. A barn would be perfect, one of those wedding barns where dogs were welcome, and a band with a fiddle provided the entertainment. Wouldn't it be cool to arrive in an old-fashioned horse carriage, while the groom rode in on a horse? No fancy menu either. A cookout, perhaps, with the only concession to fancy for mouth-watering desserts and a stunning wedding cake.

Smiling, Keira crossed the parking lot, and jerked when she bumped shoulders with an older gentleman. "Oh, I'm so sorry. This place is so fabulous, I didn't pay attention to where I was going."

She'd recovered, the incident pulling her out of this daydream. These ideas of her own wedding fantasies popping into her head, what a silly notion. But she couldn't deny it; Reid was making a convincing case for believing in her own fairytale once again. During the past three months, he had snatched every second of her free time, just as he'd promised.

Making good on his word, he'd adopted Bones. He'd even let her rope him into volunteer duty at the shelter, though not without grumbling, but in turn, Reid had convinced her to walk with him and Houston and Matt. And she'd gotten to know their likes and quirks and their offbeat humor. Beyond that, they were an accepting bunch. Challenging at first, but they'd coached her, supported her when her legs wobbled, and feet blistered. But hey, she'd lost a few pounds along the way, and how could she complain about that?

Exploring each other in every imaginable way, she'd learned what made Reid smile and what made him blow a fuse. But granted, she'd given him a fair share of figuring things out, too. A familiar heat dropped into her stomach and mushroomed as thoughts of the silly argument from this morning flashed through her mind.

She entered the courtyard pressing her lips together, or else risked looking like a loon smiling to herself amidst the tour group coming her way. There was something to be said about the unbridled passion of make-up sex. His touch, the feel of his skin against hers, his scent, the way his voice scraped, an imprint on her brain that would last forever.

The tour groups passed, giving Keira a view of tall green columns of evergreens and planters brimming with colorful flowers. She stepped into the building's massive foyer and gaped at the opulent Old World display of elegance.

"Keira." Emily's voice, and then her friend was beside her. She'd been waiting for Keira in the luxurious lobby. A second group of visitors tromped down the grandiose staircase. Tomorrow this would be Emily's stage, descending to exchange promises with Ryan waiting for her at the bottom.

Her sweet friend. Shutting her eyes, Keira squeezed Emily in a tight hug. Behind her lids, a pool of memories rose like a flashflood—of that first hospital meeting, to becoming Emily's maid of honor, and everything in-between.

"You're not crying, are you?" Emily pulled back, tears blinding her own vision.

"Who, me? Never." Keira smiled and brushed the water from the corner of her eyes. "Hey, this is amazing," she diverted the attention back to the splendor of the large hall. At the reception, tucked behind the staircase, Keira checked in, conscious of how terribly she'd miss her friend. Because Emily would still be on her honeymoon when Keira took to the road with Reid, this would be their last chance for girl-time.

Reid's proposal to join him on the cross-country walk had shocked Keira speechless. Although taking a break from teaching had knocked on her brain for a while, making it a reality had been overwhelming at first. So much to consider—her house, her dogs, her volunteer work.

But it had been Emily and her endless questioning that helped forge the decision. What if she didn't go? What would she miss out on? Would she have regrets passing up this once-in-a-lifetime experience? Keira tossed it around, stewed on it, and solutions formed as it became clear: she wanted to do this. The walls of her charming little town had been closing in for a while. More than that, however, she wanted to be with Reid; wanted to walk for Heroes Rise.

If Emily felt weepy, she didn't show it. "Let's get you settled so we can head to the Spa. I've made a massage appointment for both of us." A blazing smile, and Emily clasped her hands. Her eyes shimmered, but Keira detected no more tears, just joy and happiness. This afternoon belonged to the two of them—free to explore the castle grounds, dine in the opulent ball room/dining room, and cozy up in the Bourbon bar tonight, chatting about anything and everything.

Today they'd luxuriate in celebrating their friendship, because tomorrow would be unzipped and loaded with emotion.

***

"You look stunning, Marshmallow. Are you ready?" In busy mode, Keira fussed with Emily's veil. When her friend took a deep breath, they hugged one final time.

"Okay. Let's do this." Falling into her resolute attitude kept herself and the bride from tearing up. Handing Emily her bouquet, she opened the bedroom door, leading her to where the bridesmaids and Ryan's uncle waited near the top of the staircase landing. He would hand off the bride, as Emily had no family.

And suddenly Roberta Flack's silky voice announced the wedding procession with "The First Time I Ever Saw your Face." A hush settled over Keira's mind and her heart connected with Emily's, feeling it quiver and squeeze. Was this how *forever* felt?

The faces of the wedding guests, seated below to both sides of the staircase, faded as she strode ahead of Emily. Concentrating on not tripping in these high heels, she glanced at Ryan waiting for his bride, so dignified and earnest, flanked by his groomsmen. She searched for Reid's face. When she found his eyes raking over the soft curls touching her shoulders and the silky seafoam of her one-shoulder dress, the swarm of butterflies inside her stomach lifted off at once. How handsome he looked—clean shaven, the adorable cowlick jazzing up that sexy smile, and the blue of the shirt brightening his eyes. Keira averted her gaze, focusing on the bridesmaids ahead of her. Just a few more steps.

During the ceremony, she'd caught Reid's gaze, unsettling her in a pulse-speeding way. It was a short ceremony, and before she slipped into daydreams, the concluding words, "You may kiss the bride," shifted her thoughts.

With a champagne reception, a photo session inside and outside of the castle, and dinner in the ballroom, the party gathered to move to the rooftop terrace where the music already pulsed.

The first dance, the cake-cutting ceremony, and the D.J. whipped up the atmosphere when he announced, "All single ladies, please move to the right side of the dancefloor, put your hands up in the air."

Since Ryan and Emily's was an intimate wedding, only five single ladies lined up with giggles and smiles. Emily's eyes gleamed, her smile a beam of sunshine reaching out to her friends, and she turned, throwing the bouquet at the count of three.

A blur of lavender and pink streaked past, and Keira closed her eyes. When soft blossoms thudded against the palm of her hands, she didn't think, just closed her fingers around it.

She opened her lids, and with eyes round as tennis balls, stared into Emily's smiling face. She'd caught the bouquet, and as superstition has it ... *Holy Smoke!* She'd caught the bouquet.

***

Pat's parking lot was the center of activity as Reid strolled in with Keira and Houston. The upbeat tunes of Alan Jackson's rendition of "Good Time" rolled out from the event tent at the end of the lot. At the opposite end, four burly guys sweated over a huge grill on wheels, its smoky flames infusing the air with a sizzling aroma. And over at the refreshing station serving ice-cold water, sodas, and beer, a line snaked out. Vendor tables and information booths packed the remaining space and adjacent lot.

"Hey, over here." Matt, his wife, and the boys sat at an outdoor table, heaps of smoked ribs, corn on the cob, and baked beans in front of them.

"Nice turn-out." Reid scanned the crowd, but the party atmosphere was deceiving. It was National Suicide Prevention Week.

"Yes," Houston agreed. "Pat did a fantastic job putting this thing together."

"BBQ and live music," Emily chimed in. "What's not to like?"

Pat had organized this BBQ festival to raise awareness on the taboo subject of suicide that claimed lives daily, nationwide and in his hometown. For Houston, Reid, Matt, and Keira it was also ground zero. In just about two hours they'd start their cross-country tour. And there was no more fitting place than to take off from Pat's Place.

Pat popped out from the tent, his bald head slick with sweat. Spotting the new arrivals, he waved, motioning to meet in a shady spot outside the tent.

Matt leaned into his wife, said something, and joined Pat and the guys.

"Look at this," Houston gestured across the lot, then punched Pat's shoulder. "You pulled it off, man. This is fucking amazing."

"Ah, thanks, man." Pat, whose wrestling champion appearance and attitude left no doubt he was in charge at the bar, slid a palm over the shiny dome of his head and offered a half-smile. "It's because of you and your lofty ideas," Pat punched back in that good-natured way men use when showing emotions was uncomfortable.

"Excuse me." Houston swiveled around when someone tapped him on the shoulder.

"Alyson, Darling." He grabbed her in a hug. "You came to town to see us off?"

"Oh, Miller. You're leaving town," Alyson smirked. "I wouldn't miss it for the world."

Leaning into Keira, she cupped her right hand to her mouth, "Hun, it's not too late to change your mind. Are you sure you want to hang out with the Three Stooges for a year?"

At the table, Matt's boys had finished chomping their ribs, and Matt moseyed back to his family where his wife cleared a pile of Dixie plates and empty bottles. These days he appeared relaxed, happy even, although Reid knew Matt's demons still clawed on his mind, appearing at unpredictable times.

The boys' energetic head-bobbing caught Reid's gaze, and he smiled. Matt held his wife's hand as he signaled the team he'd be inside.

Keira twisted and turned, her eyes scanning across the parking lot, darting from here to there. "Dadgummit, where are my parents?"

That restless feeling swirling inside her would keep her humming until they'd hit the road, Reid knew. He'd felt this same restlessness before each deployment. She'd get through it; Keira was tough as nails. Spunky, too. A most attractive quality, until she pushed his patience meter into the red zone.

Reid cringed. Just two days ago they'd cleaned the cabin together, and without asking, she'd turned one of his favorite T-shirts into a cleaning rag. Yes, it was shapeless and faded and a sweat-stained piece of clothing, but damn, it had pissed him off. He didn't have to explode, but that's what happened. The next thing he remembered, she'd stomped off, slamming the door. She came back fifteen minutes later; the steam had fizzled. He'd been in the kitchen, scrubbing the fridge when she'd come up behind, curled her arms around his middle and rested her cheek against his back. "Hey," she'd said. "It was a good shirt; I'm sorry." And holy cow, making up had never been sweeter.

As Keira craned her neck, wearing a T-shirt, shorts, and hiking boots, Reid saw the heartache flowing next to excitement. She'd be all right, and he wanted to tell her that. But this, crossing the country on foot, leaving her town, and saying goodbye to her family, was a big deal. The children had returned to school three weeks earlier, but Keira had not. She'd chosen to be with him; chosen the unknown. In less than two hours, they'd walk out of this parking lot together.

And it swept through Reid like a thunderbolt—he loved her. His chest flamed with the intensity of the realization, and he pulled her against him, saying the only thing he could to calm her nerves. "They'll be here soon, Mossy."

He'd expected his own parents any moment now, too. They'd arrived yesterday afternoon from Florence and had stayed with the Millers at their invitation. Helen had planned a family farewell party with the McCabes and the Flanigans at her home.

"Your mom knows how to throw a party." Keira shot a look at Houston who answered with a sly grin. "Even your dad cut loose," she said, poking Reid in the ribs.

"Hey," Alyson tugged on Houston's arm. "The may is here."

Houston's head snapped up. "He's scheduled ͭ a speech."

"Oh, there's mom and dad." Keira bounced on her heels. "I'll bring them inside the tent. You guys want to go greet the mayor?"

"Yes ma'am, boss lady," Houston smirked, but he, Alyson, and Reid set off to do just that.

Houston's parents, Tessa, and the McCabes came into the parking lot as Houston and Reid shook hands with Mayor Denning.

"Sam, good to see you," Helen Miller greeted the mayor and introduced Amanda and David McCabe, but not before she hugged her boy and kissed his cheeks.

As everyone moved inside the tent, Pat went into the bar and grabbed a bottle he kept for special occasions. A farewell to a group of friends as close as a family was such an occasion.

Inside the tent, the band stopped playing. "Thank you ... you guys are awesome," the lead singer cut through the applause. "We're honored to play here today, considering the seriousness of the event, and the kick-off to the cross-country trek of a special group of people you're all familiar with."

In the front row, Reid's fingers slid between Keira's.

"But before I ask Mayor Denning to the stage," he paused and looked at Reid. "I'd like to introduce a track some of you have heard right here at Pat's. But for the few of you who haven't ... well, I'd like to welcome Reid McCabe of Heroes Rise to the stage to give you 'Boots.'"

Amidst whoops and shouts, Reid pushed to his feet, sauntered up on stage, and took the guitar someone handed him. Strumming the first chords, the chatter inside the tent flattened. Tessa set the GoPro to live stream and recorded.

"There's a whisper in the breeze

"Reminding me of home ..."

Scars Of the Past: Book 3 In The Oak Creek Series

The chatter died, until Reid performed the last line of the Heroes Rise theme song.

"Step by step, take a walk in my boots ..."

Applause broke after a moment of surprised silence, and Reid handed the guitar back. As he looked at the people seated in the front row, he smiled at the wave of love rolling over him. Even Helen Miller wiped the corners of her eyes.

Back in his seat, Reid slid his arm over Keira's shoulders. Pride beamed in her eyes as she leaned in to peck his lips. A glance at his parents and he saw his dad's hand cupping his mom's shoulder. Sniffles reached his ears on both sides.

The mayor took the stage next. And true to his reputation, Denning didn't miss any opportunity to talk. Although butts wiggled in seats, his address of the national and local rate of suicide was heartfelt and on-point. The speech finally ended.

"And with that, and I speak on behalf of the residents of Oak Creek, I wish you farewell and God speed."

The mayor shook hands on his way out, the band took a break, and the tent emptied.

Amanda McCabe sobbed. "I'm fine, Mom," Reid assured. "These are happy tears, right? Because of you and dad getting me through the rough patches, building me up, I'm better than fine. I'm great." He gave her an affectionate hug and kissed her cheek. "Don't worry about me."

Tears and sniffles, mixed with chuckles, surrounded him. Keira and her parents, Houston poking fun at his mom and Alyson, and Matt hugging his wife and his boys. Pat caught a smirk from Reid as he poured his special blend into plastic cups. He just shrugged his shoulders in a "what can I say" gesture.

"A toast," Pat announced, his booming vo¡ demanding attention.

"On this road to your dreams,

May your confidence never fade,
And your boots never fall apart"

Chuckles rose, lightening the mood. "It's time," Houston said. "Let's get the mutts."

"We'll wait here," Helen said, glancing at the McCabes and Matt's wife.

"A'ight. We'll be back in a few."

Weaving behind the tent, they took the alley running behind Pat's over to Miller's Construction office. In front of the office sat the Jeep, packed with water, cases of meals that didn't need preparation, protein snacks, sleeping bags, first aid kits, sets of extra hiking boots, and everything else they'd scratched off the packing list. Attached to the rear, a large American flag swayed back and forth on a gentle breeze.

Rucksacks sat in the back seat. Today they wouldn't need them, because in Houston's estimation, they'd make it to their first stop by seven o'clock. His uncle's house. The dogs ran circles when Houston unlocked the office door. Something was up, and they smelled it.

"Ready, boys?" Reid snapped a leash on Bones. For now, he'd let the mutt walk, rid himself of the overabundance of energy. Later, when he tired, Reid would carry him on his back, in the harness he'd purchased for this purpose. He didn't worry about Yard; the dog was a godsend.

"Hey, stop the smooching," Houston called as Reid cradled Keira's head, kissing her lips, but Reid didn't pay attention.

"Are you ready, Mossy?" He searched her eyes for traces of doubt and only saw the glitter of excitement.

"I've never been more ready for anything." Only truth rang in her low tone.

God, he loved her. The way she smiled at him; he felt the overwhelming urge to kiss her again.

"Got that," Tessa squealed, yielding the GoPro she'd snatched from Houston, and yelped when Reid's hand shot out and clamped around the back of her neck.

"This," he warned, "is not going on social media."

"Too late, it's streaming live." Tessa's mischievous laugh told him she was taunting, which she confirmed when he took her in a playful headlock and rubbed his knuckles across her mane. "Lighten up, Reid. Your followers will love to see that stuff."

"You're done." Houston grabbed the GoPro, ending Tessa's fun.

As the group spilled out of the office, Reid handed the Jeep's key to Matt. "She's all yours; we'll meet you back at Pat's."

When they got back to the bar, friends and strangers had lined up along Main Street in a grand farewell. Veterans wearing legion hats held street banners, and the chubby hands of tots in their mother's arms waved American stick flags.

Overwhelmed by the people who came to cheer them on, Reid's throat knotted. Yeah, they'd promoted Heroes Rise, had seized every opportunity to talk about their mission, given interviews, but this ... ? He swallowed hard and imagined Houston had to be bursting like a smashed pumpkin at the support of his hometown.

The patriotic scene was the perfect background for perky Mindy Thompson from WKAY and her cameraman, waiting to interview Houston and Reid.

"Houston, Reid ..."

"Smile." Reid elbowed Houston, but he didn't have to. Mindy's curves showed off a stylish pencil skirt and silk blouse as she hotfooted in tennis shoes toward them. Her hand clutched a microphone.

Amused, Houston and Reid answered a few questions, until she wrapped up the interview and wished them good luck. Afterward, friends, neighbors, and even a few strangers shook hands and uttered their well-wishes.

"Crunch time." Reid pointed to his military-style wristwatch as Bones pulled on his leash.

"I'll leave now." Alyson's hand cupped Houston's arm. "Keep your eyes on the prize Miller."

Reid smirked at the bewildered expression on his friend's face when she grabbed his neck, pulled him to her, and smacked a kiss to his lips. "One for the road," she said, and pushed through the crowd.

Emotions thickened at the final farewells, and suddenly Reid's dad clutched him tight, patting his back. "I'm so proud of you," he muttered with that telltale catch of suppressed tears in his voice. "Take care of yourself, Son, and be damn sure to take great care of that sweet woman by your side. And you," he bent to Yard, "take care of every one of them."

Reid gripped Keira's hand and squeezed. Despite the frog lodged in this throat, his chest expanded, and something took flight, soaring sky-high.

And he knew with absolute certainty, he didn't need two legs to be happy.

ACKNOWLEDGMENTS

Writing a book is a lonely affair, but it takes a village to publish one. Many minds come together to read, suggest, advice, and help make a dream come true.

My dream, 'Scars of The Past' is the third book in the Oak Creek series. Yet, I am blown away once again by the support I received from the writing community.

A huge thank you to the Bard's Corner, my writer's and critique group. Your support and encouragement is outstanding and your critique is spot on. Member and critique partner, Gail Kamer: Reading my chapters—one-by-one—pointing out details, tossing suggestions, and listening to questions along the way made a huge difference. Thank you!

And Jim Corbit, Bard's member and editor: You made my head spin, but your critique was always thoughtful, kind, and filled with great suggestions. The editing expertise you applied to my story is valuable beyond measure. You took my words and made them shine. Thank you!

Ann Leslie Tuttle. Your developmental edits changed my book in ways I never thought possible. Cutting over ten thousand words from my manuscript was a real eye-opener. Now I know what the phrase 'Cut your Darlings' means, but you knew it had to be done. And I agree. The story is so much better for it. Thank you!

There are many more individuals who lent their support and expertise. Thank you, Amanda with Lalinc Proofreading for crossing the t's and dotting the i's, Andie Hansen for making the interior look fabulous, Marisa from Cover Me Darling for this astonishing book cover, Robbie Blanford for sharing your knowledge on my EMT question, and Katie Marks for answering questions on establishing a non-profit organization. Thank you!

And to my husband, a twenty-six-year Army veteran. Thank you for your unwavering encouragement and patience. For your faith in me finishing this particular story, even though I came close to giving up a time or two. For your patience in answering my endless questions, for your understanding when dinner consisted of take-out once again, and for leaving me to it when my writing stretched into the early morning hours. I love you infinitely.

CONTACT THE AUTHOR

I'd love to hear from you. Please email your comments and questions to Stubblefield45@gmail.com
    Facebook – *https://facebook.com/BKStubblefield1*
    Twitter – *https://twitter.com/thedogtale*
    Pinterest – *https://www.pinterest.com/bstubblefield*
    Amazon – *https://amazon.com/author/birgitstubblefield*
    Website – *https://BKStubblefield.com*

Join my newsletter, and receive a FREE copy of my short story *Second Chances.*
    https://BKStubblefield.com

ABOUT B.K. STUBBLEFIELD

B.K. Stubblefield is a writer with a passion for dogs and dog rescue. Her dog, Harper, provided the inspiration for her first non-fiction book, Rescued: A Tale of Two Dogs.

B.K. Stubblefield was born and raised in Germany, where she met her husband. Supporting his military career, she moved between Europe, and the United States for many years. Now she makes her home in a small town in rural Kentucky, where she draws inspiration for her Oak Creek series from the slower pace of small-town living. Her favorite things to start her day are early morning walks with Harper.

Coffee, chocolate, and popcorn are the three must-haves when writing. Tacos are optional.

Made in the USA
Columbia, SC
20 June 2021